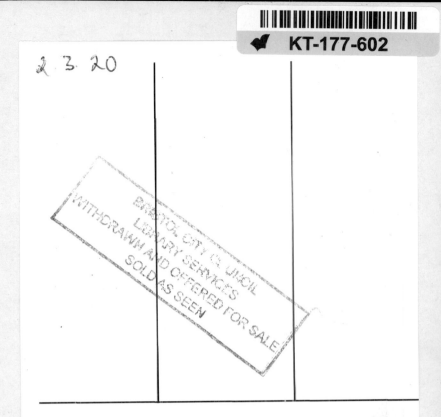
Please return/renew this item by the last date shown
on this label, or on your self-service receipt.

To renew this item, visit **www.librarieswest.org.uk**
or contact your library

Your borrower number and PIN are required.

Libraries**West**

By Sylvia Broady

The Yearning Heart
The Lost Daughter

To the air ambulance nurses of the WAAF who have inspired me to write this book. I wish to thank them for their service

The Lost Daughter

SYLVIA BROADY

Allison & Busby Limited
11 Wardour Mews
London W1F 8AN
allisonandbusby.com

First published in Great Britain by Allison & Busby in 2018.
This paperback edition published by Allison & Busby in 2019.

A CIP catalogue record for this book is available from
the British Library.

10 9 8 7 6 5 4 3 2 1

ISBN 978-0-7490-2364-5

Typeset in 10.5/15.5 pt Adobe Garamond Pro by
Allison & Busby Ltd

The paper used for this Allison & Busby publication
has been produced from trees that have been legally sourced
from well-managed and credibly certified forests.

Printed and bound by
CPI Group (UK) Ltd, Croydon, CR0 4YY

Chapter One

Hull, East Yorkshire, 1930

The rain lashed at her face and body, her thin cotton nightdress clinging to her bare legs, her shoeless feet hitting the hard pavement, but she didn't stop running. Fear gripped her heart, and every bone and muscle in her body. Terrified, she glanced over her shoulder, seeing a dark shadow looming. Was it him? Panicking, she ran faster, the pain in her chest almost at bursting point. She could still see his dark, evil face as he lunged at her. Ahead, she could see the faint glow of a light: the police station. *Help me! Help me! Save my little girl, my little girl!* The words reverberated in her head.

Stepping out into the road, she stretched out her arms to propel herself even faster. Then screeching and skidding noises on wet surface and the sound of screaming filled her whole body and mind. The impact, the pressure of metal against her thin body sent her up into space. She felt herself flying over the cold, sodden street. And then the silence of oblivion swallowed the pain and terror of her anguished body.

* * *

The man in the black saloon car slammed on his brakes. 'Bloody hell!' he yelled, his voice juddering with shock.

The duty policeman hurried from the station. 'What's happened?' he asked.

'I didn't stand a chance!' the driver wailed. Both men stood staring down at the still body of the young woman.

'Is she a gonner?' someone asked.

A middle-aged woman knelt down by the side of the young woman and took off her coat, placing it over the cold, wet figure. She shouted at the useless men. 'She has a pulse. Get an ambulance – quick!'

The woman's voice galvanised the men into action.

'Who is she?' asked the policeman.

They shook their heads and mumbled, 'Don't know.' No one seemed to know who the young woman was.

No one took any notice of the big man, well wrapped up in his jacket, muffle and flat cap, standing on the edge of the gathered crowd, surveying the scene and listening to what was being said. Then he silently slipped away.

Back at the house in Dagger Lane, the man quickly wiped up the blood and set the furniture right. Going upstairs to the bedroom where the little girl was sleeping, he stood for a few moments just watching the gentle rhythm of her breathing. He felt nothing for her. She was just a kid, a damned nuisance as far as he was concerned, and she had no place in his life. He needed to get rid of her. Going downstairs, he sat on a chair and rolled a cigarette, lit it and drew heavily, contemplating what to do next. With any luck, his useless bitch of a wife would die. He didn't want to be tied down to a woman and a bairn; his biggest mistake was marrying her. He liked his freedom and to have any woman he fancied.

He must have dozed off for the next thing he knew was the kid bawling its head off, crying for her mammy. 'Shut your bleeding noise,' he bellowed up the stairs.

'I want a wee-wee,' the little girl cried.

He was just about to race up the stairs to shake the living daylights out of her, when he stopped. An idea just dropped into the lump in his head he called a brain.

He galloped up the stairs to the little girl's bedroom.

'Mammy,' she sobbed. Her tiny, convulsed body shrank away from the big man.

'Shurrup and stop moaning.' He snatched her up from the wet, sodden bed, clumsily wrapped her in a blanket, and clattered downstairs and out into the street.

'Everything all right?' asked the next-door neighbour. She'd heard the banging, clashing and shouting last night and the bairn crying for her mammy this morning.

The big man was just about to give the nosy neighbour a mouthful of abuse when he stopped and thought, and then said, 'It's the bloody missus, she's gone off with another bloke and left me and the bairn to fend for ourselves. I've ter work so I'm tekkin' bairn round to her granny's.' *That'll give the bloody old hag something to gossip about*, he thought, as he hurried down the street, avoiding going near to the police station.

The child, frightened in the big man's huge arms, shut her eyes tightly, put her thumb in her mouth and sucked.

Arriving at his wife's mother's house in Marvel Court off Fretters Lane, the big man rushed in without knocking. Four bairns were sitting round the kitchen table eating a basin of watery porridge each. Wordlessly, they all stared at him. Their mother, Aggie, who was in the scullery washing the pan used for the porridge, spun round at the sound of heavy feet crashing into her kitchen.

'Ted, what's up?' She was surprised to see her son-in-law for he rarely visited – he wouldn't have been her choice for her daughter to marry. He was too rough and full of himself – she might be poor, but she had standards. Then she noticed the bairn in his arms.

At the sound of her granny's voice, the little girl began to cry. 'Mammy,' she hiccupped.

Ted thrust the child into the startled woman's arms. The lies came easy to him. 'Your bloody daughter's upped and left me for another bloke, and I'm off ter work, so you look after the brat.' With those words, he turned and stalked from the house.

Aggie fell onto her chair by the kitchen fire, holding the wet bundle. The little girl, arms locked around her neck, sobbing onto her bosom.

Finally, getting over the shock, Aggie unfastened the tight arms from her neck and, with an edge of her pinafore, she wiped away the snot from her granddaughter's nose. Then she rocked her gently until her sobbing ceased.

All the time, her children went about their daily routine, not speaking a word, not wanting the wrath of their mother's tongue or a smack across their ears. Their breakfast finished, the three boys went off to school and the girl to work in a shop.

Feeling annoyed at being left with the care of her granddaughter, Aggie discarded the little girl's sodden nightdress and bathed her in tepid water in a bowl in the scullery stone sink. She found a vest, knickers and a dress, all old and tatty. 'They'll 'ave ter do for now,' she muttered. One thing was for sure, she wasn't going to have the bairn shoved on her. No! She had her whack of looking after her own bairns with no help from anyone. Come tonight, she'd take the bairn back to Ted and let him sort out her care.

She glanced at the clock on the mantelpiece. It was a wedding present from her father and it reminded her of happier times. That was all she had left: memories of when she was a young married woman with high hopes until the Great War changed everything. Her Albert came home a broken man, only good for bedding her, and then he died, leaving her with seven children and another on the way. She lost three of the bairns to diphtheria. Life became a brutal, harsh struggle with poverty and hunger, a never-ending daily toil to survive, and she was still doing it – struggling! She couldn't cope with another bairn, not at her age. Besides, she had advertised for a paying lodger and a middle-aged man who worked at the flour mill was coming in a fortnight. That would give her chance to buy a second-hand bed and turn her front room downstairs into a bed-cum-sitting room. She'd given up the pointless idea of having the front room to be used only on special occasions. What occasions did she have, anyway?

'Time I was going to work,' she said to the little girl who sat on the floor, her eyes brimming with tears.

Aggie had two daily cleaning jobs, one during the day at a big house on Baker Street and the other one was in the evening, cleaning offices down Bowlalley Lane. There was no way she could take the bairn with her to either job, and she wouldn't leave her in the house on her own, so she carried her to a neighbour's house. 'I just can't understand our Alice leaving her bairn. She is so devoted to her,' she said to the old widow, Mrs Yapham.

Mrs Yapham, who liked to sit at the window to pass her days and to earn a bit of money by keeping an eye on working mothers' children, tutted and said, 'Bring me a packet of ciggies back with yer.'

'I suppose,' Aggie replied, grudgingly. She'd make sure she got the money back off that lout, Ted. 'It's a right mess,' she said. 'Men are so bloody useless. They've no idea about bairns. Our Alice hasn't got the sense she was born with buggering off with another man. Though I can't believe she'd leave her bairn behind. It's not like her.'

Later on, when Aggie had given her children their tea of bread and dripping, she bundled the little girl, Daisy, up in a blanket and, taking her daughter Martha with her, set off to see Ted. As they trundled along, Aggie was getting fraught and Martha was now carrying a scared bairn who hid her face in the blanket.

'Bloody men,' Aggie muttered under her breath. She felt too old and exhausted to have to be looking after another bairn.

Martha kept quiet. All she thought about these days was how soon she could escape her mother's grasp. And she certainly wasn't going to marry a fellow and be a drudge and have too many bairns to look after. No. For the past few months she'd been working an extra hour most days and, so that her mother couldn't take the extra pence, she left the money safely at the haberdashery shop. Mrs Jones, the owner, had agreed to keep these secret savings and not to mention it to Aggie.

'We're here, thank God,' Aggie said. She hammered on the front door and, when no answer was forthcoming, she shouted through the letter box. 'Ted, open this bloody door.'

'Mammy,' Daisy whimpered, sobbing into the blanket, trying not to make a noise. She didn't like her angry grandmother. She wanted Mammy.

Aggie banged on the door again.

'He's gone.' It was the next-door neighbour, Mrs Green.

'What do yer mean?' Aggie snapped. She had reached the end of her tether and she had to go to work this evening.

'He came home from work and banged about, and the next thing, he was off with his bag on his shoulder. I asked him where he was going. Said he'd got a ship and was off to see the world. I said, "But what about yer bairn?" He just laughed in my face, the callous bugger.'

After a cup of tea at Mrs Green's house, Aggie went off to work and Martha made her way home with Daisy.

Once home, Martha had instructions to put the dirty clothes in to soak in the stone fire boiler, then to see to her three brothers who were used to being left on their own in the early evenings. They had made a den under the table and were playing at wild Indians. Upstairs, the three boys shared a bed in the back bedroom and Martha shared a bed with Aggie in the front bedroom. It was into this bed that Martha put the sleeping child. The beds were covered with old blankets and their coats, but they were never warm enough and the palliasse was torn and lumpy. They had no other furniture. What they once owned had either gone to the pawnshop or had been chopped up for firewood. But, according to the authorities, they were lucky to have a whole house to themselves. One thing Martha could say about her mother was that she always paid the rent; even if they went hungry, she kept a roof over their heads, so they would never have to resort to living in an overcrowded house with other families. Many a week they'd lived on potatoes and bread, and once, when Aggie cleaned out a boat on the dock, they'd lived on bananas all week. This house, her mother was fond of saying, was for her old age. It was Aggie's dream to take in a paying lodger so that she'd only have to work during the day and have the luxury of having the nights to herself.

'Is our Daisy living with us now?' asked Jimmy, one of the twins. Martha shrugged, she didn't have an answer.

Everyone was in bed when Aggie returned home from work. The wet clothes hung on the pulley above the fire and she sat by the dying embers, drinking a mug of weak tea, re-patching her work dress and thinking. What was she going to do about Daisy? She hadn't the strength to bring up another bairn, she didn't want to, nor did she have the money to do so. She gave a heavy sigh. When her lodger started paying her money, she'd be able to give up the evening job. She rubbed the aching stiffness of her arthritic knees. No more scrubbing floors for her.

After a restless night, with Daisy wriggling about between her and Martha, and wetting the bed, Aggie felt more tired than when she went to bed. Her temper was sharp, and everyone kept out of her way.

It was left to Martha to haul the palliasse to the open window and to take an upset Daisy, who kept crying for her mammy, downstairs. This pulled at Martha's good nature and she felt guilty, and decided that with the extra money she earned today, she would buy food and hoped that Aggie wouldn't ask where the money came from.

For a whole week Aggie left Daisy with Mrs Yapham when she went to work. But the next day, Mrs Yapham was taken ill and was not able to look after Daisy. There was no one else available. 'I'll have ter tek yer with me, so you best keep quiet,' Aggie threatened Daisy.

The Melton family lived in a tall, three-storey Georgian house with iron railings fronting it and steps leading down to the basement, which was the entrance Aggie used. Baker Street was a prosperous area in Hull and Aggie was lucky to have found employment with such a fine household. But, to her credit, she was a good and reliable worker. This morning, her employer, the lady of the house, Mrs Melton, was at home.

'Drat,' muttered Aggie. She pushed Daisy into the outhouse at the back where the washing tub and mangle were kept. Mrs Melton rarely ventured into the basement and never into the outhouse. Aggie spread out a piece of sacking on the stone floor. 'You can go ter sleep, and no noise and be a good girl.'

Aggie tied on her work apron and set about her daily tasks. She was a good, methodical worker. And, as the morning passed, she went to check on her granddaughter who was fast asleep, curled up and sucking her thumb. She shut the door and went back to her work, and became so absorbed in her tasks that she forgot about her granddaughter until she heard an almighty crash and a child screaming.

Rushing to the outhouse, she collided with Mrs Melton, who had also heard the noise. 'Sorry, madam,' Aggie said.

'Good gracious, what is happening?'

Aggie gave her employer a look of alarm and ran towards the outhouse. Breathing heavily, she pushed open the door to see Daisy, her clothes soaking wet, crouching in a corner, and the washtub tipped over and water flooding the floor.

Aggie covered her mouth with her hands at seeing the chaos

of the scene. Her first thought was that she would lose her job.

Mrs Melton was behind her and, at first, speechless.

Half an hour later, with the mess in the outhouse cleaned up, Daisy, wrapped in a towel while her clothes dried, sat at the kitchen table drinking a glass of milk and eating one of Cook's shortbread biscuits.

Meanwhile, Aggie took off her work apron, which kept clean her wrap-over pinafore that she wore like a uniform and hid the old, patched working dress. She tidied back her grey hair, which she wore in a bun at the nape of her neck and knocked on Mrs Melton's sitting-room door. She was asked to enter and, as she did so, she bobbed a curtsey. This was not usual for her to do, but she thought it might help. Aggie told Mrs Melton every detail of how she came to have her granddaughter staying with her. When she had finished, the room filled with an uneasy silence.

Then Mrs Melton spoke. 'Do you know where your daughter is?'

'I've no idea where she's gone,' Aggie said, desperately. 'It's the bairn. I can't work and look after her, and I need my wages from you to feed and clothe my own bairns, and to pay the rent. I don't know who else to turn to.' Aggie lowered her eyes, but not before she saw the look of sympathy on the face of her employer.

'Have you spoken to the authorities?' Mrs Melton asked.

Aggie gulped. She mistrusted the authorities who would come snooping around. They'd once tried to evict her from her house. 'No, Mrs Melton,' Aggie answered, demurely.

'Very well, leave it with me and I will see what can be done to help your awkward situation.'

'Thank you, madam,' Aggie replied, dipping her arthritic knees. And before the mistress changed her mind, she then scuttled from the room. In the passageway, she heaved a great sigh of relief. Her job was safe and soon Daisy would be gone.

Chapter Two

The bright light hurt her eyes and, when she tried to move, her head ached. After a while, she tried to focus her eyes, but she could only see white clouds billowing around her. She felt weightless and her body seemed to be floating away. She was in heaven. She had died. A great pain of fear gripped her before darkness surrounded her again.

When she next opened her eyes the darkness was still around her. But, as her eyes became accustomed to the gloom, she was surprised to see a sleeping figure in a bed next to her. She didn't know they had beds in heaven. Then she saw a glimmer of light. It was coming from a small lamp on a table and sitting at the table was a woman in nursing uniform. *How strange*, she thought.

As if aware of the young woman waking up, the nurse left her post and quietly came towards the bed. 'So, you are awake at long last,' said the nurse in a soft voice. She checked the patient's pulse and blood pressure, and seemed satisfied with the results.

'Where am I?' asked the patient, in a barely audible voice.

'You are in hospital. You were involved in a road accident. What's your name, dear?'

Words formed on the young woman's dry lips, but no sound came from them and the skin on her face felt taut, and her eyes hurt with the effort of focusing. The touch of the nurse smoothing the bedcovers lulled her back into the safety of sleep.

When she next woke, it was to see a doctor and a nurse standing by her bedside. The nurse held a chart, and both she and the doctor were studying it. At the sound of stirring from the bed, both looked down at the young woman.

The doctor spoke in a brisk tone. 'Young woman, you have made a moderate recovery, considering your serious injuries.'

'My injuries?' the patient asked. 'What injuries?'

'You were involved in a traffic accident and you suffered critical injuries: internal bleeding, damage to your back and pelvis, a broken leg and a fractured skull, and you have suffered a certain amount of memory loss.' On seeing the fear on the patient's face, he continued in a softer voice. 'However, under our excellent nursing care, your health will be restored, given time.' He smiled reassuringly at her. Then he asked, 'Can you recall anything of the accident? Or your name, so that we can contact any family members you may have?'

The young woman looked puzzled, the pale skin of her face puckered in concentration, then tears filled her eyes and she bit on her lip but didn't speak. She closed her eyes, trying to remember who she was. Or was she trying to forget who she was? She wasn't sure what she felt because everything was so mixed up in her aching head.

The doctor and the nurse must have assumed she was asleep, because they began to discuss her case and she could hear them as they stood at the foot of her bed.

'Very odd,' said the doctor, 'that no one has reported her missing.'

'I understand that the police made enquiries, but no one came forward to identify the woman,' the nurse replied. Then they moved on out of earshot.

For a long time the young woman kept her eyes shut, but she was not sleeping. She was trying to think. Fragments of words seemed to be floating around in her head, but she couldn't grasp what they were.

Over the days that followed, she became known as Mrs Thursday, so called because she was admitted on a Thursday night to the cottage hospital on the eastern fringes of the city after a road accident, wearing only a nightdress. She shuddered at the thought, and a sense of being wet and cold filled her with fear. So, why hadn't anyone come forward to identify her? Did she not belong to anyone?

As each day passed, Mrs Thursday developed a strong determination to get better and pushed herself hard. But nothing could take away this strange feeling of not knowing who she was. Someone, somewhere, was waiting for her, someone needed her, but she wasn't sure who. Her broken leg was healing slowly, the pain in her back became easier and each day, with the aid of two sticks, she managed to walk around the ward. She still suffered from headaches, but was told by the doctor that, gradually, they would cease. He was quite concerned about her amnesia and she'd overheard him discussing this with another doctor.

'It is as if she does not wish to recall her past. And why was she running through a cold, wet street in just a sleeping garment?' One doctor had suggested that it could have been a form of sleepwalking.

Today, accompanied by an orderly, she was allowed to take a short walk in the grounds. Stopping for a rest, she leant on her sticks to admire the view of the green fields beyond the grounds.

She felt a jolt. A spark of recognition of something from her past, she felt sure. She tried to recall it, to reach out to it, but it vanished. Tears wet her lashes, and she felt agitated and angry. 'I want to know who I am,' she cried out.

'There, there, Mrs Thursday,' said the orderly, glancing at her watch. 'Time for your rest now.'

Exhausted, she lay on her bed, but sleep refused to come. Her mind was whirling like a spinning top as she tried to recall names, but they were elusive as they fluttered in and out, and she couldn't catch hold of them.

Eventually, she drifted off to sleep, but the same dream she'd dreamt before plagued her mind. And she experienced a sense of foreboding, something so dark and frightening. Always it was the same evil-faced man who towered above her, driving her into a black hole of fear.

The same terrifying dream occurred again that night, but it was different because a child appeared. She was hiding in a corner and, just as the man was about to pick her up and throw her in the air, a woman screamed out loud. Mrs Thursday woke up, sobbing and fighting for air. She clutched at the night nurse who had hurried to her bedside, crying, 'Don't let him hurt her.' She could taste the fear in her mouth and feel it crawling on her skin, and the strong smell of beer filled her nostrils. Wildly, she lashed out with her arms.

'Shush, you're safe,' the nurse soothed, beckoning to the probationer nurse. 'Call the duty doctor,' she ordered. Then she held the sobbing woman in her arms in an attempt to quieten her, so as not to further disturb the other patients.

The doctor came. 'A nightmare, I believe,' said the nurse and then watched as the doctor administered a sleeping draught.

The nurse stayed by Mrs Thursday's bedside until she slept and then she went back to her post to write up her report.

The woman slept until mid-morning. She was regularly checked by the probationer nurse who reported to the staff nurse that Mrs Thursday was awake.

'Don't just stand there wasting time,' the harassed staff nurse admonished the probationer. 'See to the patient.'

The probationer, Judy, was a willing worker and soon had the patient toileted, washed and bedlinen changed, and prepared a late breakfast of tea and bread and jam.

The woman lightly touched Judy on the arm and said, in a quiet voice, 'Thank you.'

'That's all right, Mrs Thursday,' said Judy, cheerfully. Then she scurried off to return to her task of cleaning out the lavatories or she'd miss her dinner break.

A few days later, in the afternoon, Mrs Thursday was sitting up in bed, reading a magazine passed to her by the woman in the next bed. It was visiting time and a lonely hour for her, because no one came to see her. It seemed that she was alone in the world, but somewhere . . . If only she could remember. The nightmare dream blocked her way and stopped her from moving forward.

She tried to immerse herself in the story she was reading, but her interest waned. She flicked over the page, seeing an article on fashionable dresses, coats and hats to suit all tastes. Had she ever worn clothes like these? She traced her fingers over the garments, willing a spark of recognition to ignite, but nothing happened. She couldn't languish for ever in a hospital bed – she had to find out who she was and then, maybe, the nightmares would go away.

'Alice Goddard, fancy seeing you here.' The voice cut into Mrs Thursday's thoughts.

Startled, she looked up to see a middle-aged woman standing at the foot of her bed.

Oblivious to Mrs Thursday's bewilderment, she continued on. 'Is yer fancy man coming to see you, then? I wouldn't mind a look at him. Is he a film star? He must be for you to leave that bonny daughter of yours. Don't you miss her?' the woman gabbled.

Mrs Thursday stared at the woman, her mind blank.

'Is there something wrong, Mrs Thursday?' said the ward sister, coming to stand by the side of her bed, having heard the visitor's loud voice.

'So, that's who yer calling yerself.'

'Madam, could I have a word with you in my office?' the sister asked, politely.

'But I'm here to see my friend, not her.'

'I will only take a few minutes of your time. Please, this way.'

Mrs Thursday watched them go, puzzled. The woman seemed to know her and called her a strange name. Alice Goddard. It meant nothing to her.

The ward sister was in Matron's office having a welcome cup of tea with her as she reported her findings. 'It appears that this woman is a neighbour of Mrs Thursday's mother, a Mrs Agnes Chandler, and the woman we refer to as Mrs Thursday is her married daughter, Mrs Alice Goddard.'

Matron replied, 'We must inform Mrs Chandler immediately. I will see to that. You must inform the doctor and he must be present when the patient, Mrs Thursday, is told of the facts as we know them.'

* * *

Aggie Chandler was having a well-earned snooze before teatime, when a loud knock sounded on the door. At first, she ignored it. Then it became more persistent. 'All right, I'm coming,' she muttered.

On opening the door, she saw a police constable standing there. 'Mrs Agnes Chandler?' he asked.

The first thing that flew into Aggie's mind was one of her lads had got up to mischief. 'Yes,' she replied, her face set in anger.

'Your daughter.' He glanced down at his notebook. 'Mrs Alice Goddard is in the Cottage Hospital suffering from loss of memory and you are requested to identify her.'

Aggie stared open-mouthed at him, lost for words.

The constable continued, 'You are to report to the matron at the hospital as soon as possible.' He shut his notebook and waited for Aggie to confirm.

She nodded, then said, 'Me bairns. I've ter get their tea.'

'You go, Aggie. I'll tek care of bairns.' It was her next-door neighbour who was standing on her doorstep, listening to the constable's words.

Aggie, still in her working clothes, arrived at the hospital out of breath and told her story to the porter on duty. He directed Aggie to the matron's office.

Matron was pleasant but efficient as she explained the facts and then escorted a confused Aggie to the ward where her daughter had been for the last six weeks. The matron's story differed from the story that Ted had spun her. In her heart, Aggie never believed that her Alice would leave her daughter to run off with another man. Things were in a right mess and how could she tell Alice about her daughter? Her heart sunk down to her shabby boots.

Matron glanced at her, saying, 'This must have been quite an ordeal for you.'

Aggie was shocked at the figure of the young woman lying in the hospital bed. She was so thin and pale, a shadow of the Alice she knew. At once she was by her side, clutching at the thin, frail hand that rested on the bedcover. 'Oh, my Alice! What's happened to you?'

The woman in the bed stared, looking bewildered at first and then a spark of recognition flickered across her eyes. 'Are you my mother?' she whispered.

'Of course I am and you're my Alice.' One of the probationers brought a chair for Agnes to sit on and she sank wearily onto it.

'Do I live with you?'

'No, you're married.'

A dark shadow crossed Alice's face and fear filled her eyes as she slipped further down into the bed.

Matron put a hand on Agnes's shoulder and said, quietly, 'Let her rest for now. It has been quite distressing for you both.' She led Agnes back to her office where a ward-maid served them both a cup of tea.

Agnes's hands were shaking as she held the cup of sweet tea to her parched lips. After a few sips, she spoke. 'I never expected to find Alice in hospital. Will she be all right?'

Matron smiled and said, reassuringly, 'Alice's injuries have almost healed and will have no lasting effect on her health, however . . .' She paused, choosing the right words. 'It was her loss of memory that was causing the most concern. However, now you have identified her and she recognises you, she should recover quickly.' She rose to her feet, saying, 'Thank you, Mrs Chandler, for coming. You may visit your daughter tomorrow afternoon.'

Agnes murmured her thanks. Slowly, she made her way home to check on her lads and that Martha was home from work to make sure they were cared for. She didn't want anything else to happen. She was getting too old for worry. Since Albert had died, that seemed to be her lot: work and worry. And just when she thought she was turning a corner, trouble pounced on her.

Chapter Three

When her mother had gone, Alice closed her eyes. She wasn't asleep, but she wanted to think. She must try to remember how she came to be in hospital. She felt sure it was to do with the dreams, the nightmares she'd been having. All she knew was what the doctor had told her, that she'd been involved in a motor car accident and was only wearing a nightdress when admitted to hospital. So, had she been sleepwalking or running away from something or somebody? The scenario played over and over in her mind until her eyelids felt so heavy, as if someone was standing on them, that she finally succumbed to sleep.

'You've had a good night's sleep,' said the nurse who came to check on Alice the next morning.

Alice yawned and stretched, then said, 'Have I really slept right through the night?'

'Yes. A good sign that you are improving,' the nurse replied.

Later, after breakfast, washed and wearing a clean nightgown, Alice did, indeed, feel so much livelier in body and mind. She sat on her bedside chair trying to recall things from her past. A child's cry interrupted her thoughts and she turned, but there was no child to be seen. She eased herself up from the chair reaching to see further round the ward and nearly overbalanced. A probationer nurse came hurrying to her, steadied her and stopped her from falling.

'Do be careful,' she said, taking hold of Alice's arm and lowering her gently back onto the chair.

Settled and safe, Alice said, 'I thought I heard a child crying.'

The probationer glanced round and replied, 'Children are not allowed on the wards. Perhaps the sound came from outside.' She motioned to the open window.

Strange, Alice thought, *it was as if the child was quite close by.*

Later that afternoon, Aggie came to see Alice. She wasn't in her working clothes and had made an effort with her appearance, wearing the only coat she possessed and her best black felt hat to match her coat. Her boots were well polished, but the soles were thin and needed mending. She had been hoping to buy a new pair, but her lodger, now installed, needed a wardrobe, something she hadn't thought of. She sighed heavily. Soon, the lads would need new boots too. She'd be glad when the twins left school and were working full-time. At the moment, both earned a few pence by running errands for neighbours and, when someone wanted to put a bet on a horse they'd act as bookie's runners, taking care to avoid police constables.

Entering the ward, Aggie forced a smile on her face. She was dreading having to tell Alice about Daisy. 'Now then, lass, how are yer today?' she said, sitting down on an uncomfortable visitor's chair by her bedside.

Alice replied, saying the one thing that kept reverberating in her head, 'I heard the voice of a child, a little girl's voice. Do I have children?'

Aggie caught her breath and swallowed hard, not sure how to tell her daughter the truth so, instead of answering the question, she asked one of her own. 'What do you remember?'

Alice closed her eyes, remembering, and said out loud, 'It was a dark, wet night and a man, a big, frightening man, was coming after me.' The voice inside her head became louder and she heard the distinct cry of a little girl. 'Have I a daughter?' She opened her eyes wide to stare into Aggie's horrified ones.

'Yes,' Aggie muttered. 'Ted brought her to me when—'

Alice cut in. 'Ted, is he my son?'

'Lord, no! He's yer husband. He brought little Daisy to me, telling me you'd run off with another man.'

Fearfully, Alice looked round the ward, saying, 'I don't want to see him.'

'He's long gone. Heard he's got a ship and gone off ter see the world.'

Alice relaxed and said, 'I wish children were allowed to visit. I'm longing to see my little girl. Tell her I love her, won't you?'

Aggie felt her blood run cold. She couldn't meet her daughter's gaze, so she bent down, pretending to pick up something from the floor. After more stilted conversation, the bell rang for the end of visiting time. Quickly, she was on her feet, saying her goodbyes, with a promise to visit at the weekend.

Alice watched her mother hurry down the ward until she disappeared through the door. 'I have a daughter,' she said to the woman in the next bed.

'That's nice, love. What's her name?'

'Daisy.' She whispered the name over and over to herself, smiling happily. She couldn't wait to see her.

The next day, the doctor and the ward sister, on their daily round of the wards, stopped at the foot of Alice's bed and picked up her chart to study. 'I am pleased that your memory is returning and, if all goes according to plan, we will soon be discharging you.' He smiled at her and they moved on to the next patient.

Alice felt a warm glow of excitement. She was longing to see her daughter and hold her in her arms. All afternoon she thought about her daughter, remembering her fair curly hair, big blue eyes and a lovely smile. And then she frowned. Would her daughter know her after all these long weeks apart? *What if she doesn't?*

'Bairns never forget their mammy,' said the woman in the next bed when Alice confided her fear.

Reassured, that night her dreams were sweet. The big, horrible, frightening man had disappeared, hopefully gone from her life.

On Sunday afternoon, Alice, her face shining with happiness, waited for visiting time. At last, the door opened and visitors came streaming in. Alice was surprised to see a young woman come to her bedside. Puzzled, she studied the young woman, watching as she sat down on the chair.

'It's me, your sister.'

Alice stared at the young woman who was smiling at her, and then a hint of recognition flickered and she knew. 'You are Martha!' Her face lit up with pleasure, and she held out her arms to embrace her. Both young women settled back. 'Where's Mam?' Alice said, looking round.

Martha's face became sombre and said, 'She's sorry, but she has to get the lodger's washing and ironing done.'

'A lodger?' Alice queried.

'Yes, he pays her for board and lodgings each week, so that she doesn't have to work of a night. She said she's getting too old for that.'

Alice nodded, saying, 'I suppose it makes sense. What's he like?'

'Bit of a stuffed shirt. He won't bother me because, as soon as I'm eighteen, I'm moving out.'

Alice looked at Martha and could see how grown-up she now was. Now, with family business out of the way, she asked, 'Tell me how my Daisy is. Is she missing me?'

Martha looked startled by the question. 'Daisy? I don't know. Why should I?'

Now it was Alice's turn to look startled as she responded, 'But she lives with you. Mam said Ted brought her to your house.'

Martha looked down at the highly polished wooden floor, wishing it would magic her away. But she couldn't just get up and run. Mam had left her to do the dirty work. She hadn't told Alice. At last, she raised her head, took a deep breath and let it out slowly, and then said, 'Mam took Daisy to the authorities.'

Stunned, Alice felt her insides turn to ice, and then she spoke. 'Authorities, why?'

Martha shrugged, feeling ill at ease. She stuttered, 'Mam said she couldn't cope with another bairn.'

'How could she do that to her own granddaughter?' Anger, mixed with fear for Daisy, filled her.

'Ted told her you'd run off with another man. She did what she thought was best.'

'But, I didn't run off. I've been in hospital all the time.'

'Sorry,' muttered Martha, wishing she was anywhere but here.

Alice fell back on the pillow, her eyes filling with tears at the thought of Daisy being with strangers.

For the rest of the hour, the sisters barely spoke.

When the bell rang, Martha jumped up from the chair, saying, 'Goodbye.'

'Wait,' Alice commanded. Martha stood stiffly, anxious to be gone. 'Tell Mam I need to see her on the next visiting day. I need to know all the facts.'

When her sister departed, Alice slipped further down the bed, wondering how she would get through the time until the next visiting day.

Later on, when the nurse was doing her rounds, she remarked, 'Your blood pressure has risen.' Alice didn't reply. 'Any reason?' asked the nurse.

Alice shook her head. She didn't want to speak about it.

The days passed so slowly and, at last, it was visiting afternoon. As the visitors entered the ward, there was no sign of Aggie.

After twenty minutes, a lone figure moved slowly down the ward. Aggie stopped at the foot of the bed, staring down at Alice, and then said, 'I believed Ted when he said yer ran off with another man. What was I to think or do? I had to find help.'

'I need the details, so I can go and get my daughter back from the authorities.'

Aggie, still standing, shrugged and said, 'I ain't got any details.'

'You must have something?'

'No, they didn't give me nowt.'

Alice sat up straight. 'They can't just take a child without the necessary forms.'

'Well, they did,' Aggie replied, stubbornly. 'If I'd known you were in hospital, I would have come to see you and sort it out. But nobody told me nowt.'

'I didn't leave Daisy on purpose, I was going for help.'

'Yer did. That's why Ted brought her to me,' Aggie shouted.

The woman's visitor at the next bed frowned at her.

Ignoring her, Aggie continued, 'I'm sorry. I really didn't know what ter do.'

Alice stared at Aggie, barely comprehending.

Aggie pulled her shawl closer around her neck and huffed. 'All I know is she has gone to a good home. And, before yer start, I don't know where.'

'But you must know.'

'I don't know. I was at my wits' end. What do yer think I could do? I've enough hardship in my life without tekkin' on yours.' Then she muttered, 'I'm sorry, lass.' She screwed up her face, suddenly remembering something. 'They said it was only for now, till yer came back.' Redeeming herself, Aggie stood up to leave.

Alice sank back on the pillow.

Aggie was hurrying along the corridor when someone called her name. 'Mrs Chandler, may I have a word with you, please?' Matron stood in the doorway of her office.

Aggie was taken off guard and stared open-mouthed, wondering, *What now?* She followed Matron into her office and sat on a chair in front of the desk. She felt self-conscious of her appearance in her work clothes, and wished she'd put on her coat and hat.

Matron smiled politely and said, 'Your daughter, Mrs Goddard, will soon be discharged into your care. Do you require any help with arrangements?'

Aggie just gawked.

Matron continued, 'I can arrange for transport to take her to your home and have a nurse accompany her.'

'But she can't,' Aggie uttered in a squeaky voice.

'Do you mean you wish to accompany Mrs Goddard from the hospital?'

'I ain't got no room for her. Me house is full now I've taken in a lodger.' She stood up, pulling her shawl tightly around her. 'I'm sorry,' she mumbled, and took flight from the office and the hospital.

Once outside, she realised she was trembling from the top of her grey hair to the tip of her worn boots. She needed to get home and have a cup of strong tea.

Aggie's bad news took its toll on a distraught Alice. Her temperature shot up and so did her blood pressure. The nurse, recording this on Alice's chart, asked, 'Have you been upset?'

Tearfully, Alice blurted out about what Aggie had told her about her daughter, Daisy. 'I need to find her.'

'Of course you do, but you must stop fretting and concentrate on a full recovery, and then you can find where your daughter is.' The nurse made Alice comfortable and then she went to report to the sister about the deterioration of Alice's health and the probable cause of it.

After a consultation involving all the hospital staff concerned, the consensus was that Alice would benefit from a few weeks of convalescence. The nearest one with a vacancy was Bridlington, on the east coast, about twenty-five miles away. Arrangements were made, and Alice was told this was in her best interest, if she was to make a full recovery.

Chapter Four

A nurse accompanied Alice to the convalescent home. And on the journey from the hospital, in a transport vehicle to Paragon railway station, she searched the children playing in streets and down alleys for Daisy, her beloved daughter. Her thoughts seemed to be rambling in her head and her big question was how could Ted have deserted their innocent child? If only she hadn't run from the house. But this attack had been so vicious, worse than the others, and she'd feared for her life and Daisy's. If only she could have foreseen the terrible consequences that had followed. Everything – the relentless brutality she'd suffered, and why she was running to the police station for help – flooded back to her, though she had no recollection of being hit by the car. Fate had dealt her a hard blow. Now, her paramount aim was to find her beloved daughter.

The train ride was uneventful. Alice sat quietly, staring out of the window, her companion, a nurse in her thirties, said she was glad of some peace and was happy to read her novel.

They arrived at the Regency Convalescent Home Bridlington,

which was situated facing the promenade and the North Sea. By now, it was mid-afternoon and Alice felt tired. After a welcoming cup of tea, she was shown up to the room that she was sharing with another lady. The walls of the room were painted a restful shade of pale green and the bed linen was pure white, in contrast to the dark chest of drawers and the wardrobe. She went to sit down on the edge of the narrow bed that was hers and dropped the old attaché case containing a few essential clothes, donated to her by the hospital charity, at her feet. The bed felt soft and inviting to her touch as she ran her hand over the coverlet. She untied her boots and eased her weary body down on the bed. She thought that at once, on leaving the hospital, her strength would return, but she felt absolutely drained of energy. A gentle breeze drifted in through the open window, playing with the curtains, and the peaceful sound of the sea lapping onto the sand soon lulled her to sleep.

She slept so soundly that she didn't wake up when her room-mate came to bed.

The next morning, after a good night's sleep, she felt refreshed in body and mind. Her room-mate said a quick hello and left the room. Alice washed and dressed and went down for breakfast. She was shown to a window table with three other people. There was a retired schoolmistress, who was recovering from a delicate operation, a shop assistant, recovering from an eye operation, and a nurse recovering from a back injury. The nurse, Evelyn Laughton, was the patient with whom Alice was sharing a room. She was tall in comparison to Alice, and she had warm brown eyes and dark wavy hair cut in a bob. Alice took an instant liking to her. They chattered quite amicably, though Alice mostly just listened to the others talking. She wasn't ready, if ever, to talk about her missing daughter or her estranged husband.

After breakfast, Alice set off for a solitary walk along the promenade. Though the sun shone, a cold wind was blowing off the sea. All the clothes she had were from a charity that helped destitute people. She hadn't realised that there were such good people willing to help. If only there had been someone from whom she could have sought advice, or spoken to, about her husband's cruel treatment of her. But a married woman was expected to make the best of her marriage, good or bad, so she'd suffered in silence until . . . She shuddered, stopping to lean on a railing, and to look out to sea and the far horizon. Tears filled her eyes. She yearned to hold her daughter close and keep her safe. Where was she? And who was she with? Did they love and care for her, and treat her well? She desperately hoped so.

One day, Evelyn asked Alice, 'May I walk with you?'

Alice hesitated, because she wanted to walk on her own with only her thoughts for company, but it would be rude to refuse, so she smiled and nodded.

They strolled in silence towards the north end of the town, which was livelier, with more people about, taking the fresh sea air.

It was Evelyn who spoke first. 'What will you do when you leave here?'

Without thinking, Alice replied, 'Find my daughter.'

'Your daughter?'

Tears wet Alice's lashes and she felt so sad. Gently, Evelyn took hold of her arm and led her to a sheltered area with wooden seating, away from the prying eyes of other people.

Alice unburdened herself and told Evelyn her sad, worrying story. When she finished, she felt a great relief to be able to tell another person of her suffering and her missing daughter.

Evelyn showed compassion, but she was also practical. 'First, you will need somewhere to stay. Has anyone spoken to you about what you will do when you leave here?'

Alice shook her head.

'I can arrange for you to see the matron in charge of the convalescent home. She may be able to help.'

The next day, Alice waited with trepidation outside the matron's office. She'd only spoken briefly to the matron when she first arrived and then seen her when she made her daily rounds. Alice checked her appearance in the small mirror on the wall. Her fair hair was still raggy and patchy from her head injury, but she'd combed it to hide the scar. Her face shone clean, and now showed a touch of pink on her cheeks from the fresh sea air on her daily walks. The dark-green dress she wore was of fine wool, with neat collar and cuffs – though rather faded, it was serviceable. Once, she surmised, it must have belonged to someone with money and class.

She jolted as the door of the office opened and a plain-looking woman dressed in grey said, 'Matron will see you now.'

Alice entered the office. Matron was sitting behind a large oak desk, writing. She didn't look up and the only noise in the room was the scratching of her pen. Alice's gaze took in the sombre room of dark brown walls where there hung a row of photos of past matrons of the establishment. Alice could feel the leg, which she'd broken in the accident, begin to hurt with standing still. Placed near to the big desk was a chair, which looked inviting, and she longed to sit down on it, but dared not until she was asked.

'Mrs Goddard.' The voice from the desk spoke.

Alice pulled her body up taller and gave her full attention. 'Yes, Matron,' she replied, hoping her voice didn't betray the nervousness she felt.

'I understand you are homeless and without funds,' the matron stated, bluntly and directly.

'Yes, Matron.' She felt ashamed at her predicament. Not only did she not have a home or any money, she had also lost her daughter. What kind of woman and mother was she? A lump caught in her throat and she swallowed hard, not wanting to cry and show such weakness before this competent and astute-looking woman.

'There is not much to offer you – there is the workhouse.' Matron looked at her.

Alice's heart filled with dread at the mention of the workhouse and she felt the hairs on the back of her neck prickle with shame at the thought of being an inmate there.

'However,' Matron continued, 'there is a live-in position at Faith House, in Hull, a home for fallen girls. As you have experience of being a housewife, part of your duties will be to instruct the girls in how to manage certain aspects of a home and prepare them for life once they leave Faith House. The girls can be difficult and may not want to conform to life in an institution.' A faint smile touched her lips as she said, 'I know from first-hand experience, as I once held a position there. It is hard work and the hours are long, with not much free time for being off-duty. Are you capable of this?'

Surprised and wide-eyed at such a challenge, Alice answered, 'Yes, Matron,' and then added, 'I will do my very best.' She would have liked to have asked how she should go about reuniting with her daughter. For now, she would have a place to work and live. And, in her free time, she would find out where Daisy was.

Alice went to look for Evelyn and found her in the sitting room reading. Quietly, she entered the room, curbing her excitement of getting a job.

Evelyn looked up and closed her book. 'Come and sit down, and tell me your good news.'

'How can you tell it's good news?'

'By the sparkle in your eyes. You've looked sad and been subdued all the time you've been here.'

Alice sat down and told Evelyn what had transpired with the matron. She finished by saying, 'Thank you, Evelyn, for all your help.'

Evelyn smiled and said, 'We must keep in touch because I will want to hear how you get on at Faith House.' They exchanged addresses. Evelyn was a nurse at the infirmary in one of the men's wards and lived in the nurses' quarters near Prospect Street as her family lived in the market town of Beverley, which was too far for her to travel from daily.

On her last day at the convalescent home, Alice set off alone and turned right for her walk towards the south end of the town. She strolled along the promenade and went further than she intended, to where there were fewer people about and the sands were deserted. Feeling tired from walking so far, she sat down on a wooden bench facing the sea. There were no screeching gulls, so it was quiet and peaceful. She looked towards the sea, mesmerised by the incoming tide gently lapping on the fringe of the golden sands, its white frothy foam reminding her of her childhood days when she bathed in a tin bath in front of the fire. She'd create lots of bubbles to cover her budding body, which gave her privacy from the prying eyes of her young siblings. There had been no privacy in a small, crowded house.

Then her thoughts turned to Daisy. Would she be fretting for her? Alice felt determined to find out where her daughter was. As soon as she returned to Hull and settled into her job, she would make plans and start her search. She rose from her seat and walked along the promenade, feeling light-hearted and positive. Someone, somewhere, would know where Daisy was.

In a big house in the village of Elloughton, on the outskirts of Hull, in a large pink bedroom full of fluffy toys, a little girl, in a bed of snowy-white covers decorated with rosebuds, cried for her mammy. Every night the pillow was wet with her dewy tears.

'She's wet the bed again, madam,' said the housekeeper.

Mrs Cooper-Browne set down her breakfast cup, her brow furrowing. 'I'm at a loss what to do with her. I'll speak to the doctor again. See that she's bathed before you bring her down.' Dismissively, she turned to pour herself another cup of tea.

The housekeeper went back upstairs to bathe the little girl and dress her in one of those ridiculous frilly dresses.

'I want Mammy,' the little girl cried, sobbing and hiccupping as if her little heart would break.

The housekeeper gently wiped the child's eyes. 'Now, try and be good for Mrs Cooper-Browne and then I'll let you help me bake jam tarts.' She kissed the top of the golden curls and took hold of the girl's hand to take her downstairs to that cold fish of a woman who was pretending to be a mother.

'Poor little mite, she's fretting away,' said the housekeeper to her husband as he came into the kitchen from his gardening duties. 'She should be with her own mother.'

He lit a cigarette and mumbled, 'Nowt to do with us. We just do the job we're paid to do and don't you forget it.'

She turned away, feeling so helpless.

Chapter Five

Alice journeyed back to Hull by train and walked from the station, through the city centre, crossing over the River Hull by the North Bridge, to the area of Witham. Arriving at her destination, she stood on the pavement looking up at Faith House, a rescue home for fallen girls. It was an imposing late-Victorian three-storey building of local brick. She glanced to her right down Holderness Road, which led to East Park where, when she'd saved enough money for the tram fare, she would take Daisy and . . . She brushed away the single tear trickling down her cheek.

Gripping the handle of the small attaché case tightly, and ignoring the fluttering of apprehension in her stomach, she marched up the steps to the front door. The heavy brass knocker sounded loudly, and she felt surprised at her strength to make it do so. A young girl in a dark-blue dress and white pinafore opened the door.

Without hesitation she stated, 'I am Mrs Goddard and I've an appointment to see Matron.'

She was ushered in and asked to wait in the hall, which had a beautiful wooden carved staircase, something that she had never seen before. Within a few minutes, she was shown into Matron's room. She was surprised, for it was nothing as austere as the matron's office at the convalescent home. It was small and cosy, with a table and upright chairs, a couch, various ornaments, pictures adorning the walls and a welcoming fire burning brightly in the fancy iron grate. Matron looked a pleasant woman with a round, smiling face. She rose from her chair to greet Alice.

'Please, Mrs Goddard, sit down,' she indicated one of the upright chairs. 'I am Matron Bailey.' Both seated, she asked, 'You have a letter for me?'

Alice withdrew from her handbag the envelope addressed to Matron Bailey and handed it to her. While she waited for her to read its contents, Alice experienced a warm and friendly feeling surrounding her.

'I see you've had a difficult and trying time,' Matron Bailey said, quietly.

Alice glanced at Matron's soft grey eyes and her kind face, the very opposite of the matron at the convalescent home.

'The girls in our care have faced a life of degrading hardship and, in the two years they are with us, we teach them skills to survive and to live a better life. While your experience of domestic life is invaluable to our teaching, the girls are my principal consideration. Therefore, I must stress to you that you do not talk about' – here she paused, then continued – 'the upsetting experiences you have endured. Is that understood, Mrs Goddard?'

Alice sat up straight and answered in a clear voice, 'I understand, Matron Bailey.' This was a relief to her because she didn't want to talk about her troubled past life. She wanted to keep it private until she set out to find Daisy and then she would tell whoever she had to.

'Excellent,' Matron said, and then rang a bell on her desk. The same girl who had opened the door to her entered the room. 'Show Mrs Goddard to her room.' Matron handed over a large iron key to the girl.

Alice followed the girl up the staircase and along a corridor to a room at the end. The girl opened the door and then gave the key to Alice, bobbed a curtsey and then, without speaking, turned and walked back down the corridor.

Speechless herself, she stood on the threshold of the room. Never in her whole life had she had a room of her own. She closed the door and looked around with pleasure. It was square-shaped with a tiny window with a pull-down blind. She crossed the bare, wooden floor and opened the blind to see a view of a small courtyard and nearby rooftops. She turned and went to sit on the iron bedstead. Its covers were neatly folded at the foot of the bed and a pillow rested at the head. There was a small table and chair, a chest with drawers, and on the top there was a bowl and ewer. The walls were painted with plain white distemper. It was at that moment that she wished she had a photo of her beloved Daisy. She closed her eyes and visualised her daughter: a bonny little girl with blonde curly hair and eyes the colour of the bluebells, which grew in the woodland area of the park where she loved to skip along the path, her childish voice happy and joyful, calling, 'Mammy, look at me.' A choking sob rose in her throat. Alice looked round for a distraction and jumped from the bed, went over to the ewer and, pouring cool water into the bowl, she rinsed her face.

Feeling refreshed and looking forward to the challenge ahead, she opened her case and took out her belongings: a change of undergarments, a winceyette nightdress, a clean blouse, two embroidered handkerchiefs and a pair of lisle stockings, which were a present from Evelyn. She wore a grey woollen skirt and a linen print blouse, her only pair of wool stockings and a pair of sensible boots. All of them were second- or third-hand, donated by a charity for destitute women. Her only new personal possessions were a brush and comb, given to her by a group of ladies called Companions of Compassion, who regularly visited the convalescent home. She placed these on top of the dresser and tidied her clothes away into the drawer.

On top of the table was a large piece of card. She sat down on the chair and picked it up to read what was written. It was a list of rules and duties, which were intended for the smooth running of the home in the interest of the girls. Alice studied them. She would be on duty from six-thirty in the mornings until nine-thirty in the evenings, and she was entitled to one afternoon and one evening per week off-duty. Mealtimes were breakfast: 7.30 a.m., dinner: 12.30 p.m., tea: 4.30 p.m., and supper at 9 p.m. Her duties were to begin tomorrow, while today she had to familiarise herself with the layout of the home, and she would meet the girls and other members of staff. At all times, when she left her room, her door must be locked and the key must be on her person.

Smoothing down her rumpled skirt, she patted her hair into place, which was now cut into a neat bob. She then took a deep breath and let it out slowly, as she was taught to do at the convalescent home. This helped to calm her and now she was ready for whatever came her way. She opened the door and locked it behind her, slipping the key into her skirt pocket. Then she walked briskly along the corridor and down the stairs.

The smell of cooking greeted her; a surprisingly tantalising aroma was something she hadn't expected from institution cooking. Her stomach rumbled and felt hollow. She hadn't eaten at all today, except to have a cup of tea before starting off on her train journey. She'd felt rather nervous at the thought of coming here, but she need not have worried. Matron Bailey was welcoming, though Alice imagined that she could be strict. And the house felt like a home, a happy home, though she mustn't become complacent and take things for granted. She was here to work. This was her first job since before she was married, when she'd worked in a greengrocer's shop.

She shuddered at the memory, because that was when she'd met Ted. He would often stop by the shop to buy a carrot for his horse. He drove a horse and rully and worked for Hopkins Brewery, and workers were allowed a ration of beer a week. He asked her to walk out with him on a Sunday afternoon. He had been quite a charmer in those days and her head had been turned by his manner of making her feel special. They'd walked to the pier, a popular promenade for young people to meet. She was only sixteen and had never walked out with a boy before. Ted was older, twenty-one, and lived in lodgings in a rooming house where the food was poor and he was fed up of living there. He wanted home comforts and a bed mate. After they'd been walking out for over a year, he asked her to marry him. Her mother, Aggie, thought she was too young to marry, but Ted charmed her mother round by taking her to the local pub and plying her with port and lemon. When she had plenty to drink and a good sing-song round the piano, Aggie agreed for them to be married on Alice's eighteenth birthday. Ted was shrewd: if they married, then they would become eligible to rent one of the Hopkins Brewery houses. Alice, for her part, was thrilled at the thought of having her own house and to be away from her mother's rules. Aggie still had four younger children at home and Alice had to hand over most of her wages to her mother each week.

At first, married life was pleasing. Ted earned good money, so they never went hungry, and she never minded him spending his nights in the pub. On Saturday nights, he'd take her to the music hall, which was rather rowdy, but fun. Then she became pregnant and was sick for the first few months, and the smell of cooking would turn her stomach. Once, when Ted came home and she hadn't cooked him a meal, he went berserk, lashing out at her. She'd shouted at him and then he stormed off to the pub and came home drunk. He wanted to make it up and she had to endure his insensitive use of her body. It was after then she always made sure, even if she felt unwell, to have a meal on the table for him when he came home from work. Taking pride in her home, she kept it spotlessly clean, which was the only consolation she had, apart from her baby growing within.

Ted took no part in the preparation for the baby. It was she who painted the spare bedroom wall with a pretty primrose-coloured distemper. In the evenings, when he was at the pub, she would sew curtains for the window and covers for the cot, all with material that she'd bought from the market stalls around Holy Trinity Church. Here, she did her main shopping and always looked for a bargain, loving the smell of fresh apples in season. She'd learnt the art of thriftiness from her mother, who was always short of money.

A voice broke into Alice's reverie. 'There you are, Mrs Goddard, finding your way around?'

Alice turned to see a smiling face. 'Yes, thank you, Matron Bailey,' she replied, dutifully.

'Come with me to the dining room.' And Alice followed.

The girls and the other staff were already seated and, when Matron entered, they all stood up. She motioned for them to sit down and said, 'This is Mrs Goddard, our new assistant. Tomorrow, she begins her duties.' Then she made her way to take her seat at the head of the staff table and Alice sat at the vacant place on the end of the bench. Matron said grace and the meal was served by the girls, who took turns by rota.

Alice had felt hungry before, but now nerves fluttered in her stomach and her appetite deserted her. Then she remembered to do her deep-breathing exercises, hoping that no one was watching her. She spooned a small morsel of food into her mouth and she began to eat the rest of the tasty bowl of stew and dumplings, which was followed by rice pudding. She felt so much better and she'd enjoyed the food. She sipped a cup of water and glanced round at the other staff, five females of varying ages. The girls were about forty in number. She knew that Faith House was supported by a charity, with money from a Mr J. P. Steadman, a stalwart benefactor, in memory of his late wife.

After dinner, Alice was being given a quick, detailed account of the work of Faith House by the deputy matron, Miss Bird, a thin reed of a woman, with, true to her name, small, bird-like eyes. Her first words to Alice were, 'My friend wanted to work here, but you got the job. Who pulled the strings for you?'

Alice didn't answer and sensed that they wouldn't be friends.

She followed Miss Bird to the back of the house where the laundry room was situated.

Miss Bird droned on in a monotone. 'The girls spend two years in the home. Their ages range from as young as ten up to sixteen, and they are given a good training in laundry work and other housekeeping duties. This equips them to earn a living once they leave here.'

Alice noticed how hard-working the girls were and they seemed to have satisfaction in a job well done. The bedding was spotlessly clean and was now being pressed with irons heated on top of the copper stove. Suddenly, one of the younger girls dropped a sheet she was folding, and her face took on a scared look as Miss Bird was bearing down towards her.

'What have I told you before, you lazy girl? You haven't the sense you were born with.'

The girl, frightened, tried to pick up the sheet, but dropped it again. Miss Bird raised her hand to deliver a blow. But Alice was quicker. She stepped in between the girl and the deputy matron.

The other girls in the room stood ridged, not daring to move or speak.

Although Alice's insides were trembling, her voice was strong and firm. 'It needs two pairs of hands and I will help you,' she said to the stunned girl. 'It is not a task for the deputy matron, don't you agree?' she said to the startled Miss Bird, who, without a word, turned and left the room.

That night, as she lay in bed, Alice realised that she'd made an enemy on her first day. For the rest of the day, after the incident, she had been expecting a summons to Matron Bailey's office, but it didn't happen.

After suffering brutality at the hand of her husband, a man

who, according to their marriage vows, was supposed to love and protect her, one thing she did know for certain was that she wouldn't tolerate violence ever again. And she thought of her daughter gone from her. If only she'd stood up to Ted, retaliated, then Daisy would still be with her.

Chapter Six

Two whole weeks had passed and life at Faith House was hectic, with an intake of six new girls assigned to Alice, so there was no time to take off-duty periods. Her first task with the girls was to delouse their infested hair, burn their clothes and see that they scrubbed their bodies clean in the tin tub in a small room off the kitchen. And then she found clothes to fit them from the store – clothes that were donated. Now, looking clean and presentable, she led them to the dining room.

At first, the girls just stood, not moving forward to sit down at the table as she indicated. She glanced at them, wondering what the problem was.

Then the tallest girl spoke. 'What do us 'ave ter do, missus?'

'Do?' Alice asked, puzzled. And then she understood. 'While you are at Faith House, for your two years of training, you will each receive four meals a day.'

'Frigging hell,' said the girl, amazement filling her pale, angular face. And there was a buzz of expletives from the other girls as they hurried to sit down at the table and to tuck into a meal of tasty vegetable soup and thick chunks of freshly baked bread.

Alice sat quietly, observing. Although she came from a poor background, her mother always adhered to her quote 'Cleanliness is next to godliness' and instilled this in her children. So, she tried not to be shocked and judgemental at the state of the girls' bodies. But what appalled her most was the vile language they used, more what would be expected from navvies than girls. Though, she suspected, mostly it was bravado, if they had to survive in the world of prostitution they had inhabited.

Three weeks later, she had her first afternoon off. Outside the home, Alice breathed in the fresh, welcoming air and turned in the direction of her mother's home. When Aggie had visited her in hospital, she had been very evasive about the whereabouts of Daisy. Alice had an inkling Aggie knew more than she was willing to reveal. If she was to find her daughter, she would start with her mother.

At this time of day, late afternoon before teatime, Aggie would be having a much-needed rest. Alice knew her mother always worked hard to bring up her children, but the most important ingredient was missing: love. Perhaps Aggie had no concept of love, or did not feel it for her children, because she always said 'Yer get no medals for having bairns.' It was left to Alice, when she was the eldest girl at home, to give her siblings a hug, a cuddle or words of love, but only when their mother was not around.

She called into the shop on the corner of Fretters Lane and bought a pennyworth of sweets for her siblings and a twist of snuff for Aggie.

'By heck, where've you come from?' asked Mrs Mumby, shopkeeper, rising from her stool from behind the counter. 'Still with yer fancy man, are yer?'

Used to Mrs Mumby's ways and not taking offence, Alice answered truthfully. 'I've been in hospital, put there by that shark of a man Ted Goddard. It was him who started the rumours, so be sure to tell everyone what he did – and he's the one who deserted our daughter, not me.'

'Well I never,' Mrs Mumby replied, eager to pass on the best bit of gossip she'd heard all week.

Leaving the shop, Alice turned into Marvel Court, a narrow paved strip, neither terrace nor street, and with nothing to emulate marvel, and lucky if you caught the light or sunshine. Some of the dwellings were three storeys high and held more than one family or were rooming houses. The Chandler family lived in one of the smaller houses with a kitchen and front room downstairs and two bedrooms upstairs, and a small yard at the back with its own lavatory. Some neighbours stood on doorsteps having a gossip, often their only luxury. They stared open-mouthed at Alice as she passed them by without a word. Then she heard them even before she was out of earshot. 'Well, how dare that slut show her face in this respectable court?'

Alice walked on smiling. Soon, Mrs Mumby would tell them the truth, with embellishment by her, of course.

She reached her childhood home. The door was unlocked, and Alice entered, calling, 'It's me, Mam.'

Aggie was dozing in her chair by the unlit fireplace. Opening her eyes, she stared blearily at her daughter. 'Oh, it's you,' she greeted, and she pulled herself up straight, coughing and spluttering.

'Here, I've brought you this.' Alice handed Aggie the twist of snuff, but kept the sweets for when her siblings came home from school.

When her mother had taken the snuff and looked more settled,

Alice wasted no time. 'I need to find Daisy and you know where she is.' She stood over her mother, something she'd never done before, but along the way, she'd become toughened by life.

This took Aggie by surprise. 'I know nowt,' she mumbled.

'Yes, you do.'

'I've ter think of me job. I can't say nowt.'

'So, your employer, Mrs Melton, knows something.'

Startled, Aggie sat up. 'Don't ask her. I'll lose me job and me bairns will starve.'

'Don't worry, I'll not mention you. I'll just go and ask her advice. After all, she is a pillar of society.'

Alice stayed to see her three young brothers, the twins, Harry and Jimmy, and the youngest, Charlie. She made a fuss of them and they watched in awe as she shared out the boiled sweets, in a rainbow of colours. 'Goodies!' they all exclaimed, looking with fondness at their big sister.

'It'll spoil their tea,' Aggie grumbled.

But Alice knew that the tea would only be bread and dripping, and her brothers were always hungry. She wished that she could have brought them more.

She stayed until Martha came home and received a welcome hug from her. 'Sorry, I can't stay, I have to be back at work,' she told them all.

'I'll walk to the end of the court with you,' Martha said.

Outside, in the damp air, Martha said, 'I never believed you would leave little Daisy and run off with another man. It just wasn't you. I hope you find her.'

The two sisters walked side by side, Martha doing most of the talking. 'I've got plans for my future and it doesn't include getting married and having bairns.'

Before they parted, Alice said, 'We'll meet up and have a proper chat when I have a free night off.'

Alice hurried back to Faith House, not wanting to be late back so Miss Bird would have an excuse to give her a ticking-off.

The new girls were proving rather difficult. Hetty, the tall girl with dark corkscrew hair, was the instigator. 'I didn't wanna come here. I was earning good money. Bloody do-gooders, they know nowt. Now, I'm expected to wash mucky clothes and go ter bed when the Bird tells me. It ain't right.'

When Miss Bird entered the laundry room to check on Alice's progress, the girls became silent, except Hetty. 'I wanna go home,' she pouted.

Alice watched as Miss Bird clenched her fists and her face reddened as she shouted, 'You, girl, are the lucky one, so be grateful to be not leading a life of wickedness.'

Hetty merely laughed. 'What's wrong with a bit of you-know-what and getting paid for it? I'd pull me bloomers down for any man if he's got money.' She squealed with laughter. 'If I wore any.'

Suddenly, Miss Bird took hold of a bar of carbolic soap and rammed it into Hetty's laughing mouth. Hetty spluttered, choking as the soap stuck in her throat.

Alice acted quickly and banged Hetty hard on the back, and the soap shot out of her mouth, slithering across the wet floor.

Miss Bird started screaming vile expletives, not in keeping with her position as a deputy matron in charge of girls. The girls, including Hetty, all backed away to the furthest corner of the room. Miss Bird continued, getting angrier and lashing out with her arms like a woman deranged.

Alice caught hold of one of her arms in an attempt to restrain her, but the woman's anger seemed to release a hidden strength. Then Alice pulled out all her reserves of energy and gave Miss Bird a hard slap across the face. Shocked, the woman stilled and then began to cry like a baby. Alice, herself, felt shocked.

A calm voice from behind said, 'I'll take charge of Miss Bird.' It was Matron Bailey. 'Mrs Goddard, you stay with the girls.' Taking hold of Miss Bird's arm, Matron led her from the room.

The girls, all ashen-faced, remained huddled together. They were well used to seeing violent men, but not a woman who went crazy.

'Come along, girls,' Alice said kindly. 'Let's finish quickly, then we can have a nice mug of tea.'

It was Hetty who moved first and spoke. 'Sorry, missus, I was only having a bit of fun.' Quietly, the girls got on with their work and Alice helped them to finish it.

She checked the kitchen to see if it was empty before leading the girls into it. She made a big pot of tea and they all sat round the well-scrubbed table, quiet at first. Then Alice started up the conversation. 'Do any of you sew?' They all shook their heads. 'Tonight, I will show you how to sew and to make garments for when you leave.'

'Do you mean proper clothes?' Hetty asked.

'Yes, while you are staying here, you will learn how to make your own clothes, except for coats and hats, and footwear and stockings. They are bought and are very expensive, so you will have to look after them with care.'

After their refreshing tea break, the girls went happily back to the laundry to start on the ironing and putting the sheets through a press.

In the dining hall, at teatime, there was no sign of Miss Bird.

No one mentioned her, so Alice assumed that she was resting.

From about 7 p.m. until time for the girls to retire at 9 p.m. was recreation time. Alice showed them the well-used patterns and small samples of material that were in use. 'So, when your two years are up, you will be kitted out with a set of new clothes and, with your laundry training, suitable positions will be found for you.' They looked suitably impressed, but not Hetty – she would take some convincing not to return back to her old way of life.

Other evenings, they enjoyed a sing-song around the piano, embroidery and knitting. Hetty taught a few of the girls to play cards for buttons.

The next day, it was announced that Miss Bird had left Faith House for health reasons and had been admitted into a sanatorium.

Matron summoned Alice into her office. She felt jittery. Perhaps she was going to be asked to leave for slapping Miss Bird across the face. All Alice could think about was that she needed this job to earn money for a home for her and Daisy. Once she found out where her daughter was and had visiting rights to see her, and by the end of two years at Faith House, she calculated that if she saved the majority of her wages she would have enough to rent a place and have an income to live on until Daisy went to school. Then, she could look for employment to fit around looking after her daughter. Never again did she want to be in the position of some other woman looking after Daisy.

Alice knocked on Matron's door and was asked to enter. Inside, she stood to attention and was surprised by the warm smile Matron Bailey offered her.

'Sit down, Mrs Goddard.'

Alice did so, wondering, her heart pounding, her hands clammy. She sat on the very edge of the chair.

'I will come straight to the point,' Matron said. 'Now that Miss Bird is no longer with us, we have a vacant situation for a deputy matron. In the short time that you have been with us, you have shown great fortitude and strength of character, and I feel that I can rely on you. Therefore, Mrs Goddard, I am offering you the position of deputy matron. Do you accept?'

For a few moments, Alice felt stunned. This was not what she was expecting to hear. However, she answered quickly. 'Yes, Matron Bailey.'

'Excellent. I will inform the trustees, who will then grant you an amendment to your wages.'

Alice felt puzzled and asked, 'Please, Matron, what does amendment to my wages mean?' She could not afford to take less money.

'The trustees will adjust your wages in accordance with your status as deputy matron. In other words, Mrs Goddard, you will have an increase of money.'

Alice left Matron's office feeling so much happier than when she'd entered. Her dream of providing a home for her and Daisy might come true sooner than she first thought. As she walked down the corridor, the spring in her step was light and positive.

Mrs Cooper-Browne engaged a nanny to be in charge of Daisy. Moira Stockwell was the daughter of a vicar and the most suitable candidate to apply for the position. She was thirty, a plain woman with bony features, and not a threat. They were in Mrs Cooper-Browne's sitting room and the good lady was listing Moira's daily duties.

When she stopped speaking, the room was silent, except for the scratching of Moira's pencil as she scribbled down the last of the list of duties in her notebook. She gazed at the list, panic rising. Would she be able to complete everything in a day?

'Have you any questions, Miss Stockwell?'

Moira hesitated and then blurted, 'When is my day off?'

'Day off! Miss Stockwell, you are on a month's trial. If, after that time, you are suitable, then we will discuss your day off.' She rose from her chair, the interview over. 'My housekeeper will show you up to the nursery to meet your charge.'

Meekly, Moira followed the housekeeper.

Daisy was standing on a chair, looking out of the window. She turned with a smile on her face, saying, 'Mammy.' At the sight of the strange woman, she began to cry, sinking down on the chair, her little body quivering with sobs.

Chapter Seven

On her free afternoon, and feeling quite optimistic, Alice made her way to Mrs Melton's house in Baker Street. For a few seconds she pondered which entrance to use. And then, without hesitation, she marched up the steps to the front door, lifted the shining brass knocker and rapped on the black painted door. As she waited, she did her breathing exercises and soon felt relaxed and confident.

When the maid opened the door, Alice stated in a clear voice, 'Deputy Matron of Faith House to see Mrs Melton.' She handed the maid a card she'd made herself, with her name and rank written on it.

She was ushered to wait in a small anteroom. She stood in the centre of the room, hoping her mind wouldn't go blank.

Mrs Melton entered and sat down on a chair by the window, but didn't offer Alice a seat. She spoke in a cold voice. 'How can I help you, Deputy Matron Goddard?'

Alice spoke clearly, 'Thank you for seeing me, Mrs Melton. I have come about my daughter, Daisy Goddard, who I understand you have placed with a family—'

Mrs Melton put up her hand, interrupting Alice. 'You are the woman who abandoned her child?'

'I am Daisy's mother. I was involved in a road accident and was in a coma. I stayed in the hospital for two whole months recovering. It was my husband who abandoned our daughter. Now, I wish to know where she is and to see her.'

'Please sit down, Mrs Goddard,' said Mrs Melton, indicating a chair. Then she continued, 'When you went missing, Daisy was placed with a foster family for a short period and, when there was no trace of you, we had to do what was best for the child. A very respectable and responsible childless couple agreed to adopt Daisy as their own. And they have provided Daisy with a loving, stable home. The adoption was legal, and Daisy is their daughter now.'

As Alice listened, she felt as though Mrs Melton was talking about someone else. It didn't seem possible that anyone could do that, to take away a child as their own. She jumped to her feet. 'I need to see my daughter. Now! I am her mother.'

'Mrs Goddard, whatever your circumstances were, you abandoned her, a helpless child, to survive on her own, making no provisions for her welfare. What kind of mother does that? It is too late.' Mrs Melton stood up. 'There is nothing to be gained by prolonging this conversation. Therefore, I must ask you to leave.' She pulled a bell cord.

'Can I at least see my daughter, please?'

'No, you have relinquished all rights. Good day, Mrs Goddard.'

Outside on the cold, hard pavement, Alice felt shocked that someone could adopt her child without her consent. She couldn't bear the thought of not seeing Daisy again. There must be something she could do. Daisy was the baby she'd given birth to and to have her taken – stolen. It didn't seem possible that anyone could do this, so how could it be allowed to happen? Surely, this was not legal? The upper class seemed to look down on the working class as if they had no rights, no feelings.

She stood for a while and then, as the shock lessened, anger filled her, and she turned and strode purposefully towards the corporation offices. She was determined to have her daughter returned to her.

Inside the building, she waited her turn in the queue. The man on the desk looked tired and strained and she could smell his stale, unwashed body odour. 'Yes?' he said abruptly, shoving bits of paper around. He didn't look at her.

'I've come about my daughter, Daisy Goddard,' Alice said in a clear voice.

He looked up then and said, 'Your daughter?' He glanced past her. 'Where is she?'

'Someone has stolen her from me.' Her voice was strong, but her hand trembled as she pushed back a stray strand of hair from beneath her hat.

'And who is this someone who has stolen your daughter?'

Alice told him everything from the night of her accident to her visit to Mrs Melton to reclaim her daughter.

He stared at her in disbelief and, remembering his manners, said, 'I'm sorry to hear that, but there is nothing I can do to help. If these good people have taken her on as their own, you should be grateful. Next.'

'No!' She wasn't going to be dismissed like a piece of rubbish. 'I wish to speak to someone in the adoption department.' A hush fell in the waiting area. She could feel people staring at her, and her body ran icy cold and she shivered. But she stood her ground.

After a glance around the room, the clerk, not wanting any

more unpleasantness to deal with that day, relented. 'Take a seat,' he barked.

Head held high, Alice sat down on the wooden bench and waited, and waited. If they thought she would grow tired of waiting and go, they were mistaken.

Almost two hours later, her name was called and she entered the adoption office. She wasn't offered a seat, but after sitting down for so long it was a relief to stand up.

She repeated her story to the adoption officer, telling him from the time she was fleeing from her cruel husband to get help at the nearby police station to when she was involved in a road accident and, as a result, lost her memory and spent months in hospital. Her health recovered, she found out that her husband had deserted her and gone to sea, and no one knew where Daisy, their daughter, was. 'I went to see Mrs Melton, my mother's employer, and she told me that Daisy had been adopted. You must have records of this and I wish to know where my daughter is, please.'

The man didn't speak, but rose from his chair and went over to a filing cabinet and came back with a thick ledger. He flicked through it, going through the motions of searching. There was no record of an adoption of a Daisy Goddard, not by the authorities, though private adoptions still went on. The authorities did not have the financial resources, or the manpower, to carry out an investigation.

He shut the ledger with a bang, making Alice jump. 'I'm sorry, Mrs Goddard, but we have no trace of your daughter being adopted through this department. As I see it, you abandoned your child and some kind person has taken her in and given her a good home. And now you want her back, but who's to say that in the future you might not neglect your child again? I should let her be.' He stood up and went to open the door for her.

In a trance, Alice walked out of the office with no hope. Speechless and shocked, she felt the aching crush on her heart and her breathing came out in short bursts, and she felt as though she was choking. A man pushed her aside as he entered the building, muttering an oath. She stumbled out into the street and leant against the brick wall for support. The whirling in her head spun faster and her knees gave way, and she slumped down into an undignified heap. People hurried by, ignoring her. As she came round from her faint, she heard a woman comment, 'Drunk. Disgusting.'

It was an old man who helped her up. 'Come on, missus. Let's be having yer.' His face was creased with deep wrinkles, but his grey eyes were warm and concerned.

On her feet, Alice slowly came to her senses and dusted down her skirt. 'Thank you,' she uttered, her voice strained with shame. As she began to walk, her legs wobbled.

'Here, take my arm, missus.'

She did and was grateful. He walked with her to the tram stop, a luxury she could ill afford, but she wanted to go and see Mrs Green, her old neighbour, to see what she knew.

At the tram stop, she thanked him again, and told him her name and asked his. 'Tom Barker.' What he said next astounded her. 'You be Ted Goddard's missus. I was sorry to hear he got the sack, but if yer fiddling selling beer that's the risk yer take.'

She stared at the man in amazement. This was news to her about Ted. 'I was told he'd run away to sea.'

'The big jerk, fancy leaving a pretty girl like you.'

Alice felt embarrassed and then relief as the tram drew up to the stop. 'Thank you,' she said to Tom as she boarded the tram.

As she walked down Dagger Lane to see Mrs Green, she spied her on her doorstep looking out for someone to talk to and to have a bit of gossip with, because what else was there to do for an old woman? Alice had brought her a twist of snuff, knowing she liked it.

'Well I never, if I go to the top of our street, this is a nice surprise! Bless you, come on in.' She wasn't going to let the neighbours hear what would be said. No, she'd save the gossip for later.

'It's my Daisy,' Alice said as soon as they were inside the spotlessly clean kitchen, with the kettle on the hob, ready to boil.

'We'll have a cup of tea, love. Then yer can tell me all about it.'

Alice sat on the edge of an upright chair waiting for Mrs Green, who bustled around making tea and going to the pantry for her cake tin. Her cake tin was legendary. If anyone was having a really bad time and had no food to feed their bairns, Mrs Green would give them pieces of cake from her tin. Sometimes, when money was tight for her, the cake tin would only have crusts of baked pastry, but, nevertheless, always welcome to a starving bairn, woman or man. Alice had much to thank Mrs Green for; there were many times she'd fed her and Daisy.

Tea was poured, and Mrs Green offered Alice a thin slice of sponge cake with a spreading of jam. It tasted delicious, and Alice thought it would be a good idea to teach the girls at Faith House basic cooking and baking.

'What was yer saying about your Daisy?' Mrs Green asked.

'Do you know where she is?'

'I thought yer mam took her.' She had heard rumours of a family taking her in, but didn't know how true it was.

'No, someone is supposed to have adopted her, saying that I, her mother, had abandoned her, as if I'd do that to my lovely Daisy.' A sob escaped Alice's lips and tears filled her eyes.

'Now then, love, don't tek on so. Have yer been ter see t'bobby?'

She inclined her head in the direction of the police station.

Alice jumped up from her chair. She hadn't thought about going to the police station. 'Mrs Green, you're a treasure. I'll go right now. Thank you for the tea and cake,' she called as she opened the front door.

Hurrying down the street, she turned the corner to cross the road to the police station, when a cold shudder passed through her body. She stopped and stared down at the rough road surface. She didn't want to relive that terrible night and its extreme consequences that had shattered her life and the life of her daughter.

Inside the station, it smelt cold and dank. Why was it, she thought, that authorities of whatever kind deemed that waiting clients should sit on hard wooden benches? She sat down and waited, tapping the toe of her boots, willing the police constable on duty, dealing with enquiries, to hurry up. The man sitting on her right smelt of strong tobacco smoke and the man on her left kept hiccupping and reeked of strong beer. Alice averted her eyes away from his leering look at her. She pulled into herself and perched on the very edge of the bench, and was thankful when it was her turn to approach the duty constable.

'I'm Mrs Goddard and I was involved in an accident just across the road a few months ago and my daughter has gone missing.' She blurted out in one breath.

The constable looked at her fully for the first time. 'I remember that, I was here. You look all right now, missus,' he said. Glancing down to the log book, he flicked back the pages to the night in question and quickly read his report.

Alice, feeling impatient, said, 'My little girl, Daisy, was at home with her father. It was him I was running away from.'

'You left your little girl?' He looked accusingly at her.

A lump rose in her throat and she caught her breath. Anger and sadness gripped her heart. Was it always going to be like this? 'I was coming to you for help.' She couldn't keep the bitterness from her voice. 'I was knocked down by a car and I was in hospital. I was unconscious for a long time and lost my memory. My husband should have looked after our daughter, but he deserted me. And he spread rumours that I had run away with another man, which wasn't true. It's him that abandoned our daughter and me. I don't know where my little girl is. She'll be crying for me, missing me, so I need to get her back. Can you help me, please?'

He scratched his bald head and thumbed through the log book. 'Nobody has reported finding a little girl.'

'He told my neighbour that he'd taken her to my mother's, but she's not there any more. 'I believe that a family have taken her in and I need to trace them.'

He closed the log book. 'Somebody must know who they are.' *Sounds a bit far-fetched,* he thought. He had four girls, and two lads who were always up to mischief, and he'd like someone to take them off his hands, but not permanently.

'What was she wearing?'

'Her nightgown.'

'Have you a picture of her?'

'No.' How she wished she had, but she had a picture of Daisy printed on her mind. 'She's a bonny bairn with blue eyes and lovely blonde curls, and she's nearly three, but she can say her name: Daisy.'

'How much bloody longer have I ter wait?' called a rough, masculine voice behind her. 'I've a job to go to.'

'You be quiet. I won't be long.' To Alice he said, 'Mrs Goddard, call again next week to see if any information has come to light.'

Slowly, Alice walked away with shoulders slumped, her heart heavy, and every bone in her body aching with sadness.

She went back to Mrs Green's house to ask her a question about the new people living in the house which was once her home.

Mrs Green was on her doorstep talking to neighbours and Alice guessed they were talking about her. They didn't say anything at her approach, but stayed to listen as she asked Mrs Green, 'Do the family next door know anything about my Daisy?'

'No, love,' she replied, sympathetically, seeing the misery in Alice's eyes, wishing she could give her good news. 'They are from out of town and have two boys.' The other neighbours shook their heads in response.

'If you hear anything, you can tell our Martha at her shop and she will pass the message on to me.'

As she walked back to Faith House, Alice mulled over everything that had been said that afternoon and couldn't make any sense of it. It was as if her Daisy had been whisked away to a faraway land. But in her heart, Alice knew she hadn't. All people seemed to say and believe was that she, Daisy's mother, had abandoned her daughter. There was never a word said against Ted, the one who had caused untold misery. Not once had he come to see her in hospital. She might have forgiven him if he'd been sorry and repented. She bit on her lip. Her heart was breaking, but she must never give up hope to be reunited with her daughter. One day, she would find her, her beloved Daisy.

Chapter Eight

For now, Alice concentrated all her energies on the girls at Faith House. They were allocated to her care and therefore her responsibility, and by helping them, it helped to dull the pain of being parted from Daisy. Every night she devoted precious moments of time to Daisy and prayed that they would soon be reunited. She kept the cherished memories of her daughter alive by visualising the contours of her face, so, in her mind's eye, she'd trace the round, plump cheeks, her tiny pink lips, the little pearls of baby teeth, and her sparkling blue eyes. If she closed her eyes, she could imagine running her fingers through Daisy's soft blonde baby curls, feeling the touch of her silky skin, the strength of her little body when she didn't want to do as she was told and hear her sweetest word: 'Mammy'. All this she kept in the privacy of her own room, never once hinting of it to anyone.

Tonight, Alice sat with the girls in a corner of the dining room and was showing them the basic sewing stitches, tacking and running. They were using a coarse woollen material and a pattern, both donated by a supporting charity, to make a skirt for the working day.

'It too bleeding plain,' Hetty remarked. 'I like something with a bit of a frill to give the blokes a treat.' They all laughed at her sayings, as she gave light relief to a busy, dull day.

'Perhaps, when we make undergarments, we could add a touch of lace, if by chance we have some,' Alice offered. Then, to lighten the mood, she suggested they sing one of the popular songs of the day. There was a bit of discussion until they finally settled on 'Where the Blue of the Night', made popular by an American singer. Alice had never heard of the song, but the girls, surprisingly, sang in harmony. So, it became a ritual that, on sewing evenings, they could choose a song to sing, providing it wasn't a saucy one.

Alice wondered about the life the girls led before they came to Faith House. Little by little, on their evenings spent together, she gleaned bits of their previous lives and the living conditions they endured. Although Hetty was very vocal and used vulgar language, Alice sensed beneath all that roughness and bravado, there was a girl eager to better herself. The other girls had lived similar lives, often homeless and on the streets, sleeping in shop doorways or in dark alleyways. They relied on prostituting their bodies in order to pay for a bed and food. A dedicated band of people, known as the Night Saviours, rescued these girls from the streets and brought them to Faith House and other such establishments in the city.

The girls talked about going hungry and Alice could relate to this because often, in her childhood, she'd been hungry too. Although her family was poor, their mother had instilled in them good manners. Until now, Alice had never appreciated her mother, taking her for granted, and although she loved her, she'd never thought she was a good mother. Listening to these girls' stories, she realised that Aggie had worked hard to provide for her family and to give them the best life she could afford, but

71

this left so little time for love or affection towards her children.

Alice, in all honesty, couldn't blame Aggie for seeking the help of her betters when Daisy had been foisted on her by her worthless, bullying husband, Ted. With hindsight, Alice knew she should have never left Daisy alone in the house with him. She had reacted out of total fear, believing he was going to kill her. She was startled by that knowledge, which, until now, had been buried deep in the recesses of her mind.

'Missus, you've pricked yerself and got blood on yer fingers.' Hetty pointed.

Alice glanced down at the garment she was sewing, seeing speckles of blood on it and blood trickling from her finger where she'd stabbed herself with a needle. She jumped up and went into the kitchen to the sink, but Hetty got there before her and turned on the tap for her. Alice let the coolness of the water run through her fingers until the blood stopped. One of the girls brought the first-aid box and Alice dried her hand on a clean towel, and then Hetty administered a sticking plaster.

'Thank you, Hetty, and you too, Beth,' Alice said. It was only a small incident, but they had responded admirably. Regaining her composure, Alice said, 'Time for supper.'

The girls loved the idea of supper as it was a novelty to them, having never known of its existence before. They knew about the three square meals a day, although they had often gone hungry and not even had one meal, but a fourth meal of the day! Here, at Faith House, they received breakfast, dinner, tea and supper.

The girls and Alice sat around the big kitchen table. A big jug of cocoa was made and poured, and for supper tonight were slices of fruit loaf made by one of the supporting ladies' charities.

'By heck, this is a treat,' said Hetty and the other girls, nodding in appreciation.

Alice felt uplifted by the girls' good manners. She glanced round the table as they tucked in and marvelled at how well they were looking. Within a few weeks of living at Faith House, they had lost the greyness of their skin and, although they worked long hours in the laundry and on other duties, they were permitted to have a half-an-hour stroll in the garden at the back of the house after dinner and, on the long summer evenings, they could sit outside with their sewing.

The sewing group was now in advance mode, having made skirts and undergarments, like petticoats, for which Alice had managed to procure lace from one of the charitable ladies. One evening, they were making dresses for when they went to church and for a stroll afterwards, or if they were invited to a concert. Alice waved her tape measure. 'Who's first to be measured?' She looked to Hetty, who was always the leader.

'Do I 'av ter?'

'Yes, if you want a good fit for your figure.' She proceeded to measure with a well-used tape measure. 'Beth, can you write down the measurement, please?' she asked.

Beth's face turned scarlet and she mumbled, 'I can't, miss.'

Alice looked up at the girl's acute discomfort. Then she realised: the poor girl couldn't write. 'Not to worry, one of the others can do it.' But no one volunteered.

Without a word, Alice picked up the stub of pencil and jotted down on a scrap of paper Hetty's measurements.

Later that evening, when the girls went to their dormitories and to bed, the staff assembled in Matron's office to give their evening reports. When Alice gave her daily report, it was then she brought up the subject of the illiteracy of her charges.

'Because of their poor upbringing and the way of life the girls led, their education has been neglected and they are unable to write and, I suspect, are not able to read.'

No one spoke. Alice wondered if she was being too forward, too outspoken. It was strange; here she was speaking her mind, as she used to before marrying Ted. He had undermined everything she tried to do and if he couldn't do it by criticising her, he used his fists. So, gradually, she became subservient, always trying to please him, believing she was no good at being a wife, because whatever she did was never, ever right. The only good thing to come out of the marriage was Daisy. A lump rose in her throat and she coughed to hide the threatening tears.

'Mrs Goddard,' Matron Bailey said. Alice quickly composed herself and listened. 'The staff and I are aware of the illiteracy of some of the girls, but we do not have the resources or the time to deal with this matter. Providing when the girls leave Faith House they are equipped with work skills and able to sew and knit and have a good grasp of how to manage their money, that is a job well done.'

'Yes, of course, Matron. I didn't mean to imply anything, and I understand . . .' Alice became silent as she was in danger of talking herself into a big hole.

As they were leaving, Matron said to Alice, 'Mrs Goddard, before you go off-duty tomorrow afternoon, come and see me.'

'Yes, Matron.' She went upstairs to check on the girls and to see that the candles were out. When she was safely in her room, she let her thoughts take over. She wondered if Matron was going to dismiss her and her heart plummeted into despair. She didn't want to lose this position, because it enabled her to save for when Daisy was returned to her and she would have enough funds to provide a home for them both.

She slept fitfully that night, hearing the nearby church clock strike every hour. On rising, she glanced in the small hand mirror and winced when she saw the dark circles under her eyes. She splashed cold water on her face and rubbed vigorously with a piece of cloth to bring colour to her pallid skin.

Her morning was busy as usual, so she didn't have time to dwell on why Matron wanted her. At dinner time, seated at the table with her helping of liver casserole, she had no appetite, but knew it was a sin to leave food, so she had to force it down her gullet.

Afterwards, she went to her room to change out of her work clothes and into her best skirt and blouse, and then she went down to Matron's office.

She took a deep breath, let it out slowly and knocked. She entered as instructed and felt surprised when Matron smiled pleasantly at her. 'Sit down. I will not keep you for too long. I've been thinking over what you mentioned about some of the girls being illiterate. It is something which I have thought about from time to time, but what to do about it, I am not sure. Have you any suggestions, Mrs Goddard?'

Alice thought for a few moments, not quite sure how to answer, and came up with her only thought. 'Perhaps, in the evenings, if any of the girls want to learn to read and write, I don't mind teaching them basic words and helping them with their reading.' She felt her face blush and wondered if she'd undertaken too much.

Matron considered before replying, 'Perhaps if you started with your girls first? I will ask the committee if slates and chalk can be provided. Books for reading could be a problem. We will see how you progress with their writing.'

On her way into the city, crossing over North Bridge, the muddy waters of the River Hull below were busy with barges unloading their cargos and the buzz of workmen's voices drifted upwards. Down George Street she hurried and along Bond Street and then turning into Albion Street towards the library. Here, she was hoping to pick up some leaflets or brochures that might be of use to guide her in teaching the girls to write. With the help of the librarian, she had a few ideas and some helpful literature, but suspected that it might be too advanced for the girls.

Coming out of the library, she realised she was near to Baker Street and her feet seemed to have minds of their own as she walked in the direction towards the Melton house. Across the road from the house, she caught her breath, watching as a big car drew up and a chauffeur jumped out and opened the door and a well-dressed woman stepped out, alone, and entered the house. Alice ran across the road to look inside the motor car, but there was no child there. She lingered a while longer, but to no avail. All hopes of seeing her beloved Daisy faded into a mist.

With a heavy heart, she made her way to meet Evelyn. Once a month their times off coincided and they went to the little tea shop they had discovered at the bottom of Whitefriargate. It always smelt of fresh baking and, as a treat, they had a pot of tea and a Yorkshire curd cheese tartlet. Evelyn, who was unmarried and three years older than Alice, was a nurse on the men's surgical ward. Alice asked her if she was walking out with anyone. 'Not likely,' she'd replied. 'I see enough of men and their bits and pieces as it is. One day, I'm going to be a matron.'

Alice loved her no-nonsense humour. They were both quiet for a few moments, their mouths full of the delicious-tasting tartlet.

'What about you – heard anything from that wayward husband of yours?'

Alice shuddered inwardly. 'No and I don't want to. He's the reason why Daisy is missing.' She ceased to think of Ted as her husband and wondered why she'd married him. She supposed she was swayed by the promise of a house of her own, a way to escape from her poor home life. She pushed him back into the deep recesses of her mind.

Instead, she told Evelyn about her idea to teach the girls at Faith House to write and maybe to read.

'That's a wonderful idea, but have you ever thought about broadening your own education?'

Surprised, Alice answered, 'No, I've never thought about it, but it is something I could do on my nights off.'

Evelyn didn't say any more until they'd finished eating and were now on their second cup of tea. 'I picked up these pamphlets,' she said as she reached into her capacious bag and drew them out. 'I thought they might help you to find out where to go for evening classes and know what's available.'

'Thank you,' Alice said. 'You are a good friend.'

'We all need friends,' Evelyn said, rather wistfully.

Alice glanced up from looking at one of the pamphlets and reached across the table to take hold of Evelyn's hand. 'Friends for ever,' she said and was surprised to see the glistening of wet on her lashes.

'Yes,' Evelyn whispered. 'It means a lot to me to have your friendship.'

Alice wondered if Evelyn had any friends within the nursing fraternity at the hospital where she worked.

That night, when she was in her room, Alice sat at her

small table, and by the light of a candle she read the brochures and leaflets she'd collected from the library to give her ideas for teaching the girls to write. And then she read the literature that Evelyn had given her. She read until her eyes ached, but she'd come to a decision. At school, although she'd left at the age of thirteen, she was bright and had no problems with her reading and writing, and her sums. She decided to enrol at the night school in George Street and take the refresher course in basic education. As well as her benefitting from adult education, it would also be helpful for when she was instructing the girls to read and write.

In the morning, she discussed her intention with Matron to seek her advice.

Matron Bailey hesitated, but only for a few moments, then she spoke. 'My dear, Mrs Goddard, I believe you to be a very resourceful young woman with progressive ideas, which will be an advantage to the girls in our care, and also to you in your life.'

Alice smiled with relief, and then said, 'Thank you.' She'd thought Matron might object and say that she was getting above her station and being too pushy with her ideas.

That evening, she mentioned to the girls what her plans were. 'Will you be leaving us, missus?' they chorused.

'No, of course not,' Alice responded, smiling reassuringly at the girls.

But later, as she undressed for bed, Alice wondered, somewhere in her subconscious mind, what was her real motive for educating herself to a higher standard?

Chapter Nine

Alice had chosen the education institute in George Street, because it was only a brisk ten-minute walk from Faith House and just over North Bridge. By the time she arrived at the institute for the evening class, the room was abuzz with voices and almost full. She slipped off her coat and hat, damp with the night air, and hung them on a wall peg. She left her scarf on, wanting to feel its warmth around her shoulders and its added protection against the thinness of her dress. She sat down on a bench with a shared desk at the back of the room. From her bag, she withdrew her new exercise book and pencil and placed them on the desk. Glancing round, she saw it was a mixed class of mostly young people, men and women, and noticed the confident looks on some faces and their leather-bound ledgers and fountain pens. The man sitting next to her caught her eye and smiled at her and she smiled back.

Suddenly, the noise quietened as a powerfully built man, with an air of authority, entered the classroom. He introduced himself, his voice booming. 'I am Mr Hookway, your tutor. I expect full attention from you at all times. If not, there is not much point in you being here. Understood?'

No one said a word.

'Understood?' he boomed.

'Yes, sir.' Everyone answered in unison.

Alice thought his voice sounded posh, but with a hint of a dialect with which she was not familiar. For some reason, she wasn't quite sure why, she liked Mr Hookway. She was here to learn, and learn she would.

The evening progressed with Mr Hookway outlining the coursework for the term and the books they should read. Alice wrote copious notes and hoped she would be able to make sense of them later. A few students with inflated confidence raised their hands to answer Mr Hookway's questions. Alice kept quiet and listened. At the end of the two-hour session of note-taking and details of homework, there was a mad scramble to be first out of the room, mostly by the men. 'Last orders at the pub,' the young man sitting next to her said. 'I'm Johnny Mitchell.' He offered his hand.

Alice took hold of his hand, feeling its firmness. This was quite new to her and she felt it rather intimate to be holding a man's hand, especially one she didn't know. 'Alice,' she said, and then added quickly, 'Mrs Goddard.' She saw him glance at her wedding finger, but she wore no ring, it was pawned long ago to buy food.

'You're married?' he asked.

She just nodded and went to retrieve her coat and hat from the hook, and, when she turned round, he was gone.

It was dark outside and the night air chilled her body, so she marched along, hoping to be in time for a hot cup of tea in Matron's office.

* * *

The next evening she sat in a corner of the dining room with her girls. This ensured that they had privacy away from the other girls for the time being. If this project proved successful, then all the girls would benefit from the teaching. Alice was determined to achieve this. While she agreed with Matron and the benefactors that laundry work was a good job for the girls to earn their living, some of the girls could prove to be good scholars and could maybe go on to further education. One thing she had gleaned from the first session with Mr Hookway was that education could open up a new way of life. And this working-class girl, she was determined, could aspire to that. For the first time since Daisy had been taken from her, Alice felt a true lifting of her spirits.

Hetty, much to Alice's surprise, seemed to take to learning the alphabet. 'Feel like a bleeding bairn,' she mimicked, with a baby voice. They all laughed and the tension they felt about the unknown of education and learning abated.

Each word she wrote, Alice said it out loud so that the girls could identify it. Soon they began to form simple words. Beth spoke, 'Missus' – she pointed to the word 'Mam', which Alice had written on a slate – 'I used to have one of them. She was ever so tiny and one day she just disappeared. Gone to heaven, they told us. I asked the angels to bring her back, but she didn't come. Me dad, he cleared off and I ran away. I wasn't going to be shoved into a workhouse.'

The room became so silent, it was as if no one dared breathe.

Then Hetty said, loudly, 'My mam was a bugger-ooze, drunk every day, but she wouldn't clear off, so I did.' She gave a titter of laughter and the mood lightened once more.

Alice wrote on the slate the word 'cup' and she pointed to where the cups were lined up in readiness for their hot drink of cocoa.

Later, in Matron's room for the staff meeting and a cup of tea to discuss the working day, Alice brought up the subject of the girls' backgrounds. She explained how two of the girls had opened up to speak of their past lives. 'I think it is a good thing for the girls, but do you approve, Matron?'

The assistants stared at Alice as if she'd spoken a bad word.

Matron closed her eyes for a few seconds and considered, then, when she opened them, she said, 'The girls all come from troubled backgrounds, which resulted in them living and working on the streets and alleys. If they wish to talk about their past, let them, but do not force anyone to do so.'

That night in her room, Alice thought of the degrading suffering the girls must have become so used to when on the streets, and how Faith House was a haven for them, at least for two years of their lives. Hopefully, afterwards, they would earn their own living and have a place to stay.

She thought of Daisy and her heart became heavy with the ache of her loss. She wrapped her arms around herself, yearning to feel her daughter's warm body in her arms. She prayed that whoever was looking after Daisy would take good care of her, though nothing could replace a mother's love.

The weeks seemed to fly by, because the days were so full of working and the evenings were for the girls to take part in activities, supervised by staff. On her afternoons off, Alice would visit her mother and siblings, and meet up with Evelyn in the tea shop. Sometimes, as a special treat, they went to Aurora's Cafe for afternoon tea and listened to the pianist play Debussy or Chopin. 'This is very relaxing,' Alice commented, dreamily, as the pianist played 'Clair de Lune'. 'Such a lovely, haunting melody.'

On her free evening, Alice immersed herself in the night class, which she'd started to enjoy. Mr Hookway (or as some nicknamed him, Captain Hook, as in *Peter Pan*) gave out a list of six books, but they could choose to read only two of them, more if they wished. She joined the library and the two books she decided on were *Jane Eyre* by Charlotte Brontë and *Silas Marner* by George Eliot. She wasn't sure how she was going to fit in all this reading and learning as well as having a demanding job.

On two of her free afternoons in the month, she decided to go to the library reading rooms, and on the other two afternoons she met up with Evelyn and visited her mother and siblings. But, before doing so, she went to Baker Street and stood across the street from the Melton house, watching the comings and goings of people visiting, always with the hope she would see Daisy. One day a large car drew up and a woman with a child stepped from it. Daisy! She raced across the road to the child, calling, 'Daisy.' Both the child and the woman turned startled at being confronted by Alice. And to her dismay, the child was a boy with the same hair colouring and curls as Daisy. 'Sorry,' she muttered.

The woman put a protective arm about the boy's shoulders and Alice, with tears welling her eyes, hurried away. But it didn't stop her from continuing to go and watch the Melton house, because there was always the chance of seeing her daughter.

She went to see her mother and told her of the incident.

'For God's sake, you'll lose me my job,' Aggie said, banging the teapot on the table, making the cups rattle.

'Just keep your eyes open and your ears alert, and if you find out anything about Daisy, let me know.'

'Alright, then,' Aggie said, to pacify Alice.

The police hadn't been able to help with Daisy's disappearance, only to comment, 'Take comfort that she is in a good home. If we hear of anything, we will contact you at the address you have given us.'

Gradually, the structure of her daily life settled into a more tolerant phase.

Alice found Johnny Mitchell, the young man she sat next to at night class, to be very helpful. He and Alice would often discuss homework and the books they were reading, which helped her to understand them better. Then, one evening, he said to her, 'I see you walk over North Bridge going home. I live in that direction, so do you mind if I walk along with you?'

Alice now thought of him as a friend, so she answered, 'Not at all. I'd like the company.' The nights were drawing in and she didn't like walking the streets alone. Johnny had never once asked her about her husband and Alice didn't offer any information, but the saddest thing was not talking about Daisy.

She felt ashamed to think that everyone she'd approached about returning her daughter back to her were all of the same opinion: that she, Daisy's mother, was at fault. With hindsight, she should have prepared more. If only she'd told the police or the authorities about Ted's brutal treatment of her and how she feared for the life of her daughter and herself. Ted's drinking habit and temper were intensifying and his violent treatment towards her was almost daily. Somehow, she carried on, hoping he was just going through a bad phase, but her heart told her otherwise. Then it was too late.

When she'd married Ted Goddard, she naively expected him to love and care for her, as she did him in the beginning. She had no other man to measure him by. Her father, after the Great War, returned a broken man and she only ever remembered him as a quiet man who finally died in the chair he sat on each day. All five children had a hard upbringing, but there was never any violence in their house.

One evening, Ted, not liking the way she'd cooked his liver and onions, had hit her so hard that he sent her flying across the kitchen against the wall where she lay stunned. He stormed off to the pub and just left her there. She feared for the baby as she clutched at her belly. She managed to crawl, on her hands and knees, upstairs and fall onto the bed. Her head spun and every bone and muscle in her body throbbed.

She must have drifted off into a fretful sleep, because she woke up with a start to hear him swearing and banging about downstairs. She pulled herself to the very edge of her side of the bed and stuffed the sheet in her mouth to stop her from crying out.

As the sound of his feet, heavy on the bare wooden stair treads, drew nearer, her body began to shake uncontrollably. In desperation, she took the sheet from her mouth and tried breathing deeply to quell her terror. She heard more swearing and banging about as he undressed, and then he fell on the bed, his weight making the mattress sag. To her horror, he rolled her way and grabbed her, pulling her onto her back, ripping off her nightgown. The strong smell of ale and tobacco and his unwashed body nearly choked her as he pressed his face into hers and forced open her lips, his tongue invading her mouth. Then she felt his erection hard against her thigh and he gripped her buttocks, pinching her soft skin. He plunged into her bruised and shattered body, grunting and groaning as he relentlessly pounded into her. Finally, he stopped and rolled away. For a long time, she was frightened to move and waited until his breathing told her he was in a deep sleep.

Then she stumbled from the bed, picked up her nightgown from where he'd thrown it on the floor, pulled it on and crept downstairs. Closing the kitchen door behind her, she leant heavily against it, feeling the choking sobs in her throat, but not daring to cry, not wanting to wake him up.

There was enough warm water in the big kettle, so she brought the tin bowl and set it on the rug in front of the dying embers of the fire and poured the water into it. Before removing her nightdress, she listened, checking, hearing his snoring. She undressed and washed her painful body, noticing the speckling of blood down below and she prayed that her baby would be safe.

When the time came, Daisy was born safely, thanks to the diligent, loving care of her good neighbour, Mrs Green.

'Are you all right?' Johnny's voice broke into her thoughts.

By now, they had reached Faith House. 'Just a bit tired,' she answered. They said goodnight and she watched him walk away, a spring in his step. How could she tell him or anyone about what she'd suffered at the hands of Ted Goddard? If she did, would it only be to lessen her shame at abandoning her daughter? It was hard to admit, but she had abandoned her. Not willingly, but, nevertheless, she had. She should never have left Daisy to the mercy of Ted. She should have found the courage to leave him a long time ago. Where she would have gone she had no idea. But she should have done it. Now, it was too late. Daisy was being brought up by strangers. Her most harrowing question was when would she see her daughter? She was determined to stay strong, because, one day, she knew in her heart deep down, that they would be reunited.

Chapter Ten

One evening at night school, Mr Hookway announced a short break of two weeks. Alice felt disappointed, because attending night school added some degree of structure to her life and helped to ease her mind from thinking of the temporary loss of her beloved daughter.

'What will you do on the nights off?' Johnny asked as they walked homewards together.

'I'm not sure,' Alice replied. It was a warm August night and she didn't like the thought of spending her nights off in her small, airless room.

Hesitantly, he said, 'We could go to the cinema or the music hall.'

Alice couldn't remember when she'd last gone to any evening entertainment. Feeling an unexpected burst of desire for a taste of enjoyment surge through her, she answered before she could stop herself. 'That sounds lovely.'

Johnny beamed at her and her heart gave a funny sort of flutter.

Later on, in her room at Faith House, guilt shrouded her for wanting to feel the pleasure of happiness, to go with Johnny to the cinema. She also felt anxious because, in law, she was still a married woman. Should she be going out with a man to a place of entertainment? She vied with her emotions and her conscience.

She lay in bed thinking about him, liking his dark-brown, wavy hair, his warm, deep brown eyes and the feel of his hand when it accidently touched hers. He walked tall with a slight bounce in his step and she could pick him out of all the other men in the class. She felt a tingling warm glow run through her body and a quickening of her heartbeat, and was glad she was in bed, so that no one could see her.

When next meeting Evelyn, Alice decided to speak to her about going to the cinema with Johnny, knowing that she could be trusted to keep a confidence.

'What do you think, Evelyn?' Alice asked, after explaining the situation. They were in the tea shop enjoying tea and a delicious cream bun.

Before answering, Evelyn wiped her sticky fingers on a serviette. 'As long as he knows you are married and it's only friendship, I don't see the harm. But don't get up to any hanky-panky.'

Alice blushed at the thought and replied, 'There's no fear of that.'

So, she and Johnny met up. There was no need to explain to anyone at Faith House, because they would assume she was at night school. They decided to go to the Majestic picture house, because it was near to where they attended night school. The main film showing was Marlene Dietrich in *The Blue Angel*, a film of drama and music. It was the first time that Alice had ever seen a talking film, so it was quite a novelty for her. At one point in the story there was a frightening scene and, without thinking, Alice snuggled close to Johnny and gripped hold of his arm. When she realised what she'd done, she quickly withdrew, not wanting him to think that she was a loose woman. Johnny didn't comment and for that she was thankful.

On the way homewards, they discussed the film. 'It's a bit like life,' Johnny remarked, 'things happen out of your control. Don't you agree, Alice?' He stopped walking and so did she, and he looked right into her eyes.

For a few seconds she was mesmerised by the sincerity in his deep brown eyes. She glanced away and then said, 'Yes, I do.'

They continued these pleasant evenings out when there was a break in the term. Alice learnt much about Johnny. He worked as a craftsman for a local furniture maker and he was studying to take his certificates. 'One day, I will have my own business and then I will make furniture to my own designs.'

She loved his enthusiasm and his zest for life, which rubbed off on her and she told him her ambition to educate herself to a higher standard. She also talked to him about her work at Faith House and how much she enjoyed making a difference to the girls' future lives.

'Do things like that really happen to young girls?' he said, sounding appalled. 'I have a younger sister and thankfully she is not living on the streets. Mam and Dad would be shocked to hear of such things.'

There were times when she felt like unburdening herself and telling him about her daughter. What could he do or say? She didn't want sympathy or to be accused of neglect, so she kept her thoughts locked away in her heart.

Christmas preparation at Faith House was cause for everyone to be in a joyous mood and looking forward to the celebrations. Alice was also, for the girls' sake, but not her own. Christmas Eve would be Daisy's fourth birthday and she would not be able to wish her a happy birthday. In spirit, she would, and she planned to make her daughter a birthday card, though how to send it to her she wasn't sure as she didn't know where Daisy was.

'Mrs Goddard,' Matron called as Alice was about to leave the dining room that afternoon.

Alice turned back and said, politely, 'Yes, Matron.'

'As it is the season of goodwill, I have decided to invite Miss Bird to spend a few days with us. She is much recovered from her illness and I feel some Christian compassion will help her over this period. Don't you agree?'

What could she say, because she had no wish ever again to see Miss Bird? But she answered, 'Yes, of course, Matron.'

'Admirable, because I have a favour to ask of you.' She smiled kindly and continued, 'The only spare sleeping accommodation we have available is in one of the dormitories. However, it is not appropriate that a past member of staff should sleep with the inmates. Don't you agree?'

Alice felt her insides freeze and hoped this wasn't leading to where she thought it was. She felt she had no option but to reply in the affirmative. 'Yes, Matron.'

'Good, I knew you would understand. Thank you for your co-operation. I will ask the handyman to put a small bed in your room. With a little rearranging, it should fit adequately.'

Alice left the room and made her way to the laundry area. To actually have that woman so close was going to take all of her Christian understanding.

At first, Miss Bird was courteous and gushing. 'Oh! Thank you, Mrs Goddard. You are so kind to allow me to share your room.'

Alice answered in the same vein. 'Not at all. You are most welcome. I have emptied the bottom drawer of the dresser for your belongings and the handyman has found you a chair.'

Miss Bird looked towards the table, where Alice's books and exercise pad and pencil were. Also, there were offcuts of coloured card left over from making festive decorations, from which Alice had started to make her card for Daisy. She had, in her head, designed a Christmas angel.

The other woman wandered over to the table and picked up one of Alice's books for her night class studies. 'Rather highbrow for you!' she exclaimed, turning to scrutinise Alice from the tip of her toes to the last strand of hair on her head.

Alice felt a sinking feeling in her stomach. Sharing her room with Miss Bird was going to require all her efforts of self-control. She didn't answer the woman, but instead said, 'Time for tea, Miss Bird. Shall we go down?' Alice opened the door and waited for her to pass and then she closed and locked the door, slipping the key into her skirt pocket.

Down in the dining room, the other members of staff made a fuss of Miss Bird and bade her sit down next to them. Thankfully, Alice went to sit at the very end of the table. This was only the first day, but how would she survive seven whole days and nights of sharing a room with the woman?

The room buzzed with chatter, which drifted over Alice's head. She kept her gaze on the high window opposite, watching as a faint glimmer of light from an outside street lamp caught the sheen of glass, sending out hundreds of twinkling stars.

'In a trance, Mrs Goddard?' said a voice next to her.

Alice turned to see one of the assistants, a pleasant young woman. She smiled at her and said, 'It has been a busy day.' Then they both chatted about their working day and Alice was careful not to mention Miss Bird.

The next day, Alice was kept busy. As well as the usual workload, there were the ongoing Christmas preparations of making trimmings to decorate the dining and sitting rooms, and, if they wished, the girls could also decorate their dormitories. This was cause for more excitement. Some of the girls had never known what it was like to celebrate the season of goodwill.

It was evening, and Alice was surrounded by nearly all the girls in the home, all eager to do their bit and make a card or decorations. One of the cards they were making was to the benefactor of the home: Mr J. P. Steadman. Alice still had her birthday card for Daisy to finish, which she intended to do when she was in her room, later on.

Suddenly, there was a hush in the room and Alice looked up to see that Miss Bird had entered and was making her way towards her. In an effort to be friendly, she asked, 'Ah, Miss Bird, how kind of you to come. Would you like to help?' She indicated the array of activity on the table. 'We would welcome another pair of hands.'

Miss Bird's face was expressionless as she replied in a simpering voice, 'I am very tired and need to rest. May I have the key, please?' She held out her hand.

For a moment Alice just stared at the woman, aware of the girls listening and watching. 'Yes, of course,' she replied, withdrawing the key from her skirt pocket and reluctantly passing it to her.

One of the girls, Beth, surprisingly proved to have a talent for drawing and sketched holly and candles on scraps of card. 'Make a snowman,' someone instructed. She did on a larger piece of card and then stuck on little puffs of snow made from tissue paper and someone else knitted a tiny red hat and red lips. 'We need something for his eyes and nose,' she said, delving into the button bag until she found the right ones.

It proved to be a very entertaining evening and Alice forgot about Miss Bird until she went up to her room. The door was ajar and so she pushed it open and went in. A candle flickered, and Miss Bird was sitting up in bed, her hair in metal curling pins and a nightcap tied under her chin. It was as if she'd been waiting for Alice. At first, she wondered if the woman just wanted to talk to her and, if so, she would listen as she prepared for bed. The lack of privacy reminded her of when she was a girl at home and she and her siblings squabbled about who would be first to use the hot water in the bowl and the clean towel. She must remember to collect a spare towel from the laundry cupboard in the morning.

She went across to the table and stopped, aghast. Its surface was cleared of her personal things. Gone were her exercise pad and pencil, the books and the pieces of card from which she was making Daisy's birthday card. She spun round to face Miss Bird whose facial expression was a twisted sneer.

The woman spoke. 'I tidied up for you. Your books and things are in your drawer, and the rubbish I took down to burn in the kitchen fire.'

At once Alice opened her drawer. Her exercise pad and pencil and books were there, but there was no sign of the card she was making for Daisy. She faced the woman, feeling the bile in her throat rising. 'What have you done with the pieces of coloured card?'

'I've just told you.' The woman smirked. 'It was rubbish, so I've burnt it.'

'You have no right to touch my personal belongings. You are sharing *my* room as Matron requested. Please, I repeat, please, do not touch my personal belongings any more. If you do so I will demand that you leave my room, and the only other available accommodation is in one of the girls' dormitories.' She stood over the woman propped up in bed who had begun to slide down until only her head was visible.

Alice shook, feeling her tense body dripping in a sweat of anger. She retreated to her side of the room, wishing this despicable woman in hell, which wasn't a charitable thought.

When she was safely in bed, she pictured the beautiful face of her daughter, Daisy. This kept her sane. But now she had no card to give to her and this brought tears to her eyes, and it took all of her self-will not to sob out loud.

When she awoke in the morning, much to her relief, Miss Bird was not there. But it was a subdued Alice who went down to breakfast. Afterwards, she would go along to Matron's office for any orders of the day and it was part of her job to see that they were implemented.

'Mrs Goddard, Miss Bird is so sorry that she upset you. She was only trying to be helpful. I am sure you understand.'

Alice had no wish to drag this situation on, so she replied, politely, 'Miss Bird has agreed not to touch my personal belongings again, so I do not foresee any problems, Matron.'

Later on that day, when the girls were back in the laundry room, getting ready to start on the mammoth task of ironing and repairing any damaged bedding and clothes, Alice sensed that something was going on between them. They were whispering and nudging, and she caught the words 'she'll like it'.

Suddenly, Beth stepped forward, holding something in her hand

and said, 'Miss, can I give you this?' The other girls all crowded round.

Surprised, Alice took the piece of white card from Beth. It was about two inches square and as it nestled in the palm of her hand she stared down at it. She felt her body tingle and flow with pleasure. She tried to speak, but a sob in her throat stopped her.

'You do like it, miss?' Beth sounded doubtful and was starting to back away.

Alice simply said, 'It is beautiful. You did it? When?'

'The other night, miss. I'm sorry, I shouldn't have used the card. I won't get into trouble, will I?'

Alice looked at Beth for the first time and noted the stricken look on her face. 'No, of course not. We encourage all our girls to use their artistic talents.'

'What's that mean, miss?' Beth asked, puzzled.

'It means yer bloody good,' Hetty shouted out and they all laughed. 'It's just like you, miss.'

Alice studied the pencil drawing of her head and shoulders, sketched from a side view. It was, she admitted, a good likeness. 'Thank you, Beth. This means a lot to me.'

They all settled down to work, surrounded by happy vibes. The spirit of Christmas was much in evidence.

After tea in the afternoon, while Miss Bird was chatting to other members of staff, Alice slipped upstairs to her room. Here, she studied the drawing of her more closely and an idea formed in her mind. Her greatest fear was that, over time, Daisy would forget her. She retrieved her notepad and pencil from the drawer and sat down at the table. She would write a letter to her darling daughter and enclose this tiny sketch of her, her mammy, in the hope that one day Daisy would find her.

* * *

My darling Daisy,

Many happy returns of your birthday, my beloved daughter. If wishes could be granted, I would be with you and holding you close in my arms. You were taken from me as I lay ill in hospital. Be happy, my darling, wherever you are. This is a drawing of me, your mammy, so that you will never forget what I look like. Daisy, I have a picture of you, held close in my heart, so I will never forget you. Always remember that I love and cherish you and that, one day, we will be reunited.

Your loving mammy, Alice xxxx

The next day was Alice's afternoon off and her only chance to deliver her letter in the hope that it would reach Daisy in time for her birthday.

She waited in the bitter cold and pulled her thin coat closer as the snow began to fall, but still she waited. Eventually, the afternoon post was being delivered. She watched the postman put the post through the letter box of the Melton household. And then she ran across the road, kissed her letter to Daisy and then pushed it through the letter box and heard it drop onto the pile. She hoped and prayed that it would be given to her daughter.

Chapter Eleven

Christmas Eve day in the early afternoon and the ladies who supported Faith House would call and so would the benefactor, Mr J. P. Steadman. They came bearing gifts. Alice thought that Mr Steadman looked rather gaunt and his tall figure stooped, but he appeared cheerful and liked to ask the girls questions on their progress at Faith House.

He was talking to Hetty, and Matron hovered by, ready to deal with a situation if it got out of hand. But Hetty was very polite as she answered his question. 'Yes, sir, I am happy here.'

'Excellent!' he acknowledged and moved on to the next girl. He never stayed for afternoon tea, but the ladies did and so there was more polite conversation. The girls were schooled to just answer questions and not to ask them. Mr Steadman thanked the girls for the beautiful decorated card and he departed.

Matron Bailey gave a short speech. 'Thank you, ladies, for your kind generosity, which we all appreciate.' With a wave of her hand to encompass all the girls and the staff, they rose to their feet and in unison voiced their gratitude. Then, as soon as the ladies had departed, there was a rush to see what was packed in the parcels.

There were mince pies, dried fruit and spiced loaves, dainty chocolates wrapped in tissue paper, crystallised fruits, boxes of dates from a distant land, and many other edible delights. The smell of Christmas filled the air with these delightful delicacies. Matron took charge of their distribution to ensure that every girl and the staff had her fair share.

Mr Steadman had donated joints of beef and these were already cooking in the slow oven in the big coal range in readiness for Christmas dinner. The aroma was mouth-watering and tempting to the taste buds, and causing much speculation amongst the girls, Alice mused.

Alice found the Christmas Eve church service a moving experience, singing the lovely hymns and listening to the vicar tell the story of the birth of Jesus. It had been a long time since she'd attended such a service, which aroused a sense of peace within her.

Christmas proved to be a very joyous occasion at Faith House, for many of the girls had never celebrated Christmastide. Alice never revealed that for the years with Ted, neither had she.

Christmas day was hectic, and Alice volunteered to work in the kitchen. Here she was kept busy and safe, with no time to think sad thoughts and wonder what Daisy would be doing.

She was glad when the day was over so that she could escape to the quietness of her room. Miss Bird had moved into a room vacated by an assistant on compassionate leave due to a death in the family. The rest of the week fell into the routine of the house, but with the girls still in high spirits. Alice had to pull herself up sharply not to admonish them for their merriment. After all, this was part of their training, an introduction to a new and better way of life for them. Though not all girls succeeded, the majority did achieve a new beginning.

Now it was a special time, New Year's Eve, when they would celebrate and welcome in 1931. One of the assistants had made a large dish of hot punch and there was spiced loaf as well to enjoy. Miss Bird had decided to leave earlier than planned and Alice breathed a sigh of relief.

Ten minutes before midnight, Alice slipped outside. She welcomed the short respite alone as she stood in the yard at the back of the house. The clear night sky was navy-blue with a host of tiny stars twinkling and sparkling. It took her back to her childhood days when she and her siblings would wrap up warm and sit on a tumbled-down wall and gaze up at the stars, looking for the plough, the bear and many other shapes of differing sizes. Innocent days of joy mixed with poverty, but taken as the norm, and then her thoughts turned to Daisy.

What was the custom in the house where she now lived? Would she be allowed to gaze up at the stars and to see their magic? Were there other children for her to play with? Before she could fall into a melancholy mood, the door flew open and everyone crowded into the yard as the church clock struck midnight. Bells began to peal, and ships' buzzers sounded in the docks and out on the Humber estuary and the River Hull. There were shouts of 'Happy New Year!' and a few girls began to dance a jig, and there was much laughter and merrymaking.

Later, Alice tumbled into bed, wondering what 1931 would bring. Her prayers and thoughts and her hope were that she and Daisy would soon be reunited. Working at Faith House had restored her confidence and she now felt she could deal with life's situation in a more positive way. Also, she was in a stronger financial position, having saved most of her earnings. As she snuggled down in her comfortable bed, she fantasised about having a live-in position where she could have her daughter with her. By reading and researching in books in the library on the subject of 'private adoption', she became aware that the adoption of her daughter was not legal. How would that stand up in a court of law? But it would prove to be costly and she hadn't that kind of money. There must be some other way, surely? She would have to read and research further to find out more information.

It was April and the end of the first year at night class. They were to sit a written examination on English, maths and general knowledge, which Alice was dreading. When she attended school, her best subjects were arithmetic and reading, though her gasp of grammar sometimes eluded her, but she tried her best. What she hated most was domestic science, because she had enough of that subject at home, so why would she want to waste time with it at school? She would mess about and let the water in the copper boil over and then be made to stand in a corner. Here, she would pass her time away by daydreaming of meeting a prince who would carry her away to his castle and let her eat sweets all day.

When she had first started Mr Hookway's class, she wasn't too sure what was expected of herself, though she wanted to expand her knowledge of general education. As well as reading the books suggested by the tutor, she often spent time at the library reading books on other subjects. One such book told the story of nurses serving in the Great War and she marvelled at their courage and endurance as they ventured into such dangerous battle zones and nursed night and day, taking only a few hours of sleep when they could be spared. As much as she enjoyed the good work and the ethos at Faith House for the underprivileged girls, she recognised in these brave nurses the need, without doubt, that she wanted one day to train to be a nurse. Not in the same circumstances, as they served in war, nursing the wounded in some foreign country, but here, in her hometown. Here, there was the chance, always the hope of seeing Daisy.

Every night in her room, before retiring for the night, she studied everything she'd learnt with Mr Hookway. Johnny was doing the same, so they hadn't met up in an evening recently. 'When it is all over, then we will celebrate,' he announced to Alice.

When the exams were over, Alice tried not to think about them and just hoped she had passed. She couldn't settle her mind to do any more studying, not until she knew her exam results. She spent her afternoons off-duty, visiting her mother and siblings, and meeting up with Evelyn, who kept her up to date with the nursing world.

Today, she and Evelyn were sitting in Aurora's Cafe listening to the pianist playing Chopin, and when a slight interlude occurred, Evelyn asked, 'Did you have any response from the letter you posted for Daisy's birthday?'

'No,' Alice said, and was saved from saying more as the pianist began to play again.

She sat back in her chair, the lovely melody wafting over her head as she thought of Daisy. Not that she could read at her tender age, but the words would be there for when she could. Alice knew in her heart that Daisy would recognise the drawing of her mother. Another thought struck her: if the people who had taken Daisy into their home read the letter, would they consider returning Daisy back to her?

Each day, she watched for the postal delivery, but no letter arrived for her.

On her nights off, Alice would drift towards the library, to find out more information about private adoption, but there were no other books or literature on the topic. She missed not seeing Johnny and it was no fun going to the cinema on her own. Once, she did meet up with her sister, Martha, and they went to the pictures, though Martha said she had little money to spare on entertainment and preferred to spend her few coins on dancing.

At last, the evening arrived to go to the night school to receive their examination results. Alice steeled herself to sit patiently while Mr Hookway gave out the results. He just called out the names, you put up your hand and he gave the recipient a folded piece of paper. As she waited and waited, her nerves began to jangle and she felt sure they could be heard. Finally, she was the last one to receive her results. She wiped the hot palms of her hands down the sides of her skirt and unfolded the paper. As she looked, the writing jumbled up and she had to force her eyes to focus. And to her surprise and joy, she had passed all three subjects: maths, English and general knowledge.

She glanced towards Johnny and, by the big smile on his face, she knew he had passed all three subjects too. There was great euphoria in the class and only a few commiserations.

Most of the class, Alice and Johnny included, adjourned with the tutor, Mr Hookway, to the nearest pub, the English Gentleman. Alice, not used to alcoholic drink, chose lemonade. Johnny had half a pint of mild beer. They were a happy, boisterous crowd and plenty of good humour bantered around. Alice chatted to some of the other young women who she'd only ever said hello to in the past and was interested to hear of their ambitions for their future. One was going into journalism, another wanted to be a secretary.

She glanced at the clock; time she was going back to Faith House. Johnny saw her look, and came over to her and said, 'Are you ready to go?'

'Yes, I'd better.'

They said their goodbyes and wished everyone the best for their futures and shook hands with Mr Hookway.

Once out in the cool night air, Alice shivered, and Johnny did something he'd never done before, he put his arm around her shoulders and drew her close to him. It seemed the most natural thing to do. She snuggled closer and slipped her arm around his waist, feeling the strength of his body. They walked as such homewards, together, and when they reached Faith House, Alice felt reluctant to move away from the warmth of Johnny's body. But she must. Just as she was about to say goodnight to him, he pulled her back into his arms and kissed her on the lips. A kiss full of tenderness. It took her by surprise, but a wonderful feeling of happiness filled her whole being as the kiss deepened and she experienced an emotion she'd never felt before: a hungry desire for more. She wound her arms around his neck, drawing him closer, moulding her body to his and feeling every muscle and sinew as if he were naked. At last, they drew apart, reluctantly. She gazed into his warm brown eyes and saw a look of pure love.

'Alice,' he whispered as he held her gaze. 'Do you feel like I do?'

'Yes,' she whispered back. Then she let out a huge sigh and her voice was full of sadness. 'But I'm still married.' She didn't feel married, but, in the eyes of the law, she was.

'Do you love him?'

'No!' she answered. 'I don't think I ever did. The only—' She was about to say, *The only good thing was Daisy, my daughter.*

Suddenly, the front door of the house rattled, and Alice was saved. Matron stood on the step, peering out.

Alice whispered, 'Goodnight, Johnny.' And she ran up the steps and into the house.

Johnny stood for a long time, just looking at the closed door. He'd found the girl he loved and wanted to marry her, but she was already married, even though her husband had deserted her. Slowly, he turned away and kicked at a stone on the pavement. He was determined not to lose her. He'd heard of divorce, but he had no idea what it entailed or how the legal procedure worked and he didn't know anyone who was. It was not the sort of conversation he could have with his parents, who were happily married, or indeed with any colleague at work. It was a dilemma for which he didn't have a clue how to answer.

He lived in the leafy suburbs of Garden Village, where the houses, shops and facilities were built and financed mainly by the Quaker firm of Reckitt's at the turn of the twentieth century. On reaching home, he went through to the sitting room where his parents were waiting for his news.

On seeing his glum face, his mother exclaimed, 'Oh dear, Johnny! Never mind, there's always next time. Have a cup of tea, son.'

Johnny put on his best smile, not wanting to tell them why he was sad. 'Fooled you,' he said in a jovial tone. 'I've passed all three subjects.'

His father jumped up and shook his hand, saying, 'Well done, lad! Mother, this calls for a drink.'

'Yes, I'll make the tea, dear.'

'Tea be blowed, it's whisky we're drinking to celebrate.'

Johnny loved his parents and he appreciated their good intentions, but he didn't feel like celebrating, not without Alice by his side, but he must, for their sake.

He didn't sleep much that night. He could still feel Alice's body next to his, the taste of her lips on his. He loved her with a passion that he'd never felt before and he sensed that Alice returned his love. He'd been out with a few girls, but never met one who stirred him with such desire and longing. And he knew, without doubt, that Alice was the one for him. Why oh why did she have to be married? Even though she hadn't been happy with her husband and he'd now deserted her, Johnny couldn't see a way forward for them to be together, not as man and wife. If she divorced her absent husband, that would bring disgrace to her good name and he couldn't do that to her. He tossed and turned, and questions with no answers reverberated in his head.

Meanwhile, Alice was having a cup of tea with Matron, who wanted to hear her good news. So, she sat and talked and tried to be enthusiastic about her exam results, and she was, but she still felt Johnny's lingering kiss on her lips. And that was a distraction. She wanted to be alone in her room to be free to think of him, this wonderful man. He was the man who held her heart and she . . . ?

Yes, she felt the same, her heart told her so, but this was an overwhelming dilemma for them both. Was she being foolish? Wanting to love and be loved? After all, she'd just escaped from a disastrous marriage that had torn her daughter away from her. Her head spun, and, at this moment, she couldn't see a clear way forward for her and Johnny, only a muddy one.

'Wake up, Daisy,' said Moira brightly. 'Soon have you up and dressed and breakfasted, and then you can go down to see what Father Christmas has left you under the tree.'

It was Christmas 1931 and Daisy didn't feel at all excited as she went down the curved staircase with her nanny to the drawing room below. But she was worried in case she dirtied her blue silk dress. Mrs Cooper-Browne would get very angry with her if she did.

The room was full of grown-up people all looking at her. She looked for her, but mammy wasn't there. Daisy hid behind Moira's skirt.

'Come here, child.' Mrs Cooper-Browne made a show of being welcoming by opening her arms wide.

Moira steered her forward and Mrs Cooper-Browne took hold of Daisy's hand. She led her over to the large Christmas tree, which shone with brightly shining baubles hanging from its branches and on the very top, sat an angel with a lovely face.

Daisy looked up, wondering if the angel was for her. But Mrs Cooper-Browne passed her a large box from under the tree. It was so heavy that Moira helped her to undo the coloured tissue paper. Inside the box was a doll wearing a fancy red dress edged with white lace and a bonnet to match and she had big, staring eyes.

In the afternoon, Moira was going home to see her parents, but she would be back later. In the meantime, Daisy was put to bed for a nap while Mr and Mrs Cooper-Browne entertained their guests.

Daisy sat up in her bed, looking through the nursery rhyme book with colourful drawings, which was a present from Moira. The doll was perched on a chair with her face turned away, because Daisy didn't like those staring eyes looking at her.

Chapter Twelve

Christmas and New Year were so busy for Alice and she didn't have any time off for three weeks, because one of the assistants had to go into hospital for an emergency operation. She had no idea how to contact Johnny until the second week when a letter arrived for her. At first, she thought it was from Mrs Melton, giving her news of Daisy, because she had sent a letter to the woman asking for news her daughter and her whereabouts. Alice held the envelope for a few minutes before she dared to open it. With shaking fingers, she withdrew the single piece of paper. She read it twice before she made sense of what was written.

Dear Alice,

I've looked for you every day and night as I pass by. I miss you so much and cannot stop thinking about you. I do hope you are not ill.

Tomorrow night, at eight o' clock, I will wait for you outside Faith House.

I just need to see your beautiful face and to know that you still love me.

Until then, my darling.
Love, Johnny

While it was lovely to hear from Johnny, it was Daisy she really wanted to hear about. Alice gave a big sigh and sank back in the chair and closed her eyes. Her room felt stuffy and she longed to be outside in the fresh air to clear her head.

When she opened her eyes, she had come to a decision. Not an easy one to make, but a fair one. Not for her, but for Johnny.

So, the next evening, at eight o'clock, Alice went out to meet Johnny. Matron, reluctantly, had given permission for Alice to take one hour, but she must be back in Faith House by nine and resume her duties.

As she stood on the steps, she watched him walking towards her and her heart gave a flutter of pure pleasure. He saw her, and his face lit up, glowing with love. At that moment, she hated herself and something within her twisted in pain.

As he drew nearer, she descended the steps and they met on the bottom step. She looked at him, feeling unsure how to tell him of her decision. Then, without warning, he took her in his arms and kissed her passionately. The thrill, the excitement, the yearning tugged at her heart.

'Oh, how I've missed you, my darling Alice.'

Tears of emotion threatened, and she whispered, 'Shall we walk?' The road was fairly quiet and there were not many people about.

With his arm held tightly around her waist, they moved off. She cherished the nearness of his body and locked the feeling away in her heart. But she wasn't relishing what she must say to him.

For a few minutes they walked along in silence, the rhythm

of their bodies in tune. Suddenly, Johnny pulled her into a shop doorway, wrapping his arms around her, so that she could feel every bone and muscle in his strong body, and the throb of his emotions. She clung to him, wanting him just as much as he wanted her, their passion flaring between them to dizzy heights.

He whispered in her ear, 'My darling Alice, I love you so much and want to spend the rest of my life with you.'

She broke away from him, saying, 'Let's walk a bit further on.' He seemed taken aback by the suddenness of her movement. 'I need to talk to you, Johnny.' He stared at her serious face.

Ahead was a pub on the corner of a street, and they went inside and settled in the quiet snug-room. Johnny went to the bar for the drinks, for her lemonade and for him a pint of strong beer.

They drank in silence, and then Johnny said, his mood serious, 'What do you need to talk to me about?'

'Johnny, I'm married.'

'Yes, I know, but that won't be for ever.'

She turned to him, saying, 'Do you mean divorce?'

'If we want to be together, there is no other option, is there?' Then he added, 'Is there anything else I should know?'

This should have been her cue to tell him about Daisy, but she couldn't find the words. How could she tell him that she was branded a bad mother and that her daughter had been taken from her? She couldn't go through with her original plan, to tell him that she didn't want to see him any more. She knew without a doubt, it would break his heart for her to reject him. Her head told her it was the most sensible decision to make, to part from Johnny for both their sakes. But her heart overruled. She didn't want to lose him and the wonderful feeling of love flowing between them, something she'd never experienced before. He represented the very essence of good in her life and she needed him.

For her answer, she shook her head.

He breathed a sigh of relief and drained the beer in his glass. Then commented, 'We will have to take things slowly.'

He didn't need to explain; she knew what he meant.

Rising to her feet, she said, 'Matron is expecting me back in ten minutes and I can't be late.'

Hand in hand, they walked back to Faith House in companionable silence and, on reaching the steps, Johnny asked, 'How will I know when you next have time off?'

'Next week things should be back to normal.'

He smiled and squeezed her hand, and she sensed his happiness as he sensed hers.

On reaching Faith House, he held her in an embrace and kissed her tenderly. Then he turned to go home. She watched him go and then went indoors. Standing in the deserted hall, she relived the wonderful moments of being in his arms and their kisses. She traced a finger on her lips, still feeling the heat of their touch. She loved him, but she hated herself for her deception. She should have told him about Daisy.

Still no letter from Mrs Melton in response to hers enquiring about Daisy, but then there was no response last year either. On her afternoon off-duty, Alice decided to go and see her mother. She might have heard something. First, she called in the haberdashery shop where her sister worked.

When she arrived, Martha was serving a customer, so she waited, browsing, and noticed the cheap price of thread and wool. She made a mental note to have a word with Matron.

'Now, what are you up to?' Martha came to stand next to Alice. 'I haven't got long to talk. Where are you going?'

'To see Mam.'

'I'll best warn you, she's on the warpath.'

'Why, what's happened?'

But a customer claimed Martha's attention and she became busy, so Alice left the shop.

She called at the corner shop to buy sweets for the boys and snuff for her mother. The shopkeeper, Mrs Mumby, sniffed. 'I hope yer can see what's up with yer mam. She's been a right moody bugger. Sort her out will yer – she puts customers off.'

Feeling hesitant and slightly worried, Alice entered her mother's house, calling out cheerfully, 'Hello, it's only me.'

Aggie was dozing in the chair, but as soon as she heard Alice's voice and saw her daughter, she was up on her feet, her eyes ablaze, her voice cutting. 'I don't know how yer got the bloody nerve to show yer face here. Yer nowt but trouble. I'm a respectable widow and I have my standards. Yer dad died leaving me to fend for meself and look after me bairns. I never ever left or neglected any of you. I did me best.' Her outburst over, Aggie gave the fire a good rattling with the poker.

Alice stood frozen to the spot. Then finding her voice, she asked, 'Mam, what on earth has happened?'

'Don't yer ever get in touch with Mrs Melton again! She was livid to get yer letter and said if it ever happens again, I'll lose me job. And would yer be able to keep us? And besides, I've got me lodger to consider. He pays me enough money, so I've no need to work nights.'

Alice sank onto a stool. 'I'm sorry, Mam, I didn't mean to bring this onto you. I just want Daisy to know I'd not forgotten her.'

Aggie sniffed. 'I suppose yer right. Put the kettle on.'

They drank their tea in silence until the boys came home from school, so pleased to see Alice, knowing that she would always bring them a treat of sweets.

Alice listened to their chatter about school lessons, their favourite one being physical training, PT. They were good lads, but not given to learning the three Rs. They loved working with their hands at woodwork and metalwork, and any kind of outdoor sport they welcomed. Sitting back and taking it all in, Alice suddenly realised, with a jolt, that her mother was still raising three children who were wholly dependent on her. Her life wasn't easy and now she'd taken in a lodger to bring in extra money.

And I, Alice thought, sadly, *I couldn't manage to bring up one child.*

When it was time for her to go, she gave her brothers a playful scuff and then surprised her mother by giving her a hug.

Alice went back to night school to study and to take her exams to the next level of education. Johnny also went back to night school, but he was studying for his woodwork exams, which were on a different night to Alice's. Their meetings became infrequent, so that when they did meet up, being together was special.

It was a Sunday afternoon, a rare afternoon together, and the weather was a glorious, warm and sunny July day and too good to be indoors. 'Let's go to East Park,' suggested Johnny. So, hand in hand, they strolled down Holderness Road to the park. When they reached the park gates, they walked down the avenue of newly planted trees and on towards the beautiful flower beds, where they sat on a bench. 'It's lovely,' exclaimed Alice, breathing in the perfume of lavender bushes intermingled with sweet-scented pink roses. It was an oasis of tranquillity away from the crowded city streets.

Johnny twisted a stray strand of Alice's hair round his fingers and murmured, 'Have you been here before?'

'Once with . . .' She was just about to say *with Daisy*. She turned towards him, but he seemed to be unaware of her discomfort. 'Come on,' she said, pulling him to his feet. Laughing, she started to run ahead, but he soon caught her up and bodily swung her round until she collapsed in his arms. Then he kissed her full on the lips.

'So, this is your mysterious friend,' said a sarcastic female voice.

Both Alice and Johnny spun round to come face-to-face with two young women.

'Mabel,' said Johnny in his most formal voice. 'How lovely to see you.'

'And you too,' Mabel replied, 'though it was only this morning that we sat together in church. Aren't you going to introduce us?'

Alice watched the tall, dark-haired woman, so self-possessed, smiling at them, but there was a hardness reflected in her dark eyes.

Alice felt a waft of cool air as Johnny moved away from her, creating a gap between them. 'This is my friend, Alice,' he introduced.

The woman interjected, 'I am his friend Mabel. We were just going for a glass of cool lemonade.' She indicated the woman with her. 'Would you care to join us?' Before either Johnny or Alice could respond, Mabel tucked her arm possessively into Johnny's and steered him ahead. And Alice followed in silence.

Alice heard Mabel say to Johnny, 'You're a dark horse.'

They sat at a table in the small cafe and Mabel talked about Johnny's family. She lived next door with her family. 'And we are all such good friends. Why, I've known Johnny since he was this high.' She laughed as she held out the palm of her hand to indicate the small height. She went on and on, monopolising the conversation.

Alice glanced at Johnny and he shrugged. Suddenly, Alice jumped up and, catching hold of Johnny's hand, she pulled him to his feet, saying, 'Sorry, we must dash. We have an important engagement to fulfil.' Mabel nearly choked on the lemonade she was sipping.

Half walking, half running, dragging Johnny along with her, Alice didn't stop until they were out of sight of the dreaded Mabel. They went into the secluded rockery gardens where they were out of view of people passing by. Both out of breath, they clung to each other, laughing until they could burst.

'Oh, my darling girl,' Johnny said when both were quiet. 'That was the best laugh ever. She's so bossy and arrogant. Thank you for saving me. How can I repay you?' he asked with a twinkle in his eyes.

Without a word, Alice drew him into her arms and kissed him.

A few days later, Johnny was home after a busy day at work and looking forward to relaxing with a good book. He'd only recently discovered the author Somerset Maugham when perusing the library shelves. As soon as he entered the house, he could tell there was something wrong by the set lines on his mother's face. Ada, with a rounded figure and permed grey hair, took pride in her home and was always beaming and happy, and nothing troubled her.

'Well, who is she, then, this woman you were cavorting with in a public park?'

Knowing full well her meaning, he attempted at light-hearted banter. '"Cavorting", Mam? What kind of word is that?'

His mother ignored him and continued. 'Mabel told me that she came across you and this woman making a public display of yourselves. I brought you up proper, my lad.'

'Mother, we don't live in the Dark Ages and you should know that Mabel exaggerates everything. She was just plain jealous it wasn't her I was having fun with.'

'You could do worse than court Mabel. She'd make a good wife.'

'I don't love her and she's too domineering.'

'Why haven't you brought this woman home to meet us?'

'She's called Alice. We met at night school and are taking things slowly. When the time's right, I'll bring her home.'

His mother glared at him.

Later, in the solitude of the front sitting room, Johnny contemplated what to do. If he brought Alice home to meet his parents, they would be sure to ask her about her family. He loved Alice, but would his parents understand that in law she was still a married woman? His mother would be shocked, and his father wouldn't do or say anything to upset his wife.

He sat up late into the night and finally decided it would be best to wait until Alice was divorced from the brute of a husband. First, he had to be found, but if he was found, would he allow the divorce to go through? Johnny ran his hands through his hair. He had no idea how to go about a divorce and he knew no one who had done so. His mind was going round in circles.

'Still up, lad?' It was his father in his dressing gown who had come downstairs for a glass of water.

Johnny had a book by his side and said, 'Got engrossed in

this.' He lifted up the book and yawned. 'Time I was going to bed. Goodnight, Dad.'

In bed, sleep wouldn't come. His mind was in confusion. It was going to be a long night.

The next free time he had, Johnny decided to go to the reference library. In whispered tone, mindful of people studying at the tables, and not wanting to be overheard, he asked the librarian, 'A friend of mine has to write about divorce laws, can you recommend any books?'

He was given two heavy leather-bound books. 'Not for taking out,' he was told.

'I'll take notes for him.'

When Johnny found the section he needed, it made dismal reading. From the information he gathered, a woman could only divorce her husband on grounds of adultery. He read case histories and it would seem that, in law, a woman was totally dependent on her husband. He pushed the books to one side and sat back in the chair. His thoughts turned to Alice. He had to admire her for turning her life round for the better by furthering her education and working. If she hadn't, he dreaded to think what would have happened to her.

He wasn't sure if he should tell her what he'd found out. He didn't want to upset her, but sometime she would have to know the truth. He'd wait for the right moment to tell her and reassure her that no matter what, he loved her.

Chapter Thirteen

Alice continued attending night school classes, enjoying the buzz she felt at devouring the knowledge of learning and furthering her education. She loved her work at Faith House. Girls had come and gone, and it was so satisfying to help them achieve a better and happier standard of life. Many of the girls kept in touch and it was heart-warming when they brought their own children to visit. This brought back memories for Alice of her daughter, but she never gave up hope that one day they would be reunited.

She and Johnny met up whenever they could. He was now studying for his woodwork examinations, practical and theory. 'One day, I will have my own business,' he enthused to Alice. She marvelled at his ambition. His life was on a steady course.

Then, one day towards the end of the year, Matron called the staff into her office for a special meeting. 'What do you think it's about?' one of the assistants asked Alice.

'No idea, but Matron will explain.'

And she did. 'I have some very sad news. Mr Steadman, our dear benefactor, has died.' A low ripple of shocked voices reverberated around the room. Matron held up her hand for silence and said, 'I am not sure how this will affect Faith House, but when I have more news I will inform you. I will send a card of condolence to his family on everyone's behalf.'

'Didn't know he had a family,' someone voiced.

'I believe there is a cousin,' Matron answered.

A week later, Matron Bailey, representing Faith House, was a mourner at Mr Steadman's funeral, which was held at Holy Trinity Church, his place of worship. He was a well-respected man, having served on many worthwhile committees and he was also a Justice of the Peace.

Faith House continued to function as normal in the following months, but the undercurrent of doubt for the future was felt by the staff, and eventually some of the brighter girls picked up on it. Matron decided to speak to the staff about the uncertainty of the future of Faith House.

It was in the evening when the girls were safely in their beds that Matron called the staff to a meeting in the dining room. To relax her staff, tea and slices of fruit loaf were served. After about ten minutes, Matron rose to her feet and everyone looked in her direction. She had their full attention.

Her voice was clear as she spoke. 'Since the death of our dear benefactor, Mr Steadman, his next of kin, a cousin, Mr Peterson, who resides in London, will quite soon decide whether he is to continue with the patronage of Faith House. However, in the meantime, I must have your full co-operation in keeping calm any fears that the girls might have. There is to be no gossiping, so I suggest that you discuss it amongst yourselves now and do not mention it further. As soon as I have news, I will inform you. Goodnight, ladies.' As she turned to leave the dining room, she said to Alice, 'Mrs Goddard, could I speak to you in my sitting room in about ten minutes?'

After talking with the other staff about endless possibilities of what would happen to Faith House, Alice went along to Matron's private sitting room. It wasn't very often that members of staff were invited into Matron Bailey's sitting room. Alice realised that Matron rarely took time off-duty. She was very dedicated to the work of Faith House, so this room was her inner sanctuary, her respite from her daily work.

Alice tapped on the door and Matron bade her enter. On first seeing it bathed in a warm glow from a reading lamp, it had an ethereal quality about it. It was cosily furnished with a pair of chintz-covered fireside chairs, a small gate-legged table and a bookcase with rows of books covered in green leather with gold lettering. Alice would have loved to look at them more closely but knew this wasn't the time.

'Please, sit down.' Matron indicated one of the chairs.

Alice sank into the comfortable chair, her feet resting on the clipped rug, and stifled a yawn. Until that moment she hadn't realised how tired she was.

'I won't keep you long,' Matron said. 'While we must undertake to maintain a cheerful attitude until Mr Peterson makes his decision, as you are my deputy, I can tell you in confidence that the committee fear the outcome will not be in our favour. It seems that Mr Peterson does not share Mr Steadman's views of helping those less fortunate in life. So, you see, Mrs Goddard, it is most important to keep up the morale of the staff and the girls.'

Alice felt shocked and a shiver of ice ran through her veins, but keeping her voice steady, she answered, 'Of course, Matron, I agree.'

Back in her own room, Alice wondered what would happen to the girls already in their care. And then it struck her: what about her own future?

Long into the night she was restless, her mind so active that sleep eluded her until a few hours before she must rise to start her daily duties. However, as Matron directed, she appeared cheerful, keeping the girls busy and encouraging them in their artistic and creative leisure work in the evenings and praising their efforts. Some of the girls would make fine dressmakers and, with the committee's influence, work could be found for them in the department stores or in small establishments. Alice mentioned this fact to Matron and she added it to the long list of things she needed to discuss with the committee.

At last, the dreaded bad news came. Matron called a staff meeting. 'I am sorry to inform you that, by the end of the year, Faith House will close.'

A shocked silence followed and then everyone began to talk at once.

After a few minutes, Matron called for quiet. 'Our first priority is the girls in our care. The girls who are almost ready to leave will be found jobs and a place to lodge. The other girls will be transferred to similar homes to Faith House that are situated within the city.' She paused, but before she could continue, one of the assistants spoke up.

'What about us, Matron? What do we do when it closes?'

'You must consider applying for a new position. The committee and I will give every one of you a good reference.'

There were murmurs of discontent at the uncertainty in their lives.

Alice asked a question. 'Matron, is it all right to tell our family and friends?'

'I see no reason why not. Soon there will be an article in the newspaper. Now, if anyone has extreme circumstances, please come and see me tomorrow and we can discuss how best to help.'

Over the next few days, everyone was subdued. The girls had been told the bare facts and not to worry, because their immediate future was being taken care of.

'I'm not gonna be shoved in another home,' one of the newer girls remarked. 'I'm gonna go back to me old job and please meself.' She gave a raucous laugh. 'And I can make plenty of money.'

It was inevitable, Alice thought, that some of the girls would go back to their old ways of life, but she hoped that not too many would do so.

On her next afternoon off, Alice met up with Evelyn in the tea room and told her the bad news of the demise of Faith House. 'I need to find employment where I can live in.'

Evelyn was quick with her reply. 'You could train to be a nurse and live in the nurses' quarters like I do.'

Alice's teacup landed with a clatter in her saucer. 'But am I clever enough?'

'Of course you are. Haven't you successfully completed all your studies and gained qualifications? You are an ideal candidate and just think of the worthy work you've done with Faith House.'

Alice sat for a few moments digesting Evelyn's words and then said, 'You're right. I'd love to be a nurse.'

'You will need three testimonials and I can give you your first.'

Alice's steps were lighter as she walked back to Faith House. The first person she saw was Matron, who commented, 'You look pleased with yourself.'

'Can I discuss something with you?'

'Come along to my office.'

Alice told Matron of what she wanted to do and of Evelyn's encouragement.

'I think you would make an excellent nurse. I will provide you with a testimonial and so will the committee.' She handed Alice sheets of headed writing paper and a stamped envelope, saying, 'I suggest you begin applying immediately.'

'But I am still needed here.'

'Yes, you are, and your application to train as a nurse, will take time.'

That very evening, Alice wrote off her application to the infirmary where she'd once been a patient. This was her first choice. She wanted to stay in Hull, because she never gave up hope that Daisy and she would be reunited.

She had to wait until her night off the next week before she could tell Johnny.

'That's wonderful. We might get to see each other more often.'

They were out walking, strolling with arms linked and their bodies touching.

It was a whole month before she received a letter from the infirmary administrators with reference to her application to train as a nurse. She'd been granted an interview and had to wait another long month.

Meanwhile, she continued with her work at Faith House. She would miss the girls she had worked so closely with, but she was pleased with how they had adapted to being trained for a better life. Only the one girl, the one who had been outspoken before, returned to her old way of life. None of the other girls wanted to go back to being used, to prostituting their bodies. They had learnt to value themselves.

Alice stopped in her thoughts of the girls. She had learnt to value herself, but at the same time she knew that what you want in life, you don't necessarily receive. Her blessings were the love of a good man and the promising career in nursing. She still prayed for Daisy each night, that she was happy with her new family and well cared for. She must now accept this for, if not, she would ruin her own life, as well as those of others.

Alice presented herself at the infirmary in good time before her interview. She wasn't the only person being interviewed for there were eight other women. As she glanced around the plain, white-painted room with two rows of wooden benches, her heart sank. The other women were younger than her. Did this lessen her chance of being accepted?

Finally, it was her turn and she was ushered into the office. There were three women sitting behind a long table. Alice remained standing as there was no chair to sit upon. Two of the women were in nursing uniforms. She guessed they must be senior nurses, but was not sure what rank they were. The other woman was wearing a tweed suit and blouse. They were studying Alice's application form and her three testimonials. She stood rigid, feeling a cold sweat around the collar of her high-necked blouse. It began to trickle down her back, and then she got cramp in her foot, but she dared not move.

Suddenly, the three women looked up at her and began to ask her questions. As she answered, her confidence grew and her passion for caring came shining through. It seemed that her experience in working long hours with the underprivileged girls stood her in good stead.

'You have the ability and the stamina that we require in the dedication to nursing,' was their consensus. 'However, you are a married woman and, though we are given to understand that you are separated, if you resume your married status, you must inform us immediately.'

'Yes, of course.' She had no intention of ever living with Ted Goddard again and she ceased to think of him as her husband.

'Now you will be taken to the classroom where you will sit an entrance exam.'

Alice's heart plummeted. Would her further education learning be enough for her to pass the exam?

Her anxiety must have shown on her face, because the woman in the tweed suit said, 'I am sure that, with your ability, it will not be a problem for you.'

She sat the exam and then returned to the waiting room, along with three other girls who had also sat the exam. Her stomach rumbled with hunger, not that she could have eaten anything, though she would have welcomed a cup of water.

It was her turn to re-enter the interview room. The panel of three had the results of her exam test before them and were studying it. She gazed at the painting on the wall above them. A scene from the Great War, of nurses taking care of injured patients in a tent, which acted as a makeshift ward, and through the open flap of the tent she could see a mud-churned field. And she thought, how dreadful to have to work in such conditions. Thank God it couldn't happen today. If she'd passed her exam, she would be working in sterile, warm conditions.

'Mrs Goddard . . .'

The official voice quickly brought her back to the present and she looked at the three faces before her. She waited for their verdict.

'Mrs Goddard, we are pleased to accept you as a probationer nurse.'

She was to receive a formal letter in the post with instructions of her duties, uniform and other necessaries she was required to buy.

Alice felt both happy and sad at the same time. She would miss the girls at Faith House. They had come to be like family to her. Already Matron was liaising with members of the committee who would oversee the girls' placements in work and secure safe lodgings for them.

At supper, one evening a few days later, Alice found herself sitting next to a very quiet Matron and it struck her that she had never mentioned what she would do when Faith House closed.

As if reading her mind, Matron turned to Alice and said, 'My sister has recently been widowed and she has offered me a home and work, which I have accepted.'

'Does she run a home like Faith House?'

Matron smiled and answered, 'Not quite. It's called the Whistle and Flute.' And on seeing Alice's puzzled look, said, 'It is an old coaching inn on the way to York.'

Each day, Alice looked for the post and at last her letter from the hospital arrived.

She had a list of clothes and books she needed, and a contract. She was to be paid the annual sum of £18, plus all her meals, accommodation and laundry facilities. The training would take three years and at the end, if she passed all her exams, she would qualify as a state-registered nurse.

Alice went to Matron's office and showed her the nursing contract. Studying it, Matron remarked, 'It all seems to be in good order.' She looked up and smiled at Alice. 'I am so proud of you, Mrs Goddard, and feel that we, here at Faith House, have had a part to play in your occupational development.'

That evening, Alice penned a letter to Mrs Melton, giving details of her change of circumstances and her new address. Then she added that she was happy in the knowledge that her daughter, Daisy, was safe and being well cared for.

As she posted the letter, Alice knew that she would give up everything she possessed to have her daughter back and to hold her close in her arms.

Chapter Fourteen

The cold January wind sent icy shivers through Alice as she arrived at the side entrance to the infirmary. Johnny had arranged with a friend who had a van to transport her and her trunk, on loan from Matron Bailey, to her destination. Although the driver was a nice middle-aged man, he didn't like to speak when driving. She wished it had been Johnny, though she was grateful for the transport as she wasn't certain how else she would have got there with her trunk being too heavy to carry on a tram.

The driver carried her trunk into the porter's lodge for safe storage until she knew where the accommodation house was. The porter directed her to the waiting area for the new intake of probationers.

On entering the room, Alice felt very nervous, rubbing her clammy hands down the sides of her skirt. The walls of the room were painted white and the only light came from two high windows letting in a shaft of sunshine. On a bench sat six other girls, waiting patiently, but not one smiling face. She went to join them.

Suddenly, the door burst open and in rushed a red-haired girl, bringing a cloud of smoke with her as she puffed on her cigarette. 'I didn't know we could smoke,' said one of the girls. And she hastily fished out a packet of cigarettes from her handbag and offered them around. Two of the girls took one. Alice shook her head. She'd never had the money to buy them, but right now she could smoke one to steady her jittering stomach.

'Put those out, immediately! I will have no smoking!' a deep, cutting voice boomed.

All eyes turned, staring at the large nurse who had entered the room from the inner door. The smokers quickly put out their cigarettes.

'Stand up.'

They all scrambled to their feet. The nurse marched around them, looking them up and down as if she was selecting them for the guillotine.

Alice suppressed the urge to let out her breath in case she made a noise and drew attention to herself. Instead, she bit on her lip and looked straight ahead.

'I can see that I will have my work cut out, keeping you lot in order. But, if anyone steps out of line, well . . .' She smiled, sardonically. 'I'll make your lives hell.' She continued walking around them, sizing them up. Then, as suddenly as she appeared, she went.

No one moved or spoke, expecting her to come back. Then the red-haired girl piped up. 'The trouble with her is that she's never had a bit of the other, and who would want her?' Someone tittered.

About five minutes later, the nurse came back jangling a bunch of keys. She spoke in the same cutting voice. 'I am Sister Marshall and I am in charge of the probationers' dormitories. You will all abide by my rules. Is that understood?'

'Yes, Sister Marshall,' they muttered in unison.

'Now, follow me.'

They filed out of the room, no one daring to make eye contact in case they laughed out loud. To Alice, it was like a film she'd seen about a group of delinquents being brought back to order. Never did she think it would be like that training to be a nurse. Of course, there would be discipline; there had to be, because of the patients' needs.

They were assigned four to a dormitory. Alice, the red-haired girl and two others were in one. The dormitory was almost as sterile-looking as the waiting room they had just vacated. Four metal bedsteads with bedding folded at the foot of each mattress, a locker by each bedside, and four tall cabinets, all painted white. Alice chose the bed in the far corner hoping it would give a modicum of privacy. Over the years at Faith House, except for a short spell, she'd had a room to herself. A small touch of doubt crept over her and she hoped she hadn't made a mistake.

Sister Marshall came to demonstrate how to make a bed with precision. 'If it is not done to my exactness, this is what I will do.' With a quick tug of the bedding, what she'd just made up now lay in a heap on the floor.

Wide-eyed, they all stared at the pile of bedding, not daring to utter a word.

'Now, follow me down to the training room.'

The red-haired girl walked behind Alice and whispered, 'It's like the effing army and she thinks she's the sergeant major.'

Alice suppressed a giggle. She liked this girl's outspoken manner. She reminded her of Hetty at Faith House. Already she was missing the girls. Soon, they would be settling in to their new lives after leaving Faith House. Matron Bailey had promised to keep in touch with Alice and to let her know the date the girls would be leaving. Hopefully, she would be able to see them beforehand and to wish them every success for their futures. She remembered reading in one of the books borrowed from the library 'Time waits for no man', which was true because time is something you cannot stop from moving on. 'Oh, sorry,' she said as she bumped into the girl in front of her, not realising they had arrived at the training room.

Surprisingly, the room was not sterile. It was not unlike the room she'd attended at night school. Only this time, there was no Mr Hookway, but a stern-looking woman, standing in front of a blackboard, assessing them as they filed in and took their seats. Alice sat next to the red-haired girl who introduced herself as Crystal Whitmore.

'Crystal!' Alice exclaimed, stifling a giggle.

'Talli to my friends. My mother was mad about drinking out of crystal glasses,' she joked, her laughter lines crinkling around her eyes.

Alice covered her mouth with her hand and bit on its flesh.

'Attention everyone!' Stern Face bellowed, introducing herself as the tutoring sister. 'There is no talking unless I ask you to do so. Understood?'

'Yes, Sister,' they chorused.

Alice averted her eyes from Talli, who made a low growling sound.

Alice listened to the introduction of the training course given by the tutoring sister and tried to take it all in, but there was so much to digest. The knots in her stomach tightened. There was so much information to remember, but she was determined to succeed and become a qualified nurse.

They were given a short break for a much-welcomed cup of tea and, during the break, the probationers chatted to each other. Alice felt the knots in her stomach disappear as she learnt that they all had the same worry. Jane, a tall, slim girl who was in the same dormitory, voiced, 'Don't worry, information will all be given out again in small bites.'

'How do you know?' A glamorous, blonde-haired girl asked, cynically.

'My sister is a nurse and she's done the same training.'

Later that night, in the noisy dining room, they ate an evening meal of some kind of stew. Alice chewed on the tough meat, thinking how spoilt she had been at Faith House. Back in the dormitory, the four girls began preparing for bed. Beds were made up and waiting for the inspection from Sister Marshall. In she marched. Each girl stood to attention at the foot of their beds. She pulled off the bedding of the small, dark-haired girl who looked as though she was about to dissolve into tears. Alice could feel her heart pumping faster as Sister approached her bed, but she just sniffed as she walked around it.

When she'd gone, no one moved or spoke. The small, dark-haired probationer sat down on the edge of her now unmade bed and, in a voice barely a whisper, said, 'I'd go home, if I had a home.'

Alice went to her and said, 'Come on, I'll help you remake your bed.' The other two girls pitched in and soon they were all safely in bed before the Marshall, as they nicknamed the sister, came to switch off the lights.

In her bed, Alice couldn't sleep. Her mind was so full of all the information given that day. Her eyes became used to the gloom of the room, which was enhanced by a shaft of light coming under the door from the nightlight in the corridor. She could now see her nurse's uniform set out on the chair, ready to wear for the start of duties at seven in the morning.

She must have drifted off to sleep, for she was aroused by the clanging of a bell in the corridor. Then their door was thrust open and the bell ringer entered. All four jumped from their beds, nearly falling over each other and then there was a mad scramble for the communal washroom and lavatory. Dressed in her uniform, Alice wrestled with her cap, as did the others, except Jane.

Seeing their plight, Jane showed each girl in turn how to turn the flat square of starched material into a resemblance of a nurse's cap.

They joined the queue for breakfast, which consisted of a mug of lukewarm tea and a scraping of butter on a chunk of bread. The probationers sat at a bare wooden table on wooden benches, pushed tight against the wall at the far end of the room, while the hierarchy, the sisters, sat at a table with a clean white cloth and were served by maids.

Alice couldn't help but compare it to the dining room at Faith House, where it had been so much more civilised. Maybe the food here would improve, but she doubted it.

There was no time to linger as they hurried to the training room, where they were to be given details of their timetable for the week. Also, they would be assigned to a ward. Alice wondered if she might be on Evelyn's ward. She'd only caught a glimpse of her in the dining room and had no time to talk.

In the training room, their timetable for the week was chalked up on the blackboard. Alice copied her duty details into her notebook. She would be assigned to a women's ward. Not Evelyn's ward, which was men's surgical.

Later, when she entered her assigned ward to present herself for duty, Alice was greeted by an agitated staff nurse. 'Don't just stand there, go and get a bedpan.'

She looked round to see which way to go for this object, when a woman's voice from a nearby bed whispered, 'Over in that corner, love.' She pointed to a door.

Alice smiled her grateful thanks and hurried off. She found a row of neatly stacked bedpans, grabbed one and then went to find the staff nurse. She couldn't see her anywhere, but from a bed with a curtained screen around it, she heard a moaning voice. 'Bloody hurry up.'

She poked her head through a gap in the curtains to see a red-faced woman, straining.

Quickly, Alice got the woman on the pan and then dived out, closing the curtains shut to give the woman privacy.

Then someone else shouted for a bedpan and she found herself running to the sluice and back again, and taking the offending objects back to empty. She thought she was doing well, considering she hadn't being given any specific instructions or tasks to do, when—

'I will not have running in my ward,' the strict voice reprimanded.

Bedpan in hand, Alice half turned round to see the ward sister glaring at her. 'But I was busy.'

'Do not answer me back. Speak only when I ask. What is your name?'

The smelly pan weighed heavy in Alice's hands and she feared that she might drop it. 'Alice Goddard,' she said, making to move away.

'Stop, Goddard. You do not move until I say so.' Then Sister must have realised what was about to happen. She waved Alice away, saying, 'Then come to my office.'

Task done, Alice walked slowly through the ward, having to ignore a woman's plea for a glass of water, but she was relieved to see another nurse going towards the woman.

She tapped on the door marked 'Sister Ashley' and waited. A voice within said, 'Come.' Alice opened the door and entered.

The office was dominated by a huge desk and behind it sat Sister Ashley, her head bent as she wrote in a ledger. Alice took the advantage to peer around the room, seeing an upright filing cabinet and rows of nursing books. On the wall was an enlarged framed photograph of a nurse in old-fashioned uniform standing in a tent with rows of beds placed side by side

'My mother, she was a nursing sister during the Great War.'

Alice was surprised to hear the proud tenderness in Sister's voice. So, she was human after all. Though in the next instance, she wasn't sure, when Sister launched into what was expected of her at all times.

Later, in the probationers' common room, which was very basic, with cream-painted walls, a small table and about a dozen mismatched chairs, the four room-mates sat, sprawled out, resting their aching bodies and exchanging what they had done on their first day of duty.

'I'm landed with a right fiery sister,' Talli said, yawning.

'Tough luck,' Jane offered.

Eventually, they all drifted away, and Alice found herself alone in the room. Someone had left a newspaper behind and she settled to have a quiet read of it. It made a change from the nursing manuals she had to read and study. She was just about to flick through to the pages with the cinema listings in the hope that she would get a night off in the near future and spend it with Johnny, when the headline caught her eye.

The article was about a man called Hitler, who seemed to be causing unrest in Europe. A strange cold feeling filled her, and she thought about her father who had come back from the Great War a broken man. Although he tried his best, he had not been able to enjoy his family. The Great War was a war to end all wars. So, there was no chance of another war. Everyone said so. Alice had no reason to disagree, but she felt an uneasiness that she couldn't explain.

Chapter Fifteen

Alice found the work of being a probationer more demanding than she'd anticipated, but she was determined to succeed and qualify as a nurse. She worked long hours and was frequently having to forgo her off-duty time, which she didn't mind, except it meant not seeing Johnny.

However, this evening, she was hoping to be free from seven o'clock and to forgo her supper in order to meet him. Looking out of the dormitory window at the rain-soaked street, there would be no chance of a walk together. She wasn't much of a pub drinker and neither was Johnny, but what other option was there? She voiced this thought to Talli, who had just entered the room.

'Now, if it was me, I'd go where it was nice and warm and dark. Go and see a good love story at the pictures. You can sit in the back row and have a kiss and cuddle.'

'That sounds a lovely idea,' Alice enthused, her face lighting up, then remembered. 'I have to be back by ten and I hate missing the end of a film and so does Johnny.'

'No, you don't have to. Take your torch and just flash it up at the window and I'll come down and unlock the door for you.' And so, it was agreed.

Alice, dressed in her new fitted camel coat and cream beret – an extravagant buy bought with the money she saved when working at Faith House – felt smart and fashionable. But because of the torrent of rain, she had to make do with an old black umbrella.

Standing against the shelter of the porters' lodge wall, she waited for Johnny. She was unaware of his approach until she heard a low wolf whistle. Instantly she was in his arms, their lips meeting in a passionate kiss. 'It's been a long time,' he murmured.

She told him of the plan and they quickly set off to one of their favourite cinemas, the Majestic. If anyone had asked her the name of the film or what it was about, she could not have told them anything about it. On the back row, Alice snuggled into the warmth of Johnny's body. His arm slipped under her coat and his hand cupped her breast. She felt waves of pleasure fill her body and her heart. She reached up to him, her lips seeking his and the intimate probing of their tongues sent her up into dizzy heights. She knew Johnny was aroused as much as she was, and nothing could mar her happiness to know she was loved in return. Never had she expected or realised that the intimate side of this closeness could be so special between a man and a woman. Real love felt so wonderful. She wanted to dance and sing at the top of her voice.

She never thought of her marriage to Ted. It was as if it had never been, except for one bright star, her daughter, whom she would never forget.

At the short interval they talked, or at least Johnny did. 'Alice, I love you so much. It hurts to be parted from you. I want to wake up in the morning to find you by my side. I want you as my wife in the fullest sense.'

She looked deep into his eyes and saw the same longing she felt. 'I love you, Johnny, but we have to be patient, for now.'

He sighed and said, 'I know.'

For the rest of the film, they held hands, but neither could concentrate on the action showing on the screen.

He walked her back to the porters' lodge and they said goodnight with a long and passionate kiss. They clung to each other, not wanting to part, but knowing they must. 'I have to go,' she whispered. 'Talli's waiting up for me.' They drew apart and made a promise to be in touch soon.

Still with her head and heart saturated with love, she walked round to where the dormitory window was. She shone her torch up at it and waited. Nothing happened. She shone her torch again, flashing it from side to side. Still nothing happened. She began to despair, when the side door opened. She hurried forward, saying, 'I thought you'd forgotten.'

The responding voice was cuttingly sharp. 'What is the meaning of this?'

Alice came face-to-face with Sister Marshall. And she was jolted back to reality. 'I . . .' she stammered. Words failed her.

'Hurry up inside, Goddard. I shall report your deplorable conduct to Matron in the morning.'

Alice ran up the stairs and into the dormitory. All three girls were asleep, though Talli was lying on top of her bed. Gently, Alice shook her and told her to get into bed.

'Good, you're back,' mumbled Talli as she got into bed and was fast asleep in an instant.

Alice undressed and slipped between the sheets. She closed her eyes, but sleep escaped her. The thought that whirled in her head and wouldn't go away was: would she be dismissed?

It was the first thought that greeted her in the grey mist of morning. Had she made another mess of her life? If she was dismissed, what would she do? She wasn't in a position to marry Johnny and nor could she foist herself on her mother. She could end up on the streets like those poor fallen girls who she had cared for. She had acted irresponsibly and all for the love of a man she couldn't legally marry.

'You got in all right?' Talli said as she stirred awake.

Alice glanced at her and just nodded. It wasn't her fault.

She couldn't face breakfast; instead, she went outside to catch a breath of fresh morning air before reporting to Matron.

She was kept waiting a full thirty minutes standing outside Matron's office. Now, feeling completely numb, with the event of her dismissal imminent, Alice felt like a condemned prisoner.

At last, she was told to enter. She stood before Matron's desk and looked straight ahead, her heartbeat racing, her body sinking to its lowest depth, and her mind frozen.

At first, Matron's voice was low and soft and even more surprising were her words. 'I trust, Goddard, that you will never repeat such a mistake again. Your conduct as a probationer nurse must be exemplary at all times.' Now her voice became authoritarian. 'I will not tolerate such behaviour from my probationers. The rules are there to be obeyed if you want to succeed to be a qualified nurse. Understood?'

Alice's body and mind switched to auto and she responded, 'Yes, Matron.'

'Your off-duty privileges are curtailed for one month. I do not want to see you again.' She then picked up her fountain pen and proceeded to write.

For a few seconds Alice stood motionless, before she realised she was dismissed. Quietly, she left the office. Once outside, she breathed a sigh of relief. She was reprieved. She hurried away to her ward. If need be, she would not hesitate to polish, scrub, fetch and carry through the night.

She found out, by listening to the second-year probationers, that, for a few pence, the porters would act as an unofficial collecting point for letters. So, she was able to keep in touch with Johnny and him with her.

She concentrated on her nursing training and was satisfied, for the time being, with writing words of love and funny happenings on the wards to Johnny. She delighted in reading his replies to her, which were often the lyrics of a love song that filled her heart with pure happiness.

'Scrubbing again,' Talli moaned to Alice. 'Just look at my hands!' Both examined their red, sore hands.

'Come on, get a move on,' came the chilly voice of the staff nurse, 'or you'll be late for your lecture.'

They had all been given a small hard-backed book in which to write their lecture notes, and each week the nursing tutor would inspect it and mark any corrections to be made. For Alice, this wasn't a problem as she had been used to taking down notes at the night school. She missed the freedom of her nights spent there, and it was where she and Johnny met. In between checking her notes on her dinner break, she also managed to pen Johnny a few lines, mentioning the happy times they spent together.

Poised with her pencil in mid-air as she checked her notes, she sighed, saying to Talli, 'It gets repetitive writing about the daily routine of the ward all the time.'

'Think of when we are qualified, the nursing will become more satisfying.'

'You're right.'

Later on, passing the laundry building, she was pleasantly surprised to see one of the girls from Faith House. 'Hello, miss.'

Alice turned round to see Beth. 'How lovely to see you,' she said and gave her a hug. 'How are you doing?'

Beth wrinkled her nose. 'It's all right, miss. I've got good lodgings and the missus treats me as one of the family, and I've got Christmas Day off, so that's great, ain't it?'

'Yes, Beth, it is.'

'What about you, miss, where are you spending Christmas Day – with your young man?'

Alice hadn't realised that the girls at Faith House had known about Johnny.

'No, I'm on duty.' The words tripped off her tongue. 'Must go. Lovely to see you, Beth, and take care.'

Alice hurried on. Johnny had never mentioned any Christmas arrangements to her. She was due a rare Sunday afternoon off and they were planning to stroll to the pier and maybe take a ferry across the river to New Holland. She would bring up the subject of Christmas Day then.

They were fortunate with the mid-December weather. The winter sun shone bright and the sky was a palate of vivid blue. Wrapped up warmly, they strolled with their arms linked, happy in each other's company. On reaching the pier they saw the ferry was just leaving. They watched it steam away from up on the top deck of the pier, tracking its progress across the Humber estuary. A strong gust of wind whipped round them, and Alice caught hold of her beret just in time. Johnny pulled her into an embrace and she felt his strong body melded into hers as they kissed, their arms locked around each other.

Suddenly the wind blew colder and, laughing, holding hands, they ran down the steps and across the road to the small tea shop.

Inside it was warm and cosy and they sat at a window seat, but couldn't see out, because of the condensation on the windows. The waitress came to take their order and they decided on a pot of tea, cheese and pickle sandwiches, and two Yorkshire curd tartlets. While they waited, Johnny traced his finger on the condensation on the windows and wrote *I love you*. Alice wrote back *I love you too*. Under the table, they held hands and looked into each other's eyes. The spell was only broken when the waitress arrived at their table.

They tucked into the delicious afternoon tea and Johnny said, with his mouth full of Yorkshire curd tartlet, 'This is just like my mother makes.'

Alice asked, innocently, 'How is your mother?'

Johnny looked at her in surprise and answered, 'She's well, thank you.'

'And your father and sister, how are they?' By the uncomfortable expression on his face, he knew what she really meant.

He cleared his throat. 'It's difficult,' he said.

'But I am not really married. I've been deserted. And, one day, you intend to marry me, so it only seems natural for me to want to meet your family.'

'But I've not met your family.'

His words startled her, but he was right. Her mother would not approve.

He reached across the table and placed his hand on top of hers, giving it a gentle squeeze, hating to see her upset. 'Don't let's spoil our lovely afternoon together. I'm happy just knowing that you love me as much as I love you.'

She forced a smile and said, 'You're right.' And she proceeded to tell him about seeing Beth working in the hospital laundry and finding good lodgings with a family, and marvelling how her life had turned around. She omitted to tell him about Beth's question.

They both seemed to have run out of talk on the way back to the hospital, but they walked with their arms around each other until reaching the porters' lodge. Out of sight of any windows, he kissed her and held her in a warm embrace.

She watched him walk away, his body upright, his strides long and, as if he knew she was still watching, he turned and waved, his smile so full of love it pulled at her heart.

Slowly, she went in and up to the dormitory to change into her uniform for duty. Her mind on one thing: would they ever be husband and wife, married in law?

She was thankful that the hospital authorities knew she was married and deserted by her husband. Matron Bailey's testimonial had given her excellent references, which stated the facts of her marriage and her outstanding work at Faith House. So, to all intents and purposes, she was classed as a single woman. She knew some of the probationers had boyfriends, but not with the intent to marry, as far as she was aware.

By the time she was dressed and ready for duty, Alice had convinced herself that Johnny was right not to invite her to meet his parents. She wouldn't bring the subject up again. What was the point if it caused trouble? It was far better to let their relationship run a steady course until such time as she was free to take their courtship a step further. That was the way forward, she persuaded herself. Until she was free, the situation could not be resolved. Though, she thought, some people might believe that the very idea was a sin itself.

On reaching the ward she took a deep breath, forced a smile and pushed open the door.

Chapter Sixteen

'You are seconded to the children's ward over the festive period.' Alice stood before the ward sister in her office. 'They are short-staffed and you are the only one I can afford to let go. Sister looked sternly at Alice and then asked, 'Is there anything you are not clear about?'

A thousand questions darted around her head, but she could only catch one and answered, 'What will I do about my training classes?'

'Over the festive period, training classes are suspended and will commence in the new year. However, it is advisable to use your free time to study.'

Back on the ward, Alice continued with her menial tasks of fetching and removing bedpans, scrubbing, polishing and, sometimes, she was allowed to make a patient comfortable in bed.

'Eh, I do love me pillows shaking up,' said a sweet old woman who was in for 'me delicate bits', as she confided.

Alice smiled and filled her tumbler with fresh water. She was just beginning to get the hang of the ward routine, and now she was moving and not certain if or when she'd be back on this ward. Still, it was all good experience and that was part of the training.

That evening after a late supper, she was up in the dormitory where she wrote a hasty letter to Johnny to tell him where she would be for the next two weeks or so. Today was Tuesday, so hopefully he would pick up this letter from the porters' lodge and they could at least have some time to spend together. Her heart sank at the thought of not seeing him over Christmastime, but she supposed it solved the problem of seeing families. Letter finished, she sealed it with a kiss and hurried down to the porters' lodge to leave it in the pigeonhole. With luck, Johnny would collect it in the morning.

On her way back in, she bumped into a nurse. 'Sorry,' she muttered, her thoughts on Johnny.

'Whoa, stranger,' said the friendly voice.

'Evelyn!' Alice exclaimed with delight. 'I haven't seen you in ages.' The only contact was a wave across a crowded dining room.

They both stood aside in the corridor to let other nurses pass.

'I could do with a quick fag,' Evelyn said. 'Have you ten minutes spare?' Alice nodded. 'Good, we can go into the sitting room.'

'But I'm not allowed in yours,' Alice explained.

Evelyn grinned, taking hold of Alice's arm. 'There'll be no one there at this time.'

Their sitting room was more comfortable than the probationers' one. Alice sat on the edge of a cosy-looking chair, while Evelyn flopped back in her chair and brushed a tired hand across her eyes. Then, sitting up, she produced a packet of Gold Flake and proffered one to Alice. And, surprisingly, she took one

– as a kind of what? She wasn't sure. Evelyn passed the box of matches and Alice lit her cigarette. Drawing on it deeply, she felt, instead of the expected coughing and raw throat, a sense of relief from the stress of the day, a gentle feeling of relaxation seeping through her body.

'Are you going home for Christmas?' she asked Evelyn, who came from the market town of Beverley.

'Aye, Mother has already done her baking, enough for an army. And you?'

Alice gave a sigh, 'Working. I'm being seconded to the children's hospital for two weeks or so.'

'I did that in my first year. It's lovely yet sad, nursing kiddies.' And then she added, 'Still no news of your daughter?'

'No, she will be five on Christmas Eve,' Alice said, and swallowed the sudden lump in her throat. 'The only consolation I have is that she is with a good family who will look after her.'

Both lapsed into silence and then Evelyn asked, 'Still friendly with Johnny?'

Alice drew on the cigarette and then answered, 'Yes, I've bought him a small gift of a box of handkerchiefs with his initial "J".' Then she went on to say, 'If I miss my dinner break tomorrow and add it to my free hour, I can go and see Mam, take her and the bairns small presents each.'

They chatted about families and Alice was careful not to mention her strong feelings for Johnny and his for her, and her thoughts on not meeting his family, who wouldn't approve of him seeing a married woman. And neither would her mother approve – as poor as she was, she had standards. *Pity those standards did not include the care of her granddaughter*, she thought bitterly, though she knew it was an unfair criticism of Aggie.

The sitting-room door opened, and four nurses entered, glancing at Alice in her probationer's uniform. She bade a quick farewell to Evelyn and made a promise to meet up in the new year.

It was late Wednesday evening before Alice heard from Johnny. He'd got tickets for a dance on Thursday night and could she get the time off? As she was on a late shift that night, Alice asked the staff nurse on duty about getting the time off and having a late pass and explained that she would be on duty over the Christmas period on the children's ward.

'I'll have a word with Sister,' was her curt response.

Alice had to wait until the end of her shift before she was summoned to Sister's office. Why, whenever she had to be summoned to see a senior member of the nursing fraternity, for whatever reason, good or bad, did she feel as though she was still at school and was about to receive the cane from the headmistress? She smoothed down her apron, which was spotted with a spray of something unmentionable and hoped Sister wouldn't notice.

As she entered the office and stood in front of the desk, she wondered, not for the first time, why the senior nurses were always writing or appeared to be writing. The room was just like any other office, pale painted walls with framed certificates of qualifications, except that on this desk was a framed photograph of a family group. Alice wondered if the sister was going home for Christmas to this happy-looking family, though she'd never imagine a nursing sister having a life outside of the hospital.

'Yes, I am.'

With a start, Alice looked up from the photograph, quite unaware she was being watched. She felt her cheeks redden and bit on her lip, not certain what to say, so she said nothing.

'Goddard, I understand that you are on duty over the Christmas period?'

Looking straight ahead, Alice said firmly, 'Yes, Sister.' There was silence and her heart sank. Was her request about to be turned down?

Then Sister spoke, 'I see no reason why you should not be granted the late pass. However, you must be back in your dormitory by midnight, understood?'

'Yes, Sister,' Alice said, eager to write Johnny a favourable reply.

Only later, when the note was delivered to the porters' lodge, did Alice think about what to wear for a dance. 'I've nothing suitable.' Her three room-mates stood with her looking in the narrow wardrobe. Nothing appealed.

Talli opened her wardrobe and peered in. 'I've got this.' She held up a dress of shades of green with silver sparkling sequins. The material swayed with movement as she held it up high. Alice eyed it, not sure if it looked too grand for her. 'Try it on,' Talli said.

Alice slipped out of her uniform, carefully hanging it up as it had to last for the rest of the week, though they were allowed a clean apron each day. She stood in her petticoat, brassiere and knickers, and discarded her thick black wool stockings. Talli gently eased the dress over Alice's head and fastened the buttons down the back. Then all three room-mates stood back to admire her.

'Not bad,' said Talli, 'you'll need a couple of tucks near the waist, then it'll fit you a treat.'

There was no wall mirror in the room, so Jane and Talli held up their hand mirrors for Alice to see her reflection.

The material felt like silk and fell in delicate folds over her slim body, and twirled with her as she tried to peep at the back of the dress. 'It's lovely,' she breathed in a heavenly sigh. Then said, 'Don't you think it's too posh for me? I've never worn anything like this before.' The only dances she'd attended in the past were the school ones and in the church hall.

'No, you go and knock 'em dead.' Talli laughed.

At last the night came for the dance and Johnny was picking her up at seven. The dance was to be held in the ballroom at the top of a department store, Johnny had written.

She waited by the porters' lodge. The night was cold and crisp, and she shivered as she pressed against the wall. She was wearing her best coat over her dress and a scarf was protecting her hair. From the lodge, the smell of fresh tea mashing in a pot reached her nostrils and she would've loved a cup to warm her up. Then she saw a set of dim headlights approaching from the borrowed van, and Johnny jumped out and enveloped Alice in a loving embrace then ushered her into the passenger seat.

Soon they arrived at the venue and Alice could hear the melody of a waltz being played. As they walked in, she looked up to the ceiling and was fascinated to see a sparkling diamante glass bowl twirling around, sending stars of twinkling lights around the room. 'It's magical,' she whispered to Johnny and he squeezed her hand. Then she went off to the ladies' cloakroom.

Stripped of the protection of her outdoor clothes, Alice suddenly felt exposed. She studied her appearance in the cloakroom mirror, thinking she was overdressed as she glanced at a woman wearing a floral summer dress and perhaps more in keeping with a works dance. She glanced back at her reflection and tidied her hair. She'd curled it specially and now the curls cascaded onto her shoulders.

Back in the dance hall, Johnny was waiting for her. As she walked towards him, she felt the silky material of the dress swish around her legs and she saw the look of pure delight in his eyes and on his face. Her heart quickened with pleasure and she felt a tingling down her spine.

'You look beautiful,' he whispered. 'God, I love you, Alice.' He pulled her into his arms and onto the crowded dance floor; holding her close, they waltzed, their bodies nearly as one.

Later, a buffet supper was being served and drinks were still free and plentiful. A group of four young men were standing in the supper queue next to Alice and Johnny, and one of the men cheekily asked Johnny, 'Who's the lass you're with, then? She's a bit of a smasher. Are you going to introduce us?'

Johnny took hold of Alice's arm and, drawing her forward, he answered, 'This is Alice, my girlfriend.' She smiled in acknowledgement. 'And the less you know about these four rebels the better.'

They ignored his remark and bantered with him, 'My, you've kept her quiet.' And to Alice they jested, 'Bit of a dark horse is our Johnny.'

The playfulness carried on as they moved nearer the buffet table, when a young woman in front of the group turned round and queried, 'Are you Maureen Mitchell's brother?'

Johnny looked at her. 'Yes, but sorry, I don't know you.'

'I work with Maureen at the telephone exchange. She's always talking about you, but she never said you had a girlfriend.'

Johnny was saved from answering, because they were all now

at the buffet table where an array of party food was set out. Alice marvelled to see such a variety of sandwiches – ham, egg, cheese and chutney, potted meat – as well as savoury biscuits, pickled onions and sausage rolls.

They found a quiet corner and enjoyed their food. Feeling too full to dance, they were content to sit and hold hands, watching the dancers twirling by. The girl who worked with Johnny's sister, Maureen, drifted by and waved to them. Alice glanced at Johnny and knew he was thinking the same as her: Maureen would soon know of her existence. He didn't voice his thoughts and neither did she.

A few days later, Johnny and his mother were in the sitting room when she said to him, 'Are you ashamed of us?'

Startled, Johnny looked up from the book he was reading, not sure he'd heard his mother correctly. 'What was that, Mam?'

She repeated, 'Are you ashamed of us, your family?'

'No! Why on earth would you think that?'

'Is that woman you went to the dance with the same one Mabel saw you with in the park?'

'Yes, but what's brought this on?'

'If she's special, then why haven't you brought her home for us to meet her?'

Johnny glanced away from his mother. How could he tell her that Alice was legally married? His mother would not be able to face her friends at church who would see it as a wicked sin. And the neighbours, what would they say? All this mattered to his mother, because that was the way she was brought up and lived her standards by. She would never understand him loving Alice.

He glanced back to his mother and said in a quiet voice, 'She's a probationer nurse and doesn't have much free time off-duty.' Then he lowered his head to read his book, but read he could not. The words just lost their meaning. They jumbled up, like the thoughts in his head.

He lit a cigarette and looked out of the window at the bleak, grey sky.

Chapter Seventeen

Christmas Eve day clung cold and damp, chilling her face as Alice stepped outside to walk the short distance to the porters' lodge to pick up a message from Johnny. Her thoughts turned to Daisy. Today was her fifth birthday. To keep herself sane, Alice imagined her daughter to be wearing a pretty dress and having a grand birthday party with a cake and candles to blow out. She would be happy and laughing, and enjoying the party games of hunting the thimble and musical chairs. These Alice had read about and seen drawings of in children's books of idyllic childhoods. Her thoughts moved on to the many hours she'd spent in the library when studying, and especially on a cold or wet day. The library was always warm and cosy near to the fire stove, where she would sit and lose herself in books, oblivious to other people around her.

'Here, miss,' the porter roused her from her reverie. Her being a regular visitor, he'd seen her coming. He was always helpful and jolly and talked about his children quite a lot. And she wondered what it must be like to have a dad who was so caring. Tearing open the envelope, Alice was disappointed to see only a few hastily penned lines from Johnny of his love for her, which was lovely. Perhaps she'd expected too much from him. Something she needed to take away the sinking, dull feeling she had inside of her.

She hadn't time to dwell on her thoughts, because she had to report to the sister in charge of the children's ward. The children's ward was at the back of the hospital facing south-west and looked out onto open fields, with a veranda running the length of it. Weather permitting, the young patients would have plenty of healthy fresh air to help them recover more quickly. That was the theory of the donor of the ward, Lady Sybil Lockwood, an Edwardian beauty who lost her only daughter, Beatrice, to the disease consumption.

Alice tapped on the office door and was bade enter. She felt the warmth coming from a fire burning in the grate. 'Probationer Goddard reporting for duty, Sister,' Alice said, glancing around the small and cluttered room.

The sister, who was busy preparing for the doctor's morning round, stopped what she was doing and said, 'Ah, Goddard, welcome. We are in need of a good pair of willing hands. Sorry, but I do not have time to talk to you until later this evening. Come to my office after supper. Now, report to the Beatrice Lockwood Ward to Staff Nurse.'

Alice located the ward and reported to a harassed staff nurse, and was told to go and clean up a little girl who had been sick.

Her heart went out to the poor little mite who was lying in her own vomit. With practised ease, she gently lifted the girl from the cot and onto a chair, saying, 'Stay there, sweetheart, and don't move.' Quickly, she bundled up the dirty bedding and took it to an outer room and within seconds, she was back to the little girl. She looked about three or four and, as Alice lifted her up into her arms, she could feel the fragile bones of her thin body. The child whimpered softly and hiccupped, and Alice looked for the bathroom.

She found it, a big white bath with a wooden lid, too big to bathe this little one. Looking round, with the child's arms now tight around her neck, Alice found a small tin bath, which she placed in the stone sink. 'Now let me take off your dirty nightie,' she said soothingly. Gently, Alice eased the child's arms from her neck and undid the strings of the nightgown and slid it over her head. She sat her down on the edge of the wooden lid of the big bath while she filled a jug with warm water from a gas water geyser and poured it into the bowl. She tested it with her elbow. 'Just right,' she murmured.

All the time the little girl, no longer crying, watched Alice with big brown eyes, her lashes still wet. Tenderly, she sat the child in the tin bath and sponged down her undernourished body. Her skin was motley with signs of fading bruises on her arms and upper body, and she bore all the signs of being neglected, poor little mite. Despite all she'd suffered at the hands of her husband, Alice had never once neglected her daughter. But there are those who said she had neglected Daisy or why would she have been placed with another family? She dashed away such thoughts to concentrate on the child she was caring for.

Lifting her from the bowl, Alice wrapped the little girl in a clean towel and patted her dry. She found the cupboard with the nightgowns and dressed her. All the time, she sang nursery rhymes and the girl seemed entranced as if she'd never heard them before.

'Now, my pretty, you're all nice and clean, so now I'm going to make your bed nice.' The girl nodded, understanding.

Back on the ward, Alice sat the girl on a chair near her bed and she looked at the chart, noticing her name was Molly.

Soon, Alice had Molly tucked up in her nice clean bed and, instinctively, she kissed Molly on the forehead and was rewarded with the glimmer of a smile.

The time passed and, as well as the menial tasks of scrubbing and polishing, she also attended to the children's needs. At mealtime, she fed those who were unable to feed themselves and attended to their toilet needs, stripped dirty beds and remade them, putting children to bed, and softly, so no members of staff could hear her, she sang nursery rhymes. Not once did the busy senior nursing staff reprimand her, they were relieved to have a probationary nurse who knew what to do without having to be shown every detail.

By the time supper came, Alice was exhausted, but in a good way. A lovely sensation filled her; she'd achieved something of worth. Quite a different feeling from when she worked at Faith House. Maybe it was because of nursing young children. She couldn't really pinpoint it.

Now she was summoned to Sister's office, so she hurried to her dormitory, a trek away, to change into a clean apron and to tidy her hair.

Alice was surprised to see Staff Nurse also in the office and wondered if her new-found elation as to her worthiness was about to crumble. She stood to attention, her heart seemed to be beating faster and she felt a sinking sensation in the pit of her stomach. A stray strand of hair slipped from its mooring of a grip and brushed her cheek, but she felt unable to move her hands from her side to secure it back in place, so she looked straight ahead and waited.

'How has your first day been, Goddard?' Sister asked, pleasantly.

Alice, surprised by the question, answered, 'Very well, Sister, thank you.' Then she waited for what was to come and wondered if she was going to be sent back to the womens ward.

'Excellent. Staff Nurse said that you are a diligent and willing worker, and an asset to the ward.'

Alice remained quiet, because she was speechless. This was the very opposite of what she'd expected to be told.

Sister continued, 'Tomorrow, Christmas Day, we allow the children's parents and siblings to come in the afternoon. Only two visitors to a bed at any one time, as I am sure you are aware of the rule, but for Christmas Day, the rule is relaxed. In the morning, after the children are fed and washed, and any dressings applied and medicines given, we have a Father Christmas . . .' Alice glanced at Sister and saw a twinkle in her eyes. She continued, 'It is one of the junior doctors and so for the rest of the morning those children who are able play with their toys. After an early dinner, the children are to rest and sleep, if possible, before their afternoon visitors arrive.'

Alice was dismissed and, wearily, she made her way up to the dormitory to find only one other occupant, a second-year probationary nurse called Marlene Dawson, who had moved in while Talli was away.

She greeted Alice with a sneering voice. 'You've soon found your feet.'

Taken aback, but quick to recover, Alice answered, 'Nice of you to say so.' She smiled at the spotty-faced girl.

This seemed to throw the girl, who went to sit on her bed.

Alice sorted out her clean dress, which they had to wear for a full week, although they had a clean apron every day. She changed out of her uniform and slipped on her dressing gown over her undergarments, collected her washbag and towel, and went along to the communal facilities.

When she arrived back in the dormitory, she was relieved to see that the other girl was asleep.

Next morning, Alice was awake early and listened to the faint gurgling sound of running water coming from the pipes that ran along the wall, high above her head. It was a soothing movement, rather like a gentle stream meandering through the countryside. Not that she'd spent much time in the countryside.

It didn't take her long to be up and dressed, have her breakfast and report to the ward. She was early and yesterday she had been too busy to take much notice of the ward. But now she could see that a lot of effort had gone into the festive decorations. There were coloured garlands in red, yellow, blue and green hanging in swathes across the ward and fixed up in the centre of the ceiling. There were red and blue balloons and, at the far end, standing majestically, was a Christmas tree. Alice had never seen a real Christmas tree before. At Faith House the tree had been an old imitation one and at home, the nearest they ever got to a real pine tree was a branch to decorate.

The night staff were just finishing their duties and handing over their reports of what had happened during their shift. Alice heard one of the nurses say, 'Molly Parker never wet the bed last night.'

'That's a first,' exclaimed another nurse.

Alice went in search of Molly and found her sitting on her bed, and still wearing her nightgown. 'Wants you to dress her,' sniffed the second-year probationer, Marlene.

Wiping Molly's sticky face and hands with a warm flannel, Alice noticed that the little girl's big eyes looked at her, as if watching in case she disappeared. It was a heart-stopping look, and Alice could feel the pull at all her maternal instincts. Without another thought, she gathered Molly into her arms and hugged her, kissing the top of her baby-strength hair.

Soon, she had her dressed in a party frock of pink taffeta and, all the time she attended to the little girl, she crooned softly the Christmas carol 'Away in a Manger'. 'Now, you do look pretty,' Alice said to Molly as she brushed her hair.

Soon the ward was alive with the anticipation of Father Christmas coming with his sack of gifts, one for each child and depending on the nature of the illness of the patient.

The special hour came and Father Christmas, accompanied by Matron, entered the ward. Most of the children were excited, except those who were too ill to move about. One boy was jumping for joy on his bed and Alice saw Marlene going towards him. Just at that moment her attention was diverted, and she went to help a little boy who was trying to sit up. And then other children needed care and Molly showed her the rag doll she'd received from Father Christmas.

'It's lovely, Molly. Have you a name for her?' Shyly, she shook her head and her soft baby curls bobbed about. 'How about calling her Tess? It's a nice name,' Alice suggested.

'Tess,' murmured Molly, repeating the name a few times.

After dinner, the children were tucked up in bed to have a rest before the visitors came when Alice noticed an empty bed, the one the boy had been jumping on earlier. Puzzled, she looked round, but saw no sign of him. The other nurses were all busy, so she searched around for him and she wondered if he'd toddled into the bathroom area. She went to investigate.

On top of the wooden lid covering the bath was a sleeping boy. His little body had slumped sideward and he was in danger of falling onto the hard stone floor. In a trice, she scooped him up into her arms. His cheeks were tear-stained and his body felt cold. He opened his eyes and, on seeing her, a look of fear filled his brown eyes. Murmuring soothing words to comfort him, she said, 'There, little fellow, you're safe now.'

He must have sensed the safety of being in Alice's arms, because his arms locked around her neck.

'Nurse, what are you doing with that child?' Staff Nurse barred her path.

'I found him fast asleep on the wooden top of the bath. Poor little fellow, he was in danger of toppling down onto the floor.'

'Who on earth put him there?' she snapped.

Alice had an idea that it was Marlene, but didn't say. Instead, she answered, 'I've no idea, Staff Nurse.'

'I'll get to the bottom of this. Put the boy to bed.' With that, she stormed off.

Alice tucked the boy into his bed and pulled up the sides, so he wouldn't fall out. She decided to wash his face later on when he woke up.

Looking down the ward near to the door, Sister was talking, in an unusually low voice, to the staff on duty. Alice busied herself, checking on the sleeping children, wondering if she would be summoned to be questioned. When she looked again, the other nurses had resumed their duties and Sister was marching a red-faced Marlene to her office.

Soon it was time for the children to be woken up and made ready for their family visitors. Alice was wiping the face of Benny, the little boy who'd missed seeing Father Christmas, when she spied under his pillow a small parcel wrapped in brown paper with a blue Christmas star. She finished tidying him up and gave him the parcel, saying, 'Look what Father Christmas left for you.'

Eagerly, he tore open the wrapping to reveal the gift of a yellow toy car. His small fingers turned the wheels and a look of joy filled his face.

Alice hoped that the ordeal of being alone in the bathroom wouldn't have any lasting effect.

Time for the visitors, and she watched as Molly held out her arms to a poorly dressed young woman, her little face a glow of delight. It was such a tiny gesture, but it showed the love of the child and her mother.

Alice's heart filled with longing for her own child. She felt tears prick at her eyes and she steeled herself to smile at the happy family scenes.

There was no birthday party for Daisy this year. Instead, she was in bed with the curtains drawn to stop the bright light, reflected from the snow on the rooftops, entering the sickroom. 'This child has chickenpox and bright light will damage her eyes,' diagnosed the doctor to Moira.

Mrs Cooper-Browne refused to enter Daisy's bedroom. 'I have my guests to consider,' she had stated.

Daisy moved restlessly, wriggling and itching. She felt hot and achy and cross, and her arms kept flinging themselves about. 'I want my mammy,' she cried.

'Sit up, Miss Daisy, and I will dab those nasty spots with this cooling lotion,' said Moira and sighed. Now she wasn't allowed to go home until Daisy was well again.

Daisy refused to do as she was told, and Moira's patience began to wane.

Chapter Eighteen

Aggie was polishing her brass wall hanging with vigour. Alice was coming to see her and her brothers and sister this afternoon. Muttering aloud to herself, Aggie said, 'I'll just tell her straight. It's nowt to do with her anyway. It's my life.'

'You'll wear a hole in that if you don't stop.'

Aggie glanced over her shoulder to see her next-door neighbour. She turned away from her task and sank into her chair by the fireside. 'It's our Alice. She's coming this afternoon and I'll have to tell her.'

'What's wrong with that?'

'Since she began training ter be a nurse, she's gone up in the world. And ter tell the truth, I dread telling her.'

'Now you look here, Aggie, my lass, you've a right ter your life as well as she has hers. So, don't waste yer time worrying. It'll do the lads good to have a man to look up to.'

Aggie mulled over the words. 'Yer right. Lads have been getting a bit of a handful.' She thought of the twins. They'd been doing a bit of thieving – apples from the greengrocers and such like. If

165

the constable caught them, they would be in real trouble and that would involve the authorities who were totally useless with help when her husband, Albert, passed away. God rest his soul.

After spending time on the children's ward, and before commencing duties on the women's ward, Alice was given two whole days of leave. She indulged in an extra hour's sleep-in and the shared communal washroom was blissfully quiet. Then, she went window shopping in Hammonds department store, stopping to admire a beautiful winter coat of fine red wool with a silver fur collar. She let her fingers luxuriate over the softness of the fur and, giving a quick glance round to see if any of the sales assistants were looking her way, she removed her coat. Easing the beautiful garment off its hanger, she slipped it on and stood in front of a full-length mirror to gaze at the coat, its fit and cut showing off her slim body. 'Perfect,' she murmured.

'Yes, it is, madam, and very expensive.' Alice turned to see a sales assistant standing behind her. Her tone suggested that it was well out of Alice's income bracket. A quick calculation told her that it would take three or five years' wages to be able to afford such an extravagant garment.

She left the store and hurried through the cold streets, feeling the chilly wind whip through her coat. People scurried past with their heads down, anxious to be somewhere warm and cosy. A newspaper seller stamped his feet, a beggar sat in a shop doorway. Alice dropped a coin into his tin, wishing it could be more.

When she reached her mother's house and opened the door to feel its warmth, it was a joy to behold. Then she was surprised to be greeted by the aroma of baking. A large Victoria sponge cake was cooling on a wire tray on the table. The kitchen was neat and tidy, and she thought that Aggie looked different, but couldn't quite put her finger on what it was. 'Had a nice Christmas?' she asked, warming her hands in front of the fire.

'One of the best,' Aggie answered truthfully, smiling. She thought of the night out to see a show at the theatre and being treated like a lady.

Alice was further surprised by her mother's upbeat manner and wondered what had brought this on.

They settled down to a cup of tea and a slice of the cake. Alice's usual gifts of sweets for her brothers and snuff for her mother seemed inadequate and she wished she had more money to spend on them, but all her spare money had been spent on the family Christmas presents and for Johnny.

Thinking of Johnny, she hoped that he would receive her letter soon, which she had left at the porters' lodge for him to collect. She'd overcome her mixed feelings after reading his last short note. It was two whole weeks since she'd last seen him and she missed him just holding her close in his arms. There was something very special to be held by the man you loved.

'I've something to tell yer.'

Aroused from her daydream, Alice looked up at her mother and hoped it wasn't bad news. 'You're not ill?' she blurted. 'Or the bairns?'

'I'm getting wed.' There, it was out.

Alice stared at her mother in disbelief. 'Wed! Who to?'

Her mother answered, proudly, 'To my lodger, Mr Baker. George.'

Speechless, Alice stared at her mother. She'd only met Mr Baker twice and she found him to be very quiet with alert grey eyes behind his horn-rimmed spectacles. He would miss nothing going on and he might be a good influence on her brothers.

'Well, say something, Alice.'

Alice found her voice and said what her mother wanted her to say. 'I'm very pleased for you, Mam, and I hope you'll be very happy.' She didn't want to think of them sleeping together. Then she wondered where her sister, Martha, would sleep. Maybe she'd have the front room.

Aggie beamed. 'George has a good job and will provide for us, so there is no need for me to work. He believes a wife's place is at home and to look after her husband.'

'Have you set a date yet?'

'End of January, so that will give me time to buy a new coat and hat,' Aggie enthused.

Alice had to admit that it was a long time since she'd seen her mother looking so happy. She'd had a hard life, raising five children virtually on her own, so who was Alice to begrudge her happiness?

Alice surprised herself and her mother by giving her a hug and saying, 'I'm pleased for you, Mam.' And she was.

Later, Alice called to see Martha at the haberdashery shop, but she was busy dealing with a customer, so she browsed, looking at the lovely rolls of material, wishing she could buy something extravagant.

'Alice, what do you want?' It was Martha, now free to talk to her.

'I've just come from Mam's and she told me she's getting wed. It's quite a surprise.'

Martha sniffed, saying, 'I don't know what she wants to marry him for, he's right picky. Mam has to starch and iron his collars and woe betide if she gets an iron mark on them. And he likes his shoes blacked. He finds jobs for our Charlie to earn his pocket money, as well as lugging in the coal scuttle.'

'What about you?'

'I'm getting out, because I'll be kicked out of Mam's bedroom and he says the front room is for Sundays and visitors and no way am I going to sleep in the same bedroom as three smelly lads. I ask yer, what visitors do we have like that? The kitchen has always been good enough.'

'Where will you go?'

Martha nodded in the direction of a young, round-faced woman serving on the glove counter. 'My friend said I can share with her 'til I get something more permanent.'

When she arrived back at the hospital. Alice called at the porters' lodge to see if Johnny had replied to her letter. The porter, not the jolly one, took his time checking the pigeonholes. She shuffled from foot to foot, thinking maybe Johnny was going out elsewhere – or had he met someone else? Her heart sank, and a shiver ran down her spine, not because of the cold day, but the thought of losing him would be unbearable.

'Ah, got it,' the porter said. 'It was trapped.'

Alice murmured her thanks and hurried up to the dormitory to read Johnny's reply. Her fingers felt clumsy as she pulled open the envelope. Reading it a second time she felt her heart race with joy. He'd managed to buy two tickets for a gala dance with spot prizes at the Alexandra.

Dancing together and in each other's arms – she couldn't wait. Wrapping her arms around her body she waltzed around the small floor space of the room, bumping into Talli, who was just entering the room.

'Whoa,' said Talli, 'I'm too worn out to dance,' and went to flop onto her bed. 'What's with all the excitement?' she said, yawning. Alice showed her the letter. 'I suppose you want to borrow me dress again?'

Up until that point, Alice hadn't thought of what she would wear. Not that she had much choice. 'You don't mind?'

'No, I ain't going anywhere, except back to the ward. I just needed to rest me aching back, so I gobbled down my tea.' She looked at the small alarm clock perched on a corner shelf. 'Ten minutes I've got,' she said and shut her eyes.

Alice moved quietly, not wanting to disturb Talli. She sorted out her best underwear and her precious, only pair of silk stockings and found the hand mirror so that she could apply powder and a bright-pink lipstick and clip on the tiny drop-pearl earrings, which Johnny had given her for Christmas. Talli fastened the buttons on the back of the green dress for her and then went back to her duties.

Downstairs, Alice hurried to the porters' lodge, their meeting point. In the gloom, she saw the tiny glow of a cigarette. And then she saw him. He hastily stamped on the cigarette and held out his arms to her and she ran into them feeling not the cold dampness of his overcoat, but his lips. His lips were hot and sizzling, his kisses breathtaking and she responded, unleashing all her pent-up emotions. Her desire and her passion overflowed with happiness for this wonderful man. 'I've missed you,' she whispered as they drew breath.

'I've missed you and I never want us to be apart at Christmastime ever again.'

The Alexandra was heaving with dancers and the band was in full swing. She'd been in the lady's cloakroom to refresh her power and lipstick and now they were sitting at the table having a drink and holding hands, just content, for now, to watch the whirling scene before them. She adored the lovely ornate decorations of the marble pillars and the magnificent glass dome high above, and the fine architecture was like a grand palace. From the ceiling hung a glittering ball of many twinkling facets, sending lights of moonbeams around the hall.

Suddenly, Johnny was on his feet and said formally, 'Alice, may I have the pleasure of this dance.'

She answered in similar tone, 'Why certainly, Mr Mitchell.'

Then he swept her close in his arms and they glided onto the dance floor. Alice put her cheek next to his, feeling its smoothness and the faint smell of shaving soap. It was heaven to be in his arms. She felt so safe and secure, but she could never be Mrs Johnny Mitchell, not until she was free of Ted. She just wanted to spend the rest of her life with Johnny. The doctor had told her when she had been in hospital, after her accident, that her pelvis had been damaged and this could limit her chances of having more children, though she hoped the doctors were wrong.

They won a spot prize: socks for Johnny and a comb for her. It was a wonderful evening and she didn't want it to end. But end it must. All too soon, they were kissing goodnight. Stealthily, she slipped her hands inside his jacket to feel the tautness of his strong muscles, pressing herself against him, feeling the hardness of his body. Her own flowed with passion. 'Oh, Johnny,' she whispered. 'I wish we could be married.'

On their next meeting, they were in a quiet pub, sitting by a warm, crackling fire and she talked about trying to find out about divorce proceedings.

And so Johnny told her what he'd found out about the law. They sat in silence for a long time. Then he said to her, 'I love you, Alice. Nothing can change that.'

Alice sighed, and reached for Johnny's hand, wanting to feel his reassuring strength. Her dream of when they were married, they would have a home for Daisy, was shattered.

* * *

Spring came in with a flourish and it brought some good news. Johnny had recently joined a walking group. 'To fill in the time while you're working,' he told her. It was a Sunday afternoon and they were sitting on a bench on the top deck of the pier.

'Easter,' she said in answer to his question. 'I'll see if I can have the time off as a holiday. Four whole days together.' She smiled, dreamily.

Johnny laughed and said, 'There will be ten of us altogether and sleeping under canvas.'

'I've never slept in a tent before,' she mused and then added, 'what if it rains?'

'The tents are waterproofed, so we will be dry.'

Alice had to approach the staff nurse first, to ask to see the sister in charge. She had to remind the staff nurse twice before her request was granted. Now she stood in front of Sister waiting for her to look up from reading a report. Alice suspected that this was a ploy to undermine probationers and to deter them from asking for leave. Alice was determined to keep her outlook positive and take a firm stance.

'Four days. Do you really need all that time off?' Sister questioned in a frosty voice.

'Yes, Sister. Four days. I'm going on a walking holiday.'

'I do not know if you can be spared, all that time off-duty. Two days should be sufficient.'

Alice pulled herself up tall and said in a polite voice, 'With respect, Sister, I did work over all of the festive season, and I missed my mother's wedding because of an emergency.'

'Hmm,' Sister responded.

Alice didn't move, and she wasn't going to until . . .

'Very well, I will forward your request to Matron.'

'Thank you, Sister.'

A week passed before she heard whether Matron had granted her the four days of holiday. It had been a very trying and tiring day. A patient suffering from a nervous complaint had upturned a full bedpan onto the clean ward floor. This caused distress to the woman in the next bed who was recovering from an appendix operation and then someone else complained about the noise. The complaints seemed to magnify as the day went along and Alice, being the only probationer on the ward, had all the dirty jobs to do. And then the staff nurse told her to remake two of the beds properly.

Bone-weary and hungry, Alice was looking forward to sitting down and eating her supper. Now she'd been standing outside Sister's office for over half an hour, before she was bade enter.

'Well, Goddard, you are fortunate. Matron has granted you the four days of leave.'

Alice couldn't believe her luck. Four whole days spent with Johnny. Even though there was only a few scrapings of food left for her supper, it didn't dampen her joy. And as soon as possible she was in her room and penning a letter to Johnny with her good news. Hurrying down to the porters' lodge with the letter, she felt a surge of new energy running through her veins.

Easter couldn't come quickly enough for her and Johnny.

Chapter Nineteen

'What do you think of this?' Alice and Talli were in the open-air market by the side of Holy Trinity Church, sorting through the clothes on one of the second-hand stalls. They had a rare Saturday afternoon off-duty period together and they were having a fun, light-hearted day away from the stress of attending lectures and nursing on the wards. Alice held up a hand-knitted jumper in dark-blue cable stitch.

Talli fingered it. 'It's warm enough to keep out the chilly wind. But then . . .' she added mischievously, 'maybe you won't need it if yer got your love to keep yer warm.'

Alice felt herself blushing and said too quickly, 'There'll be none of that.' Talli just grinned. Alice made the purchase and they moved on to the next stall, and she bought a pair of thick woollen socks. She would have loved to have bought a new pair of shoes, but her old sturdy ones would have to do. She also bought a lightweight raincoat and hat, which could easily be rolled up and packed neatly in the rucksack, and a heavy tweed skirt. All her buys were from second-hand stalls or shops. *One day*, she thought, *I'll have new clothes.*

'You'll look like a schoolmistress in that,' Talli joked, holding up the tweed skirt.

'I have to be practical. It's no fun getting wet if it rains.'

They perused the other stalls: imitation jewellery, bric-a-brac, belts and braces, bedlinen, boxes of bits and pieces for a penny. Alice rummaged in this box and found a pair of shoelaces, which would do nicely to revive her old shoes.

Talli had wandered off and Alice looked round for her, when her heart gave a swift thud of fright. She stood frozen to the spot, watching the big man as he made his way through the crowds towards her. Suddenly, he stopped at a stall selling fishing equipment. He was only a few feet away from her. He said something to the stallholder, who reached to show the man a reel. It was then that she saw the man's face in full profile. She felt an almighty tide of relief flood through her veins. The man wasn't Ted.

'What's up with you? You look as though you've seen a ghost.' Talli was back, with a multi-coloured scarf wound round her slender neck.

Alice gave a weak smile and replied, 'I thought I'd just seen my brute of a husband.'

Talli stared at her. 'I thought you was a widow, because you never talk about your husband.'

'It wasn't a happy marriage.'

'So that's why you and Johnny are not getting married.'

'You are right. I'd love to marry Johnny, but being a probationer it is not allowed and I need to qualify.'

'He'll wait for you,' Talli said. She took hold of Alice's arm, saying, 'What about this? Sniff the air.'

Alice did so and the tantalising aroma coming from the local fish and chip stall filled her nostrils. Both women drifted towards the stall and the striped awning of the attached tent. 'I didn't realise I was so hungry,' Talli said.

'Me too, but I can only afford pattie and chips,' Alice said, surveying the small contents of her purse.

They settled inside the tent and sat on the narrow form with a small ledge to place their plates of food on. They sprinkled salt and the special mint sauce over their pattie and chips, and tucked in.

Licking her lips, Talli remarked, 'Much better than hospital food.' Alice nodded, her mouth still full.

Afterwards, carrying their purchases between them, they walked back to the hospital in high spirits.

That night, in the darkness of the dormitory, Alice listened to the gentle breathing of the three sleeping women. Sleep eluded her. Running through her mind was an image of Ted on the night she'd fled from him. Until today, she'd never given him much thought. She fell into a restless sleep, dreaming of faces surrounding her, suffocating her.

When she did wake up, long before the waker-up called, she was bathed in a chilled sweat. Sliding quietly from her bed, she made her way to the empty communal washroom. She slipped off her nightgown and drew water from the temperamental gas geyser into an enamel jug and filled a large tin bowl. To soften the water, she swished around her precious bar of soap, and then stepped into it. It was too small to sit down so she stood, sponging every part of her body with vigorous movements and when finished and dried, she felt refreshed and warm.

Back in the dormitory, while the other three still slept, she dressed and sat on her bed to go through her weekly lecture notes. They were submitted to the nursing tutor who would mark and appraise them. So far, she hadn't received any low marks, but she didn't like to assume that everything was perfect, so she always double-checked her notes. Attending night school had been her saviour, for it had taught her discipline and not to be 'slapdash' with her work, as Mr Hookway, the tutor, had been fond of remarking. Often, when she had a free period, she would take herself off to the hospital library to look up and study medical terminology and its meaning, so she could understand what she was writing about and what would be expected of her in the future.

She made a mental note to put her life into perspective and priority. First, and uppermost in her mind, was her quest to find her daughter. Second, was her determination to gain her nursing qualifications, and then, third, was her ongoing relationship with Johnny, the man she loved and hoped one day to marry. There was no point in worrying about what the future held, because it would only pull her down and then she would be no good to anyone.

With a spring in her step and feeling more settled in her mind, she entered the ward to begin her daily duties.

'Bedpans, Nurse,' Staff Nurse instructed her.

When Alice and Johnny saw each other one evening, over a week later, he'd arranged for them both to meet up with the walking group. 'I'm dying to introduce you. It's a mixed, friendly group and you'll like them,' he said. Then taking hold of her arm he drew her into a shop doorway and swept her into his arms and kissed her, a long, sweet, lingering kiss.

When they both came up for air, Johnny said, 'That's to let you know you are my girl, so no flirting with the other chaps.' They both laughed.

As they walked along the street, holding hands, she thought that she'd never been happier. All thoughts of her brute of a husband were banished from her thoughts. But buried deep in her heart was her daughter whom she would never forget.

The meeting was held in the small anteroom of a church hall. There were eight members including Alice and Johnny, and he introduced her. She acknowledged each one with a warm handshake and hoped she could remember who was who. Wendy and Dennis were an engaged couple, planning to marry in a few years' time when they had saved enough money.

'Are you getting engaged?' Wendy asked Alice as they were in the tiny cupboard of a kitchen making a pot of tea.

Alice drew in a deep breath before answering, 'I'm a probationary nurse so I have to qualify first.' She omitted to tell her that she was legally married to another man.

The evening progressed without any more awkward questions. It was decided for the walking group to take the train from Hull as far as Skipton railway station and then walk to the nearest camping site, which was on a farm. Then the next day they would walk to their permanent campsite near to the village of Grassington nestling in Wharfedale. Ralph, a good organiser, would make the necessary arrangements and let everyone know the cost involved.

Alice and Johnny were walking back towards the hospital. 'What did you think of the group and the plan?'

'They're nice and friendly and the holiday sounds to be an exciting adventure . . .' Her voice trailed away. She just hoped that she had enough money to pay her way.

Johnny said, as if he'd read her mind, 'I've saved extra money for us both, so you've no need to worry.'

'Oh, Johnny,' she whispered, squeezing his hand tightly. She was pleased, but not just because of his generosity with money. No, it was his generosity as a person, a man who cared enough about her to make her happy, that she loved him for.

Easter that year fell on the third week of April and the weather forecast was mixed, with the temperature falling at night, but nothing would have dampened Alice's spirits. The walking group left on the early morning train. 'We've to make the most of the daylight hours to pitch our tents,' Ralph had instructed.

Alice felt excited, like a girl on her first holiday, which she was. She didn't really count her time at the convalescent home. Her time working at the hospital, lifting patients and moving the heavy wooden screens from bed to bed, stood her in good stead to carry the weighty rucksack on her back. She wore all her outdoor clothes and packed a change of underwear and her warmest pyjamas, socks, washbag and towel, dried food, sandwiches and a flask of tea. She was in charge of the first-aid kit, and on top of all this was her rolled-up sleeping bag and a waterproofed ground sheet. Once on the train they could discard their rucksacks and sit back and relax.

Alice would have sat next to Johnny and snuggled up to him, but the men were seated on one side of the compartment and the women on the other side. They were all very jolly and one of the men started to sing 'One Man Went to Mow a Meadow' and they all joined in.

The camaraderie of the group was infectious, and Alice found herself relaxing, any doubts she might have had about fitting in quickly dispelled.

Before they reached Skipton, they had their snack to eat because, as Ralph reiterated, 'Once off the train, we must march on to make full use of the daylight hours.'

Some of the group had walking sticks and Alice wished she had one when they had to negotiate going down a steep grassy bank. She ended up sliding down in a most undignified manner on her bottom, where she promptly erupted into a fit of giggles.

The others looked at her, bemused, but all she could say was, 'If Matron could see me now.'

Johnny hauled her to her feet and gave her a fleeting kiss on her lips.

By the time they reached the farm field and the fellows pitched the tents, while the women prepared supper over a campfire, it was almost dark, the last of the daylight creeping away, but the glow of the fire flames shone and flickered red and orange, adding a mystical quality, lighting up the faces of everyone as they sat in a circle, eating their supper of sausages and beans and drinking cocoa. Alice felt so happy, it was a magical experience for her and more so to share it with Johnny. Their eyes met across the circle and she knew he was thinking the same.

After singing a couple of songs around the fire, everyone began yawning and soon retired to their tents. Alice was sharing with Wendy and Johnny was sharing with Dennis.

As she snuggled down in her sleeping bag, Alice wished she was sharing with Johnny. She'd this strange desire to look at him while he was sleeping.

Next morning, she awoke to the smell of frying bacon. Frank, the quiet chap, was happy making breakfast. Alice marvelled how soon he could make a fire to cook on. 'I was a boy scout,' he told her.

Within the hour, they had packed up and were on the move to Grassington. The campsite was near to the River Wharfe on the fringe of the village, with the added protection of a small copse of trees. The men, as before, set up the tents and the women sorted out what food provisions were needed. Alice and Wendy, armed with a shopping list and the allowance of money, walked over the bridge and into the village main street. The first thing that greeted them was the delicious aroma of fresh baking bread coming from the bakery. They bought two big loaves and three large meat pies, fresh from the oven. At the grocer's they purchased butter, jars of meat and fish paste and next door at the greengrocer's, apples and oranges.

From what she saw of the village, Alice loved it and hoped that they could explore more of it later, maybe when they had free time. Ralph had mapped out the walking routes for each day, but evenings were free after they'd eaten a meal together. 'Team spirit is the guideline,' said Ralph.

In the course of having meals together and walking side by side, Alice found conversation was easy. Frank worked in the reference library, though Alice couldn't recall seeing him there when she was studying. Ralph worked as a clerk for the railway and he was able to get a group concession. Dennis was in men's tailoring and Wendy worked at Woolworths, and the other two women were schoolteachers.

After the evening meal, Alice and Johnny went for a walk around the village, but Alice's feet were a bit sore, so they called in at the Black Horse for a drink, a shandy for her and a beer for him. They settled at a table next to where some of the local men were having a game of dominoes. Then an old man with a white beard came and sat on the spare seat next to Alice and Johnny. He nodded to them and soon he was in conversation telling them a bit of the history of the village, which was once a lead mining village. He was an interesting character and it was late by the time they arrived back at camp.

To her surprise, she found the tent empty and Wendy's sleeping bag missing. She heard whispering coming from Johnny and Dennis's tent next door. Suddenly, Johnny lifted up the flap and came in. Alice looked at him, wondering what was happening. Johnny just grinned and hauled in his sleeping bag and gear and explained, 'It seems that Dennis and Wendy have, erm . . . things to discuss,' he finished in a flourish. 'So, my lovely girl, you are stuck with me as your sleeping companion. Sorry to be a nuisance.'

Alice didn't know how it occurred, but suddenly they were in each other's arms and kissing and touching. It was as if a lid had been lifted off the genie pot. All their pent-up emotions surfaced and there was no way they could be stopped.

Suddenly, they were both naked, not feeling the chill of the night, because their bodies were on fire with a hungry passion of love and desire. She felt Johnny's hot lips kissing every part of her body and her most sensitive and intimate parts. She arched her body to his, feeling the strength of his manhood and wanting him with a power of urgent desire she didn't know she possessed.

'Alice,' he whispered in her ear, 'are you sure?'

Her answer was to reach down and guide him to her.

They made love with frenzied urgency and it was over in a matter of minutes. For a while they both lay exhausted and then Alice propped herself up on her elbow and leant over to kiss Johnny. This time their loving came more naturally and leisurely and so satisfying. 'Bliss,' she murmured in his ear.

Alice got her wish. As they lay in their sleeping bags, she gazed at Johnny sleeping beside her and her heart overflowed with joy and love for him, this wonderful man who loved her.

Little did she realise at the time, this act of love for each other would become just a memory and no chance of being repeated.

Life over the next few years continued and nursing kept her busy and she felt a sense of achievement when she passed her nursing exams. She and Talli had opted to stay at the infirmary as it suited them. Alice because of Johnny and she wasn't sure about Talli, who joked she loved the senior nursing staff.

Each year, on Daisy's birthday, she posted her a card. There was never any acknowledgment, but she liked to think that her daughter received her cards and would know who she was. She still went to Baker Street, not to loiter, but to walk slowly by a few times, observing the comings and goings, though sadly, she never saw her daughter. She had made enquiries many times at the authority's offices just in case someone came across a document relating to Daisy, but there was no paper evidence. It would seem, if this was the case with Daisy, a private adoption was just that, private to the party concerned. From what she had read in the reference books in the library, she wasn't sure this was legal and she would need a solicitor to represent her. Her friend Evelyn had made enquiries through her family solicitor and was told to search for details would prove very costly, way out of Alice's reach. She could never earn enough money. And there was no guarantee the outcome would be positive. But she would never give up hope to be reunited with her daughter, believing no one disappears for ever.

Chapter Twenty

It was now 1939 and the newspapers were full of the forthcoming event of war. The jolly porter commented, 'There'll never be a war, because the Great War was a war to end all wars.' Thoughtful, he drew on his pipe, and then added, 'That Hitler has nowt ter do with us.'

'Um . . .' snorted the other porter. 'Bet yer a week's wages, before year's out, it'll come.'

On seeing the alarm in Alice's and Talli's eyes, the jolly porter twisted two fingers to his forehead indicating that the other porter was balmy in the head. This brought a smile to their faces and they hurried on their way. They loved the banter between the two men.

But later on that week at 11.15 a.m. on Sunday 3rd September . . .

'Shush,' someone said as Alice and other nurses entered their sitting room.

They all crowded in to listen to the wireless.

The prime minister, Neville Chamberlain, was broadcasting to the nation. '. . . *Germany has invaded Poland and Hitler refuses to withdraw his troops, so consequently a state of war exists between us. Our country is now at war with Germany . . .'*

When he had finished his speech, the only sound in the room was the crackling of the wireless. Someone turned it off and the room became a babble of voices with everyone talking at once. 'What do we do?' shocked words were uttered.

'Quiet.' A voice of authority rang out and instantly the room became silent. A senior sister stood in the doorway. She stepped into the room, closing the door behind her and then addressed them, enunciating each word clearly. 'First and foremost, you are nurses and you will conduct yourselves in a manner befitting your position. Do you all understand?'

'Yes, Sister,' they answered in subdued voices.

'Matron will issue a statement later. Now, please return to your duties and do not alarm the patients.' With a swift glance around the room, as if she was remembering every face, she turned and left the room.

Alice only heard the last part of King George's speech to the nation, which was broadcast later, and she thought how sad his voice sounded . . . *'And if this principle were established through the world, the freedom of our own country and of the whole British Commonwealth of nations would be in danger.'*

Alice remembered her own father as only a shadowy figure, coming home from the Great War battle-weary and never the same man, never well enough to enjoy his children. He was proud, said he didn't mind, because that war was a war to end all wars. All she could feel was the futility. He'd sacrificed his health and been robbed of his family life – and for what? This made a mockery of his beliefs. Hot tears stung her eyes and her heart felt leaden. She also thought of her mother and what a struggle she'd had to nurse a sick husband and, when he died, to bring up her children single-handedly. Aggie then went up in her estimation.

'So, what will this war bring?'

'Pardon?' Talli had come up beside her. 'Talking to yourself?' She slipped her arm through Alice's.

'How will the war affect us and our families?'

'Don't let's worry about it. It could be over in the flash of Sister's knickers.' They both laughed and the mood lightened.

All that Matron had to say was that the hospital would function as normal. However, posted in each ward, as well as the usual weekly list of duties and times for each nurse, would be updates as to anything appertaining to the current situation of war.

Martha Chandler had left her mother's house, with no regrets. She didn't like George Baker, he was too strict, but then her mother thought he was the moon and stars and had married him to provide security in her old age, so she said. As Martha hurried along to Collier Street where she lodged with her friend, Sally Richardson, she felt quite light-hearted. At last she felt as though her life was on the up. At work she wore a smart navy dress with white detachable collars; Sally's mam did all her washing and provided a good hot meal every night.

Today, Sunday, she'd been for a walk to the Victoria Pier with Morris Jefferson; he worked in the packing department at Hammonds. Martha smiled, feeling happy. Morris was of medium height, a good few inches taller than her with blonde, wavy hair, bright grey eyes and very good-looking. They had tea and cake in a cafe and she felt like an American film star for she wore one of her new cotton summer dresses, pink with sprays of white flowers, white gloves and sandals and, daringly, she wore no stockings, loving the freedom of bare legs, because at work they had to wear thick lisle stockings. In the evening, she and Sally, with their boyfriends, were going to the cinema. It was the boys' turn to choose which film to see. She didn't mind, because they sat on the back row and kissed and cuddled with no one from behind telling them to behave.

'It's only me,' she called out as she entered the house through the back door, which was the custom. The front door was only used on special occasions, like weddings and funerals, or if the vicar called. In the kitchen, Sally and Mrs Richardson were sitting with glum-looking faces. 'What's up?' Martha asked, staring at them both.

Mrs Richardson wiped away a tear with the corner of her best Sunday apron. It was Sally who answered. 'It's war. Prime Minster said on the wireless that we're at war with Germany. It's that madman Hitler who's the cause of it.'

Martha sat down on a chair with a bump. 'What does it mean?' She wasn't sure what war was. Did you have to go and fight the Germans in the street, and if so, what with? The only fighting she knew was in the school playground when you had to have a go at the bullies to show you weren't frightened of them.

'It means total misery,' Mrs Richardson answered. 'I still remember the Great War. I lost three of my brothers in the same battle. My mam never got over it. God rest their souls.' She wiped away another tear.

'Do we have to stay in tonight, Mam?' asked Sally, glancing sideways at Martha.

'No!' her mother exclaimed, banging her fist with anger on the table, making the teacups bounce and rattle in their saucers. 'You lasses go out and enjoy yourselves while yer can. Bugger the war.

I'm going to the Star of the West and I might even get drunk.'

Both girls looked in amazement at Mrs Richardson because she never swore, was never angry, and was never seen drunk.

Martha and Sally met up with their respective boyfriends and went to the cinema. If you were to ask them which film they'd seen none of them could have answered, because all they talked about was the war. 'I can't wait to fight and to see action,' said Morris.

'Me too,' said Sally's boyfriend.

On her two-day break, after being on night duty for two whole weeks, Alice went to see her mother in the afternoon and arranged to meet Johnny in the evening. She spent some of her savings on buying her mother a cut-glass vase, and a bunch of golden chrysanthemums.

'My, this is a turn-up for the books,' Aggie said, her face beaming as she admired the vase. She held it up so that the rays of autumn sunshine coming over the roof of the scullery and through the kitchen window could catch the glass, sending a rainbow of colour through the glass and projecting it onto the far wall.

To see her mother looking so happy and healthy gave Alice a lift of spirit, a nice quirky feeling within.

Aggie put down the vase and then she glanced at Alice, her face darkening. 'What've yer done?' Though she no longer worked for Mrs Melton, she thought there might be trouble if Alice made contact with her again.

Alice sighed. Taking off her coat, she hung it on the back of a chair and then said, 'The war. I now realise that Dad dying and you bringing us up single-handed must have been so hard for you.' The two women stared at each other.

Then Aggie spoke, 'You surprise me. And you forgive me for Daisy?'

Alice gave a quick intake of breath. She hadn't thought that far ahead. Then she saw the look of pain in her mother's eyes. Quickly, before she changed her mind, she answered, 'Of course I do. Now put the kettle on.' Feeling tears beginning to well up in her eyes, she picked up the vase and flowers and took them into the scullery where she busied herself, allowing the tears to trickle down her cheeks.

The two women chatted about the boys, who responded well to having a man in the house. 'George's really good with them. He teaches them to play cards and dominoes.'

'What about the war, Mam?'

Aggie shrugged. 'Ain't nowt ter do with me. George is too old ter fight and the lads are too young, so I ain't gonna worry about it.'

Alice smiled, this was something new. 'How's Martha doing?'

Aggie sniffed. 'All right, last time I heard. She doesn't visit much, not since she began working at that posh store, Hammonds,' she said, sniffing again.

'I'll have to go and see her at this posh store.' *Good luck to her*, thought Alice.

Later, Alice met Johnny. They had a walk towards the old town of Hull and found themselves on the high street when it started to rain. They were near to the Black Boy pub, so called because of its connection with the smuggling two hundred years ago. Alice had never been inside the pub before. The interior was dark, barrels were used for tables and it was full of rough, weather-beaten-looking seamen, some sounding foreign, probably from the nearby docks, having their cargo discharged and enjoying the beer until the next tide when they would sail.

The landlord, a burly man, built like a rugby player, beckoned them over and he spoke to Johnny. 'Nice snug upstairs, mate, for you and yer girl.'

They went up the narrow staircase to the upstairs room, which could have been a sitting room, judging by the settee and easy chairs with a couple of small tables. There were two old women sat in the far corner drinking glasses of stout. They looked at the young couple and carried on talking. Alice sat on the settee and Johnny went back down the stairs to bring up their drinks.

When they were both settled down, out of the eye range of the two women, Johnny put his arm around Alice and drew her near and kissed her. When he released her, he gave a long sigh and whispered to her, 'I want to make hot, passionate love to you.'

'And I do to you,' she whispered, placing a provocative hand on his thigh.

Somebody coughed, and a middle-aged couple had entered the room. Hastily, Alice removed her hand, picked up her shandy and took a sip, feeling her heart racing and her blood rushing through her veins.

They got round to talking about the war. Alice told Johnny, 'Nothing much has changed at work, except that the maintenance men are busy fitting the windows with heavy blackout material fixed to a wooden frame to be put in place each evening before lights are lit so it will mean more work for us.' Johnny nodded his reply and seemed lost in thoughts. Alice looked at his studious face. 'Penny for them?' she asked.

'I was thinking what would be the best service to enlist in – army or air force? Not the navy, because I'm not much of a sailor.'

Alice sat up straight and faced him. 'What do you mean, "enlist"?' she demanded, not liking the sound of it.

He took hold of her hand and answered in a measured voice. 'If I enlist now, I can choose which force to go in, but if I wait I could be shoved anywhere. You understand?' he pleaded, not wanting to upset her.

'But you might not be needed for war,' she stammered. 'Why do you have to do it?'

'Because I'm an able-bodied man and not in what would be classed as a reserved occupation.' If truth be told, he liked the idea of going to war. He could see it as an adventure. 'If we were married, I wouldn't be enlisting.'

It felt like a slap in her face. She had no answer for him.

The walk back to the hospital was quiet, both lost in their thoughts.

They didn't have a home of their own and what time they spent together was only snatched moments, though they were cherished. Legally, Alice thought, she was still a married woman, so it was her fault that they could not marry. And, there was no chance of her divorcing Ted Goddard unless the law changed.

The was a light on in the porters' lodge and they could hear the sound of music coming from the wireless. Quietly, they went round the side of the lodge and Johnny drew her into an embrace and kissed her long and passionately, as if to reassure her that everything would be fine.

But, as she watched him walk away into the night, her heart felt heavy with the uncertainty of what the future might hold for them both if this war continued.

Chapter Twenty-One

Hetty Ward, since leaving Faith House, and with Alice's guidance, had enrolled at the same night school that Alice had attended. Hetty now worked in a sweet factory on a packing line on piecework, so that the more boxes she packed, the more money she earned and saved. The lodgings found for her were down Lime Street, where she had a whole bedroom to herself – never in her life had there been such a luxury. Mrs Johnson, her landlady, was a strict person and if Hetty wasn't in by ten o' clock at night, she was locked out. It happened a few times and Hetty didn't like spending nights huddled in a doorway, because during the night some jerk always came along and asked how much she charged. She never, ever wanted to go back to selling her body. She'd learnt self-respect. So, she began to charm Mrs Johnson by cooking the occasional meal, buying her a bunch of flowers and doing jobs in the house, until, eventually, much to Hetty's delight, Mrs Johnson relented and allowed her to have a front-door key.

On Saturday nights she went dancing with the girls from work and, sometimes, the friends she'd made at night class, and oh, how she revelled in her new-found freedom. Tonight, they were at the Advent Dance Hall where the band was in full swing, and then it slowed down to the tune of 'Love is the Sweetest Thing'. Hetty was dancing with a tall, lanky young man who had bad breath. He pulled her into a tight hold and began singing in her ear. His voice was smooth and suggestive, and Hetty knew what that meant.

They were dancing the last waltz and he asked, 'Can I take you home, sweetheart?'

She played it coy, but he was persistent, so she said, 'All right, I'll meet you near the counter.' She pointed in the direction where soft drinks had been served during the night. 'I'm just off to the cloakroom.' She didn't want a man in her life telling her what to do and bossing her about. No fear. She moved swiftly away and found her friends, grabbed her coat and handbag, and hurried out of the dance hall with them, laughing as they made haste. They always looked out for each other, especially warding off undesirable men who tried to get fresh with them.

The next day, Sunday 3rd September, Hetty was busy ironing clothes. She didn't mind, because she'd had plenty of practice at Faith House and it saved her landlady a job as she suffered with a bad back. Mrs Johnson was twiddling the knobs of the wireless. Hetty was humming a tune when Mrs Johnson suddenly said, 'Be quiet and listen.'

The prime minister was speaking. Hetty stopped ironing and sat down on a kitchen chair. This sounded serious. When he'd finished his speech, neither woman spoke.

Then Hetty broke the silence. 'What does he mean about war?' She knew about gangs fighting, but knew nothing about countries warring.

And before Mrs Johnson could reply, the kitchen door burst

open and the next-door neighbour came in shouting, 'I'll swing for that bloody Hitler, upsetting everyone.'

'Now then, don't get yer knickers in a twist. Sit yer body down,' Mrs Johnson placated.

'But I don't want another war.' And she began to cry. With big sobs racking her thin body.

Hetty jumped up to put the kettle on to make a cup of tea, because she didn't know what else to do. She hoped war wasn't going to interfere with her new-found freedom of enjoying herself.

At work the next day, everyone was talking about Hitler and war. The handyman with an arm shot off in the Great War and who suffered with his nerves became so upset that the foreman sent him home.

In the canteen at dinner time, Hetty munched on her meat paste sandwiches, listening to the gossip going on around her. 'My man's gonna join the navy 'cause he wants to see the world,' one girl boasted.

'I hope he can swim.' Someone sniggered.

At night school on Tuesday, Hetty had handed in her assignment to the tutor, Mr Hookway, for marking the previous week. As she sat at her desk, checking a row of spellings, her mind drifted to her lack of schooling during her childhood.

Her childhood, if you could call it that, was spent looking after her seven younger siblings while her mother slept off her drunken stupor during the day. Then, when Hetty escaped at the age of twelve, it was to fall into the hands of a man who said he would look after her. He was a bully, a pimp who preyed on vulnerable girls, and he set her to work on the streets as a prostitute. She'd shared a room with five other girls in a hovel of a house. Once she tried to run away from him, but he caught her and thrashed her until she couldn't stand up. She'd spent two whole days in a filthy bed with only water to drink. She never did it again and for four years her body was abused nightly.

Her salvation was being taken off the streets by a band of good women who brought her and other girls to Faith House.

'Daydreaming, Miss Ward?' It was Mr Hookway standing by her desk.

'Sorry, sir.' She saw in his hand her assignment and her heart did a flip as she waited to hear the worst.

'Your progress is steady, but there is opportunity for improvement. I shall expect perfection from your next assignment.' Without another word, he laid the papers on her desk.

As she glanced at them, she could see he was fond of the red ink. At that moment, she wished she could talk to Mrs Goddard about it, for it was she who had encouraged her to take up adult education. But she was busy nursing long hours. The girl next to her, one of her pals, nudged her and said, 'I'll go over it with you.'

Hetty mouthed, 'Thank you' and flashed a grateful smile.

Talli was on the ferry crossing the Humber to Hull. She'd been home to Barton for two days, visiting her elderly parents, and because of all the talk of war, they had told her some devastating news which kept reverberating around her head, making her feel dizzy. It had never bothered her that she was an only child and that her parents were much older than her school friends' parents.

After a lovely meal together, the table sided away, when they were sitting comfortably, Talli saw a look pass between her parents and then her mother nodded to her father. He coughed and tapped his pipe on the fender side and began to twiddle it in his fingers. Then he coughed again and spoke. 'You know we love you, Crystal?'

Talli stared at her father's solemn face and wondered what on earth he was going to tell her. Then it hit her like a flying shovel. 'You're not going to die?' She felt the colour drain from her face.

'No, lass!' he said. 'Nowt like that.'

She looked into his rheumy, pale-grey eyes and said, 'What, then?' She was feeling baffled by all this strange talk and wished her father would get to the point. Then he lowered his head away from her direct gaze and seemed to lapse into a world of his own.

Her mother, Anne, leant across from her chair and patted his arm, giving him comfort and whispered, 'William.'

He seemed to remember where he was, lifted up his head and spoke, 'Crystal, love. You like your name?'

Talli nodded, not sure where this conversation was leading to.

William gave a weak smile and said, 'Your mother named you.'

Talli glanced at her mother, but she was looking down at her hands folded on her ample lap.

William looked at a point above Talli's head and said, his voice dreamy, 'You were just a tiny bundle when she brought you to us, all red and crinkly, but with the sweetest rosebud lips. She cried when she left you and we promised to take good care of you and to look after you until she came back.'

The room filled with silence as if the three of them were not breathing. Talli could feel the tightening of her throat and the hammering of the pain in her chest as she looked to her father and then to her mother. She found her voice; it was a croak, but her voice. 'Do you mean you are not my parents?'

'Your mother was our daughter,' Anne said. 'She was a wild girl, but with the voice of an angel. Against all of our common sense and because of the endless arguments with her, we let her go with a band of actors and singers who toured around the country

196

performing plays and concerts. One day she arrived home with you in her arms and asked us to look after you. She never returned.' Anne's eyes filled with tears and Talli remained speechless. Then Anne continued, 'She was killed in a train crash near to London and so was your father, he was an actor with the company. They were never married. She said they didn't need a piece of paper to declare their love for each other.'

Finally, Talli spoke. 'Why didn't you tell me this before?'

'There was no need, but now with the advent of war, just in case anything happened to us, we wanted you to know,' Anne replied.

'What was my mother's name?'

'Isabella, but she liked to be called Bella.'

'Bella,' Talli whispered, liking the sound of her mother's name. 'And my father's name?' she asked.

It was William who answered. 'Gerald, but we never knew his surname.' Then he rose from his chair and went over to the wall cabinet and produced a bottle of brandy and three glasses. His hand trembled as he poured out a liberal measure for each of them.

Later on, Anne went upstairs and brought down a fancy chocolate box, which held photographs of Bella, from a young age to growing up. Then there were postcard-size studio pictures of her posing, wearing various costumes. 'She was very talented,' Anne said with pride. Talli gazed at the pictures of the beautiful woman, her mother, still unable to take in the overwhelming news.

The jerking of the ferry berthing alongside the pier shook Talli from her reverie. Her head was still spinning, that her parents were not her parents, but in fact her grandparents. She would always think of them as her parents for she had known no other and she loved them dearly. She would have loved to have known Bella and wondered if she was like her. The photograph

Anne had given Talli was one of Bella before she'd left to go with the touring concert company and Talli gazed at it for the twentieth time. The photograph was sepia-coloured, giving Bella a dreamlike appearance as she looked at the camera from under her long, dark eyelashes. She looked flirtatious, Talli thought, and wished she had known her.

'Move along!' one of the ferry's crewmen shouted. 'Time to disembark.'

Talli slipped the photograph securely into her handbag.

Three months had passed since war was declared against Germany. Things were changing at the hospital. Alice and Talli moved to a new dormitory, which they had to themselves.

'Just look at this: a handbasin! What a luxury. No more rushing to the communal washroom in the mornings,' Alice exclaimed with delight.

'No, you just have to fight who's first to use it,' Talli moaned.

Alice glanced at her friend. Ever since she'd returned from her visit to her parents, she didn't seem to be herself. Unable to see her friend looking so miserable and downbeat, Alice asked, 'What's wrong, Talli? Can I help in any way?'

So Talli told her story and Alice listened in silence. All she could think of was her own daughter, Daisy. Would they ever be reunited? Mentally, she shook herself and put her arm around her friend, saying, 'What a sad story, for your birth parents to die so young. I'm sorry, Talli. Bella sounds a lovely, vivacious person and not unlike you. Have you any photographs of her? Talli showed Alice the treasured photograph of Bella. 'She's beautiful, just like you. What you need now is a frame, so it can stand on top of your bedside cabinet next to the one of your parents. They must have been so devastated to learn of Bella's death, so you must have been a great comfort to them.'

'They are both darlings and I love them so much.'

After that, Talli brightened up, but Alice knew she would still be thinking of Bella.

Alice was now nursing on the men's surgical ward and Talli was on a women's surgical ward. And Alice was pleased to hear that her friend and mentor, Evelyn, was now a qualified nursing sister.

Lying awake in bed, Alice reflected she'd come a long way since first going to work at Faith House. She continued to keep in touch with Matron Bailey and they corresponded by letter on a regular basis. Miss Bailey, as she now was, kept busy with her village church and ran a group for mothers and babies, as well as helping her sister to run the inn.

As Alice drifted into sleep, her thoughts were of Daisy. On her last day off-duty, she'd plucked up courage and knocked on the Melton kitchen door to ask about Daisy. A young scullery maid answered and said that the Melton's grandchildren were going to the country for safety, but she didn't know what they called them.

Walking away, Alice absorbed this news and thought about Daisy. She would be ten this coming December. Tears filled her eyes and she let them run unheeded down her cheeks. Her heart ached with this yearning to hold her daughter close in her arms. And never let her go.

'Alice, whatever is the matter?'

Alice looked up through wet lashes to see Evelyn standing before her. Gently, she felt the guiding hand lead her away to a nearby teashop and sit her down.

She dabbed her eyes and composed herself, looking into Evelyn's anxious ones.

'Do you want to tell me what has upset you?' her friend asked. She listened quietly while Alice unburdened herself of her guilt over her missing daughter. And as always, she sympathised with Alice and then added, 'My dear, take comfort that in all probability, Daisy will be safely in the country away from any harm. And hold on to the fact that, one day, she will learn the truth about who her mother is and return to you.'

'Thank you,' Alice whispered.

February 1940, and more children were being sent to the country for safety. In crocodile formation, Daisy marched along the station platform with the other children whose parents were not with them. Mrs Cooper-Browne had said she was far too busy with her war work to spare the time. Daisy's eyes welled with tears as she glimpsed children being kissed and cuddled by their mothers and fathers. She half closed her eyes to play her pretence game, to conjure up an image of a pretty lady with a smiling face and make-believe it was her mammy. She didn't tell anyone, because they would laugh at her. It was her secret.

'Come along, girl. Stop dawdling,' said the bulky woman in charge.

On the train, Daisy was squashed on the bench seat next to a little boy who had wet himself and began to cry for his mammy. Daisy delved into her school satchel and gave him one of her fairy buns, which Cook had made for her.

'Thanks, miss. He's my little brother and I've to watch out for him,' said the tall boy sitting opposite them.

Daisy glanced across at the boy who looked about her age, twelve. 'Would you like a bun?' She proffered him one.

He hesitated and then reached out to take it, nodding his

thanks. He wolfed it down and then he said, 'Mam was too poorly to make us owt so we're starving.'

Promptly, Daisy took out her sandwiches, wrapped in greaseproof paper, and she shared them with the two boys, and they finished off with swigging from a bottle of home-made lemonade. This made Daisy laugh, because she had never drunk from the neck of a bottle before and she was glad that Cook forgot to pack a beaker as this was more fun.

The older boy looked at the label tied to a buttonhole of her coat and read it. 'Daisy, that's a pretty name.'

She felt her cheeks flush scarlet, but he didn't seem to notice. No one had ever told her that her name was pretty, and this lifted her heart. Boldly, she asked, 'What's your name?'

'Wilf, Wilf Holland and me little brother is Micky.'

'I'm Micky dripping,' the little boy said. 'It's me nickname, but Mammy doesn't like it.' At the mention of his mother, his eyes filled with tears and his bottom lip started to quiver.

'Look at the cows in the field, they are lying down,' Daisy said to distract him.

He clambered from his seat and pressed his nose to the grimy window as the train steamed through farmland.

'How many can you count?' she asked.

He began counting, his tears forgotten.

Wilf winked at Daisy and she smiled at him, a warm infectious smile and he grinned at her, showing a strong set of white teeth. She sat back in her seat feeling happy. She liked the brothers and hoped that she would be billeted near to them.

As it happened, both Daisy and Wilf were picked to live on Grange Farm, about a mile out of the small Lincolnshire village of Osbournby, and Micky went to live with a mother and daughter in a cottage in the village. When not at school, Daisy was to help the farmer's wife in the kitchen and around the yard and sleep in the house, while Wilf was to help the farmer on the land and he was to have sleeping quarters above the stable.

The farming couple, Mr and Mrs Jessop, were strict but fair and Daisy loved her tiny bedroom under the eaves. She blew out the candle, so no light was showing, and opened the curtains wide. Stretched out in her cosy bed, she could see the clear night sky full of twinkling stars and her thoughts turned to her real mother. And she wondered if her mother could see the same stars as she could see.

Chapter Twenty-Two

Johnny Mitchell faced his parents and, on seeing his mother's bottom lip tremble at the news he'd just imparted, he said softly, 'It's not for ever, Mam.'

'But why do you have to join up now?' Ada Mitchell demanded.

Johnny looked to his father for support and Len Mitchell took the hint, clasping his wife's hand. 'Now then, Ada, it's like the lad said, it's not for ever.'

Ada wasn't easily pacified. Johnny took hold of her other hand and said, 'I've joined up now so that I can enlist in the RAF and not be recruited into whichever service they'd send me to. I don't fancy being a sailor on the high seas or a soldier fighting in combat.'

'You mean you want to be a pilot?' Ada sound mortified. 'Up in the air?' Tears threatened her pale-grey eyes.

'Come on, Ada, how about dishing up the Sunday dinner? I'll come and give you a hand. Our Maureen will be home soon,' Len said, ushering his wife towards the kitchen.

Left alone in the sitting room and to his thoughts,

truthfully, Johnny didn't know what role he would be playing in the RAF or indeed what he was qualified to do. He worked with wood, loving the feeling of creating something of beauty. In the workshop was a large glass window, which let in the natural daylight and he was always fascinated by the sky and its different moods. It gave him inspiration, especially when crafting a fine piece of furniture. His love of the sky was his main reason for wanting to join the RAF, as well as fighting for his country. He wanted to be up there in the clouds, to be in the vast expanse of the sky, day or night, but he couldn't explain this mystical feeling to his parents.

He had mentioned his intention to sign up for the RAF to his employer, Joe Makepeace. As well as being his boss, Joe was also his mentor, nurturing him from a young apprentice, and who knew that one day Johnny intended to have his own business.

Joe's response had been, 'If the country needs you, Johnny, so be it. There'll always be a job here for you afterwards.'

Johnny wondered if Alice would understand his need. It would be midweek before they had a chance to meet up. He wished that their courtship could be out in the open. He would have loved to have brought her home to meet his parents, but they would be shocked to know that he was seeing a married woman, even though her husband had long deserted her. And he had never met her mother or her siblings. One thing he did know for sure was that he loved Alice and wanted to spend the rest of his life with her. He was positive that she felt the same as he did.

Wearily, Alice climbed the stairs to the dormitory and hoped that her room-mate was not there, because she wanted some time to herself. She pushed open the door and was relieved to see the room was empty and, kicking off her shoes, she lay fully clothed on her bed and closed her eyes. Johnny's words had come as a shock to her. He would soon be commencing training for the RAF. She knew that's what he wanted to do, but she hadn't realised it would come so quickly. She admired him and understood why he was joining the RAF, but he was so much a part of her life that she was going to miss him terribly, like losing a part of herself. She had no real claim on his life, because the law stated that she was still legally married.

She thought about the walking holiday where they had first made love and wished he was here in bed with her. She had been tempted to sneak him up to her bed when Talli was away, but the home sister could pounce at any time and it would mean instant dismissal for her. She couldn't afford to mess her life up, not when she had come this far.

She sat up in bed as an idea began to formulate in her mind. It would take some planning and . . .

'You look in a pensive mood.' It was Talli. Alice didn't hear her enter the room. They had become quite close, like sisters, ever since Talli had confided to her about her parents being her grandparents and her birth mother, Bella, long since dead. Alice, in turn, had told her about her estranged husband and her love for Johnny and them not being able to tell their respective families. But there was one thing Alice could never talk about and that was her daughter, Daisy, who had been taken from her and adopted into another family. There were only two people outside the family who knew her story and they were Evelyn and Miss Bailey. She didn't count those connected who'd taken Daisy. Often, she'd thought about telling Johnny, but it never seemed the right time. As much as they loved each other, their relationship was fragile; telling him now would only add to that fragility. Now the law had changed and in favour of the wife divorcing her husband for cruelty and desertion. Once she was divorced then she would be free to tell him. She wanted their marriage to be built on trust as well as their love for each other. Now with the advent of war, their future would be unsettled for a time with their enforced separation.

Alice smiled at Talli, her eyes twinkling merrily as she explained, 'I'm going to plan an illicit weekend away with Johnny.'

'Tell me more,' Talli enthused, sitting on the edge of Alice's bed.

After much discussion between the two friends, Alice decided on Scarborough, a beautiful seaside resort further up the east coast. Here, they would have anonymity and enjoy the bliss of spending every minute of every night and every day together. She would have to negotiate with the ward sister for those precious days off-duty. In theory, they were not supposed to have man friends, but sometimes rules were wavered, though this ward sister was known for keeping to the rules.

'What will you say to Sister?' Talli asked.

Alice's reply came swiftly. 'I'll tell her the truth.'

Talli's eyes widened. 'Is that wise?'

'Yes! I shall say I'm going with a friend who has been called up, which is the truth, and keep my fingers crossed she doesn't ask who.'

'Make sure she's in a good mood before you ask.'

The next time Alice and Johnny met, they went to the cinema where they liked to sit on the back row so they could snuggle up to each other with no fear of blocking anyone's view behind them. 'What do you think?' she whispered to Johnny, after outlining her plan for them to have an illicit weekend away together.

'Alice, my darling, you are a genius. I'll keep my weekends free this month. Just let me know when.'

Suddenly the warm touch of his lips brushing her cheek aroused her senses and sent tingling sensations down her spine. Instinctively turning to him, her lips found his, caressing gently at first and she felt her passion rising as their bodies crushed together and became inflamed with desire. As his hands cupped her breasts, she felt an overwhelming urgent need of him. Then, reluctantly, with a huge sigh, she drew away from him, conscious that they were in a public place.

When the film finished and the auditorium lights went up, Alice rooted in her handbag for her lipstick and powder compact and hastily retouched her make-up and ran her fingers through her untidy hair. Johnny just grinned at her and she playfully dug him in the ribs. Men never seemed to care about their appearance like women did. Leaving the cinema, they strolled along, their arms linked, towards the nurses' home. There was only time for a quick goodnight kiss as Alice had to be indoors by ten o'clock and she didn't want to be late and lessen her chance to have time off-duty.

As they parted, Johnny whispered in her ear, 'I can't wait to sleep with you again.'

His words sent shivers of pleasure through her whole body and she tucked them away in her heart to cherish.

A few days later Alice approached Sister Jones. She was a tall, thin woman in her late thirties who never had a hair out of place. She was dedicated to nursing and very rarely took time off. Alice chose a quiet spell near to the end of her night shift and put her request for three days of leave one weekend during the coming month. She crossed her fingers behind her back as she told Sister the reason for her request.

Sister studied Alice, who felt sure she could see into her mind and read it was with Johnny she wanted to spend the weekend.

'I will see how you progress this week, Goddard, and then I will make my decision.'

'Thank you, Sister,' Alice said dutifully.

The next evening when she went on duty, the night staff conferred with the day staff. There was only one new patient, a man. He was in a side ward and was recovering from an emergency operation for appendicitis. Sister Jones said, 'Goddard, I want you to take care of Mr Barker and monitor him through the night.'

Alice went to check on her patient. The man, in his late sixties, was sleeping. Not wanting to disturb him, she gently felt his pulse. Glancing down at his face, she frowned. The man looked familiar to her, but she couldn't place him. She studied his chart and noted his name: Mr Thomas Barker. She felt sure she knew him, but wasn't certain where from. This puzzled her.

Later on, in the early hours of the morning, Mr Barker began vomiting and Alice quickly attended to his needs. Cleaning him up and making him comfortable, she checked that the knee pillow was in place to support his thighs. His pulse rate was higher, and she held his hand until the restlessness of his body settled and his breathing was even, then she checked again and his pulse was normal.

Through the night, Alice had other duties to perform, but she kept a constant watch on Mr Barker.

The time came to wake the patients up with a cup of tea, for those who could have one, and prepare them for the day ahead before the day staff came on duty.

Mr Barker's eyes opened when Alice was at his bedside. 'How

are you?' she asked. His reply was to give a slight nod. She attended to his bodily functions and gave him a gentle wash to freshen him up, checking that the dressing and the tube were still in place after his operation. He didn't stir much or talk, because of the effect of the anaesthetic and soon he drifted back to sleep. Alice filled in the patient's chart and wrote up the necessary notes for the changeover to the day staff.

Alice monitored Mr Barker's condition over the next few nights and on the fifth night he was wide awake. She quickly read his chart to bring her up to date. 'How are you feeling?' she asked him as she righted his pillow, which had slipped down, and made him comfortable.

'Much better, Nurse.' Then he stared at her, his words jolting her. 'You be Ted Goddard's missus.'

Her heart gave a funny lurch and she felt the colour from her face blanch away. 'How do you know that?' she whispered.

'I worked with him.' He put out a bony hand to touch hers. 'You've nowt to fear from me, lass.'

As she gazed into his concerned-looking eyes, Alice realised where she'd met Mr Barker before. 'You're the man who helped me to the tram stop when I was feeling unwell.'

He nodded in reply. 'He's been back, yer know.'

It took all of her resolve not to cry out at these words and she stood still, immobilised with fear. Quickly, she regained her control. She was a nurse and her paramount duty was to care for patients. She forced herself to ask, 'Where is he now?'

Mr Barker shrugged. 'He only came for a reference from the boss and to collect money due to him and then he went. I heard he'd got a boat sailing to South America, but I don't know how true that is.'

Mr Barker began to tire, so Alice checked his pulse and temperature and settled him down to sleep. He appeared to be making a good recovery after his emergency operation.

Later, Alice was having her meal break in the staff dining room and was glad of the quietness. She sat barely touching her food as she thought about Ted Goddard. If only she'd known he had been back in the city, she would have made every effort to ask him for a divorce. He had no family that she was aware of or any special friends, so there was no one whom she could ask about his whereabouts or a contact address for him.

She went to see his foreman where he'd worked. Waiting until the yard was clear and all the horse and carts were out on their rounds, Alice went across the yard and knocked on the foreman's lobby door. Not waiting for an answer, she stepped inside and stood on the threshold of the small, square room with a window, which looked out onto the coming and goings of the yard. The foreman was making himself a pot of tea and getting ready to settle down with his morning paper.

'Who are you?' he growled, not taking kindly to being disturbed and especially by a woman. 'What do yer want?'

Alice didn't hesitate. 'I'm Alice Goddard and I want to know the contact address of Ted Goddard, my errant husband.'

The man eyed Alice up and down. 'Why?'

'To divorce him.'

The man laughed and began pouring out his tea into a pint-size tin mug and then said, 'I gave him a letter just addressed "To whom it may concern" and we've no forwarding address for him. I asked if he fancied going down ter pub and he said he had nowt to hang around for and he went. That's all I know, missus.'

Alice studied the man's face and knew he was telling the truth. 'Thank you,' she said, closing the door behind her.

Outside, she stood for a moment. As much as she wanted a divorce from Ted Goddard, the knowledge that he had been back in the city unnerved her slightly. Then she pulled herself up straight and strode forward. It was imprinted on her mind, never to be frightened by that man.

Chapter Twenty-Three

Alice felt anxious. Sister Jones had not yet given her permission to have three days' leave and it was now the beginning of the last week of the month. However, she had gone ahead and booked the hotel room in Scarborough for this coming weekend. She understood how busy the ward was with the outbreak of war with Germany and the uncertainty it created, but she desperately wanted to spend time with Johnny before he began his RAF training.

'You should challenge her,' Talli advised Alice. Both women were in the dining room snatching a well-earned tea break, which was pure luck as they worked on different wards and times didn't often coincide.

'I'd thought of that, but I don't want a right-out refusal, which she would be bound to give.' Silence prevailed between them and Alice looked into her cup of weak tea and drank the remaining. She stared at the tea leaves left at the bottom of the cup and spoke. 'Can you read tea leaves?'

Talli looked at her friend. 'You mean as in telling your fortune like Gypsy Rose Lee?' Neither woman had dared to go into the fortune-teller's caravan at Hull Fair. Alice nodded and Talli picked up the cup. She pretended to study the tea leaves and, putting on a mysterious voice, she began her prediction. 'Do I see an "N" or could it be a "Y"?' She swirled the tea leaves around.

Alice sat on the edge of her seat, waiting, willing. She could stand the suspense no longer. 'Can I have time off, or can't I?' she blurted out, but Talli continued to study the leaves.

'I'd say it's a yes,' said a loud voice. It was the kitchen hand come to clear their table.

Alice nearly jumped off her seat, she was so intense. Then she found her voice and said to the woman, 'Can you read the tea leaves?'

'Nope, but there's nowt wrong with me hearing.'

Both nurses looked at her and said in unison, 'What do you mean?'

She looked over her shoulder, but no one was within earshot. 'I'm invisible, see.' That was hard to imagine with her big bulk. 'I hear things like these two ward sisters discussing a certain nurse Goddard who wanted time off to spend with a friend who's going into the forces. "A likely tale," one said, but the other sister reminded her that she was young once.' With that, she whisked their teacups away and departed to her kitchen.

Alice and Talli stared with astonishment at the retreating figure and then burst out into peals of laughter.

At the end of her night shift, Alice was summoned to Sister Jones's office. Aware that her apron was none too clean after such a busy time on the ward, she stood before the sister's desk and waited for her to look up. Whizzing through her mind was the prediction – was it true or just a wind-up? The core of her stomach knotted and instinctively she touched it with her hand and just as quick drew it away as Sister spoke.

'Goddard, over these last few weeks you have worked diligently and therefore, I grant you your three days of leave.'

When she realised that the sister had decided in her favour, her whole body relaxed and she promptly replied, 'Thank you, Sister.'

In a daze, she went up to the dormitory to write a note to Johnny, telling him the good news and then took it down to the porters' lodge for him to pick up on his way to work.

They arrived at the Scarborough Hotel in the late morning to be told by the owner that it was to be requisitioned by the military and they couldn't step over the threshold. Standing outside on the cold stone steps, Alice and Johnny both looked so disappointed. She twizzled the brass ring on her marriage finger, and he ran his hands through his hair.

The owner's wife appeared and scowled at her husband. She was more helpful. She handed them a piece of paper, saying, 'This is my sister's address with directions, and she has a spare room and will put you up for your three nights. She'll be glad of the extra money.'

They walked up the narrow streets and down narrower passages of the old town of Scarborough and found 6 Dimple Lane, which overlooked the harbour. Mrs Eves, a fisherman's widow with a pleasant smile, beamed at them. 'Come in,' she said as she held the cottage door wide open.

Alice was feeling tired and just wanted to rest her legs and so was grateful for the warm welcome.

'Just leave your cases there and come and have a cup of tea, and I've just made a fresh batch of scones,' their landlady said.

Soon they were seated in the tiny sitting-cum-dining room with a blazing fire and the delicious aroma of baking. Alice and

Johnny looked at each other, relief on their faces. He reached for her hand and gently squeezed it.

Mrs Eves bustled in with an overloaded tea tray and Johnny jumped up to assist her.

After they had eaten their fill, Mrs Eves showed them up to their room. It was dominated by a big brass iron bedstead covered in a snowy-white counterpane decorated with embroidered pink roses and bright green foliage, a washstand with basin and ewer, and an Edwardian wardrobe with a panelled mirror, which reflected the lightness of the white painted walls.

'It's lovely,' Alice whispered.

Mrs Eves smiled, a faraway look in her soft grey eyes, and said, 'Aye, it's special.'

And Alice had the feeling that this was the room, the very bed, which Mrs Eves had shared with her late husband.

'I'll cook an evening meal for six-thirty and you can have a key to the front door, so you can come and go as you please.' She produced an iron door key from her apron pocket and passed it to Johnny. Then she turned and left the room, closing the door behind her.

They heard her footsteps descend the creaking stairs and both Alice and Johnny stood silently until they heard the downstairs door click shut and they turned to each other. Johnny cupped his hand under Alice's chin and kissed her lips, with his other hand he drew her close and she could feel his rapid heartbeat, which matched hers. Their kissing was gentle at first, then becoming urgent as she slipped her arms around his strong physique, wanting more of him. Then within seconds, they were both undressed and on the bed, their bodies becoming one, enriched with their love for each other.

For a while afterwards they lay, neither wanting to break the spell. Then Johnny said softly, 'I love you, Alice.'

She turned to him and with her fingers she traced the dark hairs on his chest and replied, 'I love you too, Johnny.' She felt so good inside, so perfectly contented in the knowledge that this was the man she wanted to spend the rest of her life with. She hoped this war wouldn't last too long and keep them apart.

They weren't inhibited with each other's bodies and it seemed so natural to be naked in each other's company. When they had made love in the tent on their walking holiday, it had been in total darkness. She ran her hand further down his body and he grabbed it, 'Later,' he whispered and brushed his lips tantalisingly across her breasts.

They dressed quickly and went out into the February sunshine and, hand in hand, Alice and Johnny walked along the Scarborough seafront. Wrapped up warmly against the wind blowing off the North Sea, it brought a healthy colour to their cheeks. They stopped to look out to sea, mesmerised by glinting silver on the rippling waves. 'They look like fairies dancing,' murmured Alice. 'It's beautiful.' Johnny took advantage of the moment and she felt the soft touch of his lips on hers. Was this a promise of more to come?

The sands were deserted, except for a lone man with a dog. They watched for a few minutes as the man threw a stick and the dog retrieved it, again and again. Johnny glanced up at the sky and said, 'The sun is hiding behind those dark clouds. Come on.' They set off at a brisk pace. They had walked north to south along the promenade and now they were heading north again, back the way they had come.

Coming to the harbour, they stopped to chat to an old

fisherman who seemed oblivious to the cold and was mending a trawling net. He eyed the young couple, saying, 'It's a bit early for summer season.'

It was Johnny who answered. 'I'm reporting for my RAF training next week and we wanted to spend time together before . . .' His words trailed away as he felt the tightening of Alice's hand in his.

The fisherman nodded, understanding. 'Warring is never easy. Them bloody Germans have started with us already. Last Thursday three trawlers were fired at by enemy planes, but the fourth trawler was armed and retaliated, and the Germans buggered off.' He paused as if in contemplation and then said to Johnny, 'The sooner you get up in the sky, the sooner we'll beat 'em.' He turned back to mending his net.

In silence, Alice and Johnny moved on, both deep in thought and relieved to reach the welcome of Mrs Eves and her cooking. They mentioned to her what the fisherman had told them. 'That'll be old Jasper Aysgarth. He likes to chat with folk; it stops him from feeling lonely. Aye, enemy has started attacking our trawlers, but fishermen are a hardy breed and know how to deal with disaster.' She bustled round them, serving generous portions of meat pie, a pie with a crust that melted in your mouth, and plenty of fresh vegetables and rich gravy, followed by lemon meringue.

After they had finished, she came in to clear the table and to bring in a pot of tea. Turning to depart from the room, she said, 'The room is yours, so make yerselves comfy.'

'But what about you?' Alice asked, not wanting this kind woman to be driven from the room.

'I love my kitchen and cosy chair, and I have my knitting and I listen to the wireless, so don't fret about me.' She beamed at them and left them alone.

Johnny sat on one of the easy chairs and as Alice sat at his feet with her head resting against his legs, she stared into the fire and watched the glorious red and gold flames dancing. She daydreamed, imaging that she and Johnny were in their own home by their own fireside and was hit by an overwhelming feeling of happiness, and she wrapped her arms tightly around his body, holding it close, keeping it secure.

The only sound in the room was the occasional crackling of coals. Johnny touched her hair and tingles of pleasure ran from her scalp and down her back. She looked up to see his smiling face looking down at her. 'Time for bed,' he said softly.

He put the fireguard in place and turned off the large oil lamp, and carried the smaller one upstairs to their room.

They prepared for bed, both in tune with each other's needs as if it was something they had done countless times before. Lying side by side, hands touching, Alice thought how different this was to the cramped conditions of their first coupling. Suddenly, Johnny leant over to kiss her and instinctively they were embracing, not the frenzied lovemaking of earlier, but a tender, gentler mood and both taking time to explore each other's naked body, glistening in the glow of the oil lamp. She ran her hands over his firm chest and down to the narrowing of his hips, her fingers lingering, tantalising. He pulled her closer, so close she felt his breath travelling across her breasts and down to the roundness of her stomach. She couldn't contain herself any longer and arched her back, drawing him into her, their rhythm as one. Suddenly the oil was spent, and the lamp went out and darkness wrapped them in a veil of mystery.

The next morning Alice was awake first and she watched Johnny in sleep. A lock of his dark hair had fallen onto his forehead and the shadow of a new growth of hair was visible on his face. She slipped from the bed, washed and dressed, brushed her hair and applied cream to her face, along with a touch of pink lipstick. When she glanced back at the bed, Johnny was awake, watching her. She blew him a kiss; she would have loved to get back into bed with him, but she could hear Mrs Eves moving about down below and the aroma of frying bacon was drifting upwards.

She drew back the curtains of the small lattice window and gazed out across to the harbour down below and beyond to the swell of the sea. Johnny had jumped from the bed and was standing behind her looking over her shoulder at the view. He kissed her neck and she could feel his naked body pressing against her and she was tempted to fling off her clothes. Instead, she said, 'Nearly time for breakfast.'

'Spoilsport,' he replied, moving away from her. She heard the splashing of water and him humming a tuneless tune.

After they'd eaten a hearty breakfast of eggs, bacon, sausages, black pudding and mushrooms, plus hot cakes and a pot of tea, they set off to brave the elements of the weather and went down to the harbour to watch a trawler coming in on the tide. As they watched, there was quite a lot of commotion going on around the trawler and soon a crowd gathered. They couldn't get near enough to hear what was being said and had to wait until, gradually, word was passed along.

'Crew's been damn lucky,' said a big man.

'Why, what's happened?' asked Johnny.

'German plane machine-gunned a trawler, but skipper says no damage done, although one of the young 'uns is in shock.'

Alice hung on tighter to Johnny's arm, her face pale. On seeing that there was nothing they could do, Johnny said, 'Shall we go up to the castle?'

Both lost in their thoughts, they walked upwards. Just seeing what was happening so close to home had shaken them both. Whether they liked it or not, the war was here to stay until Hitler could be stopped.

Alice now really knew how Johnny felt about joining up so soon, but she was determined to make the rest of their time together special in every way. She tugged his arm to halt his steps and he looked at her. 'I love you, Johnny Mitchell, and don't you ever forget it.' And then she kissed him full on the lips, much to the amazement of a man in a suit and a bowler hat passing by.

Chapter Twenty-Four

All too soon, the time came for Johnny to report to his training camp. On his last free day, he went to meet Alice. He felt torn two ways. The very thought of leaving Alice behind filled him with the blues, but on the other hand, excitement gripped him, a feeling of exhilaration he'd never experienced before. He was going into unknown territory.

As he approached the hospital porters' lodge, he saw her waiting for him and his heart did a quick somersault. When she saw him, she smiled a smile full of love that lit up her whole face. He realised with a pang that he didn't have a photograph of her and she didn't have one of him. On reaching her, he embraced her, feeling the slight tremble of her body. Her lips looked inviting, but the porter was watching them, so he gave her a fleeting kiss on the cheek and took hold of her hand, and they moved away.

'Where are we going?' she asked as they began walking towards the town centre.

'We, my darling, are going to find a photographer's shop.'

'A photographer's shop?' she said, mystified.

'Yes, I've just realised I haven't got a picture of you and neither have you one of me. Every day I'm away from you, I want to look at your smiling face to remind me how beautiful you are. And of course, for you to see how handsome I am,' he teased.

The doorbell jangled as they pushed open the shop door. A middle-aged woman was at the counter and looked up as they entered. 'Good afternoon, can I help you?' she asked in a pleasant voice.

Johnny explained about the photographs they required.

'Just one moment,' she said and went through a door at the back of the counter.

A man emerged wearing a dark apron and said, 'Yes, I can take your photographs now and I can have them ready for tomorrow.'

'Tomorrow?' Alice and Johnny replied in disappointment.

'That is the quickest time I can develop them.'

Alice was the first to recover, saying to Johnny, 'I can collect them and post yours on to you.' And so, it was agreed.

They were ushered into the photographer's studio. He talked to them all the time, which helped to relax them, and their moods were soon full of gaiety and laughter. First, they sat together on a sofa and Johnny slipped an arm around Alice's shoulders, drawing her close, feeling the soft warmth of her body against his. Next, they had separate ones taken, standing by an occasional table with a vase of artificial yellow roses placed on its surface. As Alice stood, gazing into the camera, Johnny blew her kisses and he watched her face light up just the way he loved to see it.

Through the next five years and through his darkest hours, that photograph of Alice kept him sane and hopeful.

* * *

More children were being evacuated to the countryside. Alice watched as a subdued party of schoolchildren with labels attached to their coats made their way to the train station. 'Where are they going?' she asked a lady helper.

'To the country for safety,' the helper replied. 'Come along, children, no dawdling.'

As the children passed by, Alice searched their faces for signs of her daughter. Her insides stirred with guilt – would Daisy recognise her? Would she know instinctively that Alice was her mother?

Alice watched the children disappear from sight and she turned towards Marvel Court to visit her mother.

Aggie seemed more contented these days, Alice thought, as she sat down to receive a welcome cup of tea. The twins were working as messengers on cycles for the GPO and bringing in a wage and Charlie was a part-time errand boy for the local butcher, plus Aggie had her housekeeping allowance from her husband, George. Alice glanced around the kitchen, noticing a new picture on the wall above the new green chaise longue.

Aggie followed her daughter's gaze. 'Nice, ain't it? George bought it. It's the Last Supper. George is a bit religious.' Aggie smiled with satisfaction. 'We go to church on Sundays, so I can show off my new coat and hat. I'll go and bring it down to show yer.' Off she went up the narrow staircase coming back down in moments with the garments.

Alice sat back while an animated Aggie showed off her new midnight-blue wool coat and matching hat, sporting a paler blue bow. She'd never seen her mother so happy and so smartly dressed. She rose from her chair and hugged Aggie, saying, 'I'm so pleased for you, Mam, that life is good to you.'

'Just as long as that Mr Hitler keeps away,' Aggie stated.

Alice hoped so, not wanting to see her mother's new-found happiness put in jeopardy. Her thoughts turned to Johnny and on a sudden impulse she told her mother about him.

'You, Alice!' Aggie exclaimed after listening to Alice's story of meeting Johnny and her love for him. 'Does he know yer married?'

'Yes. When I divorce Ted Goddard, then Johnny and I can marry. He's a good man and I love him,' she added, blushing.

'Well I never,' Aggie gave a big sigh. 'I can't deny you happiness. You have my blessing.'

Alice swallowed hard to ease the lump in her throat, but tears wet her lashes. Her mother had never spoken such kind words to her before and Alice sensed a new understanding between them. Though she had long forgiven her mother for the part she played in letting Daisy be taken, she had never forgotten.

Alice stayed until Charlie came home, seeing how he'd grown and was now too big for his sister to kiss him. The twins would be home too late for her to see them as she had to be back at the hospital for night duty. She did manage to see Martha and exchange a quick few words. She seemed happy living in her lodgings and was still enjoying her freedom. So, it was with some satisfaction, knowing her family members were happy and safe, that Alice made her way back to the hospital.

Later, she took a well-earned break after caring for patients recovering from operations for varying conditions, including helping a patient with a broken leg and arm after an accident on the dock where he worked. The big, brawny man needed the lavatory, but was being obstinate, refusing to have a bedpan. When she told him the alternative was for her to take him to the bathroom, he argued, 'I ain't having no woman take me to the lavvy.'

'Mr Jordan, I am no stranger to a man's bodily functions,' she replied crisply.

'Aye, but—'

'No buts, Mr Jordan. It's me or the bedpan.'

He muttered and swore under his breath, but he allowed her to help him, though he blustered and cursed all the time. By the time she'd returned him to his bed he was exhausted and as soon as she had checked his wounds and tidied the bed, he was sound asleep. She was pleased he was, because, come the morning, how would he react to her washing and shaving him?

As she sat in the dining room, her hands cupped round a mug of cocoa, she half listened to the conversation going on around her. Then someone asked her a question. 'Sorry, what did you say?' she said to the nurse.

'We're thinking of joining up, are you?'

'Joining up? What to?' she asked, not following their meaning.

'We're thinking of joining the Princess Mary Nurses.'

Alice sat up straight, now paying attention to what the two enthusiastic nurses were saying. 'I've not thought about joining up, so I'll stay here because they'll still need nurses.'

'Yes, but joining up will be an adventure,' the two nurses chorused.

Alice glanced up at the wall clock. 'I must go. Good luck!'

When she caught up with Talli and asked her what she thought of joining up to one of the nursing units, her answer caught Alice by surprise.

'Yes, I'm considering it. It's a chance to travel and meet a dashing young officer or two.'

Even her friend Evelyn had already made application to join

the Queen Alexandra's Imperial Military Nursing Service.

They sat in their favourite tea shop and Alice wondered if this would be the last time they would meet up. 'It's a posh-sounding organisation,' she said.

'QAIMNS for short, and nursing is nursing whatever the name or rank,' Evelyn replied. 'Nursing is my life and I'm eager to expand my knowledge. What about you?'

'Nothing strikes me as urgent at the moment. I'll stay here for the time being.'

Evelyn poured out more tea for them both and, changing the subject, said, 'How does Johnny like the RAF?'

Alice didn't answer at first, but sipped her tea and when she spoke her tone was subdued. 'He didn't make it to the RAF.' Evelyn raised her eyebrows, but didn't speak and Alice continued, 'He's now training with the Parachute Regiment. He's cut up about not being in the RAF. His ambition was to become a pilot as he has a thing about being up in the vast sky amongst the clouds. He'll be coming home on leave soon and that's another reason why I'm staying put – so that I can see him.'

'Have you met his parents yet?'

Alice shrugged. 'No, not so far. I am going to take him to meet Mam and my brothers.' Alice told Evelyn about Aggie's happiness and her change of heart. When the two friends parted they promised to keep in touch whenever possible. Alice's heart felt lighter and her step not as heavy as she walked through the busy streets.

Johnny's leave turned out to be two short days and then he was going for more advanced training. Alice was surprised by his upbeat mood. 'I'm going for parachute training,' he enthused.

They were walking towards the small park where they could talk in peace and afterwards they were going to Aggie's for tea and then on to a night at the cinema. Alice let him talk, pleased that he'd got over his disappointment at not being accepted for the RAF. Finally, he was talked out and they sat down on one of the park benches.

Johnny put his arm around her, drew her close and kissed her. The fresh smell of him was tantalising and she savoured the passionate feel of his lips on hers and the closeness of his warm, strong body next to hers. 'Remember Scarborough?' she whispered in his ear and then a plan began to formulate in her mind.

Johnny brought bars of chocolate from the camp store as a treat for the family. Aggie did them proud by providing a delicious tea of ham and pickles, newly baked bread and apple pie and custard, and beer for the men. Johnny was in his element, regaling the boys about his training routine. He certainly had a way with words, Alice thought, as he embellished the mundane training exercises.

After tea, they walked to the cinema and were ensconced on the back row with their arms entwined around each other, their bodies touching. She felt the arousing caress of his lips on hers and knew she wanted more from him.

Johnny whispered in her ear, his voice urgent, 'Alice, I desire you. I need you.'

'Come on, then.' She rose and he followed her, shuffling past the other courting couples on the back row.

'Where're we going?' he asked.

Alice's reply was to take hold of his hand and lead him.

The night was warm and balmy, and the moon hid behind fleeting clouds, seemingly knowing what the lovers required.

She headed towards the park and they squeezed through a broken fence and on to the seclusion of sweet-scented bushes and the softness of springy grass. Without hesitation, Johnny laid down his jacket and Alice dropped onto it, holding up her arms to him, drawing him down to her waiting body.

They made love with all the passion of a first time and then lay in each other's arms.

Then Johnny began feathering her lips with light kisses, building up a crescendo of undiluted urgency. She arched her body to his, responding with every touch, every caress of their love for each other. They made love, indulging each other's needs, taking their time, savouring every precious moment to hold in their hearts for when they were apart.

'Happy?' asked Johnny as they left the park the way they'd come.

She looked up into his adoring eyes and replied, 'I will cherish this precious time together.'

They were both subdued, for the not knowing when they would be together was best left unsaid.

As they parted at the hospital gate, Alice held on to Johnny's hand, reluctant to let go. 'Write to me when you have your new address.'

'As soon as I can.' Then, ignoring the porter, he kissed her tenderly. 'I love you, Alice,' were his parting words.

'Love you, Johnny,' she whispered.

She stood very still, tears clouding her eyes as she watched him walking away until she could see him no longer. And then she experienced an intense feeling of desolation and loneliness, which rocked her whole being. She gave a big sigh. She'd felt like this when she realised that Daisy had been taken from her.

Daisy blossomed on the farm, the result of fresh air and good, wholesome food, which Mrs Jessop cooked. After school, Daisy cleaned the dairy where the cheese and butter were made, fed the hens, dried the pots, and completed any other task that Mrs Jessop asked her to do. Wilf spent his time with Mr Jessop and, during the summer months, worked until darkness fell.

Both Daisy and Wilf had Saturday and Sunday afternoons free, so they spent the time together, happy in each other's company. In the summer months, they explored the countryside, finding a hidden stream and making a boat out of old timber left from a long-ago storm. Or they would lie in long grass and look up at the sky, hoping to see the bombers take off from a nearby RAF station. The winter months, they went to the Saturday matinee at the picture palace in Sleaford and on Sunday they went to the church Sunday school, which generated enough attendance stars on their cards to go to the Christmas party.

Then, one day, Daisy found Wilf up in the hayloft and he refused to speak to her, and she wondered what she had done wrong. Having no appetite for adventuring on her own, she went to help Mrs Jessop by peeling the apples for a pie and she learnt the reason why Wilf wouldn't speak to her.

Mrs Jessop spoke in a low voice. 'He's received sad news. His mam has died, and he's upset. She was in fragile health, so that's why she couldn't visit him and his brother. Give him some space to mourn his loss.'

Wilf didn't come for his tea, but Mrs Jessop put a plateful aside for him and told Daisy to leave it at the bottom of the barn steps and shout up to him. So, she did this, but there was no response from Wilf.

Daisy went to sit in the yard away from the kitchen door and out of sight. She sat with her knees drawn up and looked up to the sky to watch the fluffy clouds drift on by. She understood the reason for

Wilf's mam not coming to visit, but she didn't understand why no one had come to visit her. Mrs Cooper-Browne would be too busy, and she didn't really count as a mother, but somewhere, someone was her real mother, so why didn't she come to see her? Tears pricked her eyes and she let them fall, trickling down her cheeks unheeded, experiencing a feeling of loneliness deep down within her. She cried for the mother who was only a fleeting and distant memory. 'Why don't you come and find me?' she sobbed, her heart breaking.

Chapter Twenty-Five

The war began to escalate and was no longer referred to as the 'Phoney War'. By 1941, the city of Hull with its many docks, shipyards, railway networks and industrial areas became a main target for the German bombers. Between the 3rd and 9th of May, this resulted in large-scale attacks on the city and 400 deaths were reported, with many more injured.

Alice went from working a day shift on one ward and then a night shift on another ward with just a short break in between. Wherever she was needed, she went. One evening she was passing from one ward to another along a dark corridor with no visible light showing, when she stopped to look out of a small window. She could see the sky lit up with fires raging from buildings hit by bombs and down below the fearless firefighters were risking their lives to keep the fires under control, to stop them from spreading to other buildings and causing more destruction and deaths. Her thoughts flew to Johnny and she wondered where he was, knowing that at this precise moment he could be parachuting into enemy territory on a mission. She said a silent prayer for his safety and for all the other paratroopers. He could never say in his letters where he was or what operation he was on, so instead he wrote about the weather, food – or lack of it – and the great comradeship that existed with the other paras.

Suddenly, the clanging bell of an ambulance as it screeched to a halt outside the hospital shook her out of her reverie and she hurried on, knowing she would be needed. On the ward, she made beds ready for the injured and checked the supply of dressings and other equipment required.

'Nurse Goddard, theatre number one, immediately,' ordered the ward sister.

Alice didn't have time to think that she'd never helped at an operation before, she just went. But what met her caused bile to rise in her throat and she coughed, mentally steeling herself. It was a man with part of his leg and arm blown away. The surgeon, who was past retirement age, nodded to her and expected her to follow procedure, and so did the anaesthetist. Dashing aside her thoughts of nervousness she quickly scrubbed up and gowned, and began to check that all the necessary instruments were sterilised. In her mind, she recalled her probationary training in the event of having to attend an emergency operation.

'Ready?' the surgeon addressed Alice.

Alice nodded her agreement.

It was a long, arduous operation and it wasn't until the patient was in the recovery ward that Alice realised how exhausted she was.

'Well done, Nurse,' said the surgeon. 'Your name?'

'Goddard, sir.'

Alice slept soundly for five whole hours and then she was up and dressed, and ready for duty. Reporting first to the ward sister, she then went to check on Mr Jameson, the patient whose operation she'd assisted in surgery. He was in his late forties and she stood for a few seconds noting the gentle rhythm of his breathing and then she studied his chart for his progress. An after-operation infection of the wound could cause problems. They had managed to save his leg, but his arm was amputated above the elbow. She wondered if he had a wife and family and how would they all cope. Momentarily she shook herself. It wasn't easy to be detached from the patient, but there was so many injured that she had to curb her emotions and concentrate on nursing the patient back to good health, and then let the authorities concerned deal with his welfare.

After that operation, Alice was often called to assist in the operating theatre. She found it quite fulfilling and challenging, and experienced a sense of achievement when an operation was successful. Sometimes this was not always the case and nothing could be done to save the life of a patient. One day the surgeon, Mr Outhwaite, said to her, 'Goddard, have you thought of joining one of the military hospitals?'

The thought had crossed her mind now that older women, who were nurses before marrying and raising a family, had answered the call to return to nursing. But one thing held her back: Johnny. Whenever he was granted leave, she wanted to be there for him, to see him, to love him, but was she being selfish when so many servicemen and women were separated from their loved ones?

In the end, Johnny venjoyed being in the Parachute Regiment. He passed the high standard fitness medical examination and along with the other five who had also passed, went to Ringway Aerodrome near Manchester for a parachute training course. He and a para named Geordie from Newcastle became pals. Geordie had worked in shipbuilding and was the same age as Johnny, but where Johnny was dark-haired, Geordie's hair was ginger. In training, they soon developed how to land sure-footed. 'Like our moggy back home,' remarked Geordie.

The dropping zone was Tatton Park and Johnny revelled in the experience, though once Geordie was dropped in a lake, a miscalculation by the navigator. To make up for all the thorough and precise training was the welcome relief of a dance for all services put on by a local committee.

Geordie, who didn't have a girl waiting back home, was soon on the dance floor. Johnny held back, thinking of Alice and wishing she was here to hold in his arms. Then after a few pints of beer, he thought, why not, it's only a dance. Then he let swing and danced with a different girl every time.

Before embarking on his latest mission, Johnny wrote a hasty letter to Alice. They were not told many details, but he sensed it had all the hallmarks of a hush-hush campaign, so he only voiced his thoughts to Geordie and not to his other comrades. Then they had three weeks of special, rigorous training on Salisbury Plain. He loved to feel the sensation of the air whizzing past him and his parachute opening and then bracing for the drop. The parachutes were packed by the WAAF and each WAAF signed their completed parachute. They prided themselves on packing correctly, not wanting to be responsible for loss of life if the parachute didn't open.

Without notice, the paras were transported up to Scotland for advance training, including dummy exercises, then back to Salisbury before they were finally ordered to be ready. After a slight delay, they were ready for take-off in Whitley aircrafts, which carried ten men. Their destination was an area of the French coast. They were issued with a Sten gun, a light sub-machine gun, which proved easy to fire.

Johnny climbed up into the plane and shuffled up to make room for the other paras as there was no seating. He felt Geordie next to him and, in the confined space, they struggled into their lightweight sleeping bags to keep out the cold. Then they were airborne, the third aircraft to take off.

Their drop was off course and they were landed a good few miles from where they should be and so, under the command of their officer, they made their way across the terrain and through a wood to meet up with the rest of the paras on the operation.

Ahead they heard gunfire and were ordered to spread out and stealthily move forward to stop the enemy from advancing on the paras further up the line. What they were unaware of was the Germans coming up behind them until it was almost too late. Geordie was hit in the leg and crashed to the ground. Instantly, Johnny was by his side, seeing the blood oozing from the gunshot wound. From his pack he extracted a strapping and fastened it securely around the injured leg. He looked at his pal's ashen face and saw the pain as he bit on his lips, so as not to cry out. Johnny pulled Geordie into a nearby bush out of sight and administered a shot of morphine. 'I'll be back,' he whispered. Then he was gone.

It was over an hour later when Johnny crawled through the undergrowth of the wood to where he'd left Geordie. 'Come on, pal, let's get you up.'

Geordie muttered incoherent words. Johnny heaved him to his feet, and Geordie yelped and swore with pain as soon as the foot of his injured leg touched the ground and his body crumbled. 'Leave me,' he muttered.

Ignoring his words, Johnny took a deep breath, summoned up all his strength and hauled Geordie back up, pulling his arm round his neck and anchoring his own arm around his pal's middle body, taking his weight. Johnny then extracted a tiny compass from a button on his tunic and they began moving in the direction of the beach, the pickup point by the navy.

Their progress was slow over rugged terrain and Johnny didn't know where his strength came from, but he was determined not to leave Geordie behind to the mercy of the Germans. But by the time they reached the clifftop leading down to the beach it looked deserted. Johnny eased his pal down on a grassy patch and then scrambled down to check the situation. Keeping to the sides of the cliff, he advanced, his Sten gun at the ready, but all was quiet, too quiet, and Johnny's heart sank. They were too late. The pickup had gone ahead, and they were left stranded.

Back up on the clifftop, he once again hauled up his pal, first checking the compass to move inland with the hope that they might come across a barn or outhouse to hole up in for the night. He listened for any sound of gunfire or a vehicle on patrol, but the still night was filled with an unnatural silence.

Night was giving way to early morning. Nothing stirred, not even the sound of an animal or a bird penetrated the silence. Johnny was beginning to despair of finding a place to rest, when he spied a barn looming out of the half-light. Both men crashed out, but first Johnny checked Geordie's injured leg. It didn't look good and needed medical attention straight away or he was in danger of losing it. He administered the morphine taken from Geordie's bag, which he'd left behind in the bush, so at least he could have a few hours of sleep.

At the sound of the barn door opening, Johnny woke with a start and aimed his Sten gun, which he'd slept with in his arms, to the figure of an old man silhouetted in the open doorway with the aroma of fresh coffee and warm bread hovering around him. He came forward with his offerings to them, which they devoured with thanks. Johnny knew only a smattering of French, but enough to understand that the farmer and his wife would be shot if they were found to be harbouring the paratroopers. The farmer collected the used mugs and the cloth the bread was in and hurried away.

'We've two choices,' Johnny said. 'We carry on and risk you losing your leg and being shot, or give ourselves up.'

'You go,' Geordie muttered through his pain. 'I can't go further.' He fell back on the straw and closed his eyes.

Johnny stood up. He knew damn well that without medical attention his pal would lose his leg or, worse still, he'd die. He went over to the open doorway and saw a line of German vehicles advancing down the road in their direction. He went back to sit beside his pal and from his top pocket he withdrew his last two cigarettes and lit them, giving one to Geordie.

The hospital had taken a direct hit during the night and now it was a mopping-up procedure. They had been fortunate that there was no loss of life, but a porter had been injured by falling debris. Alice was anxious to have time off to see her mother and family, because she'd heard that a bomb had been dropped in their area and she needed to know they were safe.

It was late afternoon before she was free for a couple of hours' respite. Throwing on her coat and tying on a headscarf, Alice made her way to Marvel Court. Relief flooded her being when she saw the front of the house intact. She burst in through the front room to the kitchen to find it in utter chaos. The window had blown in and there was glass littering every surface. Out in the yard, the surrounding wall was a heap of bricks and dust. Aggie, wearing a wrap-around pinafore, was trying to clean up the fireplace so that a fire could be laid and a kettle boiled for a much-needed cup of tea. The gas main was cut off. George and the twins were in the yard trying to make it safe and secure so they could get to the lavatory. Then she saw Charlie sweeping up glass from the floor, his knee bleeding having been cut by it.

She bent down to him and said, 'Come on, Charlie, sit on the chair and I'll remove the glass, or it will fester.' He didn't take any persuading and she could see signs of fear lingering in his big brown eyes.

She finished the sweeping up of the glass, George boarded up the window and Aggie had got the fire going and soon the kettle was on the boil.

'At least we've still got a home,' Aggie said. 'Mrs Mumby's shop has gone.'

'Is she . . . ?' Alice began.

'No, she's at her daughter's.'

Relieved that her family had survived, including her sister who had also come to the house to help out, Alice hurried back to the hospital to freshen up before she went back on duty.

As she reached the porters' lodge, she saw a flush-faced young woman approaching who, on seeing Alice, rushed up to her.

'Are you Alice, our Johnny's friend?'

Alice felt her insides go icy cold. 'Yes,' she whispered.

'I'm Maureen, his sister. He's missing, presumed dead,' she blurted and then burst into tears.

Alice clasped a hand to her mouth to stop the scream from coming, and then she was enfolding the girl into her arms as she sobbed, holding her close. But Alice remained dry-eyed. Filled with numbness, she felt as though she was slipping down into a deep crater where there was no escape. No ending.

Chapter Twenty-Six

Up in her room, Alice automatically prepared for duty. She felt numb with shock and just wanted to curl up on the bed and hide away from the horrors of war. But she had patients to nurse, so there was no time to think about the terrible news that Maureen had told her. Downstairs on the ward she listened to the day staff giving their reports of the day's happenings. Because of the continuing bombing of the city, new patients were being admitted at all hours of the day and night, and the staff and resources of the hospital were stretched to the limits and well beyond.

'Come along, Goddard. Are you going to stand there all day?' tutted the ward sister.

Alice mentally shook herself and hurried off to check on the notes of the new patients. All through her night shift, she attended to the patients' every needs: changing dressings on wounds, cleaning up after a mishap with a bedpan, taking temperatures, monitoring blood pressure and holding a man's hand as he cried for his dead wife who was killed in a bombing raid.

'She went back ter house to get her handbag with bairn's birth certificates and our marriage lines. I never saw her again.' Big tears flooded down his cheeks.

Alice soothed back a stray strand of his greying hair. 'I'll make you a nice cup of tea.' Tea, she thought, when all the poor man wanted was his wife, the mother of his children back.

Through the night she worked tirelessly, not stopping for a break, carrying on until the day staff came on duty. Exhausted, she couldn't face the dining room, she didn't want to speak to anyone, so she went up to her room.

Stripping off her uniform, she flung herself on the bed, hoping for sleep to come to her before Talli came up. But sleep eluded her. Maureen's words kept reverberating in her mind – *Johnny is missing presumed dead* – until she could bear the pain no longer. Then a thought slipped into her mind: Johnny wasn't dead. He didn't feel dead. He could never be dead. They had their lives before them to be together for ever and ever. She must get up and go to church and pray for his safe return.

She jumped from the bed and began to scramble around for her outdoor clothes when she caught her foot on the corner of a blanket, hanging from the bed, and tripped, falling face down, her body splayed out. Suddenly, her held-back tears of emotion began to overflow and she couldn't stop them. She felt her tired body convulse with a terrible pain for which there was no known medical cure.

How long she laid there she wasn't sure, nor did she hear Talli come into the room.

'Alice, are you hurt?' Talli dropped onto her knees beside her friend. She managed to lift Alice's head to see her tear-streaked face. 'What's the matter?'

Alice uttered one word. 'Johnny.'

Talli eased her into a sitting position and held her close until her sobbing and her body stilled. Then, gently, she helped her friend to her feet and, sitting her on the edge of the bed, she brought a cool damp flannel and began to pat Alice's red, blotchy face.

Feeling calmer, Alice said, 'I need to go and pray for Johnny to come back to me.'

Recognising her friend was still in shock, Talli went along with her wishes and assisted her to dress, and she herself quickly changed out of her uniform.

Linking arms, they set off for the nearest church of Saint Luke's, only to find it had been damaged in a bombing raid and was unsafe to enter. So, they made their way to Holy Trinity in the Market Place. On the way they passed more devastation where once there were homes, factories, shops and now only piles of rubble. Children played amongst it, looking for shrapnel and any other mementoes to collect. They didn't know the significance of war and, as Alice glanced at them, she was glad they didn't. Even the smell of decay and burnt-out ruins didn't seem to bother them. A horse and cart passed by with a load of old furniture, on its way to replace someone's lost possessions. People went about their business, seemingly to accept that they must get on with life, but not able to mask the fear and heartache of war.

Neither of the women spoke until they reached Holy Trinity. Relief was in Alice's voice as she whispered, 'It's still here.'

They went inside and at once Alice felt the tranquil peace. It was like entering a different world from the war-torn one outside. She noticed a couple sitting quietly with their heads bowed. She caught the aroma of candle wax burning and the comforting fragrance of beeswax, and saw a woman polishing pews on the far aisle. A curate was coming towards them and, without a word, guided them in the direction of a small chapel. Alice smiled her thanks and knew that, in these troubled times, he was used to people coming to the church to find solace.

She squeezed Talli's hand and went to kneel at the small altar, while Talli sat on a seat at the back of the chapel. Alice tried to find the words to pray for Johnny, but they became jumbled up in her head. Every time she thought she had the words, they took flight. Then after what seemed an eternity, she found them. 'Dear Lord, please bring Johnny safely home to me.' Then, after a thought, she continued, 'I make a vow to dedicate my services to nurse the sick and wounded forces that are fighting in this terrible war and to go wherever I am sent. Amen.'

For a long time, she remained at the altar until a discreet cough came from Talli. Alice rose stiffly to her feet and saw two women, both wearing black, waiting to pray at the altar.

Outside, Alice and Talli linked arms once again and made their way to a tea shop. 'One where I can get a sticky bun,' Talli said.

Once inside, they sat at the table drinking tea. Alice couldn't face food and Talli, unabashed, scoffed both buns.

'I'm joining up,' Alice stated.

Talli, her mouth full of bun, spluttered crumbs over the tablecloth. 'Where did that come from?'

Alice shrugged, not wanting to reveal her real reason. 'The time's right. We've more married nurses coming to work at the hospital, so I can volunteer to nurse the wounded servicemen.'

'That means you leaving Hull.'

'I know, and it doesn't matter where I go now.' She felt tears prick at her eyes.

Talli cut in, 'So, we'll join up together.'

About a month later, Maureen came to see Alice and she feared the worst when she saw her. 'Johnny?'

Maureen gave a watery smile and blurted, 'The Red Cross have been in touch and he is a POW. You can write to him and the Red Cross will deliver letters, but it takes time.' She thrust a scrap of paper into Alice's trembling hand.

Alice stood a long time staring down at the scrap of paper. Then she turned and hurried to her room to write a letter to Johnny and, as she wrote, tears splashed onto the sheet of paper.

Hetty Ward sat on the train going up to Durham. She wanted some excitement and adventure in her life. She was on her way to the ATS training centre. The train was crowded and sitting next to her was another young woman who fell into conversation with her. Hetty learnt she was heading to the same place and she introduced herself as Jill Kirkby. She was small and petite, with long light brown hair, pale complexion, bright blue-grey eyes and an infectious grin. While Hetty also had a grin to match, this is where the similarities differed: Hetty was taller with dark hair and dark eyes, and her complexion was olive-coloured. She knew who her mother was but not her father, and she didn't think her mother knew who her father was either. Not that she was bothered about them. From an early age she'd learnt to look after herself, though falling into prostitution was degrading, she realised that now. Her saving grace was Faith House and Mrs Goddard, who had been instrumental in pointing her onto the right path, so that she could achieve more in life and value herself.

Jill interrupted Hetty's thoughts and said, 'I live in Goole with my parents and I have four brothers older than me, so it's good to have you as my friend. What about you?'

'Have a sandwich; my landlady, Mrs Johnson, made them and she is the only family I've got.'

'It's like being at school again,' Hetty grumbled as they, the new recruits, were herded around like cattle going for milking. They were queueing to collect their uniforms. 'Better than I thought,' appraised Hetty as she held up her uniform, 'though there's nowt glamorous about these shoes and stockings.' The stockings were thick and the shoes heavy.

'Like me granny wears.' Jill grinned.

The training was rigorous and that's when the shoes came in useful. 'Bloody walked miles,' Hetty muttered as she examined her sore feet. They'd spent hours at lectures about gas and the importance of carrying a gas mask at all times.

'So, you won't feel like dancing tonight,' Jill said.

Hetty's face lit up. 'Dancing – where?'

Jill tapped the side of her nose and then whispered in Hetty's ear and her eyes lit up.

The dance was to be held at a nearby village hall. They had to wear their uniform, were not supposed to go outside and, having been driven there, would be taken back again under escort.

Inside the hall, the makeshift band belted out a tune and soon the girls were dancing with a new partner each time. Hetty had no desire to break the rule and go outside with any man for a quick kiss and fumble, because she knew what it might lead to. No, she respected herself and long ago she'd decided that the only man to touch her would be the one to marry her, if she married. She watched Jill go off with a uniformed man and she went to the makeshift counter, which was acting as a bar, and ordered an orange juice.

'Would you like a gin in that?' said a male voice from behind her.

Hetty glanced over her shoulder to see a man in RAF uniform. She didn't know what rank he was, because she wasn't familiar with them yet, but she was quick to reply, 'No, thank you.' She'd seen what drink had done to her mother and had no wish to travel that route.

'Well, at least let me buy it for you,' he persisted. So she did, and they sat down at a table close to the dance floor.

For a while neither spoke, they just watched the dancers. Then he said, 'I'm not much of a dancer, but . . .'

His words faded as Hetty turned in her seat to look at him and saw raw shyness etched across his young face. She smiled at him and said, 'I'm not much of a dancer myself, but if you're willing, I am.' And she held out her hand to him.

His face lit up with unexpected pleasure and, hand in hand, they went to join the other dancers. 'I'm Bob,' he said, his eyes level with hers. They were the deepest blue, and his hair was fair and wavy, but cut short to meet regulations.

'And I'm Hetty.' She saw the querying look in his eyes. 'Short for Henrietta.' He grinned at her and held her closer.

They danced together for the rest of the night. He was training as ground crew at a nearby airfield. 'I was a car mechanic before I joined up,' he told her.

'I think I'd like to learn to drive,' Hetty said.

'I'll teach you,' he joked.

At the end of the evening, she said goodbye to Bob with a kiss on his cheek and he squeezed her hand. Parting from him, she tapped her handbag where, on a flap of a cigarette packet, were all his contact details. She'd promised to write to him once she knew where she would next be going.

She and Jill both had shown an interest in driving. 'Heavy vehicles, so hope you are not thinking you'll have a cushy number driving top brass around,' they were told. So, they were sent down to Greenford, the depot of the Royal Army Ordnance Corps. Here, they took driving lessons in a 30 cwt Bedford. They both passed the driving test and then they were posted to one of the largest vehicle depots. Now Hetty felt the war had really begun for her. It was hard but rewarding work.

'All that training and being pushed around was well worth it,' said Hetty.

'Hope so.' Jill yawned as they tumbled into their bunks. They shared the long room, which once had slept schoolgirls, with ten other ATS women.

Hetty sniffed her hands. 'I can still smell petrol on them.'

'Pretend it's perfume,' was Jill's sleepy answer.

Alice looked around the small room she'd shared with Talli. She didn't have many possessions, only her clothes and her nursing certificates, and the treasured photograph of Johnny. She put her hand on her heart, feeling the tightness, the pain of Johnny missing from her life, but her gut instinct told her somewhere he was alive, or was it just a foolish notion? She wasn't sure any more, because those who brought love into her life were so cruelly taken from her. Daisy was long lost to her, the daughter she had borne and nurtured and loved – still loved. Nothing could ever take away her love for her daughter, a love that was locked securely in her heart.

Talli burst into the room in a flurry of excitement. 'Ready?' She glanced at Alice's small attaché case. 'I've managed to scrounge a couple of cheese sandwiches to take with us and hopefully we'll get a cup of tea on the train.' She chattered non-stop.

Alice felt a tinge of sadness creep over her. She was moving on to another phase in her life and yet she felt she was leaving behind those she loved. Not her mother and family, because they would always be here for her. No! It was Johnny, the love of her life, and Daisy, her daughter who she should be taking care of.

Where was Daisy? Alice hoped with all her heart and love that she was safe and wondered if she'd been evacuated along with all the other schoolchildren from the city to the countryside. She would be twelve years old on Christmas Eve. Alice felt the stirring of pain lodged deep within her and momentarily closed her eyes trying to picture Daisy as she would be now, but couldn't. Hot tears pricked her eyes and she said a silent prayer: *Be safe, my darling daughter*. Then she picked up her case and followed Talli from the room.

'She's wet her knickers, miss,' said the big girl, sitting next to the unfortunate little girl. They were in the classroom of the village school.

Daisy, one of the older children in the school, was a prefect, which meant doing the menial tasks that the teacher didn't like to do.

'Daisy Cooper-Browne,' snapped Miss Holderness. She'd come out of retirement to teach these evacuee children. She hadn't expected much from them, given that their schooling had been interrupted too often by German bomber raids on the city of Hull and surrounding area, but to deal with wet knickers! 'Deal with the child.'

Daisy slid off her seat to take care of the unfortunate girl. 'Come along,' she soothed, but not walking too close to her, because the pee was running down her legs and into her socks. The other children sniggered as Cora slowly made her way to the front of the class. She kept her head down, no longer able to use her once lovely red hair to hide behind, it having been hacked off by the woman who she was billeted with.

'Come along. Stop dallying, girl,' Miss Holderness said, irritated at the disruption to the class.

Daisy didn't mind taking care of the girl, thinking back to her younger days when she'd had little accidents and the housekeeper was kind to her. 'I'll take you to Cook and she'll wash and change you.'

'My tummy hurts,' the child hiccupped.

'Oh dear!' said a harassed cook and doer of everything. 'Not another one,' she exclaimed as they entered the kitchen.

Daisy glanced at a boy, about the same age as the girl. His most outstanding feature was his hair, the colour of a carrot. He was sitting at the wooden scrubbed table with a towel wrapped around his trunk, peeling potatoes, and gave them both a cheeky grin.

'You're nowt but skin and bone,' Cook observed as she washed the girl's thin, tiny body.

'I'm hungry,' the little girl whispered.

Within ten minutes, Cook had removed and washed the offending garment, which was now drying next to the boy's trousers. The girl was sitting at the table, also with a towel wrapped around her thin little trunk and eating a chunk of newly baked bread and drinking a glass of milk.

The boy picked up another potato to peel and handed it to the girl.

Daisy smiled at Cook and said, 'Thank you,' and then departed back to the boring lesson in the classroom. She would have rather stayed in the kitchen and helped.

Chapter Twenty-Seven

Alice and Talli enlisted in the Women's Auxiliary Air Force. They were travelling on a crowded train to RAF Gloucester, a tedious, cold journey, and they were standing for most of the way. 'You'd think someone would give up their seats,' muttered Talli.

Alice glanced down at the sleeping soldiers and guessed not. 'Have one of these.' She proffered a paper bag of barley sugars.

'I could do with a cup of tea.'

Alice turned away from Talli's grumpy-looking face. She'd love a cup of tea too, but the one station they'd stopped at which was handing out cups of tea was hopeless, because by the time they'd fought their way to the tea stand on the station platform, the guard was blowing his whistle for departure.

Suddenly, the train gave an ungainly lurch and Alice felt herself being jerked forward to press close to a sleeping airman and, as she felt their bodies connect and smelt his male scent, she pictured Johnny. Touching his face and feeling the grizzly growth of days of stubble, she whispered his name.

The airman, now fully awake, said, 'Sorry, love, I'm not Johnny.'

He patted his knee for her to sit on. 'But we could get to know each other.'

Embarrassed, Alice muttered, 'Sorry,' and quickly removed her hand from his face. She retreated to staring out of the corridor window, her body turned away from any passing serviceman. She felt this yearning for just a touch of Johnny; she couldn't and didn't want to think of him as a prisoner. She wrote most days to him, but so far she hadn't received one in reply. She took comfort that he was alive and that's all that mattered to her. When she settled down in a permanent post, she would write to Mrs Melton to inform her of her new address, so she could contact her at any time.

When they arrived at their destination, having been driven from the railway station in a truck that hit every pothole on the road, it was dark, and the kitchen was closed. There were eight other women and they were clustered in an anteroom awaiting instructions. No one spoke. Alice felt like they all looked, disheartened and wondering why she'd volunteered for the WAAF. Hopefully, her nursing skills would be of use and she began to speculate whether she should have tried to enlist in the Queen Alexandra Nurses or the Princess Mary Nurses.

Suddenly, a welcome sound came from the corridor outside the room, the rattling of a tea trolley. The door burst open and a cheerful voice called out, 'Tea up!' There were cheese sandwiches as well. Everyone began talking and soon the room was buzzing.

After snatching a few hours of sleep on an uncomfortable iron bunk, they were herded to a room to be kitted out in their uniform. Standing in line, they were told that they would be training as drivers.

'We're trained nurses,' Alice said indignantly to Talli.

'I'd quite like to drive,' Talli replied.

Unbeknown to Alice, she was overheard by one of the officers.

A week later, after a gruelling training of marching, square-bashing and saluting, both Alice and Talli found themselves on the move. This time they were sent down south to an RAF hospital.

After a journey through the night on a train with no interior lights, snatching intermittent sleep and feeling and looking weary, Alice and Talli arrived at the RAF hospital. It was a large house commandeered by the authorities and standing in wooded grounds, near to the south coast.

'I could do with a bath.' Talli sighed.

'Me too.' Alice couldn't remember when she last had a soak in a bathtub. It was a far and distant memory.

'Come along, don't stand there all day,' said a brisk voice. 'You are here to work.'

Alice turned to see a woman of about forty, in a smart, dark-blue dress, white collar and cuffs, and a white hat, and a pair of deep brown eyes surveying them critically. Alice stood to attention and out of the corner of her eye she saw Talli do the same.

'I am Matron Hackness.' The woman spoke as she walked around them. She sniffed and stood back from them and said, 'Goodness knows where you have both been, but before you present yourselves on my wards, please, clean yourselves up.' With a flick of her wrist, another uniformed woman stepped forward and Matron Hackness departed without another word.

'Follow me. I'm the housemaid-in-charge and I will show you to your quarters.' She was a small, plump woman in her late forties, at a guess, Alice thought as they trooped after her.

'This is heaven. A wish granted,' said Alice ten minutes later, as she luxuriated in the deep bath of hot water. 'Though I'm not sure about this carbolic soap.'

Talli was busy drying her hair with a rough towel. 'Just pretend it's an exotic perfume.' They both laughed.

'Come along, now,' said the housemaid-in-charge. 'Matron needs you both on the wards.'

'What about something to eat?' Talli said. 'I feel sick.'

'Oh, you poor dears,' she exclaimed. 'You can have a sandwich and a cup of tea.'

Both nurses refreshed and fed, and in their new RAF blue nurses' uniforms, presented themselves to Matron Hackness in her office. After instructions on the protocol of nursing different ranks of the RAF, she led them to a large ward, which had been, in the house's glory days, a ballroom.

At a quick count, Alice whispered to Talli, 'Twenty beds.' All were occupied, and she was eager to start work, to nurse – that's why they were here. She caught Talli's eye and guessed she was thinking the same. However, they remained polite and listened and then followed Matron as she exercised her position. Then she introduced them to Sister Garton, who was in charge of the ward.

Suddenly, there was a commotion outside and, glancing out of the window, Alice saw a field ambulance with the back door open and the attendants bringing out a man on a stretcher. She could see blood oozing from his leg. Her first instinct was to go out to the ambulance and assist, but Matron was already delegating nurses.

'He won't be coming on this ward,' said Sister Garton. 'He's an officer.'

'Can't mix with the likes of us,' said a narky voice from the nearby bed.

Alice glanced at the young man who had an arm up in a sling contraction. She flashed him a smile and he winked back at her. This was going to be different from nursing in a civilian hospital where every patient was treated the same – military was different. The higher ranks took precedence over lower ranks by having private rooms and facilities. Never would they be placed in a ward of twenty beds.

Nursing in a military hospital, while the basics were the same as she had nursed back home in Hull, Alice found the injuries the patients suffered were horrific. The worst were the amputees, those who had lost limbs and were maimed for life.

'It amazes me how they keep so cheerful,' Alice said to Talli as they sat down to a meal in the staff dining room. It really was a dining room, with its crystal chandeliers still in place, though there were bare patches on the wall where paintings had been taken down and stored away.

Talli, who was busy tucking into the tasty meat-and-potato pie, laid down her knife and fork and replied, 'They have to, I suppose, or lose the will to live.'

Both women retreated into silence and Alice's thoughts turned to Johnny. Did he suffer and have life-threatening injuries? She'd rather have him maimed for life than not at all, still believing he was alive somewhere in occupied territory. Then her thoughts turned to Daisy – would she ever see her again? Daisy was her secret locked away in her heart, but one day she would be able to turn the key.

After the meal, they were on their way back to the ward when a commanding voice said, 'Goddard, report to the operating theatre.' Turning, Alice saw the ward sister. 'Quickly, now. We have an emergency.'

Alice hurried to the operating theatre, which was very basic compared to the one she'd assisted in at the hospital back home. Nevertheless, the procedure was similar, and she scrubbed up, put on a protective apron, then ensured that the necessary instruments and equipment were sterilised and in the correct order. It was an amputation just below the knee of a young pilot officer. The aircraft had been hit by enemy guns and although the pilot had managed to land his plane and save the lives of his crew, his left leg had become trapped in the cockpit amidst tangled metal and was severed.

On seeing the pilot, who only looked in his early twenties, she gasped inwardly, then bit her lip and recovered her equanimity and alertness, and began concentrating on the procedure of the operation. The surgeon was a military man and used to the severity of war injuries. Alice would never understand why one human being would want to inflict injury on another. But that was war and her duty was to nurse those wounded and bring comfort to them.

After the operation, she felt exhausted and drained of all energy, but while the room was being cleaned by the domestic staff, Alice had a quick cup of tea and a sandwich and then reported back to the operating room. The next operation was the removal of shrapnel from a shoulder and was not as harrowing as the previous one.

About a week later, Alice was nursing in the officers' rooms. 'Nurse, can you assist me, please?' called a male voice.

She was passing by the open door of one of the rooms and stopped to see what she could do and entered the room. A young, pale-faced man was trying to heave himself up in the bed. She recognised him as the pilot officer who'd lost his leg below the knee. Smiling cheerfully at him, she helped him to a comfortable position and then checked his chart and saw that his wound was starting to heal up.

'I've had a letter from my girl, Nurse.' He pointed to an envelope on his locker top.

She looked up from studying the chart into his pain-filled grey eyes. 'Have you?' she said, guardedly, sensing his sadness.

'Will you read it to me, Nurse?'

She didn't ask the question 'why?', because she had an inkling of what was written. 'If you wish,' she replied. She picked up the envelope and withdrew the single sheet of paper and glanced at the few lines of words written. She had to bite on her lips to stop the tears threatening to well up in her eyes. How could his girl write such a letter just when he needed her the most?

She looked at his face and saw it crumple. Instinctively, she went to him and put her arms around his shoulders and held him close while he sobbed. It was then she let her own tears fall.

After that, Alice made a point of attending to the young pilot officer whose name was Malcolm Fleming and would often spend her off-duty periods sitting by his bed and reading to him. His mother lived in the far north-west and only made the journey once to see her son. His two brothers were also fighting in the war and his father was on war duties as well, so he had no other visitors. When the weather was fine, Alice would push him in a wheelchair and take him around the grounds. 'The fresh air will bring colour to your pale skin,' she told him, when he started to object.

One day, in the officers' common room, Alice popped in to see Malcolm. 'Get me away from this.' He nodded in the direction of where one of the other officers was talking with his young lady. They were holding hands and looking into each other's eyes.

Alice went to fetch a wheelchair and said to Malcolm, when she had got him settled into it, 'I'm sorry, I will not have time to take you out, but—'

'Why not?' Malcolm cut in, his expression black.

'Because today I am extra busy.' She didn't want to tell him about the young pilot who was so badly injured that his operation would take most of the day and whose survival was uncertain. 'But I have a surprise for you,' she said to him as she wheeled him into the main hall. 'This is Amy and she would love to take you out.'

A young, dark-haired girl, with a heart-shaped face and a wide smile, came forward and Alice introduced them. Amy was a girl from the village and one of a band of volunteers who, in their spare time, came up to the hospital to help with patients and take them out in the grounds.

Alice went off to prepare for her duties in the operating theatre but, before doing so, she glanced out of the window. Down below, in the gardens at the back of the house, were Malcolm and Amy. She was talking to him and then they both laughed. Alice smiled. It was good for the young pilot to be with someone of his own age.

Of late, he was becoming too attached to Alice and that wasn't good for his mental well-being, especially when the time came for him to move on . . . She sighed. Until then, she would always be there to nurse and care for him, as she was for all the patients in her charge.

Chapter Twenty-Eight

Talli was excited. 'Me, Prince Charming, I can't believe it.' The hospital was putting on a Christmas show for the patients who were unable to go home or, as in some cases, had no home to go to, having been bombed out in enemy raids on towns and cities. And there were those who were far from home: Australians, Poles and Canadians serving alongside the RAF, all fighting for the same cause. Both Talli and Alice had elected to be on duty for the Christmas period and would take their leave in the new year, 1943.

It was Talli who had suggested this to Alice. 'It's a time for children and we've no children,' she enthused. And then on seeing the sad look cross Alice's face, she said softly. 'Sorry, was you thinking about Johnny?'

Alice's answer was, 'Come on, I'll be wardrobe mistress. I'm no good at acting or singing.'

It also became Alice's job to enrol those men able to help with the making of props for scenes. This preparation caused a good-feel buzz amongst the patients. They seemed to forget, for a time, their injuries and wounds and to just enjoy the simple pleasures of life, like splashing with a paintbrush.

As for Talli, she practised her singing as she went about her ward duties. One day, an Australian airman was negotiating a corridor on a pair of crutches, with both his legs encased in metal contraptions, when she came along, singing.

'Why do you have to be so bloody cheerful?' He scowled at her as she drew level with him.

She stopped singing and stood by his side, commenting, 'Yes, you are right. Why should I be so happy singing when my mother and father are both dead and I am an orphan of the storm?'

He stared at her with a confused expression on his ashen face, which was now becoming a fetching shade of pink. 'Sorry,' he muttered.

Talli shrugged, a mischief twinkle in her eyes, as she asked, 'How's your singing voice?'

He gaped and then said, 'I used to sing in a choir back home.' His eyes lit up, transforming the jagged lines of his face to give a glimpse of the real man beneath.

'You're just the man I'm looking for,' she enthused, starting to walk along the corridor, matching his pace as he began to manoeuvre with the aid of his crutches.

Later on, Talli went to the common room and found Flight Sergeant Jeffery Sutherland – Jeff to his fellow men. She sat down next to him in his wheelchair and told him about her grandparents, who had brought her up as their child when her own parents had died. 'My parents were entertainers and travelled around the country, so I guess I take after them, although I can't remember them.'

Jeff, in turn, told her about his life. 'I come from Tasmania, but I'm of Scottish descent – my ancestors were sheep farmers in the Highlands and my father carries on the tradition.'

'Are you going to be a farmer after the war?' she asked.

'No, it's not the life for me. I fancy the entertainment business.' He grinned at her and said, 'We could become a duo.' They both laughed at the daft idea.

The weeks leading up to the festive season were a joyous time for the patients and, because they were engaged in an activity that was nothing to do with war, they relaxed. This was great for morale and the healing process of mental and physical wounds. Some men, with the help of women volunteers from the village, took to sewing costumes as naturally as flying the skies. Even the stern-faced ward sisters became pleasant human beings.

The concert, based on *Cinderella*, was to take place on Boxing Day, but first there was Christmas Eve. It began with a choir of children from the local school and members of the church congregation. It was to be held in the largest common room, which could accommodate the beds of the patients who were bed-bound. Suddenly, the chatter stopped as the lights of the room went out and it was in complete darkness. From afar came the sound of children's voices singing a beautiful Christmas carol, 'Away in a Manger'. As they entered the room, each child carried a small lantern with a candle inside and the room became bathed in a wonderful glow of warm light. Talli glanced at Jeff, who was standing by her side, balancing on his crutches and saw tears glistening on his lashes. He must be missing his folks back home, she thought, and she reached out and gently rested her hand on his arm.

Before the children went home, each child was given a small bag of sweets. The congregation from the church stayed to join in with the singing and they brought with them to celebrate mince pies and hot punch. And the vicar said a prayer for an end to the war and everlasting peace to all.

Later, as Talli and Alice came off-duty, Talli remarked, 'It's been such a lovely evening.' Alice agreed, but Talli was thinking of the stolen kiss from Jeff. She had held him close, so that he could balance against her body. But what was playing through her mind was the feeling of pleasure that had rippled through her body at his nearness to her. It was a feeling she'd never experienced before when she'd kissed a man. Talli sighed with contentment; it had been a memorable evening.

Christmas Day, after the usual round of ablutions were dealt with, brought plenty to eat and drink, crackers they had made to pull and fancy paper hats to wear, and for those who were able, a walk in the cold, fresh air. 'Must blow those cobwebs away,' Matron had stated.

Talli walked with Jeff and they stopped in the shelter of a wall. She lit two cigarettes and put one of them to Jeff's lips. They didn't talk; they had no need, for the nearness of their bodies said it all.

Boxing Day, and anybody who was taking part in the concert was either singing to themselves or muttering their lines. Once again, the use of the large common room changed. It now had a stage and curtains at one end and one of the airmen manning the lights, while the musical director managed the wind-up gramophone. Action, go. It began. Talli felt her voice tremble at first and then it became stronger as she sang, and Jeff's deep baritone voice complemented hers. There was plenty of audience participation and clapping and joining in with the singing. Talli caught a glimpse of Matron, sitting on the front row, singing along. It was a light-hearted concert with a feel-good factor, and the patients from far-away countries quite liked the British sense of humour. It was certainly a Christmas to remember.

Talli and Jeff drifted out into the unlit corridor and kissed with such passion, a long, long kiss to seal their feelings for one another.

'When the time comes for me to leave, will you write to me?' Jeff asked.

Talli looked into his eyes and saw and sensed the seriousness of his question. She touched his lips with the tip of her finger and whispered, 'Of course I will.' They were just about to kiss again when . . .

'Nurse Whitmore, you are needed,' came a stern voice.

'Coming, Sister. I was just assisting Flight Sergeant Sutherland. I didn't want him to fall.' She gave him a mischievous grin.

'Thank you, Nurse,' he said.

During the preparations on Christmas Eve day, Alice had managed to slip away. She walked along the quiet country lane, passing a cottage from which smoke curled upwards and the aroma of baking coming from an open window tantalised her tastebuds. Further on, she stopped to have a chat with an old man walking his dog. Coming to the end of the lane, she turned right, through the lychgate of the church and along the path to the huge door, which squeaked as she pushed it open. Inside she felt the welcoming sanctuary of tranquillity. For a few moments she breathed in the atmosphere. Would she find the peace her heart so desired here in this place of worship and prayer? She was fighting an inner conflict with her emotions and she needed to resolve them. Moving down the centre aisle the scent of freshly gathered winter greenery filled her nostrils with its heavenly perfume. Tall candles glowed, their flickering light sending shadows onto the stone walls and pillars. A woman was arranging flowers near the altar and Alice slipped unnoticed into a pew. She sat quietly for a while with her eyes closed. It wasn't until she heard the woman leave the church that she rose to her feet and walked down the aisle to the altar where a candle stand was placed. Alice picked up the taper and lit it from a burning candle and then she lit her first candle for her daughter Daisy's birthday today. How the years had flown by and now she would be almost grown-up. Alice felt her heart miss a beat and she prayed that her beloved daughter was safe and one day they would be reunited. And then she lit a candle for Johnny that one day they would be together.

She sat down on the front pew and watched the candles' slender flames curl upwards. And, casting her gaze upwards, she saw to her surprise a star twinkling above the altar. Mesmerised, she stared up at it for some time until a voice behind her spoke.

'It looks very real, doesn't it?' It was the vicar and he came to sit next to her on the pew. 'One of our parishioners made it. It's a star for his son who was killed on the beaches of Normandy. It's his way of dealing with the anniversary of his son's death.'

Alice turned to him, her eyes glistening with tears. 'It's beautiful,' she whispered. She and the vicar sat in silence for a few minutes and then Alice rose, saying, 'I must get back to the hospital. Thank you, I feel more at peace with myself now.'

And she did. As she walked back along the lane to the hospital, her heart didn't feel so heavy. And there was a welcome surprise for her: a letter from Johnny. As soon as possible, she escaped to her room to read it. She tore open the envelope and read the words. Those loving words she'd yearned to see for so long. She read in between the censored words that he was well, loved her and missed her. She reread them again, savouring every word, thankful he was alive and able to write to her.

* * *

On New Year's Eve, Alice was on night duty; in a couple of days, she was going for a short visit to her mother's house. All the windows of the hospital blackout blinds were drawn each night by a volunteer. Tonight, Alice carried a small lantern as she went round the twenty-bedded ward, checking on each patient. 'Nurse Nightingale, will you come and soothe my brow?' whispered one cheeky chap. Alice smiled and did so, adding to the mood of well-being. Placing the lantern on the table in the centre of the ward, she settled down to write up her notes. All was quiet, except for the gentle rhythm of breathing and the odd snoring sound.

She had written up almost two pages, when, from the far corner bed, was the sound of a scream of terror. Alice hurried down to the patient. He was a ground crew airman who, when a plane had crash-landed, had, without fear for his own safety, jumped onto the wing of the plane to rescue the unconscious pilot just in time before it exploded. They were both thrown with the blast and the pilot was now in a specialist burns hospital, while his saviour was here.

By the time she reached his bed, he was screaming the words 'I'm coming!' He was struggling to get out of the bed and it took all of her strength to hold him down and to stop him from hurting himself. And then he was sobbing uncontrollably. She pulled the wooden screen around the bed and put on the night light. He was bathed in sweat, his nightclothes clinging to his frame. His cries had alerted other staff and a doctor with unruly hair and eyes still with sleep in them appeared at the bedside.

The doctor quickly checked the notes then left, returning within minutes to administer medication to the man, James Thomas. Alice bathed James's face and neck with cool water and, with the help of the doctor, put him into clean nightwear. When the doctor had gone, Alice sat by James's bedside and held his hand. She stayed with him until she was certain he was in a deep sleep. She made her rounds more frequently to check on James and to make sure that the other patients were now settled and asleep after the disturbance.

When morning arrived and the ward was beginning to wake up before the day staff came on duty, he was still fast asleep and, on the advice of the doctor, she let him remain so. Alice made a note on his chart and in the notes for the day staff for James to have a light meal and a drink when he woke up.

After she'd had her rest and eaten, Alice went on the ward to see how he was and was delighted to see him sitting up and chatting to the man in the next bed. While he was being nursed for his superficial injuries, his mental injuries of the terror of that incident would take time to erase from his mind.

Alice went up to her room to pack her case for her short visit to her mother's home. Although Agnes wasn't good at reading and writing, Alice had written to her as a courtesy, but to make sure her mother was aware of her daughter's planned visit, she'd also written to her sister.

Luck was on her side and Alice breathed a sigh of relief as she settled in a seat on the crowded train. For the long journey, she had a packet of sandwiches and a small flask of tea given to her by a volunteer from the village. Also, she had a book to read, one of her favourites, *Jane Eyre*. She also had a request to consider from Matron Hackness, who would require an answer on her return.

Chapter Twenty-Nine

After a long journey home from the military hospital, Alice arrived at Paragon Station feeling travel-weary. It was about four in the afternoon and already the daylight was fading fast. Everywhere looked grey and murky, even people passing by seemed to fade and become part of the landscape. She stood for a few moments surveying the devastation of the city centre. Her heart ached for her once beautiful city; she hadn't appreciated it until she was far away from it. Glancing round, where once stood shops, banks and homes there were now just piles of rubble and utter destruction. It was hard to take in and she hadn't realised that Hull had been bombed to such an extreme intensity. Listening to the wireless back in the nurses' sitting room, or reading a newspaper, there were no reports of such bombings and raids on Hull.

She crossed the road to buy a newspaper from the old man on the corner of the street. Quickly, she flicked through the pages. There was nothing. She glanced at the newspaper seller and he was watching her. 'Why is there is nothing about Hull being bombed?' she questioned.

'Because they think we don't bleedin' exist,' he replied angrily. 'It's about bleedin' London all the time, as if they are the only ones suffering.'

Alice agreed with him.

As she passed by yet another bombed ruin, the strong smell of dust caught at her throat and she coughed and sneezed. A few children were scavenging amongst the dirt of fallen bricks and mortar for signs of treasure or a souvenir of war, like a piece of shrapnel. She heard the whoop of joy as a boy held up his find. She couldn't help but smile, thinking of the boy's innocence of war and all its atrocities.

She pulled up the collar of her coat and turned right, threading her way through darkening streets towards her mother's home in Marvel Court. She hoped she was expected and that her mother and sister had received her letters. Martha was now working shifts in a munitions factory and Alice had no idea of her work schedule, but she was here for three whole days, so there was a chance to catch up.

Her steps faltered, and she stared at the gaping hole where once a shop had stood. A rise of panic filled her as she hurried on towards her mother's home. 'Oh,' she gasped with relief as she ran the last few steps, pushed open the front door and stepped inside. She leant against the closed door and dropped her case to her feet. She put her hand over her heart to steady its erratic beating. Over the last few years she'd seen many war-damaged buildings and she'd had to steel her heart against the severe injuries of the patients in hospital, but when it was close to home and someone you knew who had lost their home and livelihood or maybe their lives, it made a much bigger impact on her.

'Who's that?' called a voice from the kitchen.

'It's me, Mam.' Alice passed through the front room to the kitchen to be greeted by Agnes, who was making dumplings for the stew which simmered on the stove.

'Oh, it's you, Alice. Put the kettle on.'

Alice slipped off her coat, leaving it on the back of a chair, and did her mother's bidding. This was as warm a welcome as she would get.

Soon the two women sat by the fireside drinking tea. 'The baker's shop's gone, and Mr Jordan – is he all right?' Alice's voice trailed away.

'No, poor man, he copped it two weeks ago. He would never go to the shelter, because he feared the shop would be broken into.' Aggie gave a big sigh. 'What's the point of money if you're killed?' Then she poured them more tea and brought Alice up to date with family happenings. 'I'm right proud of the twins. Our Harry and Jimmy are in the navy, and our Charlie is in the army.'

'I can't believe how grown-up they are now,' Alice said, staring into the flickering flames of the fire, thinking of Daisy and wondering what she looked like now. Did she still have her lovely baby curls?

'Aye, well, time stands still for no man,' Aggie remarked, glancing up at the clock on the mantelpiece. 'George will be home soon. He likes his tea on the table.' Alice raised an eyebrow at her mother, who replied, 'He's on fire-watch tonight.'

'Where am I sleeping?' Alice asked.

'Why, the lads' bedroom, of course.'

'I'll take my case up out of the way.' She would have liked to freshen up, but that would have to wait until George had gone to his fire-watch duties.

In the early hours of the morning, Alice was woken up by the wailing sound of the sirens. Hastily, she scrambled into her clothes and went downstairs where her mother was waiting.

Aggie was organised, having had plenty of practice and she was armed with her handbag, which held her marriage certificates and the children's birth ones, ration and clothing books, insurance documents and pictures of her sons in their uniforms, but not one of her daughters, Alice and Martha. She also had a shopping bag, holding her knitting, sandwiches and flask of tea, and a bottle of smelling salts.

They both hurried to the brick shelter in the next street, one of many dotted around the city, though residents in some parts of the city had Anderson shelters built in their gardens. Alice was surprised how clean and fresh-smelling the shelter was. The concrete floor was scrubbed to perfection and the bunks had clean blankets and pillows, which were for the children to sleep and the infirm. 'We take turns to keep it clean,' Agnes said, proudly.

Once the children and the infirm were settled down, the women liked to sit and gossip, knitting or sewing as they did so, hands never idle. Alice listened as she tried to make sense of knitting a sock on four needles. The women swapped recipes and ideas to make the most of the meagre rations. One woman was telling how she'd made jam from turnips. No one took notice of the noise overheard as the defence guns sounded, but then came an almighty crash and bang, shaking the foundations of the shelter. 'That was close,' someone murmured.

'Could be the dock,' someone else said. Alice looked round as the women continued with their knitting, not dropping a stitch. She marvelled at their matter-of-fact attitude and their fortitude. And she felt an immense pride that her mother and these ordinary working-class women had such grit and determination to carry on in the face of danger.

At last, the all-clear sounded and they began to pack up their belongings. Alice carried a sleeping child in her arms as she walked alongside her mother and neighbours towards their homes. When Marvel Court was in sight, she heard a sigh of relief come from everyone. Tonight, their homes had been saved, but the docks had been hit yet again. The night sky was ablaze with flames of red and orange as firefighters fought to bring the fires under control. Alice wondered how many people had been injured or killed, or homes lost.

The next day, Alice went to see her sister, treading carefully as she negotiated debris strewn over roads and pavements from last night's raid and witnessed people trying to salvage what they could from their damaged homes. Martha was at her lodgings and busy getting ready to go to a dance with her friends. They chatted a while, Martha telling her about the good times she had going to various dances and meeting up with servicemen, either home on leave or stationed nearby. In return, Alice told Martha about the pantomime at the hospital and little funny anecdotes.

'Don't you go dancing?' Martha asked.

Alice shook her head and replied, 'No, though they do have some dances in the village hall, but I'm always too busy to be involved.' She could have added that she had no desire for dancing, not since Johnny was reported to be in a POW camp. One day, when this terrible war was over, he would come back to her. She held on to that belief and it kept her sane.

Time to say goodbye and the sisters hugged. They didn't have much in common as both their lives had taken different paths. 'Whatever happens,' Alice said, 'we will always be sisters.'

Alice walked towards Baker Street to the house of Mrs Melton, the woman responsible for having Daisy privately adopted. There was always a chance that one day she might tell her where Daisy was and with whom. By now daylight was fading and there were no lights shining from windows or on the street. It felt eerie and she shivered, pulling the collar of her coat closer. As she rounded the corner to the street, she blinked hard and a sudden trembling ran the full length of her body and back again. She moved forward, trying to focus her eyes to see, but it wasn't there. There was just a gaping big hole where once the house had stood.

Without hesitation, she knocked on the door of the next property. It was a while, seconds which felt like minutes, before someone opened the it. A woman peered out from the half-opened door. 'Yes?' she enquired.

'The house next door. Mrs Melton . . .' Her words trailed away when she saw the sorrowful look on the woman's face.

'Sorry, they all perished. They refused to go in the communal shelter and stayed in their basement and it had a direct hit.'

The woman began to close the door and Alice put out a hand to stop it and blurted, 'Did you know of the little girl, Daisy? Mrs Melton arranged her adoption and I'm trying to find her.'

The woman looked puzzled and said, 'Sorry, I don't know what you are talking about.' And she shut the door.

Alice felt the painful tightening of her chest and she put her hand on the wall to steady herself as the strong wave of devastation filled her. She wanted to hold her daughter in her arms and never let her go.

After a few minutes, with her head bent, she began to walk away and didn't see the figure of a man looming up behind her. Her steps were slow as she thought of her child and she hoped with all her heart that Daisy, wherever she was, was safe. For now, that was her hope.

She suddenly became aware of the heavy footsteps behind her. She glanced over her shoulder and could just make out the figure of a heftily built man in a dark uniform. She quickened her steps and so did he. She hurried along down a deserted Savile Street crossing Victoria Square towards Whitefriargate and still he was behind her. She felt a pain in her side with hurrying too much and fear pulled at her. But then something strange happened to her. Anger!

She stopped and turned round sharply. All her years of dealing with difficult patients had made her aware of being able to defend herself whenever necessary. Her eyes blazing with fury, she challenged the man. 'And which part of your anatomy do you want me to cut off?'

The man stopped in his tracks, bamboozled by this sudden turn of events. He seemed to have lost the power of speech and his step faltered. She watched him, and was about to hurry on, when he spoke.

'My, who would have thought it, little frightened Alice sticking up for herself!'

She stared into Ted Goddard's bleary eyes and smelt the pungent stench of beer from his breath. He looked rough and unshaven, the odour of body sweat and dank earth seeped from him as if he'd been sleeping in a ditch. She didn't reply to him, but stood her ground and glared at him, no longer feeling intimidated by him.

He seemed to sense her fearlessness and it must have unnerved him because his arm, half raised to hit her, fell back by his side. 'I need money,' he growled.

Still, she didn't speak and instead looked directly into his eyes and then she spoke one word. 'Why?'

'I've ter get away,' he whined.

She repeated the one word. 'Why?'

'Because they're bloody well after me.' His voice was between a howl and a gripe.

'Why?'

'For God's sake, woman, just give me the money.' He made to grab her handbag, but she was too quick for him.

With a force she didn't realise she had, she swiped him hard across his face with the bag. He yelled with pain and his hand went up to cover his nose, and she saw blood squirting from between his fingers. She knew that being a nurse she should do something to alleviate his injury, but at that moment in time, she was taking a bizarre pleasure in seeing him hurting. So, she just stood there, as if in a suspended time frame, and looked at him – after all, it wasn't life-threatening. It was nothing compared to what she'd witnessed while nursing servicemen injured in battle. She turned away from him and walked, his moans and groans becoming fainter.

Next day, she read in the local newspaper that Ted Goddard had been arrested for desertion. The next time she was back in Hull, she would see a solicitor to see what divorce entailed and what it would cost.

Chapter Thirty

Back at the military hospital, Alice was summoned to Matron Hackness's office where she was introduced to Senior Medical Officer Norton, a man with an inbuilt serious expression on his thin face. Then, wasting no time, Matron asked, 'Staff Nurse Goddard, have you made your decision?'

Standing to attention and looking straight ahead, Alice replied, 'Yes, Matron. I will volunteer.'

'Then I have no hesitation in recommending you for air ambulance duties.'

Alice answered all the questions that the officer asked and, just when she thought they were done, he fired one more question. 'You will be the only nurse on the aircraft and you will have injured men unable to walk. You must get all the wounded safely on board in a matter of minutes. How will you accomplish that?'

Alice recalled her probationary nursing days when she had to serve meals to a full ward of about thirty patients and every meal had to be hot and so she sought the help of those patients who were mobile. 'I will recruit the walking wounded to help, sir.' Behind her back, she crossed her trembling fingers.

'Excellent,' replied the officer.

Later, Alice and Talli were in the common room, both relieved that they had made it. 'A chance to fly,' said Talli. 'If I didn't get through, I was going to apply to drive an ambulance, but to fly in one is more glamorous.'

Alice laughed, saying, '"Glamorous" is not the word I'd use. You watch too many of those American films.'

Within days, Alice, Talli and two other nurses were transported down to an RAF station in Wiltshire. Here they joined a squadron of other WAAF nurses on air ambulance duties. They trained hard, having to have flying experience before taking up their posts. The first time Alice went up in the plane, a Dakota, she felt sick. She sensed that the young non-commissioned pilot was showing off his skills.

So after a few times up in the air with him and his aerobatics, she approached the pilot in the village pub where she and Talli were having an evening off-duty. Talli was playing darts with a couple of the other WAAFs and Alice was half watching them when in walked the pilot whom she was gaining flying experience with. 'Can I buy you a drink, sir?'

Surprise showed on his face as he recognised her and this unexpected pleasure. 'Sure, a beer, please,' he replied.

They settled down in a quiet corner and Talli gave her the thumbs-up sign. Alice sipped her lemonade and smiled at the wisecracks coming from some of the ground crew members who'd just come into the pub. She put down her glass and said, 'I feel safe with you, up in the air, and I know you are an experienced pilot.' He looked quizzically at her, a smile playing on his full lips and she continued, 'As I am an experienced nurse.' He opened his mouth wide and laughed. As he did so, she said, 'I could operate on your sore tonsils, if you wish.'

He promptly shut his mouth and stared at her. 'How do you know?' he said and glanced around to see if anyone had overheard Alice's observation, and then his boyish face crinkled into a smile, and he said, 'Point taken.'

She finished her drink and rose to her feet and saluted him, not sure if this was correct or not. Before he could say anything, she went over to where Talli and the others were.

After that the pilot and she became friends and there were no more aerobatics.

Before they embarked on their first mission, they were given a pep talk by a medical officer and were told to be ready for duty. They were to receive an extra eight pence a day flying pay. 'Not bad,' said Talli as she chewed on her allowance of gum.

Alice didn't like the chewing gum and swapped it with Talli for extra barley sugar, but the treat for her was the orange on the days that she flew, and she couldn't remember last having tasted one. She loved the sweet, tangy taste of the orange and enjoyed letting the juice dribble slowly down her throat and she savoured every single segment, making it last as long as time allowed.

'Goddard, Whitmore,' the officer called out, 'prepare to leave at first light.' There was a hush and then everyone began talking. The officer held up his hand for quiet and then spoke, 'You will be taken to collect your gear and parachute and then retire to your quarters. You will be called early in the morning.'

And it was early. 'Blimey!' said Talli, rubbing the sleep from her eyes. 'I feel as though I've only slept a few minutes.'

Alice hummed to herself as she hurried off to the ablutions. She felt so alive and thrilled at the thought of the unknown and doing work she loved. She hadn't felt like this in a long time, not since the bad news about Johnny. And then she thought of Daisy and the hope she nurtured deep in her heart that one day they would be together.

After breakfast, carrying their medical equipment in their panniers and dressed in their blue flight suits, they hurried towards the waiting Dakotas. Alice was surprised to learn that the plane was full of ammunition and supplies for the troops fighting at the front. She had wondered why there was no Red Cross sign visible on the plane. Now she knew why.

At last, Alice was airborne with the pilot and three other crew members. She couldn't tell in which direction they were flying, because the windows were blacked out. The flight was bumpy and there was nowhere for her to sit, so she perched on what she later found out was a bomb. But nothing bothered her; she felt no fear. She had a job to do and that was paramount in her thoughts and her doing.

They landed on a makeshift airstrip in Belgium and Alice could hear the sound of gunfire in the near distance. As soon as the cargo was offloaded, she had the wounded men on board, and they were airborne and on the way back to base.

The first thing she was asked by a chirpy soldier from her home city of Hull was, ''Ave yer a cup of tea, luv?'

'I've got an urn full,' she replied and gave him a mugful of sweet, slightly stewed brown liquid. After a long draught, he licked his lips in appreciation. Next, she began to administer medication to those in need. One young soldier was in a delirious state and thought she was his mother. So, when she'd redressed his chest wound and given him medication for the pain, she gave him a gentle kiss on the cheek, saying, 'Have a sleep, now.'

One soldier with a leg amputated below his knee asked, 'Will you go dancing with me?'

She smiled at him and replied, 'I'll save the first dance for you, sweetheart.'

'I'll hold you to that,' he said. But as she checked his stump, he winced with pain. It was covered in sores and the skin was rubbed away. For now, all she could do was to put a soothing cream on it, redress it and give him pain relief medication. He held out his hand to her and she took it in hers and squeezed it.

Soon they were back at base and the wounded were on their way to hospitals. Alice gave her report to the medical officer, with recommendations she thought were necessary. Both she and Talli were of the same thinking as they were nurses with a great deal of experience and expertise.

'It's your job to obey orders, not to suggest what to carry on aircrafts,' the medical officer barked at Alice and Talli when he read their reports and sent for them.

'Sir,' said Alice, politely, 'then we cannot be held responsible for the wounded dying on our watch.' She wanted to add 'so that will be your responsibility', but held her tongue and looked at a picture of King George on the wall above his head.

'Dismissed,' he said curtly.

'Old windbag,' Talli said, once they were a safe distance away from the office.

'He'll come round, because he won't want deaths on his conscience and, besides, it won't look good when he wants promotion,' Alice prophesied.

And she was right.

The medical officer issued a statement, pinned to the air ambulance nurses' noticeboard: *Forthwith, all nurses will now carry morphine syrettes and oxygen. It is the responsibility of each nurse to check that all their medical equipment is in order.*

'Not before time,' a WAAF commented as they all stood around the noticeboard. Alice and Talli exchanged a knowing glance.

There was a dance arranged in the NAAFI one Friday night a few weeks later. Alice wasn't sure about going. 'Don't be a spoilsport,' Talli admonished. So, she relented and brushed her WAAF uniform and polished her black lace-up shoes, which were rather unflattering for dancing. She undid her hair that was coiled round ribbon like a half-moon sausage that was serviceable for duty. She brushed it out and was surprised to see how long it had grown, sweeping past her shoulders. She remembered long ago having it cut in a bob when she'd worked at Faith House. She wondered about Miss Bailey and how she was surviving the war, and the girls. Did they all go on to have better lives? She hoped so. She knew Hetty had joined up and was driving big trucks and that Beth, the girl who had drawn the picture of her, had married. That was the picture, together with a card, that she had posted to Daisy, care of Mrs Melton, though she never knew whether her daughter had received it.

'Are you gonna daydream much longer?' asked an impatient Talli. 'Here, put some lipstick on.' She handed the precious tube to Alice.

She painted her lips and said, as she looked in the mirror at the gash of red, 'It makes my face look pale.'

'You'll soon flush up when you get dancing. Come on.'

When they arrived, the NAAFI was heaving with dancers twirling and jitterbugging and the band was on top form belting out the latest music from America. They squeezed through the throng of dancers and were making their way to the bar when they were intercepted by two airmen and swung off their feet.

Alice didn't realise that she had so much energy as she kept in step and beat with the airman. Coming to the end of the dance, she was just about to walk away when he caught her arm.

'Come on, I'll get you a drink.' He pulled her through the crowd to the bar where his mate and Talli were already waiting. The two men turned to attract the attention of the barman.

'I'm not sure about this,' said Alice. She felt disloyal to Johnny, although she didn't mention it to Talli.

'Bullshit!' Talli exclaimed. 'Think of it as doing a service to war work, keeping our lads happy.'

Alice laughed out loud just as the two men turned round with drinks in their hands. 'That's the spirit, girls. Live and laugh for today for tomorrow might not come,' the airman said, as he handed Alice a beer, 'and maybe a kiss or two.' He winked at her.

'This is welcomed. I'm parched,' she said. 'Thank you.'

They spent the rest of the night with the two airmen and had great fun and a few kisses and cuddles. When they went to the next NAAFI dance, the two airmen were not there. 'I wonder if they've been posted or . . . ?' Alice didn't finish the rest of the sentence – what was the point? So, after that, a kiss and a cuddle she was happy to give, but no further.

'The last thing we want is to be pregnant,' said Talli. 'Not like that poor bugger Maisie. She's well and truly in the family way and the man, if she can remember which one, is nowhere to be seen or found.'

About two weeks later, Talli flew out on a mission ahead of Alice, who had to wait for more uploading on the plane and so she was a good thirty minutes behind. Their destination was the

Netherlands, somewhere near to the German border. When the Dakota that Alice was in touched down on the narrow airstrip, they were aware of total confusion. Alice scrambled from the plane and dropped down as a sniper's bullet whizzed by her head. She lay flat in the churned-up, muddy soil; the smell of a musty, coarse damp stench of earth filled her nostrils and she clamped her mouth shut and waited. There was an exchange of fire from the British troops and soon the Germans retreated.

Alice cautiously got to her feet and looked around. Reinforcements arrived and the wounded, hidden in a dugout, were now being brought out safely. It was then she saw her.

'Talli!' she cried. But Talli didn't move or respond. Alice ran to where her friend lay crumpled on the ground. She fell to her knees and felt Talli's pulse. It was weak and there was blood coming from her shoulder. Quickly, from her bag, Alice produced a dressing to stem the flow of blood. She needed to get her on board immediately. She looked round, surveying the scene. The crew were busy unloading, and the crew of the other Dakota were doing the same now the shooting was over. She was on her feet, shouting to a man who only had a superficial wound to his face. 'I need your help.'

Between them, they lifted Talli into Alice's Dakota and rested her on one of the lower bunks. 'Thanks. Can you make sure that those able to walk get aboard the first Dakota?'

'Sure,' he replied.

Talli was coming round and moaning in pain. 'You're safe,' Alice soothed as she lifted her head to administer morphine for the pain. 'I'm going to leave you while I get the wounded aboard. Try to keep still.'

Outside, the soldier helping was making slow progress, but

Alice soon had the others aboard and settled and had given medication to those who needed it. Now she must get aboard her own plane and give her attention to those most seriously injured.

When she got round to Talli again, she was pleased to see her friend awake and reassuring a soldier in the opposite bunk who was saying that he wanted to go home.

The radio operator had alerted the base of the incident and the number of wounded, including one of the nurses. So, when they landed, there were ambulances and medical staff to meet the injured and take them to hospital.

'I don't want to go,' Talli protested.

But Alice was firm in her response. 'The quicker you go to hospital and have your injury attended to, the quicker you will be back on duty.'

'You sound like a bloody matron,' Talli said, but she managed a quirky smile.

Back in her quarters, after attending the debriefing and washing the mud off her face and discarding her uniform, Alice sank down onto her bed, exhausted. But sleep wouldn't come. All she could think about and hear in her head was the gunfire and bullets whizzing by her as she had flattened her body, face down in the mud. It hit her like a cricket bat, the reality of war and her own mortality, over which she had no control. So, there was no purpose in worrying. She gave a big sigh, turned over and was soon sound asleep.

Chapter Thirty-One

Talli was in hospital for almost three weeks. As well as being hit by a bullet, her shoulder suffered damage from her falling on sharp stones and was fractured. The bullet had been removed from her shoulder and, after having physiotherapy and rehabilitation, she was given leave to go home. It felt strange to be nursed rather than to be the nurse. Since Jeff Sutherland had returned to base having been nursed by Talli, the Australian flight sergeant and Talli had been writing to each other. Letters were spasmodic, but nevertheless they were in touch. From her hospital bed she wrote to him, but had no idea how long it would take for the letter to reach him wherever he was. All she had for him was a BFPO address, so after being home for two days and being fussed over by her grandmother like a newborn lamb, she was surprised and delighted to see him.

'I've a whole forty-eight hours to spend with you,' he said when Talli's grandmother had gone to the kitchen to make a pot of tea. 'And I want to make the most of it.' He put a hand tenderly under her chin and, looking into her deep hazel eyes, he kissed her. 'That's just a taste of what's to come,' he whispered. He drew back to his chair as Mrs Whitmore entered the room bearing a tray loaded with tea and the delicious aroma of freshly baked scones. He jumped to his feet to take the tray from her hands.

'Thank you, that's kind of you.' She smiled at the young couple as she settled down in her chair to pour the tea into delicate china cups. 'Whereabouts in Australia do you come from?' she asked Jeff.

'Tasmania, near Hobart,' he replied.

'Tasmania,' she repeated almost to herself and then added, 'My maternal grandmother came from Tasmania.'

Surprised, Talli said, 'I didn't know that, Mam, you never mentioned it before.'

Her mother answered in a far-off-voice. 'There was some kind of mystery surrounding her and why she left Tasmania to come to England. I heard said whatever her secret was, she took it to her grave.'

'She sounds an intriguing woman. What was she like?'

'I never really knew her as she was old when I was born. All I can recall of her was that she sat in a chair and just stared out of the window and very rarely spoke. I thought she seemed a sad lady.'

When her grandfather came home from his Home Guard duties, they had a meal together and Talli felt content to let her grandfather and Jeff talk about flying, the different aircrafts and what was currently happening in the war. 'I reckon the Italians are on the run now . . .' She left the men to their war talk and went to help her mother to wash the dishes and prepare a bed for Jeff.

'Are you sure you can manage, luv?' her mother fussed.

'Yes, Mam, if I'm gentle with myself.' It usually felt uncomfortable when she was in bed and lying flat, so being the good nurse she was, she arranged her pillows so she was in an elevated position.

They made up a bed on the sofa in the sitting room for Jeff, because the spare room was occupied by two young brothers from the heavily bombed city of Hull across the Humber estuary. They hadn't seen Jeff, because they went straight to friends for tea.

'Gosh, are you a real pilot?' they asked, both pyjama-clad, peeping their heads round the sitting-room door as he was preparing to bed down for the night.

'Now, you two, aren't you supposed to be in bed?' sounded the stern voice of Mr Whitmore.

Jeff winked at the boys and said, 'See you in the morning.'

Before they went to school next morning, Jeff regaled the brothers with stories of flying and chasing German bombers. From the kitchen window, Talli watched as they went off to school, zooming along with satchels firmly strapped on their backs and arms outstretched like wings. Children, even in the midst of war, can be carefree and innocent. 'It's as it should be,' she murmured.

Then she felt a strong pair of arms slip around her waist, warm lips nuzzled her neck and then she felt her body being turned until she was facing him. The most wonderful feeling, like electricity, zipped through her whole body and as they held a brief second of eye contact, she knew he felt the same. Their lips met. The kiss was gentle at first and then with a passionate urgency of a longing never to let go, never to be parted, and to be together for eternity. As the sound of footsteps drew near, reluctantly, they drew apart.

Talli said, loud enough for her mother to hear, 'It's a lovely day. Shall we go for a walk?'

'Good idea,' said Jeff. 'You can show me your beautiful countryside.'

Alice missed Talli, her liveliness and the ability to make her laugh, but most of all the friendship they had shared ever since they had worked together as nurses – and more so now being air ambulance nurses. After bringing back the injured servicemen from the front line, when often they would encounter the unknown, they would share their knowledge and confide in each other and pool their resources. The other WAAFs were chatty and friendly, but it wasn't until Talli was injured and not able to carry out her duties for some time that Alice really came to value her true friendship.

With Talli away, Alice took on more duties and elected not to have any days off. At first, she felt exhausted, but then it was as if she'd gone through a time barrier, or perhaps it was that exhaustion was part of her daily life. Whatever, with her being so busy she had little time to dwell on the two people she loved most in life. Her daughter, Daisy, was adopted by another family. Alice often wondered if she remembered her real mother who gave birth to her or had she forgotten? After this war was over, Alice was determined to find her daughter. After all, she had never signed any legal documents for her to be adopted and, if necessary, she would seek help from the courts. She had saved most of her money while nursing, so that wouldn't be a problem. And she wasn't the naive woman she had been back then, and no way was she going to be put off by people in authority.

'Are you all right?' A kindly voice broke into her thoughts.

Alice looked at the woman wiping down the dining tables in the mess and then glanced around the now empty room. 'Sorry, yes, I am,' she replied, brushing away the tears she hadn't noticed sliding down her cheeks.

'Not hungry, then?' the woman pointed to the plate of half-eaten food.

Alice pushed the plate away and rose to her feet. 'No appetite.'

She turned and went from the mess to make her way to her billet and sleep.

The following days were routine, flying out to whatever area they were assigned to, though she would never get used to some of the terrible injuries the men suffered – maimed and lost limbs. One of the most horrific and saddest injuries she recalled was the young man who couldn't have been more than twenty. He wanted a cigarette, but part of his face, including his mouth, had been blown away. She understood there was an eminent plastic surgeon who could perform miracles, but all she could do for now was to hold the young man's hand and smooth back his hair, matted with blood, and administer morphine. She had to steel her heart not to cry and, always, she showed compassion, whatever their wounds were. And she would do everything in her nursing power to keep her patients alive, so that when they reached hospital there was a great chance they would receive the life-saving operation they needed.

Seemingly, to Alice, all airstrips in remote places were the same, but one thing she'd learnt was not to be complacent. Sometimes the too quiet places held hidden dangers. Today was no exception. The touchdown was bumpy over rough terrain and Alice was shaken, although she wasn't unduly worried.

On landing, Alice was greeted by a Red Cross field officer. 'Sorry, delays. I have orders for you to stay overnight. Please bring your equipment.' He instructed the crew to unload the ammunition and return to base. Alice was taken by truck to an area close to Caan where she was to bed down in a tent alongside a wounded soldier with severe internal injuries. He groaned in pain as she entered and then he was muttering. She took his temperature and found it high. She bathed him in cool water and then administered morphine and oxygen, and hoped it would give him some respite. He urgently needed an operation if his life was to be saved. All she could do, for the time being, was to make him comfortable.

She rested by his side, but didn't sleep, and wondered why the soldier hadn't been brought to the Dakota. At one stage, he woke up and thought she was his wife. He kept murmuring the name 'Joanie'. Then he tried to take Alice in his arms, still murmuring, 'Joanie.' Alice, unable to bear his pain, put her arms around him and whispered, 'I'm here.'

Tears fell unheeded down her cheeks as she held him close, listening as his breathing faded away until he gave one last breath and then he was silent. Alice felt for his pulse, but there was none. Stiffly, she rose to her feet. She needed to see the Red Cross field officer and report the soldier's death before she could perform the last act for him. Outside the tent, the air was cold, and she shivered. As she glanced around, she realised that this tent was the only one and that all the other men were either in the truck, underneath it or on guard.

The soldier on guard saw her approaching and saluted her. For a second, she was taken aback, because it had never happened to her before. However, she returned the salute and said, 'I'm afraid the soldier has died.'

He immediately roused the field officer, who came with her to the tent. After the formalities, Alice performed the laying-out procedure. Tenderly, she sponged down his ravaged body and noticed how young he was. She thought of his young wife, Joanie, and decided that she would write to her to tell her how his last thoughts were of her. Over her years of nursing, Alice had often done the laying out of patients. The first time she was frightened and then it was part of nursing so she didn't dwell on it. But, somehow, this young man was different. Was it because she had held him in her arms right until the end and he thought she was his wife?

When daylight came, a convoy of lorries bearing the wounded arrived. There had been heavy fighting and they had to make camp in a place of safety. When the Germans had retreated, it was safe for the convoy to proceed. The Dakota was on its way for the pick-up and Alice was busy checking her supplies for the journey back. She was relieved to see another nurse aboard who would help and have the extra medication needed.

'Some people will do anything for a night out with a party of men.' The nurse greeted Alice with a cheerful smile.

When everyone was aboard and they were up in the air, homeward bound, the nurse said to Alice, 'I've brought you a flask of tea and a sandwich, because I guess you wouldn't have had time for dining out. You have it while I see to the injured.'

'Thank you, and later I'll buy you a drink in the NAAFI,' Alice replied, realising that it was almost twenty-four hours since she had eaten. And then she thought of her welcoming bunk. 'Bliss,' she murmured.

Chapter Thirty-Two

Talli was back at base and Alice gave her friend a welcoming hug. 'I've missed you.' She stepped back to view Talli. 'You look amazing and I see you've enjoyed your mother's cooking.'

'Cheek,' said Talli and laughed. 'You look thinner and tired. Now I'm back to lighten the load.'

Alice studied her friend's face and saw the gleam of happiness in her eyes and remarked, 'Now I know you are pleased to see me, but who put that sparkle of light in your eyes?'

Talli grinned and replied, 'They call him Jeff. Flight Sergeant Sutherland to you. He came a-calling and made quite an impression on my parents. He had a forty-eight-hour pass just to see me.' Her expression became dreamy.

Alice sighed. Her friend was in love. 'Come on, dreamboat, we've work to do.'

And Talli took to it as if she'd never been away. 'It's weird,' she said. 'When on operations, I never feel any fear. Do you?'

'Never think about it,' Alice answered honestly.

The rest of the year passed and when they were not flying, Alice and Talli were enjoying themselves at dances in the NAAFI or in the local pub along with others from the camp. They had fun, but never took it further. In September, Italy had surrendered, and everyone wondered if it would be Germany next. But Christmas and New Year came and went, and the war raged on.

Talli met up with Jeff as both had a twenty-four-hour pass and they found a quiet hotel in the heart of nowhere with no amenities, but they had other things in mind to pass the time away.

Alice didn't take leave as she needed to save all her money for when the war ended and was quite happy doing her work. She spent any free time she had writing letters and, in particular, she wrote to Matron Bailey. She liked to keep in touch, because many of the girls who had been at Faith House also kept in contact with Matron and she, when writing back to Alice, would tell her the news of everyone. Many of the girls had married and had children, or were working, or they'd joined up in one of the armed forces. Alice was saddened to hear of one girl who had been killed when the factory she was working in took a direct hit in an air raid.

One letter, via the Red Cross, was the most unsettling of all. It was from her friend and mentor, Evelyn Laughton, who was a sister with the Queen Alexandra Nurses and stationed in the Far East. The letter had been very heavily censored. All it said was that Evelyn was a POW and she was well. Letters could be delivered via the Red Cross. Alice sat for a long time with the single thin sheet of paper in her hand before she wrote her reply. She felt angry. What was the point of interning a serving nurse who could save lives? War made no sense at all to her.

On her next flight out, everything was going according to plan and patients were on board when one man became very vocal. 'Sling the flaming Jerry off. If I could stand I'd do it myself!' Alice

292

went to see what the commotion was about. The vocal man was red in the face and shouted an order to Alice. 'Get the bloody Jerry off!' He jabbed a finger in the direction of a frightened-looking young man in German uniform.

In her most commanding voice and her face stern, she said, 'I issue the orders here, sir.' She'd noticed his stripes. 'Now, I am going to take your blood pressure, so calm down unless you want a heart attack.'

He blustered and then, exhausted, he sank back against the leg of a lower bunk.

Alice proceeded to take his blood pressure, which was high, and his head was hot. She thought it might be the start of a fever, so she administered medication and was relieved to see he remained quiet.

When she came to the German, he looked as though he was about eighteen or nineteen and as she glanced at his face, she saw the raw terror in his eyes. His name was Gunther Schumacher and he had a broken thigh bone. Gently, she examined his injury and could see the bone protruding. He clenched his lips tight, trying not to cry out and draw more attention to himself. Alice spoke quietly, telling him she was going to give him morphine for the pain and oxygen, and then she would put a firmer dressing around his thigh so as not to cause more injury or infection. He didn't understand all her words, but because her voice was soothing, he understood her meaning.

She inched along the limited space of the aircraft to the man who had been vocal earlier and she could see he was in great discomfort. 'How are you?' she asked, formally, knowing he wasn't the kind of soldier to cry out in pain and this would give him a chance to sound off.

'It's this useless, blasted foot. Can't put pressure on it,' he retorted angrily.

'I'll check to see if I can make you more comfortable.' She dropped to her knees to be at his level. She didn't remove the supportive dressing; instead, she expertly felt around it and knew that many bones of the foot had been crushed severely. She felt him wince under her gentle touch and knew he was in pain. She explained to him, 'The supportive dressing will hold until you reach hospital and I will give you morphine for the pain.'

'I don't—' he blustered and stopped when he saw her no-nonsense glance at him. Before moving on, she placed a folded blanket under his foot to make him more comfortable. She sighed under her breath. He was going to be out of action for some time.

Later, when everyone was safely off the Dakota and on their way to hospital, Alice went to give her report to the medical officer. She wrote down about the injured German soldier and the officer's objections as well as the details of the other patients. The MO looked up at her when he read the report and said, 'You were quite correct, Goddard.'

After a wash and freshen up, and wearing a bright-red lipstick, which they shared, she and Talli went for a stroll down to the pub. The landlord had some gin, from where he wasn't saying, but it tasted good with a touch of orange cordial. After a few drinks, one of the pilots began to play some lively tunes on the piano and soon everyone was having a good sing-song. Later, going back to the camp, everyone was in an ebullient mood and they all danced the conga down the lane in a long, straggly line, singing loudly as they went, seemingly without a care, with no thought to what tomorrow might bring. For now, they lived for the excitement of the moment.

* * *

There was an undercurrent buzzing in the camp. Something big was about to happen. This was towards the end of May 1944 and there was much speculation on base. In the first week of June, Alice read out on the noticeboard. 'All air ambulance flights are grounded until further notice.'

'Blimey, something big is happening,' Talli said.

Then they witnessed all planes taking off. It turned out to be Operation Overlord – D-Day. All in all, they heard that some 12,000 aircraft were involved to ensure air supremacy in bombing German defences and providing cover for the thousands of troops and over 6,000 vessels taking part. The troops landed on five Normandy beaches and took the Germans by surprise. The casualties of the Allied forces taking part were not as great as feared. The ground troops' movement forward was slow, hampered because of narrow lanes and the thick overgrowth of hedges of the French countryside. However, by the end of June, Cherbourg was liberated, and two months later so too was Paris.

Alice and Talli watched it on the Pathé News at the cinema when they had a rare night off-duty. They saw the joy on the faces of the French people as they hailed their liberating heroes.

The Dakotas were involved in picking up the wounded from the D-Day landings and were flying non-stop. Alice found herself on one of her many flights stuck overnight. Talli's plane had taken off, but bad weather and fog closed in, so the flight back was delayed. The crew were staying near the aircraft, but she was being taken by truck to a farmhouse. The driver of the truck was young and, in conversation with him, she learnt that he had just recently joined up and was only eighteen.

'I'm a man, now,' he stated, proudly, 'and I'm doing my bit for king and country.'

They arrived at the farmhouse to find a terrified farmer and his wife tied to chairs and a German officer with a gun. Alice could see that he had an injury. His left shoulder hung down at a precarious angle.

Her brain ran on adrenaline. By her side, she felt the young soldier's body brace, ready to pounce. She touched his back lightly to stop his action, knowing that the enemy wouldn't hesitate in killing him.

The German barked an order at them to put up their hands, which they did. Neither she nor the solider spoke or moved, but waited to see what the German would do next . . .

They remained immobile for what seemed a very long time. Then, suddenly, the German pointed to Alice and to the Red Cross on the sleeve of her uniform.

She stared at him, noticing that through his dirty, torn uniform, the injury on his shoulder was oozing blood and she knew what he wanted her to do. She motioned to the pannier at her feet, which held her medical equipment.

He barked an order, waving his gun at Alice and a cold shiver ran through her body and then was quickly replaced by her code of nursing and her professionalism. She picked up her pannier and moved towards him, her head held high, her gaze fixed on him, watching the hand that held the gun. He motioned her to open the pannier and he checked for a weapon. She had never fired a gun, nor handled one, but she had morphine.

'Remove,' she said, indicating his jacket and shirt, which he did with difficulty, but remained watchful of her. She hoped the solider wouldn't try to do anything heroic, not until the German was sedated.

Alice examined the wound and could see that a bullet was

lodged firmly in his shoulder, which was dislocated. She cleaned the flesh wound as best she could with antiseptic and packed it to stop the flow of blood and then applied a sterile dressing. That was as much as she could do under the circumstances, but he would need more attention and possibly an operation. As she treated him, she was conscious of the pain he was experiencing, and he would need painkiller relief.

Accidently, she brushed against his ribcage and he gave a sharp intake of breath. She glanced at him and, by the way he held himself, knew he had cracked or broken ribs.

When she had finished his dressing, she said, 'You need medication for the pain.'

'No,' he snarled and motioned for her to bring him a chair.

She heaved the solid wooden chair across to him and then he directed her to go back to stand beside the solider. She did so, glancing furtively at him, signalling for him to do nothing, yet.

Alice was tired. She never liked standing still; it reminded her of school when given detention for naughtiness. She noticed the old couple also looked tired and guessed they were as hungry as she was. She let her mind drift back in time to when Daisy was a little girl, the special days when they would walk to the park. They loved to watch the splash boat, a boat which was on runners and was hauled mechanically up the slope to the top platform. It was one penny a time and you climbed up the iron steps and stepped into the boat and sat on one of the wooden benches. And then the boat would go hurtling down, splashing into the lake below. Everyone shrieked with delight, including Daisy. Was it possible that she could remember this joy in the short time she was with her mother? Alice clung on to this tiny, precious part of her daughter's life.

The minutes passed by and then a whole hour, and Alice sensed the soldier's impatience. She was just beginning to think she had misjudged the situation, when the German spoke, rapping out an order. Now alert, Alice understood his meaning and picked up her pannier and slowly walked across the room to him. She knew what she had to do, but first she replaced the sodden dressing with a fresh one. Then she sterilised the muscle into which she was going to inject. Totally focused, she selected the syringe and the dosage of morphine from her bag and she performed the injection.

She glanced up to the German's face and saw beads of sweat on his forehead. 'It will take some time for the medication to take effect,' she said to him.

'*Danke*,' he replied.

She picked up her bag and went back to her place and the soldier glared at her. 'Wait,' she mouthed. They waited.

Soon, the German's head began to loll to one side and his eyes would close and then he would force them open, trying to keep control of the situation. Eventually, the gun slipped from his hand and the soldier pounced forward and picked it up. The German never moved.

'I'll kill the bastard,' the solider shouted, his patience at breaking point.

'No, said Alice, 'there is no need. He will be out for a long time. Untie the couple,' she instructed him. With the rope from them, he tied up the German and laid him face down on the floor.

The old couple, who spoke no English, were pleased to be free of their restraints. She began to bustle around making a meal while he put more kindling on the fire. Soon there was a delicious aroma of rabbit stew and root vegetables. They were seated at the kitchen table and, while his wife dished up, the man fetched a bottle of red wine.

All this time, about two hours, the German never stirred. Alice said to the soldier, 'Should we take him back with us to the Dakota?'

He went over to where the German lay and said, 'No, we've too many of our own chaps.'

At first light, Alice looked out of the farm kitchen window to see a clear sky. After a breakfast of bread and cheese and more wine, Alice longed for a cup of tea and hoped that the big urn of tea on board would still be warm.

The time came for them to depart and they thanked the couple for their hospitality. With a glance at the German prisoner, who no doubt would soon be coming round, the farmer reassured them that he and his wife would be fine; he had the German's gun.

Outside, Alice and the soldier climbed into the truck and had only driven a few yards, when they heard the sound of gunfire. They looked at each other. Neither spoke and they carried on towards the airstrip.

Chapter Thirty-Three

The courageous flights of the air ambulance nurses, who were affectionately named the Flying Nightingales, became well known and they were an established part of the crew who flew these missions. The men, and sometimes women, who were casualties at the front or in trouble spots, knew when they saw their plane touch down they would be safe and soon on their way home.

Paris had been liberated and now the war in Europe was over, but the Japanese had not yet surrendered. Alice and the crew of the Dakota touched down at Le Bourget, Paris and she caught a glimpse of General de Gaulle's tall figure in the distance amidst the crowds of people who were celebrating. They had no time to join in the merrymaking for, once the supplies were offloaded, they were on their way.

On one trip to France, Alice was approached by a soldier. 'Could you do me a favour?' he asked.

Alice looked at his earnest face and wondered what he meant. 'I will if I can,' she replied.

He drew a letter from his breast pocket and whispered, 'Will you post this to my girl back home?'

Alice took the letter from his outstretched hand. 'Of course I will,' she said, putting it in the side pocket of her bag. And so it became a regular occurrence to post letters from servicemen to their loved ones back home. Once, a French woman caught hold of Alice's arm and thrust a letter into her hand. Alice didn't understand the French language, accept for a few words, and the woman spoke in a garbled tongue, but Alice picked up the drift of it. 'For your daughter?' she said. Tears flooded the woman's dark eyes and she showed Alice a tiny photograph of a young girl about the age of four or five. Alice felt tears prick at her own eyes as she thought of her own daughter; if only she could post a letter to her.

'Time to go,' one of the crew shouted to her

'I will post it, madam,' she assured the woman, who thanked her profusely.

There were many flying missions bringing wounded troops home and there were terrible tales of civilian atrocities they had seen and witnessed. Hearing this, Alice felt for those who had suffered so much under the regime of Hitler.

'To think that humans could inflict such barbarisms on mankind, it's inhuman,' Alice said to Talli as they climbed into their bunks that night. 'I'm glad I'm a nurse, taking care of the wounded and helping to save lives.' This was in tune with her beliefs and thinking. 'What do you think?' There was no reply from Talli, just the gentle sound of snoring.

Away early the next day, they flew two missions back-to-back and it wasn't until the next night and back on base that Alice caught up with the news and what was happening. What interested her most was the liberation of the POW camps. A few days later, she and Talli were having a rare night off and had gone to the cinema to see a lively musical, but what caught her attention was the Pathé News. It showed earlier footage of British and Commonwealth POWs being marched from their camp by German soldiers in January and February 1945 in the bitter cold temperatures of minus 13 degrees Fahrenheit. As they watched the heart-rending trudge of the men, Alice suddenly said loudly, 'That's Johnny.' She was on her feet staring at the screen and oblivious to the remarks made around her to 'be quiet and sit down'.

She and Talli sat through the whole film again until the Pathé News came on once more. By now they had moved to sit on the front row. 'It *is* Johnny,' Alice whispered. 'I'd know him anywhere.'

Because she was not Johnny's next of kin or indeed a member of his family, she found it difficult to find any news about him. Desperate to know where he was and how he was, she wrote to Maureen, Johnny's sister. After two whole weeks of waiting, she received a reply from her.

Dear Alice,

Johnny is seriously wounded with the loss of a leg and is in a military hospital. We are not sure when he will be coming home. Mother is very upset, because she doesn't know how she can care for him as Father has had a stroke and needs all her attention. I am married and I have recently given birth to twins, so I won't be able to care for Johnny. Everything is in a muddle and we don't know which way to turn. Would you be able to help? I have told Mother you are a friend of Johnny's.

Alice sat for a long time with the letter in her hand. She was so very relieved her Johnny was coming home. But her darling

Johnny who loved walking, cycling and enjoying the freedom these activities gave him wouldn't be able to . . . Tears flooded her eyes and she couldn't allow her thoughts to be negative. Whatever life threw at them, as long as they were together and loved each other, they would survive. She gave a huge sigh and, finding her pen and paper, she replied to Maureen, giving her reassurance she would take care of Johnny because she loved him and asking her to forward on his hospital address.

Her next step would be to seek a divorce from Ted Goddard. 'I'll have to take leave to go home and see a solicitor,' she said to Talli after she'd told her the news about Johnny.

But it wasn't to be. All leave was cancelled, because they were still involved in bringing the wounded home.

He woke with a start, sweat bathing his ravaged and broken body. He felt the truck skid and shudder on the ice-packed track. Momentarily, his mind flashed back to the PCW camp and then to the march in the coldest winter months of 1945. His head half raised, he heard the sound of expletives in the Russian language as the driver righted the truck. A sigh of relief escaped Johnny's scabbed lips and he sank back on the sacking covering the floor of the vehicle. Bodies packed near him groaned and then were quiet. Johnny shut his eyes and tried to conjure up the face of Alice, but it kept slipping out of his vision. 'Where are you?' he muttered, feeling delirious with the attacking pain. His head ached, and his leg felt numb. The medication given to him by a Russian medic was wearing off. They had picked him up from the roadside where he had fallen and been left for dead by the German guards. If the Russian hadn't come along at that precise moment, he would have died. The rhythm of the rattling wheels of the truck lulled him back into the sanctuary of dark oblivion.

When next he was conscious, he felt his body lifted and loaded onto a stretcher and then into the softness of a bed, which later he was told was in a military hospital. He drifted in and out of consciousness and thought he was back in the POW camp and that someone wanted to hack off his leg.

'We have no alternative,' a man's strong voice said.

'No,' Johnny cried out. 'No!'

'Sorry, old chap, but gangrene has set in and if we do not operate, you will lose the whole leg and your life could be in danger.'

When next he awoke it was to a nurse taking his temperature. 'Alice,' he whispered and slipped back into drowsiness, contented because she was near.

'How are you feeling?' said a male voice.

Johnny stirred and opened his eyes to see a surgeon standing by his bedside. 'Where's Alice?' he asked, but no one answered.

The sister, attending with the surgeon, drew back the bedcovers to reveal a cage protecting his severed limb. Johnny's leg had been amputated from below the knee. He lay there, listening to them discussing him and it was as if they were talking about someone else. It was nothing to do with him. That night, when the ward lights were dimmed, he buried his head under the blanket and wept. He felt as though everything was crushing down on him. Alice would never want him now. He might as well have died by the roadside for now his life was over.

'Letter for you, Johnny,' said the caring voice of a middle-aged woman, one of the volunteers who came into the hospital to help in non-nursing activities, such as writing letters for those whose hands were damaged, or who had lost arms or sight. They posted letters and delivered them as well, and sometimes they would shop for presents or cards for the patients' families or, in the case of Johnny, just sit and hold his hand until his black moods evaporated.

She placed the letter on his locker and Johnny stared at it, recognising Alice's perfect handwriting. He thought back to when he'd first met her at night school when they were both raw students and how she'd taken pride in her handwriting. His heart raced, his pulse rose, and a pain caught in his throat. In the POW camp, Alice was constantly in his thoughts, day and in the black hours of the night when sleep evaded him. She was his reason for living, for surviving – and now . . . ? He raised his body on his elbows to look down at the empty space where his leg should be. Alice wouldn't want him now, a cripple for life and not a whole man. Then, with one powerful swipe, he sent the letter flying across the spotless floor of the ward and he let out a deep, throaty scream, which was reminiscent of a battle cry.

The hush on the ward was instant. A nurse moved swiftly to his side and a doctor was summoned and Johnny was given a sedative to calm him down, but he knew that when he next awoke, the problem would still be there.

When he woke up later it was dark and only a night light by the nurses' central table shone. The duty nurse must have been tuned in to his awakening, because she came down the ward, carrying the night light, towards him. 'How are you feeling now, Johnny?'

He gave a wry smile and uttered, 'Not bad.'

She checked his pulse, temperature and blood pressure, and seemed satisfied. She poured him a glass of water and asked, 'Are you hungry?' He responded with a shake of his head. She helped him to sit up and passed the glass to him.

It was then he noticed the letter, Alice's letter, was there on his locker top, waiting.

The nurse saw his glance and said, 'I'll leave the night light with you.'

Johnny stared at the letter and tears sprang into his eyes. He dashed them away, and then he heard a distinct voice within him say, 'Let me see your back, lad. Why, it's broad and strong, and you can face anything.' It was one of his mother's sayings when he left school and was going out into the scary world of work.

He reached for the letter and felt the tremble of his hand as he held it. He tore open the envelope and let out a shuddering breath and then he focused his eyes to read the worst.

My darling Johnny,
You are alive and this is all I ask for. I kept you safe in my heart until you returned to me, my darling. I am applying for a twenty-four-hour pass, so that I can come and see you. Maureen told me of your injuries and, whatever you think, nothing will shock me. I have seen too many wounded men and all that matters to me, my darling Johnny, is our love for each other and that will never dim. I just want to come and see you, to see your smiling face, to look into your loving eyes and kiss you, and hold you close, my precious man.

Johnny wept tears of joy. He read the letter over and over again and then he pressed those loving words close to his pounding heart. Never in his whole life had he experienced such intensity of love. It didn't matter whether she had got her divorce or not, because he was going to live with her as her husband and she as his wife. He might only have one whole leg and half of another, but he had two good hands, and he would work and provide for her. He loved Alice and she loved him, and that was all that mattered.

He fell asleep, a sleep full of sweet dreams of him and Alice running joyfully along the beach, the warm sea lapping their feet as the waves rippled on the sand. Then, hand in hand, they fell into the soft, silky sands and made breathtaking love and the warm sea washed over them. He woke up with a smile on his face as he thought, *Well, I haven't lost that art.* He felt an overwhelming joy of happiness knowing that the seed of life would continue to flow, and he would be with his beloved Alice. Nothing else was going to come between them. Ever.

Chapter Thirty-Four

Alice was on the train travelling down to Surrey to see Johnny in hospital. The journey was tedious and never-ending, and the train seemed to go slower – or was it her heart racing too fast? She just wanted to see him after all these wasted years of war, but her longing would soon be over. Damn, she thought, after being told she had to change trains at London and had to cross the city by bus. Sitting on the top deck, she glanced down on the people scurrying about their daily business. Britain had won the war against the terrible regime of Hitler and the horrendous crimes committed by the Nazis . . . and yet? Now the jubilation, the street parties, the dancing and singing were over, according to the newspapers and the wireless, people were now subdued. As the bus travelled slowly along, Alice noticed a woman walking along the pavement with two young children who were tugging at her skirt while she pushed a baby in a pram. Their clothes were clean but tired-looking, and the mother had a look of despair on her face and her shoulders were hunched. Alice wondered if her husband had come home from war and was back to work, or was injured and not able to work, or maybe had not returned at all. She shuddered and closed her eyes for a moment, thinking and being thankful Johnny was now safe, but as for the state of his health, that would take time to recover. She felt apprehensive and at the same time felt full of joy at seeing him.

It was late afternoon by the time she arrived at the hospital. She would have loved a cup of tea and to freshen up, but first she wanted to see Johnny, her man. He was in one of the main wards and was asleep. She approached his bed on tiptoe and when she gazed down at his beloved face, she gave a silent, inward gasp. His face was thin and ravaged by pain due to his time spent in the POW camp and having poor-quality food, and little of that, by the state of him, which showed in the deep lines etched around his eyes and mouth. Then her gaze travelled down to the cage protecting his amputated limb and she bit on her lip to stifle a cry.

Then, as if sensing her presence, he opened his eyes and said softly, 'Alice, you've come.' He reached out a thin, bony hand to her and said, 'I need to feel you.'

Tears filled her eyes, but her heart sang as she sat down on the chair an orderly had brought for her. She clasped his hand in hers, brought it to her lips and kissed it gently. 'You are safe, Johnny,' she whispered, her voice breaking with emotion. 'I love you.'

Now tears filled his eyes as he said, 'I've waited so long to hear your voice say those words to me.'

She reached out to him and kissed his lips, so cold and brittle, but that wasn't important, because what really mattered was that Johnny had come back to her. Caressing back his dark hair from his forehead, she struggled with her pent-up emotions. She wanted to lay her head on his chest and sob with relief, but for now, she had to be strong for him.

She stayed with him, holding his hand, talking until his eyelids drooped and he drifted into sleep with a smile on his face.

In the nearby village, she was lodging for two nights with a woman who was a widow, whose family had long since left home. Alice enjoyed a meal of roast rabbit with fresh vegetables.

'The vegetables are from my own garden and the rabbit came from the local gamekeeper, and in return I cook him a meal or two. Just to keep friendly, like,' the woman said. 'When you've finished, you can have a nice hot bath to wash away all that travelling.'

It was pure luxury to soak in a bath, to take as long as she liked and not have to think of having to save the water for someone else. She stretched out her legs and then it hit her – Johnny had lost part of his leg. And then her tears, which she'd held back for far too long, began to flow.

Surprisingly, she slept soundly in a strange bed, but, when she thought about it, she'd slept in many strange places and not always in a bed. Once, she and Talli were stranded in Belgium, coming under attack from a stray group of Germans who didn't know that the war was over, and they had spent the night under a hedge. It was a clear night and the sky was filled with a multitude of twinkling stars. They tried to go to sleep, but to no avail so, as there were no sheep to count, they began to count the stars and it had worked, for a time, until . . . Alice had woken up with a start to see a tiny creature of the night, a field mouse, nibbling at her hand. Being a city girl, she wasn't used to the wilds of the countryside, so for the rest of the night under the hedge she didn't sleep, but lay watching and waiting for when it was safe for them to return to the aircraft.

Next morning, coming down the stairs, Alice could smell the tantalising aroma of bacon frying in a pan. Her landlady bustled around her kitchen, happy to have someone to look after. 'Sit down and pour out a cup of tea, my dear,' she said as she bent forwards to take from the oven a newly baked loaf of bread. Alice felt her tastebuds spring into quick action at the mouth-watering smell of the hot bread.

She felt refreshed after the hearty breakfast of bacon and eggs, a gallon of tea and the bread. She could have eaten the whole loaf, but that was just a greedy thought, she mused, as she set off to see Johnny.

The night before, Alice had had a word with the ward sister to say that she only had today to see Johnny and would she be permitted to visit him for most of the day. The sister was understanding and suggested that Alice was welcome to use the staff dining room.

Johnny was sitting up in bed and looking cheerful, his face lighting up when he saw her approaching. 'Hello, sweetheart,' she said as she bent to kiss him full on the lips. Lips that, today, were warmer and not quite so brittle.

Someone gave a low whistle and a chirpy voice exclaimed, 'How about a kiss for me, love?'

Johnny laughed, and Alice turned to the man in the next bed. He had an arm missing and other injuries. She turned back to Johnny, who nodded. Alice went to the man's bedside and kissed him on the cheek and said, 'How about that?'

The man put his hand to his cheek and said, 'Shan't wash it away.'

Alice settled down on a chair at Johnny's side and reached out to hold his hand. He whispered to her, 'Any chance of you hopping into bed with me?'

She squeezed his hand and replied, 'Anytime.'

Johnny didn't seem to want to talk about his time as a POW and Alice didn't press him. If and when he wanted to talk about it, she would listen. They continued with the light-hearted banter as it took away any stilted conversation and soon they began to talk of their future together.

'As soon as I'm discharged from the WAAF and back home, I'm going to start divorce proceedings.' Though she didn't mention the fact that it could take about three to four years for a divorce to become absolute.

'Children, how many shall we have?'

These words from Johnny dealt a blow to her heart. They had never talked about children before and she felt numb with fear of the unknown. When in hospital, Alice was told that she couldn't conceive any more children, though the doctors could be wrong.

Johnny must have seen the look of uncertainty on her face because he said, 'Well, one, then.'

She smiled at him and reached for his hand, not saying anything at first and, hoping her voice sounded normal, she replied, 'Lovely idea, but let's get you better and back home first, then we can plan for the rest of our lives.'

His voice had an edge to it as he replied, 'I might be minus part of my leg and a foot, but everything else is in working order.'

Alice felt devastated. How could she have been so insensitive? There was a moment of silence between them and she was saved from replying when a cheery voice called, 'Cup of tea, dearies?'

It was one of the homely volunteers who pushed her trolley round every morning and afternoon, with never a day off. 'You're my family,' she told all the patients. She was a widow who had lost her two sons in the war.

Alice listened to the banter between the volunteer and the patients, and then she tuned out, letting her thoughts drift. She had to be truthful with Johnny and tell him that she had a daughter who had been taken from her. She was classed as a bad mother who had abandoned her child. How could she put that into words to the man she loved? But she wanted to spend the rest of her life with him, so she would have to tell him about Daisy. But would he still want her? She felt overwhelmed with guilt. His parents and sister, how would they view her, a married woman seeking a divorce and a mother who in the eyes of everyone had deserted her child to be brought up by others? What kind of person did that make her? For one brief moment, she wished she was dead. But then she was no defeatist. She sat up straighter on the chair, determined to find what had happened to her daughter and who had taken her into their home.

'What are you thinking about?' Johnny's voice brought her out of her reverie.

She looked into his anxious face and replied, 'How lucky I am to have the man I love back by my side.' She reached up to him, cupped his face in her hands and kissed him full on the lips. She felt his thin body tremble and she slipped her arms around his shoulders, gently drawing him closer and letting him rest his head on the soft cushion of her breasts. Tears pricked at her eyes, tears of joy and hope for their future.

For the rest of their day together they were content to be in each other's company, laughing, talking about the days when they first met at night school, and when she was training to be a nurse, and leaving letters at the porters' lodge. They remembered their illicit lovemaking when camping, but it was their time together at Scarborough that lingered most in their minds.

'When we are married, we'll go to Scarborough for our honeymoon,' said Johnny.

'Sounds like bliss,' murmured Alice as she nibbled at his ear.

'I'll have no ears left,' he protested, laughing.

'Ears are the fastest growing part of your body.'

'Never.'

The ward sister allowed Alice to stay until supper time, but, all too soon, the time to go came. 'I'll come again, my darling, just as soon as I have leave, and I'll write to you.' This time it was Johnny who cupped her face and kissed her lips, a passionate kiss, so full of love and hope. She didn't want to leave him, but she held back her tears.

The next morning, she was up early on her way back to camp. The train was full, and the man seated next to her tried to engage her in conversation, but she yawned and closed her eyes. She wanted to relive her precious time with Johnny. She had been there when the nurse had come to change the dressing on his stump. It looked to be healing, but there was still some rawness and it would be some time before he could have a prosthesis fitted and learn to walk on it. In the meantime, his body would be built up with food and exercise, and he would gain weight and strength. In her time of nursing in hospitals and with the air ambulance, she'd seen many amputees, and it had never touched her. Now, seeing Johnny, the enormity of such a loss struck her. 'That is the tragedy of war.'

'I beg your pardon,' said the man next to her.

Alice hadn't realised that she'd spoken aloud. She opened her eyes to look at him and, as she did so, he removed the dark glasses he was wearing. She gasped. 'You're blind.'

'Yes, I am. I was a bomber pilot and am lucky to be alive.'

She found herself telling him about Johnny and his injuries, and her work with the air ambulances, and he told her how he was training to be a piano tuner and hopefully one day would play in a band.

Then he suddenly asked, 'And what about you?'

'I'm not sure what you mean,' she replied.

'When I became blind, my other senses became stronger and I can detect in your voice that something, besides Johnny's injuries, is troubling you.'

'You're very perceptive.' And then she found herself telling a complete stranger all about her daughter, Daisy, and how she came to be taken from her. And about her intended divorce from her cruel husband, that it could take three to four years to become absolute.

His words came quickly. 'Have you checked to see if this errant husband of yours is still alive?'

'No! That never occurred to me.'

'Then you should make enquiries. And your daughter, you know in your heart what you must do.'

A station name was called out and the man rose from his seat and said, 'This is my stop. I wish you well,' and he held out his hand for her to shake.

His handshake was warm and firm, and seemed to impart strength into her. She wondered how he would manage in alighting from the train and he must have sensed her thoughts for he said, 'I have my trusted company.'

It was then Alice saw the guide dog that had been lying at his feet.

She watched him go, a young man of courage and a great inspiration to all mankind.

She felt truly humbled to have met him, the stranger on the train.

When the end of the war was declared and after all the festivities in Osbournby village, the evacuees were being sent back to their homes. Mrs Cooper-Browne didn't want Daisy back and said she was now eighteen and old enough to look after herself. She had forwarded on to her a post office savings book with one hundred pounds deposited and a brown envelope.

Daisy was up in her room, sat on the edge of the bed. She put the savings book to one side and picked up the brown envelope. She sensed it was important and she turned it over in her hands, wondering what it could contain. In her heart, she hoped and prayed it was about her mother. And how to find her. But what if it was from the authorities and they were going to make her live in another place? She wasn't ever going to do that. She would run away. Her hands began to sweat, and she rubbed them down her skirt.

Finally, she carefully wedged her forefinger under the envelope flap and opened it. Inside was a document saying that Daisy Goddard had been given into the care of Mrs Cooper-Browne after being abandoned by her mother, Mrs Alice Goddard. It was signed by a Mrs Melton. She was called Daisy Goddard, not Cooper-Browne, which she'd always thought was a daft name. And her mother's name was Alice. 'Alice,' she said out loud. 'What a pretty name.'

And then she saw it. A small pencil drawing of a beautiful young woman with a smiling face and she knew instinctively this was her mother. She studied it for some time, taking in every feature and the laughing eyes. With tender strokes, she traced a finger over the portrait and then, lifting it up to her face, she tenderly brushed her lips over it. For a long time, she sat with the drawing of her beloved mother in the palm of her hand, just gazing at it. She placed it on top of her dressing table and decided she would make a mount and frame for it, so that she could hang it on the wall opposite her bed. It would be the last thing she saw before sleeping and the first thing she saw when she woke up.

Next in the envelope were birthday cards to her from her mother, each one with a handwritten verse, telling how much she loved Daisy and that she missed her every day. She always knew in her heart that her mother loved her and had not willingly abandoned her, as Mrs Cooper-Browne was fond of telling her. She lay down on the bed, the cards clutched to her chest, near to her heart and she wept tears of joy and sadness intermingled.

Later, she went to find Wilf to tell him what was in the envelope. 'So, what shall we do now?' he asked her. Mr and Mrs Jessop's sons were coming home and there would be no room or jobs for them on the farm. And after Wilf's mother had died during the war, his father had remarried and there was no room at home for Wilf.

'I want to go where you go, Wilf,' she said, panic filling her.

'I'll always look after you.' And then as an afterthought, he added, 'We could get married.'

'But how can we do that?'

So that evening they asked Mrs Jessop if she could help them. 'It's a nice idea, but when you marry it's for life and you're both so young. Are you sure?' She looked seriously at them.

They both nodded. Daisy felt for Wilf's hand and held it tight. They knew nothing about married life and what was expected of them. The most they had done was kissing and a tumble in the hayloft. And they'd seen the pigs gave birth to lots of piglets.

'I'd better tell you about the birds and the bees,' Mrs Jessop said with a twinkle in her eyes.

Mrs Jessop arranged everything with the vicar. And Mr Jessop got in touch with his brother who owned a caravan site. He was looking for someone to run it and clean out the vans each week, and there was a cottage to live in. Mrs Jessop took Daisy into

Sleaford and helped her to choose an outfit, a two-piece costume in powder blue with a blouse and hat to match, new white sandals and a handbag, and new underwear and nightgowns. She and Mr Jessop paid for everything.

'It's the least we can do. Now you keep your savings for when you move to your own home, because there will be things you'll need.'

Daisy and Wilf arrived in the village of Fleetwick on the east coast of Yorkshire amidst a raging storm. That night they huddled together, fearful of the sea almost on their doorstep.

But when they awoke in the morning, it was to a calm sea lapping on the shore of sand and shingles. Both still in their night attire, they ran barefoot down to the sea edge and splashed about in the frothy water, frolicking like two children. And when their energy was spent they flopped on the beach, entwined in each other's arms.

Chapter Thirty-Five

On the base, things were starting to wind down. Talli was on leave and she and Jeff were visiting her parents. Alice had a feeling that wedding bells would soon be ringing. Meanwhile, she caught up with her letter writing to Miss Bailey and a letter of condolence to Evelyn's parents. The death of Evelyn had shaken her. She had perished in a POW camp in Singapore, just before the camp was liberated. Evelyn was a truly brave woman and a courageous nurse whose only vocation in life was to care for people and make them well again. The tragedy of war is that it does not differentiate between good and evil. There was so much more she wanted to write about Evelyn, but perhaps these were not the right words for her parents to read. Alice gave a heavy sigh and rose from the chair to stretch her stiff body. She gazed out of the window to see a group of pilots and crew kicking a football around, their voices high-spirited. But she could see on their faces and in their eyes the pressure of doing a job well done and the uncertainty of not knowing if they would return. Now the war was over and won, how would they settle down to civilian life? No one was exempt, from the top ranks down to the bottom, unless you chose to remain in the forces. There was a whooping cheer from the players below as a goal was scored.

She went back to her letter writing to the bereaved parents. Evelyn had been her first real friend and mentor after she'd come out of hospital. Evelyn knew about Daisy and she had never reproached her or said she was neglectful. After the end of the war that was one of the things she'd been looking forward to, talking to Evelyn again and seeking her wisdom. Sealing the envelope, she wept tears of sorrow for the loss of her dear friend.

'Cheer up, love, it might never happen,' said the woman clearing the table of the debris of the midday meal.

Alice mentally shook herself and went to check the noticeboard to see what was happening. Some of the other air ambulance nurses were also having a look.

'Don't think I can face any more,' one of the nurses said. 'I just wanna go home now.'

Alice moved nearer to see. The notice was asking for volunteers to fly out to a camp in Poland. Alice put her name forward and the next day she was airborne along with another nurse. They weren't told anything and were not sure what to expect, but nothing could ever have prepared them for what they found. This POW camp, somehow, had slipped through the net of the system.

Living skeletons. The stench of human decay was entrenched in the earth and the air around the camp. At the first gasp of the foulness, Alice choked and then ignored it. Nothing in her nursing career had prepared her for this: human degradation on such a vast scale. And yet, some of the POWs, now free men, smiled and one man gave her a wolf whistle. She answered the banter. 'You've made my day.' She smiled at the man. His body was emaciated, his face gaunt and his eyes were like two lumps of black coal, but he still had spirit.

She and Doris, the nurse she'd flown with, set about their work with other air ambulance nurses. Some men were too ill and frail to be flown home yet. A field hospital had been set up close by and nurses and doctors would see to their care until they were well enough to fly home to continue their care in hospitals in Britain.

She and Doris, with their patients, were waiting for transport to take them to the plane. As the truck drew up, a woman in ATS uniform jumped out and called, 'Staff Nurse Goddard?'

Alice, alert, said, 'Yes.'

'It's me, Hetty,' said the ATS with a wide smile.

Then Alice recognised the smart, striking-looking woman as one of the girls from Faith House. They clasped hands and then Alice hugged her, saying, 'What a pleasant surprise.' Just to see one of the girls who had come through the care and teaching at Faith House filled her with pride. She had heard of others, but it was good to meet up with one, though she wished it had been in different circumstances.

Hetty soon had everyone organised and in the truck. She drove carefully, mindful of her precious passengers. Each day she drove to the camp, so she somehow got used to the terrible sights. She was still wary of men after her abuse by them and then being forced into prostitution, but she wouldn't wish what they had endured on any man. Faith House had been her escape route and Mrs Goddard, although she'd never told her, was her mentor. Back then, she'd never heard of the word 'mentor' until she came across it in a library book she was reading and liked the sound of it.

Hetty helped with the transferring of the patients into the air ambulance, while the two nurses saw to the less able-bodied ones.

Time to head back to collect more patients who were homeward bound. 'Bye, Mrs Goddard,' she said. 'Might see you tomorrow.'

'Thanks, Hetty, for all your help, and it's Alice, not Mrs Goddard.'

Hetty jumped back into the truck, started up the engine and was soon away. Alice – so that was her name. She'd never known.

'God have mercy!' Alice said as she and Doris opened the door of a hut and stood on the threshold. The stench smacked them in the face and she thought she was going to be sick. She bit on her lip. There was no time to think about herself; she was here to do a job. *So do it*, she admonished herself. The interior of the hut was gloomy after the brightness of the outside and at first, she thought it was empty, but as her eyes became accustomed she could see two bunks were occupied.

'I'll go to the next hut,' said Doris, not waiting for a reply.

As Alice ventured across the floor, her feet stuck and bonded to whatever it was covering the hard grit surface: blood, faeces and urine, mixed with the smell of rats. She scraped her shoes on the side of a bunk and then watched where she trod.

One of the men raised himself up and said, 'He's nearly a goner. I couldn't leave him.'

She didn't speak, but passed the man a small bottle of water from her bag.

Turning to the other man, she could see that death wasn't far away. She found a scrap of blanket to kneel on by his side, and she felt for his pulse. It was faint. She then wiped his dry, cracked and blistered lips with a soothing balm and, with a sponge, she gave him a drop of water. His eyes opened slightly and, gently, she wiped away the caked crust from them. He opened his eyes wider and his bony fingers gripped at hers. She watched as he tried to form words and she bent her head to catch what he was saying.

'Alice, is it you?' The words were slurred like a man drunk.

She reeled back.

The other man, now sitting on his bunk, said, 'He keeps on about this Alice.'

She felt as though her breath was seeping from her. *Pull yourself together, you are a nurse*, a voice inside her head commanded. So she did.

'Who is she?'

'Wife, I think. Said he'd done her wrong.'

Alice turned back to the patient who lay still with his eyes open and fixed on her. 'Ted?'

His eyes blinked in acknowledgement.

This man was Ted Goddard, her husband, and he was dying. She bit on her lip to stop the tide of emotion within her surfacing. She smoothed back his hair and held his hand. It felt nothing like the feel of it when he'd dealt her blow after blow, but she had to forget all that and concentrate on now. She would never leave a man to die on his own, no matter what he'd done to her.

Suddenly, she heard the voice of Doris. 'God, what's on this floor?'

Alice looked up at her as she peered over her shoulder. 'He's not got long.'

'Poor blighter. Who is he?'

'Ted Goddard,' said the other man.

'My husband. Check his pulse, please.'

Doris stared at her. Then she stated the obvious. 'He's gone.'

Outside, Alice breathed in the air and felt the warmth of the sun on her face, then she let the tears fall. Many times in the past she'd wished Ted dead, but never for him to die in such squalor. She brushed aside her tears and went to find the officer in charge to report the death. She walked as if her body and legs were moving in opposite directions.

That night, back in her bed, she couldn't sleep. She could hear Talli's soft breathing as she slept. She wished she smoked; a cigarette would calm her nerves. Swinging her legs out of bed, she went over to Talli's bedside locker and shook out one of the cigarettes from the packet of Pall Mall kept there. 'Take the lot,' a sleepy voice said and she did. Pulling on her dressing gown, she went outside and sat on a grassy hump and lit a cigarette. Inhaling deeply, she relished the sensation and blew out a wisp of smoke and watched it as it spiralled upwards and disappeared towards the heavens. She stared up at the midnight-blue sky, full of a multitude of stars, and she thought of her daughter and whispered, 'Daisy, where are you?' Her heart ached with a yearning to hold her child in her arms and talk to her. It was then that a realisation emerged, like a door unlocking.

She was free. She was a widow. She would not be a divorced woman. So, if she didn't have to concentrate on applying for a divorce, she would have more time to devote to tracing where her daughter was living. She lit another cigarette. Suddenly, she felt the great heaviness of the burden she'd carried for so long lift from her heart. Next week she would be visiting Johnny again and she had so much to tell him.

Over the next few months, Johnny's walking with his prosthesis gained momentum with each day. It was October and the late autumn sun shone as Johnny and Alice walked with arms linked. He still had the support of a walking stick, but that didn't mar their happiness. 'We are together and that's all I need,' Alice reassured him. The path they walked down was lined with trees, their leaves in various shades of gold, red and bronze. Johnny's pace slowed, and his breathing became laboured.

Alice said, 'Look at that majestic oak, it's got a seat going round its trunk. My back aches, shall we have a rest?' With her hand, she swiped the fallen leaves off the seat and they sat down. For a while, neither spoke, but watched a squirrel foraging amongst the fallen leaves. Gradually, Johnny's breathing returned to normal. Alice was thinking of something to say that didn't entail speaking about her work and the horrors she'd witnessed or about Johnny's progress, which they'd already exhausted, when he spoke.

'I've this to show you.' He withdrew a letter from the breast pocket of his jacket. 'Read it.' He thrust it to her.

She glanced at him, trying to gauge his mood, but his face gave no trace of it. With unsteady fingers, she took the sheet of paper from the envelope and read.

Dear Son,

Dad and I are happy to hear your good news. It's time you settled down to married life. I didn't like to worry you before, but Dad suffered a mild heart attack and not a stroke as we first feared. Working all day and firewatching on nights has taken its toll on him, but he won't hear of giving up work. So, I've made the decision to take the post of housekeeper, with our own flat, for a retired couple in a large house in Wharfedale. Dad will look after the vegetable garden and do a few odd jobs — nothing too strenuous. The fresh country air will do us both good. Now it brings me to our house, which survived the bombing of our city. As you know, our Maureen is settled in to married life and has her own house, so Dad and I are offering our house to you and your future wife. What do you say?

Write back soon.

Your loving mam xx

Alice reread the letter again and then turned to Johnny. His eyes were full of joy. 'What do you think?'

'It's a generous offer. What do you think?'

'It's just right for us; it's a family house.'

'But what if we don't have children?' she blurted. He looked at her in surprise. 'Perhaps I'll be too old.'

'Nonsense, you're still young and vibrant, and you'll make a lovely mother.' He pulled her to him and kissed her full on the lips and whispered, 'All that matters to me is having you as my wife.'

As they walked back along the path, Johnny chatted animatedly about their future and she didn't interrupt. She knew she should tell him about Daisy – it was now or never. 'Johnny, I—'

'There you are,' a voice interrupted. An orderly came into view. 'Sister's on the warpath.'

'Damn,' Johnny muttered, 'I'm late for my physiotherapy session.'

Johnny went off with the orderly, and Alice went to sit in the visitor's sitting room and was thankful to see it empty. She sat, staring out of the window at the darkening sky. Was she doing the right thing, marrying Johnny, if he had his heart set on having children of his own? What would he say when she told him that she had a daughter? After the accident, her pelvis was damaged, and it was doubtful if she would ever conceive a child again. She knew that before she went back to base, she must tell Johnny the truth, the whole truth.

Chapter Thirty-Six

Alice didn't get a chance to tell Johnny about Daisy until later the next day. They walked along the same path as yesterday, but today the sky was overcast, and dark clouds hung about. When they reached the oak tree, they sat down on the circular wooden bench.

'You're very quiet,' Johnny said. 'Not having second thoughts about marrying me?'

Alice felt her heart race as though she'd just run up a mile-long steep hill. She looked out across the parkland towards the vegetable plot where the volunteer gardener was digging and fixed her gaze on his rhythmic movements, hoping to feel calmness within. She clenched her hands together in her lap, replying, 'No, but you might have second thoughts about marrying me.'

He slipped one arm around her shoulder and his lips touched her cheek with a warm caress. He was just about to lean into her, to turn her face to his, to kiss her, when she drew away from him. She sensed the tensing of his body. 'What is it?' he asked.

She dug the heels of her shoes into the soft earth to keep her steady and to try and stop her uncontrollable trembling. She looked down at her feet, as if looking for some kind of invisible sign to materialise. Slowly, she raised her head, staring across the parkland with unfocused eyes. Her voice quivered as she replied, 'It is something I should have told you at the very beginning of our courtship.' Her eyes blurred with threatening tears and she didn't dare to look at him as she whispered, 'I have a daughter, Daisy.'

A sharp breeze disturbed the leaves on the tree and a blackbird pecked at the grass, foraging for worms. Two wood pigeons swooped down and forced the blackbird away. She waited for Johnny to say something, but he remained silent. She wanted to look at his loving face and for him to tell her everything was all right and that he understood. Still, he didn't speak. Her mind began to drift back to that terrible time when she found out that Daisy had been taken from her. Every avenue she turned to find her was blocked and the consensus was that it was her fault for leaving her at home alone. But Daisy hadn't been home alone, Ted was there. If it hadn't been for his cruel temper, his physical abuse of her, his wife, she wouldn't have been running to the police station for help and the accident wouldn't have happened. If only she—

'Where is she?' Johnny's stony voice broke into her thoughts.

Instinctively, she turned to him, but he didn't meet her eyes, staring straight ahead, his body unyielding.

'I don't know.' She was just about to explain the circumstances, when he cut in.

'You don't know. What kind of mother are you?'

The threatening tears now trickled unheeded down her cheeks. She felt as if her heart was being ripped to pieces. She bit on her lips to stop the sobs from sounding out loud. He was right, what kind of mother was she? How she wished he'd support her and not be like all the other people she'd approached to find her daughter. She wanted reassurance from him. She needed his help and understanding, not his condemnation. Most of all she wanted to find her daughter. A sudden anger whirled up from nowhere within her and with his support or not, she was determined to find Daisy.

'It's raining.' Johnny's clipped tone filled the silence. He rose from the bench and so did she. They walked in silence, their bodies not touching.

At the hospital, without a word, Johnny went off for his physiotherapy. Alice picked up her handbag and nodded to the ward sister, who asked, 'Shall we see you tomorrow?'

'No, I'm going back to base.'

She set off to walk to her digs, her tears mingling with the rain on her face.

Back at base she was greeted by a jubilant Talli. 'Me and Jeff are getting married in two months and we are going to live in Tasmania.' She said it in one long breath.

Alice hugged her friend. 'I hope you will both be very happy.'

'Come down to the pub and celebrate with me tonight.'

Alice didn't feel like celebrating, but she didn't want to spoil her friend's happiness, so she agreed to go.

Later, by the time they'd reached the village pub, everyone had heard the good news.

'Fancy marrying an Aussie. Aren't us Brits good enough?' one of the pilots ribbed Talli.

Drinks flowed, and everyone was merry and good-humoured. The war was over and won, but soon all these scenes of celebration would disappear, because in the newspapers and on the wireless they talked of austerity, so everyone was making the most of the good times. 'Just propaganda,' the landlord said. He had made an excellent living from the air force base and he wanted to continue doing so for longer. He had his eye on a cottage near the sea, and a spot of fishing and drinking on the other side of the bar, telling a yarn or two.

One of the ground crew started to tinkle the ivory keys, so glasses were filled and everyone crowded around the piano for a good rousing sing-song.

At this stage, Alice slipped outside to stand in the yard. She pulled a packet of Gold Flake cigarettes from her pocket and lit up, watching the smoke curl upwards to the stars. The night sky was clear, and the stars shone and sparkled like diamonds. She could see why they were often, in a romantic setting, referred to as diamonds. She inhaled deeply and let out a long sigh. She would never wear a diamond engagement ring. 'Oh, Johnny, if only we could start again from the beginning.' Back then they had no idea that a war would intervene in their lives. Then, she'd lived a fairly naive life. If only she'd been more forceful, more demanding in trying to locate Daisy.

'What are you doing out here?' Talli's joyous voice broke through her gloomy thoughts.

'Just taking a breather.'

'I'm worried about you,' Talli stated. 'You've been too quiet since you returned from seeing Johnny. Have you two fallen out?'

Alice glanced at her perceptive friend and felt this overwhelming desire to unburden herself. She offered her a cigarette, saying, 'Have you time to listen?'

They sat on a piece of broken-down wall, facing away from the joyous activities inside the pub. Alice found herself telling Talli everything, from her terrible time living with Ted, fleeing for her life from the house, her time in hospital, and the finding out her daughter had been taken without her consent. 'The most hurtful thing for me was that everyone blamed me for leaving Daisy alone in the house and said I should be grateful that another family was willing to bring her up as their own. No one mentioned that Daisy's father should have cared for her while I was in hospital.'

There was a silence broken by the cry of an owl seeking its prey. Then Talli spoke. 'Jeepers, Alice, why didn't you tell me all this before?' She gave her a huge bear hug.

'I suppose because of the war and what we saw . . .' Her voice drifted away.

'Come on, you need a strong drink.'

She didn't really. She just wanted to be on her own, but she didn't want to spoil Talli's night. And unburdening herself made her heart feel a little lighter. She gave a big sigh. Now she must think more about the practical side of her life.

Many of the WAAFs had been demobbed and were back in civvies and Talli was among them. She was at home preparing for her wedding next month and Alice was to be her matron of honour. She'd stayed on the base, because she was in no particular hurry to go back home. Home! Where did she call home? In an ideal world, she should be getting a home together for her and Daisy to move into. But from what she'd gathered from the news on the wireless, houses – because so many had been bombed to smithereens by the Germans – were in short supply. Her only option for now was to go back into nursing and live in, and then to consider her next move.

Johnny hadn't been in touch. So, he didn't love her enough. He would want someone to give him children and she couldn't blame him. She'd written many letters to him, but she never posted them. She wondered if he'd been discharged from the hospital and gone home to the house . . . She cut off her thoughts. She must stop torturing herself, stop thinking about him and concentrate on her paramount quest to find Daisy. If it took her the rest of her life, she would find her. She contacted the Red Cross, but they were too busy working with POWs who needed their help to return to families. 'Contact us later' had been their answer.

A whole month had passed and still there was no word from Johnny. She was demobbed now and left a forwarding address back at the base for the hospital nurses' home where she was now living, just in case. She wasn't officially due to start her duties till next month, but there was a room available for her. Today, she was preparing to travel across the Humber on the ferry to Talli's parents' home for the wedding, where she would be staying for a few nights. It was a relief to get away from the nurses' quarters as most of them, especially the ones training, were much younger than her and talked of their young men. Behind her back she'd heard them refer to her as 'the black widow Goddard'. She didn't blame them, because in their eyes she was old and had no sense of humour. She wasn't fun to be around. When Talli's wedding was over, she was determined to find decent lodgings where she could make a home and then begin her search for Daisy, by contacting the Red Cross again to see if there were any other organisations willing to help her. Someone, somewhere, must know of her whereabouts.

Alice sat on the upper deck of the ferry, watching the swirling waters of the Humber until her head started to spin. She moved down to the lower deck and found a seat on the corner of a bench. She withdrew a book from her bag and opened it, but the words on the page blurred and she couldn't read. Instead, she thought of Johnny and hoped he was managing with his prosthetic limb. He was so brave to survive a POW camp and he never complained or talked about it. A great swell of love filled her, and oh, how she missed him. Her man, her Johnny. She wanted to be there for him, to take care of him and to feel his warm body next to hers.

'Good book, is it?' The woman on the bench next to her interrupted her reverie.

Alice glanced at her and nodded, turning over the page as if she was engrossed in the story. Of course, she wasn't reading it, but it helped to stop people from trying to engage her in conversation, small talk.

She went back to her thoughts, thinking of the hours she'd spent flying back and forth across the Channel bringing home the wounded and managing only on snatched hours of sleep. She remembered the horrors of the concentration camps for which she couldn't sleep, because she kept reliving what she'd seen and witnessed: the horrendous degradation of human life. Even though they were now free men, they would probably live with the memory of their incarceration for the rest of their lives and not talk about it to their families or friends. When she'd tried to ask Johnny about his experience, he would clam up and say, 'Best all forgotten.' Maybe that was his way of coping, blotting out those wasted years.

She arrived at Talli's house feeling exhausted. It was as if all the past times she'd gone without sleep were now catching up with her.

Mrs Whitmore, Talli's grandmother, fussed over Alice. 'Come and sit down, love. You look tired. I've made a nice pot of tea, and a Victoria sponge cake with butter cream and home-made plum jam. Now, tuck in.'

Alice nodded her appreciation and was soon enjoying the good wholesome food. Afterwards, she felt a warm glow of contentment as she sat in front of the fire, listening to Talli and Mrs Whitmore talking about the wedding arrangements. Their voices seemed to drift over her. She tumbled into that dreamlike time between sleep and not sleep, and it evoked a memory deep within her heart. She remembered explaining to Daisy when she wanted to know where you went when you were asleep. 'To fairyland, that is an enchanting place of dreams.' And she had replied, 'Am I there now, Mammy?' to be reassured by Alice, 'Yes, my darling, you are.'

Alice must have dozed, because the next thing she knew Talli shaking her arm. 'Come on, sleepy-head. I'll show you your room.'

The next day Alice went with Mrs Whitmore to the village church to decorate it with flowers, mostly wild ones and greenery for the altar, and at the end of each pew they tied a small posy. The day escalated into a frenzy of activity, which kept Alice busy. She swept fallen leaves from the garden path, iced fairy buns, made buttonholes and chatted with neighbours, so she had no time to dwell on things past.

Talli and Jeff's wedding day. Talli had no desire to wear a white, frothy dress and, instead, chose to wear a costume of deep blue, not unlike the blue of the WAAF uniform, but the material was a fine barathea and fitted Talli's slim figure. On her dark wavy hair was a perky hat of the same colour blue. Alice had managed to buy a second-hand dress the colour of primroses and of fine cotton material trimmed with broderie anglaise. For her hair, she wore a band of daisies around the brim of her straw hat.

The day was bright and sunny, a perfect day for a wedding and love. *Love*, Alice thought, *what is it? The love of a mother for her child and the love of a wife for her husband. Stop it!* she commanded herself. *Today is Talli and Jeff's day, so focus on that*, and so she did, though her cheek muscles ached with smiling.

She walked down the aisle behind Talli and her grandfather, passing a sea of faces. On reaching the altar and standing by Jeff's side, Talli turned to hand her posy of white roses to Alice, then she sat down at the end of the pew where she'd been assigned to sit. So intent on watching the ceremony taking place before her, Alice wasn't aware of whom she was sitting next to until she had to stand for the first hymn. She put Talli's bouquet on the ledge in front of her, but it slipped down onto the floor. The person next to her bent down to retrieve it and placed it on the seat as they stood up. It was then she saw who it was.

'Johnny!' She gasped out loud. Talli turned slightly and winked at her.

Alice put her hands together as in prayer, to stop her crying out further, and turned to gaze into those beloved eyes.

He reached for one of her hands, gently squeezed it and whispered, 'I've missed you.'

Her heart began to sing, like a bird freed from its captor. 'I've missed you, too,' she whispered to him. Then both of them tried to focus on Talli and Jeff's wedding ceremony.

Chapter Thirty-Seven

On an early misty morning in April 1946, Alice and Johnny walked hand in hand into Holy Trinity Church in their home city followed by their families and friends. To see them marry by special licence. Talli and Jeff came, and Alice wore the same outfit she wore for her friend's wedding and she carried a posy of roses. Feeling blessed with happiness, she stole a glance at Johnny, her man. He was so handsome standing beside her in his demobbed suit of navy-blue pinstripe and his Brylcreemed hair. As they entered the church, Alice breathed in the stillness of silence, and let the peace and tranquillity satiate her body and her soul. The fragrance of flowers lingered in the air and joy filled her heart. She gently squeezed Johnny's hand in hers.

The ceremony was a quiet affair in contrast to the earlier one of Talli and Jeff but, nevertheless, it was full of love and hope. After taking their vows, the vicar said to Johnny, 'Now you may kiss the bride.'

His lips on hers were tender and held a promise of what was to come.

Outside, the mist had cleared, and the sun shone brightly on the happy couple. Talli threw rose petals filched from her wedding bouquet, while Jeff took photographs with his Kodak Brownie camera, and the atmosphere was light and happy,.

Back at Johnny's home, they were greeted by the aroma of freshly baked bread made by one of the neighbours, there were newly laid eggs in a big frying pan and a joint of ham was ready to be carved. 'Your wedding breakfast,' Johhny's mother announced to the happy couple. It was washed down with plenty of hot tea and his father produced a bottle of whisky.

Glasses were filled, and Mr Mitchell led the toast. 'To the bride and groom. May they have many years of happiness ahead.'

By early afternoon, Alice and Johnny, with their cases packed, said their goodbyes to their families. Alice hugged Talli and said, 'Write to me as soon as you arrive.' Talli and Jeff would soon be setting sail for Tasmania.

When Alice and Johnny arrived in Scarborough, this time they stayed in a hotel at the south end of the resort. It was a beautiful hotel with a grand sweeping staircase, and Alice could imagine an era before the war, when ladies in ballgowns graced the once magnificent ballroom. During the war, the hotel had been used as a convalescent home for the armed forces and was gradually being renovated back to its former glory, although some patients were still in residence.

They had an early meal and then went up to their room. It seemed strange, Alice thought, she and Johnny had in the past shared a bed and made love. Now, they were married, and it felt to her like their first time. She was ready for bed, not in the satin and lace she'd have wished for, but in a cotton nightgown with faded rosebuds. Johnny was a long time in the bathroom and then it struck her like a boulder – his leg, his prosthesis. She was on the verge of going into the bathroom to see if he wanted any help. After all, she was a nurse and used to seeing prostheses and missing limbs, but he must be feeling sensitive at the loss of his leg. She understood he'd want to be independent and keep it on until he reached the bed and then take it off.

She turned the ceiling light off and put on the two bedside lamps, and then went over to look out of the window. The sea rippled calmly in the bay and in the distance she saw the twinkling lights of a boat out fishing. People were strolling along the promenade, taking in the night air before retiring for bed. She heard the bathroom door open and his unsteady footsteps on the carpet. Without turning round, she said, 'The sea looks quite calm, so that must be a good sign of the weather tomorrow. The fresh air will bring colour to our pale cheeks.' She knew she was babbling, but all the time she was listening to his movements and she knew when he had taken off his prosthesis.

Slowly, she turned and saw he was still sitting on the edge of the bed, his back to her. She tiptoed over to her side of the bed and then snaked her body over the counterpane to him. She slipped her arms around his shoulders and began kissing his neck. At first, he remained rigid and she persisted until she felt his body relaxing and then gently she moved nearer to him, twisting her body so that she could see his face. She kissed him on the lips and whispered, 'I love you, Johnny.' Together, they fell backwards onto the bed and she felt the warmth of his rising passion.

That night, they made love many times, each time taking them to glorious heights of pleasure, joy and love.

They overslept and missed breakfast, but found a cafe nearby, and enjoying tea and toast while holding hands under

338

the table and giggling like young lovers. They both admitted to each other, 'We are young lovers with a lot of catching up to do,' and they giggled more, getting sideways glances from other customers in the cafe.

The next three days they spent walking and dodging showers of rain by going into a cafe or shop and, one afternoon, they went to the cinema to see the light-hearted comedy *Here Comes the Sun* with Flanagan and Allen. The afternoon in the cinema was Alice's idea, because she could see that Johnny was tiring and she had a selfish notion for keeping him fit for the night. Their nights were spent exploring each other's bodies and then making love, deep and passionate, until they were finally fulfilled – until the next time.

All too soon, the honeymoon was over, and they were on the train home to Hull. Johnny had sent a telegram to Maureen and she would have the house aired, a fire lit and food in the cupboard to last them for a few days. They were both quiet on the journey. Alice was thinking of her new home and hoped she could run it as well as his mother. 'What are you thinking of?' she asked Johnny.

'My job! I wrote to my boss to tell him I've been discharged from hospital, demobbed and fit to start work, but he hasn't replied yet.'

She looked at his furrowed brow and the worried look in his eyes and she felt full of protective love for him. 'Don't worry. When we arrive home there will be a letter waiting for you.' She was just about to say that she could resume her nursing and bring in money, when she stopped. From what she knew of Johnny, he had pride and he wouldn't want to be kept by his wife. Certainly not. He would be the provider, the one bringing home a wage, not his wife. To be honest, she was looking forward to being a homemaker and taking care of Johnny. She had this feeling that Johnny's mother kept the house running smoothly, and if his parents visited, as they might well do, she wanted to give a good impression. There was a garden, too. She would have loved a garden when Daisy . . . A lump stuck in her throat and her eyes pricked with tears. She turned to look out of the grimy window.

As they emerged from the station to catch a bus, the city, under a grey, cloudy sky, looked even grimmer than when she last was home. On the bus, Alice noticed Johnny's face set in a hard line. She squeezed his hand.

Turning to her, he said, 'I never realised the city had taken such a hammering, so much destruction of people's homes.' His voice grew angry as he stared at this once beautiful city. 'And the fine buildings of great architecture have been crushed to the ground. How come it wasn't mentioned on the wireless when I was in hospital or in newspapers? All the news was of London and other big cities, so why not Hull?'

'I can tell you, mate.' The enraged voice came from the seat behind them. Turning, they saw an old man with fierce-looking eyes, who must have been listening to their conversation. 'Hull was only referred to as a north-east coast town. Supposed to hoodwink the Jerries, but it didn't work.'

'What a cock-eyed idea,' remarked Johnny, offering the man a cigarette and the two men chatted some more. Alice turned to gaze out the bus window, forlornly looking for Daisy.

Johnny's parents' house was in the heart of the area called Garden Village. The building of houses was first initiated by Sir James Reckitt, of Reckitt & Sons Ltd for their employees and families. He formed the private company, the Garden Village, Hull Ltd and invited other Reckitt board members to unite with him in purchasing land near to the factory. This was in 1907 and the business continued to flourish with more houses built, including amenities: shops, a library, clubs and open park spaces with plenty of fresh air for all residents. Added to this, a private company was set up to manage the estate. Alice could remember reading about Garden Village in the library when she first met Johnny, though she had never ventured to the area.

Now she was here, walking down a leafy avenue of fine houses, with gardens and so much space around each house, not cramped together like the house she was brought up in. Though now, her mother and George, and her youngest brother, Charlie, were living in a brand-new house, which had being erected in two months, a prefab. Sadly, one of the twins, Harry, had been lost at sea when the destroyer on which he was serving was sunk with no survivors. War is so brutal and senseless. His twin, Jimmy, survived and was now married with a son. Martha had travelled south and lived in London and, according to their mother, she was in the chorus line of a show.

How the tide of life moves on and never stops flowing. Daisy would now be a young woman. Alice caught her breath at the thought.

Johnny glanced at her and said, 'Are you all right?'

'Just feeling a little overwhelmed.' The truth was she just wanted to find her daughter.

'We're here,' Johnny said, putting down his case.

Alice could see by the strained expression on his face that he'd found the short walk tiring. As they went through the wooden gate, she glanced up at the big house, which was semi-detached. She'd never seen such a wonderful house. Its architecture was a work of beauty and the windows . . .

Suddenly, the front door was flung open. Maureen stepped out onto the porch and welcomed them with a dazzling smile and hugged them both. The hall was almost the same size as her mother's front room in their old house. They followed Maureen into the bright, airy kitchen where the kettle was singing on the stove. Soon, they were settled around the table with its blue checked cloth, drinking tea and tucking into spam sandwiches.

Maureen did most of the talking, though she didn't mention Johnny's lost limb. 'Sorry about the spam sandwiches. It's a bit of a bind us still being on rations. We won the war, you'd have thought the shortages would end, but now bread is rationed. I've managed to get you a small loaf and a few groceries. I've told the shopkeeper you'll be taking your ration books to him.'

'Where is his shop?' She couldn't recall seeing any shops.

Maureen jumped up and said, 'I'll come round tomorrow and take you. Must go and collect the bairns from my mother-in-law's.'

Johnny looked whacked. 'Why don't you go and have a lie-down while I check what food there is and rustle up a meal?' Alice suggested and he agreed.

Alice went to explore the house and was surprised at its spaciousness, picturing a child running around and filling it with joy. She wandered through the sitting and dining rooms, and spied a cloakroom with an inside lavatory. An image of her childhood flashed through her mind of a cold winter's day and the lavatory outside in the yard. At least they hadn't had to share the communal one. She opened the back door and stepped out into the garden. There was an Anderson shelter down at the bottom and the rest of the garden was a bit of a tangle, but it was a good area for children to play hide-and-seek. She closed her eyes and heard the shrill voices of children at play. Quickly opening them, she glanced round the garden, expecting to see children, but it was empty.

Then a voice startled her. 'Hope my bairns didn't disturb you?'

A pleasant-faced young woman was leaning over the adjoining fence. 'No,' said Alice and she introduced herself.

'I'm Sadie. The bairns have gone back to school now. If you need any help, just give me a call. Oh, I nearly forgot.' She dashed indoors and emerged within seconds. 'I've baked this for you. It's only a jam sponge.' She passed it over to Alice.

'That's so kind of you, thank you.' This act of kindness gladdened Alice's heart and made her feel welcomed.

Later that evening, after Johnny had rested and they'd eaten a meal of spam fritters, baked beans and a liberal slice of Sadie's cake, Alice fetched the letter waiting for him.

The envelope was franked with the logo of the firm Johnny worked for before the war. She watched while, with trembling hands, he tore open the envelope and read the contents. He seemed to be studying it for ages and then, with a burst of anger, he screwed up the letter and flung it down on the floor and, knocking back his chair, he went out into the garden.

She waited a few moments and then picked up the ball of paper from the floor and smoothed it out. She read it.

It stated that old Mr Makepeace had died and his son, now running the business, intended to make utility furniture and, as the process would be mostly mechanised, Johnny's skills were not required.

Alice went to look out of the window to the garden. This was a great blow for Johnny and would knock his confidence sideways. She picked up his packet of Gold Flake and lighter from the table and went outdoors.

She found him at the bottom of the garden, sitting on an

upturned old earthenware pot. He looked up at her as she approached, his eyes wet with tears of frustration. She lit two cigarettes and put one to his lips, and then she sat on a hump of dry earth at his feet. They didn't speak, but sat there until the light began to fade and the birds became silent.

Chapter Thirty-Eight

While Johnny thrashed about as he slept, Alice couldn't sleep. It wasn't because she was in a strange bed as, over the course of the war, she'd slept in many beds, beneath hedges and under the stars. The aftermath of war brought untold problems, she knew that, but Johnny being out of work she hadn't foreseen. Ever since she first met him, he'd always been passionate about his work as a wood carver and maker of fine furniture.

She dozed for a short time and then woke up. So as not to disturb her husband, who was now sleeping soundly, she crept from the bed. Slipping on her dressing gown and slippers, she went downstairs to make a cup of tea. While the kettle was boiling on the stove, she went from room to room, unable to believe that she was living in such a lovely house with so much space. She wandered into the dining room and inspected the highly polished table and the six magnificent carved chairs. It occurred to her, would she ever have six people to sit down at the table for a meal? The kitchen table was what she'd been used to. She sat down on one of the chairs and stretched her back. It was quite comfortable, so she remained there for a while, her fingers tracing the pattern on the edge of the chair. It felt relaxing and soothing, and the faint whiff of beeswax polish tantalised her nostrils. She guessed Johnny's mother had spent many hours polishing it with care.

Suddenly, her fingers touched something underneath the chair. Curious, she knelt down to see what it was and spied a piece of thin cardboard wedged in a corner. She eased it free and then sat back on her heels and read what was written on the card. *Carved and French-polished by J. Mitchell.*

'What are you doing?' It was Johnny.

'Sorry, did I wake you. Is this you?' She handed him the card.

He looked at the card and then he ran his hand over the chair. 'I made the set for Mam and Dad's wedding anniversary.'

'You did all this carving?'

'Why, yes.' He sounded surprised by her question.

It came to her, a glimmer of an idea. The kettle in the kitchen was singing. 'I've got an idea. We'll have a cup of tea and then I'll tell you.'

She sparkled with enthusiasm as they sat down at the kitchen table to drink their morning cup of tea. 'Johnny Mitchell,' she began, 'your craftsmanship is too precious to ignore. Today, we are going to your old works to buy tools and equipment, which they will no longer need, and then you are going to set up your own business making hand-carved furniture.'

He stared at her in amazement, and then said, 'I'll need a workshop.'

She glanced out of the window towards the Anderson shelter at the bottom of the garden. 'That will do for a start.'

Within the week, Johnny, with Alice's help, set up his temporary workshop. He had purchased everything he required, plus some oak wood, and just in time, because it was going to be chopped up for firewood.

Johnny got in touch with his old walking companion, Dennis Dalton, to ask him to find a shed or a hut, anything with electricity, and he promised to do so. To help finance this venture, Alice was to go back to nursing, but only part-time. 'Just until I get on my feet and the business is sound,' Johnny stressed.

He began by restoring war-damaged furniture and the customers were so thrilled to have their treasured possessions brought back to their former glory. Johnny worked hard and soon he established a thriving business, building up his clientele by word of mouth. Now he had his own workshop within walking distance of their home, his first commission to make a dining table and six chairs, plus a sideboard. It was for a titled family who lived out towards the Yorkshire Wolds. They'd remarked that they wanted to host intimate dinner parties.

Now that Johnny was beginning to make a name for himself as a traditional furniture restorer and maker, Alice devoted as much time as possible to tracing her daughter. First she applied for a duplicate birth certificate for Daisy. This wasn't a problem as many were lost during the war. She also contacted the Red Cross and the Salvation Army for their help and lodged her details and address and also the details of Daisy. Sadly, she didn't have a photograph of her daughter. The members of these organisations were understanding and sympathised when she gave them the facts about Daisy being taken from her, so very different from the authorities when she first tried to find her daughter.

The kind lady at the Red Cross centre said to Alice, 'You must realise, your daughter may not want to be found.' At the sight of Alice's stricken face, she continued quickly, 'That is the worst scenario that could happen, but it doesn't happen often. So remain positive and we will do everything in our power to help you to reunite with your daughter.'

Outside in the street, Alice felt dazed. It had never entered her mind that Daisy might not want to be found.

She reached the bus station and glanced at her watch. Johnny was visiting a client and it would be hours before he was due home. A bus was pulling into the station and she saw it was number 47, the one to where her mother now lived on the eastern fringe of the city.

When she arrived, Aggie was pleased to see Alice and proudly showed her round her new home. Alice had long since stopped blaming her mother for Daisy being taken. It anyone was guilty, it was Ted Goddard and he was now gone.

The two women settled down for tea and biscuits. Alice told her mother about what steps she had taken to find Daisy.

Aggie listened in silence and then said, 'I've never forgiven myself for what happened, but I was at my wits' end and frightened I might lose my job. If Mrs Melton was still alive, I would have no fear in asking her who she gave Daisy to. All I was told was she went to a good home. If I could turn the clocks back, I would.'

Alice watched as, with trembling hands, Aggie fumbled in her apron pocket for a packet of cigarettes.

As she sat on the bus going to the city centre, she knew for certain that she would never give up looking for her daughter, to hold her close in her arms. Through half-closed eyes she conjured up a scene in her mind of her daughter in the tin bath in front of the fire, splashing the water with her tiny hands, then lifting Daisy out to dry her wrapped in a fluffy white towel and to smell the lovely warm baby scent of her freshly bathed daughter.

'Terminus, love,' called the conductor.

She just missed her connecting bus home, so she bought a newspaper from the seller outside the station and crossed over the road to a small tea room. She ordered a pot of tea and a Yorkshire curd tartlet, and then a wave of sadness swept over her. How she missed her friend Evelyn and their afternoons spent talking and sharing. With Evelyn, she could have spoken of her innermost feelings about Daisy and asked her advice. Johnny was a good and loving husband, and said he would support her whatever she wanted to do to find her daughter and that Daisy could live with them, but he could offer no practical help because of his work. Alice supposed that Johnny longed for them to have children, but it hadn't happened. Sadly, perhaps it wasn't to be.

The waitress appeared. 'Sorry, missus. No tartlets left, rations, like, so I've brought you this.' It was a rather dried-up bun.

Alice nodded her understanding and declined the bun. Being still on rationing was the least of her worries and she managed quite well. Life had taught her how to be frugal. She sipped her tea and perused the newspaper, looking for any articles that might relate to missing children. There were none. She was just about to fold it up and leave it on the table for the next occupant, when she spied a personal column. The first insertion was from a firm of solicitors seeking the whereabouts of a person who could be a claimant of a will. She read the rest of the column, but there wasn't a daughter seeking her mother. *Another dead end,* she thought as a wave of despair hit her. She rose to go and then suddenly sat back down with a thump. The couple at the next table looked towards her and she managed a weak smile. She picked up the newspaper again and reread the column. Why not?

She scrambled in her handbag for paper and a pencil, and began to draft an outline of what she needed to say.

I am looking for my daughter, Daisy Goddard, taken from me in early 1930, born 24th December 1927. If anyone knows the whereabouts of Daisy, please contact me in confidence.

She then hurried to the newspaper offices. The receptionist was helpful and said all replies would go to the box number allocated.

'How long do you wish the insertion to be included? And do you wish for them to be posted to you or will you collect them?'

'Three months and posted, please.'

As she left the building, she felt elated and her steps were light and springy. At last she was making positive steps forward in her search to find her missing daughter.

The first month fell barren, and so did the second and third. She went to the library in town to search records to see if her daughter was named on any. With the help of the reference librarian, a very efficient woman, she trawled through the huge amount of documentation that was available, but with no luck. She was told that some records were lost or damaged during the war.

'There is a possibility that your daughter might have been placed with a family from another area,' the librarian said. 'I can give you the contact addresses and telephone numbers of newspapers in East Yorkshire.'

Alice thanked the woman profusely. Another step forward and people were so helpful. She felt light-hearted.

She hurried home, eager to start writing, but when she arrived back it was already late, and she had Johnny's tea to cook. Afterwards, she listened to Johnny talk about his day at work and his enthusiasm for a new commission he had just acquired. She was so pleased that all the hard work he'd put into making his business successful, which in her opinion was richly deserved, was now paying dividends. She still worked two days at the hospital and helped Johnny with his paperwork.

The next day, Alice was up early to write her letters to the newspaper offices in Driffield, Withernsea, Hornsea, Bridlington, Hedon and Beverley. She caught the late-morning post and walked home light-headed to wait for a response. Deep within her, she felt this positive awakening begin to stir and she knew she would receive a reply. But would it be the right one? To keep herself sane, she went out into the garden and began to attack the weeds.

Chapter Thirty-Nine

Daisy stood at the door of her tiny one-bedroomed cottage nestling just above the sand dunes and watched the evening mist rolling in from the sea. She called to her daughter playing on the beach, 'Lucy, come in now or the sea roake will get you.'

The three-year-old child stopped her search for coloured pebbles in the sand and shingle, and looked towards the mighty North Sea. And, not wanting to see the sea rogue, the monster, because that was her interpretation of what a roake was, she hastened to gather up her finds in the skirt of her dress and hurried to her mother.

Daisy waited, her eyes filled with love and fear for her daughter. Inside, the room they lived in was warm and cosy. She took a sheet of newspaper from the pile she'd brought home from work that morning to use as kindling for the fire and spread it on the table, so that Lucy could clean her collection of pebbles. She liked to make patterns with them, calling them her make-believe brothers and sisters. And so she entertained herself, while Daisy prepared a meal of fried eggs and chips, Lucy's favourite meal, with bread cut into tiny length portions, her 'soldiers' to dip into the running egg yolk.

Finally, when Lucy was washed, her golden curls brushed and in her nightie ready for bed, she would always say in her sing-song voice, 'A story, Mammy, please.' She pulled out from under the bed her most treasured book, *Rupert and the Wonderful Kite*. She had a yellow checked scarf just like Rupert the Bear, but she didn't have a kite.

'One day I'll make you one,' Daisy promised.

When Lucy was tucked up and asleep in the bed they shared, Daisy dropped wearily into her easy chair and stared into the dying embers of the fire. She was grateful for the site owner letting her keep her job of cleaning out the holiday caravans, but she wasn't sure how long her health would allow her to struggle on. She missed Wilf every single day. He had been her lover and her best friend, the only good thing that had happened in her life, and he'd given her their daughter, Lucy. And now he was gone. It had happened so quickly.

Last year, on a bright, hot, sunny day with a gentle breeze fanning the air, children were playing on the beach, making sandcastles and digging dams and some were paddling or swimming in the sea. Two young lads had got hold of an old car tyre and were playing about with it at the edge of the sea, when the breeze whipped up and the boys were enjoying being tossed about. Suddenly a scream erupted as the boys were flung into the sea and out of their depth.

Wilf, returning to the cottage, heard the shouts of fear and ran down to the beach towards the sea. Discarding his boots, he plunged in and swam out towards the boys. He managed to bring one boy to safety and laid him on the sand for him to be taken care of by the gathered crowd. Then he turned back and swam out for the other boy, but he was nowhere in sight. Wilf dived under the sea to locate him. People watching from the shore were horror-struck when neither man nor boy reappeared. By now, two workmen had come, and they swam out to where the boy and Wilf were last seen, but they couldn't find them. It was over a week before their bodies were recovered, washed up among rocks further down the coast.

Daisy felt numb with shock, but she had to carry on, because she had Lucy to care for. Every day, before his body was sighted, she kept a vigil at the water's edge, expecting him to return to her and emerge from the sea.

She continued to work and look after her daughter, taking on extra duties, which enabled her to take Lucy with her, so they were always together, never apart. Wilf had left her a precious legacy, their daughter, and she would protect her with her life if needed. No matter how hard the struggle, she would never give up her daughter, not like she was given up.

She felt ill most of the time now and was losing weight, and in desperation she had gone to see the doctor. After tests, she had returned to the surgery and the doctor told her she was suffering from the early stages of tuberculosis. 'Mrs Holland, you should go into a sanatorium for treatment.'

'I cannot leave my daughter,' she insisted, much to the doctor's disapproval.

It worried her that she would become too ill to take care of Lucy. Somewhere out there she had a mother of her own. She knew this for a fact, because on numerous occasions, when angry with her, Mrs Cooper-Browne had told her she was like her wayward mother. Mrs Cooper-Browne now had a child of her own, a son, whom she spoilt, and Daisy didn't like him. She was glad when she was told she didn't have to go back to live with them. She had always been treated as if she was a doll to dress up and looked at occasionally. Mr Cooper-Browne had been a distant figure who sometimes patted her on the head.

She began dreaming of her mother and that she was looking for her. Daisy knew what she looked like, because she had the tiny drawing of her, looking so beautiful, along with the birthday cards that her mother had sent, although they had stopped coming at the beginning of the war – not that she knew anything about them until she had opened the sealed brown envelope Mrs Cooper-Browne had given her at the end of the conflict.

She was just about to rise from her chair to tidy up and set out the breakfast things when a spasm of coughing racked her body. When it abated, she looked at the handkerchief and saw it was splattered with blood again! She flopped back on the chair, her breathing shallow. She knew she was getting worse and felt frightened of what the future held. She couldn't afford not to work, for who would take care of her and Lucy?

She closed her eyes, trying not to sob, because it would only bring on the coughing again. She must have drifted into a fitful sleep, because she was suddenly awoken by Lucy touching her arm and saying, 'Mammy, come to bed.'

She hugged her daughter, feeling the comfort of her warm body and buried her face in Lucy's hair, smelling the lingering traces of tangy sea. Then she took hold of her hand and went into the bedroom to the comfort of the bed and her daughter. She gave a backward glance at the table, left untidy with the newspaper and pebbles on it – it could wait while morning.

Despite her best intention to rise early, Daisy slept in and made a hurried breakfast for her and Lucy, allowing no time to tidy up before leaving for work and only a quick wash. Glancing in the mirror hung on the wall, she noticed her eyes were dark and sunk into their sockets, and her skin was tinged with a grey, unhealthy pallor. The pain in her chest tightened. She turned to see her daughter staring at her.

'Mammy poorly?' Lucy whispered, her bottom lip quivering.

'No, love, just a nasty cough. Have you got your dolly and crayons?' Lucy lifted up her drawstring bag, made from scraps of material.

Later that day at home, exhausted by her workload and another coughing fit, Daisy struggled to clean out the grate and to light the fire. This was her only means of cooking and all she had for today's meal were a few root vegetables. These she prepared and put in a pan with water to simmer, adding seasoning of salt and pepper and gravy browning. To make this into a tasty and satisfying meal, she would add dumplings made from flour and suet. For afters, there would be her version of pancakes made from bread, and jam sandwiches cut into triangles then dipped in batter and fried, then rolled in sugar, if there was some to spare.

Lucy's pile of pebbles was growing and on some of the larger ones she'd drawn faces with coloured crayons, which one of the kind holidaymakers had given her. Daisy had found an old wooden tray, thrown out from a caravan, which she scrubbed clean for Lucy to display her family of pebbles on.

Her child now safely tucked up in bed, Daisy set about tidying up the kitchen table. She was about to remove the newspaper, when a picture caught her eye. It was of the local infant school, the one that Lucy would go to when she was five. An awful thought flashed through her mind, one that she didn't want to think about. To take her mind off such thoughts, she sat at the table to look more closely at the picture. It was of sports day, an egg and spoon race with mothers cheering on their children. At the moment,

Lucy was happy going to work with her and playing by herself on the seashore, but soon she would need the company of other children as playmates.

She was about to screw up the newspaper for kindling when a name seemed to leap out at her. Her heart skipped a beat and she shivered. It was her name, before she'd married Wilf, and that was her birth date. It was her mother, Alice, who was searching for her. 'At last, at last!' she cried. 'I always knew she wanted me.' She never did believe that her mother had abandoned her by choice.

She felt her nerves dancing about, and her whole body tingled with a mixture of tension and excitement. She stared at the printed words and began reading them again, checking to make sure she'd read them correctly. They were the most precious words she had ever read.

Tearing a page from Lucy's drawing book, for she didn't have any writing paper, she sharpened the stub of a pencil and began to write.

Next morning, she asked Lucy to draw a picture of them both at the bottom of the letter. 'Who's it to, Mammy?'

'A lady who could be your grandma.'

'Will she make you better?' the child asked in all innocence.

Tears pricked at Daisy's eyes and she brushed them away with the back of her hand. Then she planted a kiss on Lucy's head and said, 'Time to go and post our letter.'

The postmistress was quite chatty; she liked to know about people's lives. 'A stamp and an envelope – who are you splashing out on?'

Daisy gave Lucy's hand a quick squeeze for her to remain quiet and replied, 'Just an acquaintance.' With her other hand she crossed her fingers behind her back.

The postmistress watched mother and daughter go and then remarked to her next customer, 'That young woman is looking poorly. She's all skin and bones.'

That evening, feeling tired and weak, Daisy sat on a stool outside the cottage door watching her child by the seashore, absorbed in her play of gathering pebbles. Her heart was full of protective love for her daughter, but for how much longer could she carry on working? Her only hope was her mother – though would she want them, a daughter who was ill and a three-year-old grandchild? What if she had other children? Daisy felt drained.

'Mammy, look up,' Lucy called. In the sky above, the first star had appeared shining brightly. 'Is that Grandma watching us?'

Daisy looked up and felt a flicker of hope.

Chapter Forty

Alice rushed to pick up the late-afternoon post as it plopped onto the doormat. She searched through the envelopes and the hope she'd first experienced turned to disappointment mixed with sadness. 'Not a single reply from any of the six newspapers,' she said to Johnny. Sighing deeply, she sank down on the kitchen chair. She had felt so sure she would have received a reply.

'Perhaps she has moved away from the area,' offered Johnny, sympathising with his wife's feelings. To lift the mood, he said, 'Shall we have a walk round to our Maureen's later? You can help her bath the twins for bed.'

Alice rose from her chair and went to kiss Johnny, then said, 'Yes, we'll do that.'

He slipped his arm around her waist and whispered, 'I love you, Alice Mitchell,' and she was thankful for his support.

After tea, hand in hand they strolled the short distance to Maureen's house and soon, Alice, with an apron tied around her waist, was helping to prepare the twins for bed. They were a delight. Their happy, gleeful mood was infectious, and Alice felt her depression lift. As she wrapped one of the twins in a warm towel, she felt her heartstrings ache with love for her own lost child. She realised Daisy would be a young woman now, but, for Alice, she would always be the little girl as she had last seen and remembered her.

The twins were in their cots and sleeping. The four adults played a game of dominoes and the evening passed pleasantly. As they prepared to go home, Maureen asked Alice, 'Have you any plans for your birthday?'

My birthday? Alice thought, surprised that Maureen should remember it. 'Why, no,' she glanced at Johnny, but he shook his head and she guessed he hadn't given it a thought and neither had she.

'How about I do you a nice tea, and who knows what we might get up to after?' Maureen laughed.

'Thank you, that's very kind. I accept your offer.'

On the day of her birthday, Alice was busy around the house sweeping and polishing, just in case an unexpected visitor called. Sadie from next door had been earlier and brought her a card and a pretty box of handkerchiefs. They then had a cup of tea and a piece of Victoria sandwich cake.

The morning post popped through the letter box and landed on the doormat. There were cards from her mother and sister, and one from Miss Bailey, with a chatty letter as well. Talli's card had come yesterday, saying she would write and tell her all the news when she had more time. Alice missed Talli's company and being able to talk to her about anything, but she was far away in Tasmania, settling into her new life with Jeff.

She picked up the last envelope and her heart beat faster and her body trembled. She fumbled for a chair and she eased down onto it. With trembling fingers, she slit open the envelope and withdrew the single sheet of paper, trying to read the words, but her eyes seemed not to want to focus. She took deep breaths and exhaled slowly, and her nerves stopped jangling, but her hands trembled as she read the words.

> *Dear Mrs Mitchell,*
> *I think you are my mother. I am Daisy Holland née Goddard, born on 24th December 1927. I did live with Mrs Cooper-Browne and then I was evacuated, but she didn't want me back any more. I have a daughter, Lucy, who I love dearly. Her daddy died saving two boys at sea. He was a brave and good man. I have the birthday cards you sent me and a small pencil drawing that I think is of you.*
> *Please come and see us,*
> *Daisy*

Below was a childish picture of two matchstick figures of a woman holding the hand of a little girl and there was a row of kisses running off the page. She stared at the picture for a long time, unable to believe that she also had a granddaughter. Then she looked at the address at the top of the page and saw that it was only a train ride away.

Glancing at the kitchen wall clock, she would have time to go and be back for tea at Maureen's. She whipped off her apron and put on her best coat and hat, picked up her handbag and left the house.

Sadie was sweeping her garden path and called out to Alice, 'Where are you dashing off to?' But Alice didn't hear her neighbour.

The journey by bus and then by train passed in a state of

oblivion for her. When she stepped from the train at Withernsea, she asked the guard the way to the hamlet of Fleetwick.

'Catch bus yond side of road,' he said as he went to supervise the engine on the turntable in readiness for the return journey.

But when she reached the bus stop, it had already departed, 'It went five minutes ago, love,' said an old man sitting on a bench, smoking a pipe.

Alice looked along the coast in the direction of Fleetwick. 'How far?' she asked.

'Good three miles' walk along clifftop.' He must have seen the frustrated look on her face for he added, 'Yer can hire a bike from yonder.' He pointed to a shop on the corner, which had a row of bicycles parked outside.

She was soon pedalling along the cliff path and she saw the cottage come into sight at the end of the rough, winding track. She jumped off the bike and pushed it the last hundred yards to avoid the potholes. The tangy smell of the sea assailed her nostrils and the soft, balmy breeze caressed her cheeks. She shaded her eyes to look towards the incoming tide washing against the shingles and then she saw her. Her eyes filled with tears and she held a hand over her lips to stop the sound of her cry of pain mixed with joy. 'Daisy, my Daisy,' she whispered, her emotions overflowing.

The child was unaware of Alice's presence as she was so engrossed in her search amongst the pebbles. Alice watched and saw the look of delight on the little girl's face as she held up a large pebble in different shades of red.

It was then the child saw Alice and she waved to her to come and look at her find.

Alice walked over to the little girl. 'Hello,' she said, dropping to the child's level. 'What have you got there?'

The child passed the stone to Alice, who fingered it gently. 'It's beautiful. What else have you got?'

'Look at these,' she said with glee. And together, in pure bliss, they inspected the rest of the pebbles.

Alice straightened up and felt the back of her neck go goosepimply and her nerves tense. She turned and saw a pale-faced young woman watching them from the doorway of the cottage. Alice closed her eyes for a second and then opened them. This young woman was her daughter, Daisy. Over the long years she had often thought about her finding her daughter and their reunion. Nothing would ever bring back those lost years, but now they had a lifetime together and she had been given the most wonderful gift of a granddaughter. Never again would she abandon her daughter. It wasn't intentional all those years ago, but, nevertheless, she had always felt guilty. If only she had not left her daughter on that terrible night.

Neither of the women moved. They just looked at each other, and then Alice felt the aching, the longing to hold her daughter. She opened her arms wide and her daughter ran into them. Alice held her close, feeling the warmth of her body, the smell of her hair, the taste of her tears mingled with hers.

They stood, not moving, drinking in each other, until a little hand tugged at them, saying, 'Why are you sad?'

The two women drew apart. 'We're happy,' replied her mother.

For a fleeting moment, the child looked puzzled and then said, 'I'm hungry.'

The two women each took hold of one of the child's hands and walked into the cottage.

The fire was aglow, and they toasted pikelets spread with home-made jam from the local farm, drank tea and talked and talked while Lucy played with her pebbles.

Daisy didn't tell her mother about how lonely and unhappy she'd been living with the Cooper-Brownes, but talked more about when she was evacuated to a farm in Lincolnshire. A sad note crept into her voice when she spoke of Wilf Holland. 'He was my best friend. He always looked out for me and we stayed together. After the war, we married and came to live here and work for the caravan site owner.' She stopped talking, her eyes filling with tears. Alice reached across and held her hand. Daisy continued, 'Wilf drowned when saving the lives of two boys.'

Alice let out a shuddering sigh. She should have been here for her daughter.

Then Lucy, sensing the sadness, climbed onto her mother's knee and clasped her cherub arms around her mother's neck.

After moments of silence, Daisy disentangled her daughter's arms and said, 'Lucy, this lady is your grandmother.'

Lucy stared at Alice and then said, 'I'm Lucy Holland, what's your name?'

Alice smiled at the lovely innocence of the child and replied, 'You can call me Grandma Alice.'

Both women were reflective and lost in their thoughts. Alice knew she must tell Daisy about her father, Ted, but decided to omit the horrible things and his treatment of her. So, she told her the bare facts of how she was involved in a road accident and in hospital for months and her father couldn't cope with her and with work. 'That's how you came to live with the Cooper-Brownes, but it was never meant to be permanent. When I came out of hospital, there was no record of whom you were living with. Not even the authorities knew or cared where you were.' She looked at her daughter, thinking that there might be reprisals.

But Daisy took hold of her mother's hand and squeezed it. Then she asked, 'What of my father? Where is he?'

'He was a soldier who was captured and became a prisoner of war. Quite by chance I was assigned to the POW camp to bring home the wounded. Sadly, he died of his wounds and I was with him until the end.'

Suddenly, Daisy started coughing and Lucy said, 'Mammy's poorly.'

Alice was shocked when she saw the blood being coughed up by her daughter and she held her until the spasm passed. 'How long have you had this cough?'

'Since last winter,' Daisy said, her face flushed with exertion.

'What does the doctor say?' When her daughter didn't reply, she asked, 'Have you been to see him?' Daisy nodded and closed her eyes, and Alice could see how exhausted she was. 'Tomorrow we will go to see him again.' But Alice knew what the outcome would be. She had seen the symptoms many times in her nursing life.

Chapter Forty-One

Johnny Mitchell entered the silent house. 'Alice,' he called as he went into the kitchen and then into the sitting room. He'd come home early from work to celebrate Alice's birthday. He went upstairs, calling, 'Alice, I'm home.' But the bedrooms and bathroom were empty. He descended the downstairs thinking she must already have gone to Maureen's and looked for a note, but there wasn't one. He looked at the bunch of pink roses, Alice's favourites, still clutched in his hand. He put them in a jug of water and left them on the draining board for her to arrange later.

After a quick wash, shave and a change of shirt and trousers, he hurried round to Maureen's house. Alice must be there, because there was nowhere else she could be.

'Hello. Sorry I'm late,' he called as he entered his sister's house.

The twins were sprawled out on the living-room carpet, playing with a wooden train set. Maureen appeared from the kitchen. 'You're early, Johnny.' Then, looking beyond him, she asked, 'Where's Alice?'

Johnny looked puzzled. 'Isn't she here?'

'No, I haven't seen her.'

'She must have slipped out on an errand. I best get back home, or she'll be wondering where I am.'

Back home, the house still sounded silent and empty. He searched all the rooms again and then went out into the garden and saw Sadie bringing in her dry washing off the line. 'Have you seen Alice?'

Sadie dropped the clothes into the basket and came across to the partition fence. 'Not since this morning when she hurried from the house. I called to her, but she seemed preoccupied and didn't hear me.'

Inside, he paced up and down and then went out the front door and down the garden path to look up and down the street in the hope that, wherever she'd been, she was coming home. He saw only a man on a cycle, a woman walking a dog and, at the far end of the green, children were playing, their voices full of merriment.

Back indoors, he paced up and down again. 'Alice, where are you?' he said out loud to himself.

Suddenly, the back door opened and he turned with relief, but it was Maureen. His shoulders sagged. And Maureen didn't have to ask, but she said, 'Have you rung anybody?'

One advantage of his business was that they had a telephone in the house, although it was a shared party line. 'But who can I ring? Her mother and sister aren't on the telephone and if she was there, Alice would have found a public telephone box to let me know. This isn't like her.'

Maureen made a pot of tea and poured out two cups, but Johnny didn't touch his. He kept going to the bay window and looking out, or he went outside to look up and down the street time and time again.

'Where do you think she is?' Maureen asked anxiously.

He shook his head, baffled. 'I don't know.'

'I think you should ring round the hospitals. She might have been involved in an accident.'

By now it was dark outside, and Johnny dreaded what the outcome would be. But after fruitless calls, no one answering Alice's description had been admitted to any of the hospitals that day.

Maureen went home, and Johnny slumped in a chair, but his mind was alert to every noise of the house and outside, listening for a sign of Alice's return. By midnight, he decided to ring the police to report his wife missing.

The police sergeant on duty listened sympathetically to Johnny's dilemma and took down Alice's details. 'At this stage, sir, we cannot do anything. Nine times out of ten, the person gets in touch. Perhaps some unforeseen situation has arisen and she is unable to contact you. If by tomorrow you have no news of your wife, telephone again and then we will investigate. Try not to worry, sir.'

Johnny put down the telephone and slumped back in the chair. What of the one person out of ten who doesn't return home? He covered his face with his hands and tried to think over the last few days to see if anything was amiss with Alice. But he couldn't think of a thing. She'd been looking forward to her birthday tea and wearing the new dress he had bought her. Then at the back of his mind something nagged at him, but his head buzzed with worry and fatigue and he couldn't think.

He must have dozed off for he woke up with a start, but it was only cats at their nocturnal play. He shivered with cold and his leg felt sore where the prosthesis fitted. He limped through into the kitchen to make a hot drink of coffee. Camp coffee made from chicory, but it would help to keep him awake.

Early morning light shafted through the window. He blinked and stretched up his stiff arms and then eased his weary, aching body from the chair. There was no way he was going to his workplace, even though he had orders to complete, not until Alice was safely home. He went to look out of the window and saw a woman walking across the green and his heart lurched. He dashed to the front door and flung it open, but it wasn't Alice. It was a woman he recognised who cleaned at the doctor's surgery each morning.

Back inside, he glanced at the silent telephone and then slowly he went up to the bathroom and gave his face a quick swill in cold water, then he dragged a comb through his tangled hair. He couldn't be bothered to shave or to change his crumpled shirt and trousers. Downstairs, he sat by the telephone, willing it to ring.

Maureen came round with the twins. She was going to the shops and would ask if anyone had seen Alice. And then Sadie came round to see if there was any news.

The telephone rang late in the afternoon. Johnny stared at it for a few seconds and then grabbed it. Before he could speak a voice said, 'Johnny.'

'Alice! Where are you?'

In between the sobs, she told him the wonderful news of finding her daughter and then the heartbreaking diagnosis of Daisy's illness. 'She has tuberculosis and the doctor is seeking a bed for her in a sanatorium; until then, I cannot leave her. Oh Johnny, I have just found her after all these years and she is ill. I cannot bear it.' She sobbed uncontrollably.

He heard the pips sounding and the line went dead. He stood as if glued to the spot, trying to digest what she had told him.

Maureen came through the back door with some shopping and found him still standing there with a glazed look on his face, which frightened her. 'Johnny, what is it?' He just stared at her, not speaking. She took hold of his arm and led him to a chair in the kitchen, and then she fetched the brandy from the cupboard and poured him a generous measure.

At last, he was able to speak coherently to her and told her about Alice finding her daughter after all these years. Maureen, who hadn't been aware that Alice had a daughter, replied, 'Surely that's good news?' And Johnny explained the bad news.

Alice telephoned the next morning to say she would be coming home, but only to collect some clothes and money and then she would be returning to care for her daughter.

Johnny bathed, shaved, put on clean clothes and washed the dishes left in the sink. Maureen had brought round a casserole, which was in the oven on a low heat and set the table for two. He positioned himself by the sitting-room window to watch for his wife coming. His insides felt all churned up. These few years of married life together had fallen into a settled, comfortable pattern, which they had welcomed after the uncertainty and devastating tide of war. They had overcome the fact that they would not be able to have children and got on with enjoying their lives together. Alice finding her long-lost daughter and her being ill was something he'd not expected, and he was unsure how to deal with it. Deep down he felt he didn't want to share Alice with her daughter, a selfish thought that he acknowledged he must keep buried.

He saw her. She walked with her head down and she cut a sad

figure. His love for her welled up and he rushed outside to meet her. Taking her in his arms, he hugged her.

Once inside the house he slipped off her coat and kissed her tenderly. Then he saw the sadness in her eyes and said, 'Sit down, you look all in.'

Then she blurted, 'I'm so sorry for worrying you, but there was no phone nearby and I didn't want to leave her alone. I took her to see the doctor. He said she should not delay in having treatment, if she wants to survive. So, you see, I cannot leave her, I must care for her until . . .' Her voice faded.

He put his arms around her shoulders, feeling her vulnerability. 'My darling, I understand. I will be fine. I have plenty of work to keep me occupied. But if I can help you at any time, just let me know,' he reassured her, and he meant it.

She gazed at her husband and loved him even more for being so understanding.

They enjoyed the meal together and then Alice went upstairs to pack a few clothes and other necessities. He insisted on going with her to catch her train back. He carried the case and she linked her arm with his. At the station, he helped her onto the train and put her case in the overhead luggage rack. Then he kissed her tenderly and said, 'You take care, my darling.'

Alice closed her eyes and leant back on the seat, feeling sad and weary. She'd yearned so long to find her daughter, always thinking of a joyous reunion, and now Daisy was struck down with a debilitating illness. If only she'd found her sooner and stemmed the illness in its early stages, she could have nursed her back to good health. Instead, all she could do for Daisy was to make her comfortable until she went into the sanatorium and goodness knew how long she could be there. Tears seeped from her closed eyes and wet her lashes, and she bit on her lip. She must be strong for her daughter, and there was Lucy to take care of. Alice must shield her from the harsh reality of her mother's illness.

Lucy! She jerked upright, startling the old man and woman seated opposite her in the railway carriage. What with all the upheaval of the emotional tide, she'd forgotten to tell Johnny about Lucy, her granddaughter.

Chapter Forty-Two

'Mammy's poorly.' Lucy's words greeted Alice as she entered the cottage. She dumped her case on the floor and, dropping to her knees by Daisy's side, she felt her forehead. It was burning, and her nightgown was soaked in sweat. She didn't need a thermometer to tell her that her daughter's temperature was far too high. Her nursing training kicked in and it helped to stop the guilty emotions churning inside her body and mind. All these lost years when she should have been caring for her daughter.

She pushed back a stray wisp of Daisy's hair and whispered, 'Come on, love. Let me help you to your bed.' She put an arm under both of Daisy's and eased her gently to her feet, supporting her into the bedroom and onto her bed. She filled a bowl from the cold water tap and added enough hot water from the kettle on the hob for it to be tepid. With care, she removed Daisy's nightgown and was shocked to see how thin and strained her body was. Tenderly, she began to sponge her down with smoothing strokes and gradually she felt the tension flow from her daughter's body. With practised ease, Alice slipped a clean nightgown on her daughter and straightened the bedcovers, making her comfortable.

Daisy murmured in a weak voice, 'Thank you.'

Alice watched her eyelids droop and close. For a few minutes, she watched over her until she was sure she was sleeping and not going to have another coughing fit.

Back in the living room, Alice turned to look at Lucy to see that her bottom lip was quivering and her bright-blue eyes looked sad. Alice went over to her granddaughter, holding out her arms, and Lucy tumbled off her chair and snuggled into her grandma's loving embrace. Alice kissed the top of her head and whispered, 'Your mammy's tired and she's sleeping now.'

The child looked up into her grandma's face and asked, 'Is Mammy better now?'

A sinking feeling gripped Alice and her heart ached for her daughter and granddaughter. She must try to be truthful without frightening the child, so she answered, 'Your mammy is not hurting.' She gathered the child's warm body closer to her. And, for now, Lucy accepted that answer.

A van called from the village with the two camp beds, sleeping bags and a supply of groceries, which Alice had ordered earlier.

After a light supper of scrambled eggs, Daisy was comfortable and sleeping. Alice and Lucy added toast to their meal and now Lucy was washed and changed into her nightgown. She was ready for bed and so was Alice. She must snatch sleep whenever she could. 'We're going to play a game,' she told her granddaughter, who held Alice's gaze with a look of trusting innocence. 'We're going to pretend we are on a ship.' Lucy watched her grandma place the sleeping bags on the camp beds under the table. Alice then took hold of the warm, tiny hand and said, 'This is our cabin. Shall we see how comfortable it is?' Lucy, clutching her rag doll, bobbed under the table and Alice dropped onto her knees and helped her granddaughter into the sleeping bag. She then climbed into hers and began to sing the song she used to sing to Daisy when she had been a little girl going to bed, 'Twinkle, twinkle little star'. She sang until she heard the gentle rhythm of sleep coming from Lucy.

But Alice lay awake for a long time, listening to Daisy's heavy, racking breathing. Through the night, she arose countless times to attend to Daisy after her coughing bouts, where she brought up blood and sputum. Alice used paper handkerchiefs for Daisy to cough into and then she burnt them on the fire. Then she bathed her daughter's forehead with a clean, cool cloth, gave her sips of water, boiled then cooled, checked her pulse and took her temperature, which still remained high.

The days formed a pattern of such, which became dominated by Daisy's needs.

Alice had engaged the help of a local woman to come each day and take the dirty washing. Each day, Alice changed the sheets on Daisy's bed and her nightgown – sometimes during the night as well. With the washing catered for, this gave her more time to spend with Daisy and to play with Lucy.

Alice wished that the doctor would call to say there was a bed available now in the sanatorium for Daisy. She worried her, because her daughter was eating less and less. Alice mashed up and liquified food for her and had to spoon-feed her, because she was too weak to do so herself. Daisy only just wanted sips of boiled water, no food. Alice held her daughter's thin hand and listened to her rasping breathing. She bit on her lip to keep the tears from falling. There was nothing else she could do but sit with her and wait. If only she had found Daisy earlier at the outset of her illness, she could have nursed her back to good health. Now, it was going to be a slow process and she would always have a weakness.

Lucy came wandering into the room, wanting to show her mother the blue speckled pebble she'd found. 'Look, Mammy. It's pretty, like you.'

Alice felt a choking sensation in her throat and tearing at her heart, but she whispered to Lucy, 'Your mammy is sleeping, but give her a kiss.' She lifted the child up to reach her mammy and watched as she planted a big kiss on her forehead. And then, Daisy's eyes opened, and she smiled at Lucy, her thin fingers touching her daughter's chubby cheeks. Eagerly, Lucy showed her the pebble and Daisy took hold of it and held it in the closed palm of her hand. She sank back into sleep with a smile on her face.

'You find another one, Lucy,' said her grandmother, and off she ran.

The next day the doctor called to inform them that an ambulance would come tomorrow to take Daisy to the sanatorium. 'It is quite a distance away, at the foot of the Yorkshire Wolds, where the air is fresh and pure.'

After the doctor had departed, Daisy opened her eyes and focused on Alice's face. Her voice was faint, barely audible. 'Will you look after Lucy for me?' she asked of her mother.

Alice took hold of Daisy's hand, the one without the pebble she was still clutching. 'Yes, my darling daughter, I will. I will look after her. That is a promise I will never break. And when you are well again, there will always be a home for you and Lucy with me.' She kissed her daughter's thin, papery lips.

The next day, Alice and Lucy waved goodbye to Daisy in the ambulance until it was out of sight. Then they both hunted for pebbles on the beach until the sun set, and the night began to draw a veil across the sky.

'When's Mammy coming back?' Lucy asked.

'As soon as she is better, my darling.'

'But I want her now.' Lucy bottom lip quivered, and tears wet her long lashes.

Grandmother and granddaughter sat side by side on the sand dunes. 'Look up there,' Alice said. 'You see that star, the brightest star?'

'That one, Grandma, the twinkly one?'

'Yes, that's the one. Now your mammy is in hospital and she will be able to see that star, just like you can. So, any time you want to talk to her, you look up in the night sky, find that star and your mammy will hear you.'

'Night night, Mammy,' Lucy said.

Alice put an arm around Lucy's sturdy body and held her close while they both looked up to the night sky. By now lots of little stars were shining, but there were none shining as bright as Lucy and Daisy's star.

The next day, Alice looked round the now empty cottage. Everything was packed in readiness for the journey back home to Hull. Except for their two suitcases, the rest would go by carrier. She had telephoned Johnny from the village as to when to expect her home. She didn't mention Lucy, only that she had a surprise for him. She should have told him, she knew, though somehow the words never came. She was now Lucy's guardian until Daisy was well enough to come home. Would Johnny accept Lucy into their lives? Yes, he'd wanted children of their own, but would he be willing to take on a child, a granddaughter? Her first priority and responsibility was Lucy and, come what may, she would never, ever break her promise to Daisy.

The taxi came slowly along the track towards them. 'Ready, Lucy?' she called.

'Not going,' said Lucy stubbornly, stamping her foot.

'We're going on an adventure by train. You'll like that.'

'Stay with Mammy.' Tears began to run down her cheeks and her bottom lip quivered.

'Oh, my darling.' She bent down to the child's level. 'Wherever you go in the big wide world, you will be able to look up to the night sky and see the brightest star, and talk to your mammy. She will always hear you.' She straightened up and held out her hand and Lucy took it.

Outside the house in Garden Village, Alice stood holding Lucy's tiny hand in hers. She felt faint and her heartbeat began to race. What if Johnny wouldn't accept Lucy? Up until this point she had not felt fear of the unknown. Fear, without her husband to support her with his love and understanding. But she had made a promise to her daughter to look after Lucy and she would never break it. Never.

'Grandma,' Lucy tugged at her hand. 'Who's that man?'

Alice looked and saw Johnny at the window and then he moved away. Her heart sank.

Suddenly, the front door was flung open and Johnny stood there, looking at them both.

Then he spoke. 'What are you standing there for? Come on in.' He was smiling and opened his arms to them both.

Inside, Lucy looked at the smiling man with crinkling, smiling eyes and asked, solemnly, 'Are you my granddaddy?'

Johnny sat down on the settee and looked into Lucy's round cherub face. 'Would you like me to be?'

She nodded her golden curls and reached out to touch Johnny's face and said, 'You've got whiskers.'

Over the top of Lucy's head, Johnny smiled up at Alice, his eyes full of love. He reached for her hand, holding it tight. Then he said to Lucy, 'Now you have a grandma and a granddaddy.'

Alice felt her heart overflow with love for these two precious people in her life.

The daylight was beginning to fade, and Lucy asked, 'Can I talk to Mammy?'

Together, with Alice and Johnny holding Lucy's hands, they went out into the garden to look up at the night sky and they saw the brightest star gazing down upon them.

Lucy waved, and said, 'Night night, Mammy.'

All the time Daisy was in the sanatorium, Alice wrote every week, giving her daily news of Lucy. Of what she had done, visits to the park, playing with the children next door, what food she liked to eat, and how she was growing out of her clothes. Johnny had bought a camera especially to take photographs of Lucy, so that Daisy had a pictorial diary of the development of her daughter.

It was a long year before Daisy finally came home, fully recovered from her illness. She stepped into the house, which was now her home, as if she had lived there all her life.

Alice witnessed, with Johnny by her side, the loving reunion of mother and daughter. Lucy clung to Daisy and seemed frightened that she might disappear.

And Alice wondered what Daisy thought of her, if anything. Would she reproach her for abandoning her all those years ago? Putting her hand to her heavy heart, she felt the rapid beating of uncertainty. She was just about to turn away and busy herself, when . . .

Over the top of Lucy's head, Daisy, her eyes glistening with joy, reached out her hand to Alice. The touch of her daughter's hand was so gentle but firm in hers and she felt mesmerised by Daisy's intense look. Then a thousand stars exploded around her as her daughter spoke just one word. 'Mammy.'

Acknowledgements

For a book to come to fruition, it takes many stages before publication, and without the expertise and guidance of my agent, Kate Nash of the Kate Nash Literary Agency, this would not have happened for me. I wish to thank Kate for having faith in my writing ability.

Credit is also due to the Romantic Novelists' Association. At their annual conferences, they run an excellent scheme – One 2 One – where you can pitch your writing to an agent, publisher or editor. And this is how I was fortunate enough to meet my agent and for her to represent me.

This book is written in remembrance and in gratitude to the brave and dedicated air ambulance nurses, who served in the WAAF during WWII. They flew with the RAF, carrying military supplies and ammunition on outwards journeys and returning with the wounded from the battlefields. They were affectionately called the 'Flying Nightingales'.

It was a privilege and honour for me, many years ago, to meet one of these nurses and listen to her story, which I never forgot.

On the TV there is an interesting programme called *Long Lost Family*, whose storylines I find very intriguing and have influenced my writing.

Sylvia Broady was born in Hull and has lived in the area all her life, although she loves to travel the world. It wasn't until she started to frequent her local library, after World War II, that her relationship with literature truly began and her memories of the war influence her writing, as does her home town. She has had a varied career in childcare, the NHS and the East Yorkshire Council Library Services, but is now a full-time writer.

sylviabroady.blogspot.com
@SylviaBroady